PRAISE FOR *A LIFETIME OF MEN*

Tenderly and elegantly written, Ciahnan Darrell's debut novel deftly balances with equal scope and intensity life's mundane adventures, its deep-ripping traumas, and the cataclysmic political contexts within which they take place. Readers of Darrell's beautifully sparse prose inhabit the overlapping dramas and traumas of three generations of small-town Maine women. The "lifetime of men" they endure, the social impediments with which they collide, the rebellions they wage, their successes and failures, stand on equal footing with the audacious intrigue and brutal violence of the Cuban Revolution and the US government's internment of Japanese Americans. This satisfyingly humane novel of intimacy in its public and private spheres is ultimately about stories: those we tell ourselves and those we tell others, those we discover and those we suffer, those we survive and those that survive us, even those we unwittingly harbor within ourselves, and how we persevere through and sometimes in spite of them. —Tyler M. Williams, PhD, Assistant Professor, Midwestern State University

A major new talent in American fiction. Riveting and deeply moving, Darrell interweaves the lives of three women across generations, masterfully layering monumental historical events with the delicate beauty of quotidian life. The novel explores the many kinds of love, capturing the wonderment of a new relationship as friends become lovers, the complexities of forbidden love provoking moral outrage from the community, and a lifelong friendship teetering on the brink of something more. The story explores how women challenge the societal expectations limiting them to the home, introducing the unforgettable protagonist Bo. From her humble roots in Maine, where she tramps the forest as a girl to hunt with her bow, to her dazzling success as a photo-journalist, as she captures the atrocities of the Cuban revolution and the internment camps of Japanese Americans during World War II, Bo pushes the boundaries of what women can accomplish in the twentieth century. A skillful storyteller, Darrell presents a beautifully written tale that challenges readers to honor the women in their own lives by asking for their stories. —Robin E. Field, Professor, King's College, Pennsylvania, Author of *Writing the Survivor: The Rape Novel in Late Twentieth-Century American Fiction*

The author proudly donates 10% of his portion of the proceeds from A LIFETIME OF MEN to Girls, Inc.

girls inc.

Inspiring all girls
to be strong,
smart, and bold

ISBN : 978-1-71670-791-9

Propertius Press
Martinsville, Virginia

A LIFETIME OF MEN is also available as an ebook wherever books are sold.

To
GARD for making me laugh,
JAD for her faith,
RCM Jr & LED for my beginning,
&
LAD for telling me stories

A Lifetime of Men

Ciahnan Darrell

CHAPTER ONE

Tolan's been sitting at her mother's computer long enough that the fat blocks of sunlight on the carpet have withered to emaciated fingers. She just needs to print her paper, but the essay is fifteen pages long and their printer secondhand slow. Boredom sends her eyes wandering over the photos that cover the walls, pictures of Tolan and her mother, mostly, and some of Tolan with her best friend, Tori. Tolan likes to pretend that she wants her mother to take them down, from time to time, so other people won't see them, but her mother never does, because she knows that Tolan not-so-secretly loves them, even if she's being silly and making faces.

Tolan looks at a picture of the three of them from last Halloween, and smiles. She and Tori had talked Tolan's mother into dressing up with them so they could go as the witches from *Hocus Pocus*. Her mother hadn't seen the movie, and wasn't exactly cool, so she didn't know that women's Halloween costumes tended toward raunchy, and she came out of her room in the one the girls had picked out blushing scarlet. Tolan shakes her head, chuckling. They'd taken pity on her eventually and let her hide in the car, but not before they asked one of the men handing out candy to take a picture of the three of them.

Tolan actually thinks the picture came out really well, all things considered, and there was the added comedic bonus of placing Tori, who was 5'3", between Tolan and her mother, who were 6'2" and 6'4." Even her mother, who hates having her picture taken, and probably hadn't even heard of foundation until Tori did her makeup that night, admits to liking the picture, in large part, Tolan thinks, because Tori had used concealer to hide that scar that runs from her mother's right cheek to her eyebrow.

Tolan listens to the printer rumble and reset, her knee bouncing and her hand jiggling the mouse and sending the cursor careening about the screen, document titles and program names flashing as it moves over them, spreadsheets and inventory lists for her mother's bookstore. Then a file catches her eye: '*The Tall Girl.doc*.' Tolan opens it:

Sarah woke when the window shattered. She'd fallen asleep on the living room floor. The brick landed thunderously and cartwheeled, catching the meat of her cheek as it ripped over her brow, crashing to a halt against the couch behind her. The clock ticked, baseboards creaked. She heard a car, a dog, nothing, pushed herself off the ground; a shriek of pain ripped through her as a shard of glass bit deep into the flesh of her palm.

The last three pages of her essay have slipped off the printer tray and onto the floor, but Tolan doesn't notice. She feels like she's been struck. Her mother's name is Pan, not Sarah, but that brick, the way it caught Sarah's cheek... Tolan looks back at the pictures, the one from Halloween where her mother's scar is hidden, then at the others.

It had been a game between them, the scar. Tolan would ask how it happened, and her mother would invent a wild story: she fought off fifty cannibals in the Amazon, was abducted by homicidal aliens two Fridays in a row; she got into an altercation with a conspiracy of angry lemurs.

But they'd never play that game again, now, because they couldn't, because the scar had become a brand that marked her mother as a stranger and a liar, as a woman with a secret past and false present.

The church bells are tolling six o'clock; her mother will be home soon. She emails the file to herself, collects her paper, and walks back to her room.

Her guitar is in the corner, waiting; she plays every day, especially when she's confused or troubled or frustrated. She always starts by tuning it, though it's never really out of tune. The ritual soothes her, helps her think or not think, silences the rush and babble of voices in her head.

Tolan takes it from its stand, gently, as always, but quickly, too, because she doesn't want to think anymore. Her guitar is a Patrick James Eggle Parlour Cuban that Tori gave her for her birthday. Sometimes Tolan says it to herself, repeats the five names over and over until she feels calm again. Tolan has memorized snatches of the write-up the guitar received: *"impressively grown-up... open timbre: warm, smooth... richly textured... counterpointed by a sweetly sustaining bite in the highs."*

If her mother knew what it cost she'd make her give it back, but Tori said it was no big deal. Her parents have more money than they knew what to do with.

Tolan is wondering why her mother never told her she was writing a book as she strums the first chords, but she's lost in the music by the second bar, words stealing from her lips, meek as children.

CHAPTER TWO

A little girl, eight, almost nine, shivering, half-asleep, sitting cross-legged on a raft of logs twenty meters wide, northern hardwoods looming on either side of the river as it flowed north into Canada. The girl knew from memory that there were spruce and white cedar, quaking and big-tooth aspen, tamarack, hemlock, and birch, pine, poplar, and maple, but it was an hour before dawn, now, and the trees were indistinguishable.

There was a rust-spotted bucket next to the girl, a fishing pole and a creel basket, a black tin lunch pail with two cheese sandwiches, a hard-boiled egg, and a quart of milk; there was a dog-eared copy of Chapman's *Bird-Lore*, and a tattered field guide to New England flora and fauna.

Her father would be back after sundown, sooner if he took a deer early on. In the meantime, she wasn't to leave the raft. She had a few squares of toilet paper in her pocket, and a feed-bucket to do her dirt in.

It was hard not to fall asleep; they'd left the house just after three that morning, she, her father, and two of his friends crammed into a model A/AA pickup. The last twenty miles of the trip were all logging roads, unimproved, deeply rutted swaths of mud and rock that pitched her about the cab and made it impossible to sleep. They'd arrived at their campsite around four-fifteen and her father had installed her on the raft and left. The wind was coming off the river and she didn't have a blanket, so it'd been too cold to sleep, and by the time the wind stopped and the temperature rose, she couldn't let herself fall asleep because her father wanted trout, and trout rise at dawn.

She'd never doubted that she or her father knew what a trout was until she'd started reading the field guide he'd given her and found out that trout were actually char—at least some of them—and also drum. *Salmonid: Salvelinus fontinalis* and *Salvelinus namaycush*; non-salmonid: *Sciaenidae* and *Oncorhynchus. Cynoscion nebulosus* wasn't really a trout, she remembered, then she thought about what her father would do if he came back and found her empty-handed and she told him that char were all that was biting, and she'd thrown them back because they weren't really trout, and quickly decided that she should try for the fish her father called trout, whether they were actually trout or not.

She hoped she'd get a burbot today, too, even though not even her father called a burbot a trout. *Lota lota* was the only fancy name she could pronounce out of all of them, and though she didn't want to catch one, she knew *Lota lota* was the only gadiform freshwater fish and the only member of the genus *Lota*, and that some people called it mariah, the lawyer, which made her think of a fish with a briefcase and a suit, which was funny.

Her parents argued, which wasn't funny, especially when it was about her: *It's not normal, Lester,* her mother would say. *She's coming with me, Alice. She's a girl, Lester—a girl!*

She'd seen them once, through the crack of their bedroom door. *She belongs at home with her sister!* her mother had said. Her father had ground his teeth: *Enough,* he'd said, slashing the air with the blade of his hand. *She's going. End of discussion.*

Her mother usually lost: about buying their farm, about Bo going hunting, about Bo's haircut and clothes. Bo had a dress for Sundays and church socials, but the rest of the time it was pants and a shirt.

Her mother lost even when she won: her father had wanted Hunter or Reese, but her mother had prevailed and named her Beatrix Rose.

Bo lay the pole across her lap and went through the progression her father had taught her: backing to fly line, fly line to leader, leader to tippet, and tippet to the fly. A.N.S.I., he had said. Say it out loud, Bo. Backing to fly line with an Albright knot, fly line to leader with a Nail knot, leader to tippet with a Surgeon's knot, and tippet to the fly with an Improved Clinch knot. A.N.S.I. Say it again—she had, and again, he'd said, and again, and again: A.N.S.I., A.N.S.I., A.N.S.I., A.N.S.I., A.N.S.I.

She didn't tell her father, but A.N.S.I. had gone out the window within a month. She still used the Surgeon's knot to attach the tippet, but she mostly used a Blood knot for the leader, and either a Palomar knot or a Surgeon's loop for the fly, depending on whether she wanted it tight or loose.

She was fairly certain he couldn't tie any of those knots.

"OW!"

A drop of blood slid down her thumb, catching in the creases of her palm and spreading laterally; her fingers were clumsy from the cold and she'd pressed too hard on the fly, sinking the hook into her flesh past the barb.

It was just before sunrise—she had to get it out quickly.

Bo looked around furtively—she wasn't supposed to go near the edge of the raft, but she did now, lying flat for safety and holding her thumb beneath the frigid water. When she couldn't feel it any longer, she closed her eyes, counted to three, and yanked the hook from her flesh, yelping agony and smelling metal as the world lurched and churned and blood bubbled out over her ragged flesh and down the meat of her hand, and she lunged to plunge her hand back into the icy water to keep from passing out.

Her father had only just started letting her fish unsupervised, and if he saw her thumb he'd change his mind and she wouldn't be allowed to fish while he was gone.

She pulled her hand from the river and looked down into the flesh. Toilet paper wouldn't staunch the bleeding. It was nearly dawn. She had to do something, so she unlaced her boots with one hand, holding the other away from her so she wouldn't bleed on her clothes, tugged at her pants, pulling one side and then the other until she could kick them off. She shucked her underwear; a brace of wind kicked up off the river, biting into her bare flesh. Thumb or pants first? Thumb. She wound the fabric tight around it, tied it off with her teeth, shoved her legs into the pants, leaning back and pulling them up two-handed. She jammed her feet into her boots, tried to tie her laces, failed, unwound the makeshift bandage and tore the fabric into smaller strips, re-tied it, and managed her laces.

She had a fly in the water before the sun broke free of the horizon, and all but filled her creel within the hour. Her thumb was throbbing, but she kept on casting; one or two more and she'd have her limit.

Back home, her sister would be scattering corn for the chickens, feeding the rabbits, and milking their goats.

Cattle are expensive, Bo, her father had said when they bought the farm, goat milk and rabbit meat are the future.

Bo was happier where she was, thumb or no thumb. Her father never said so, but she knew he was proud of her. It was why she got to go away with him on weekends. She wasn't supposed to know about the beer or whiskey he won off his friends by betting on her, but she did. Mr. Hanley made the whiskey in his cellar, and Mr. Abbott brewed beer in his shed. Bet you Bo can build a fire faster than you, Art, her father would say—bet you she'll dress our deer quicker than you can dress yours, Bill—bet you Bo catches more fish.

Her father would probably win a few more bottles when they got back and saw she'd made her limit.

She cinched the leather strap on her creel, fastened it to the raft with a bowline and sunk it so the fish wouldn't spoil, took off her fishing vest and disassembled her father's pole. He would have returned by now if he'd taken a deer during the dawn window; she had a day on the raft ahead of her.

An eel of nausea slithered up from Bo's ileum and coiled in her throat as she sat, and her hand throbbed, but the bleeding was staunched, mostly, and the few crocodile tears her thumb wept were no more than a nuisance. She removed the shirt she was wearing over her t-shirt, folded it into a pillow and lay down, letting the warmth of the day and the murmur of the river carry her to sleep.

Bo woke beneath a skin of sweat, hungry. The angle of the sun made it about two o'clock. She opened the lunch pail; her father liked hardboiled eggs so she left them for him and ate a sandwich, then another after she realized he'd want to eat the fish she'd caught when he got back. She halved the milk in a series of breathless pulls, wiped her mouth with her sleeve.

She had to go to the bathroom.

These were the hardest hours, waiting for her father to come back. She wanted to be moving, exploring and swimming and tracking game, but her father would tan her hide if she left the raft. Worse, he'd leave her behind the next time.

She invented games to play, counted and watched and read. She recognized a fair weather cumulus and remembered parts of a book her father had given her. She thought of her sister again, mending now, or helping their mother in the kitchen, having already mucked out the goat pen. Ruby was five years older, and smarter. She'd remember all of the book and understand what thermal convection meant, and what cloud erosion was. The only reason Bo knew the words was that her father brought her with him on his weekend trips and made her sit in one place for hours with only a field guide for entertainment. Ruby never said anything, but Bo knew she was jealous. She wished she could give her a present, but it was hard because her sister liked dresses and ribbons and had a picture of William Haines hidden amongst her things and looked forward to being allowed to wear makeup, and there weren't any of those things in the woods, and Bo couldn't make them, and didn't have any money to buy them. She'd given Ruby an eagle feather, a friendship rock, a bird's nest, bouquets of daffodils and daisies, an arrow head; Ruby always smiled and thanked her, but Bo knew they weren't things she really wanted.

Bo felt teeth and slapped at her leg, came away with a splatter of blood on her hand, flicked the crushed carcass into the river.

Ruby *hated* bugs, though she was wrong about them just like their father was wrong about the trout. Bugs were their own thing, *Hemiptera*, and the horse-flies and black-flies and deer-flies and mosquitos and no-see-ums that made Ruby frantic were not *Hemiptera*; *Hemiptera* were hemimetabolous and usually phytophagous, too, though Bo couldn't remember what those words meant. Horse flies and black-flies and deer-flies and mosquitos and no-see-ums made her father slap himself and swat at the air and say bad words.

She hoped her father got his deer today, because the flies were thick, and if he got bit all day and didn't get a deer, they'd ride home in silence, and when they got home he'd wait for her mother or sister to say something, and then explode and yell and pound his fists on the furniture and walls.

He was always sorry afterward. Bo had heard him apologizing to her mother, begging forgiveness—she'd even heard him crying, her mother soothing him, whispering reassurances.

The sun began to set, the temperature drop. Her father's friends returned, and she was able to go off into the woods and relieve herself while they built a fire. She came back and sat a short distance away; if she were within arm's reach they'd muss her hair and poke fun at her, which she hated.

Her father appeared just after nightfall, emerging from the black with a six-point buck.

"You stayed out any longer, and it'd be the middle of next week," Art ribbed. Bill cackled.

"Guess I'm just not the hunter you guys are—your deer already in the truck?"

"Go to hell, Les."

Her father laughed.

"Help me get this into the truck, Bo."

CHAPTER THREE

Lester White was twelve when his mother had the last of her eleven children. Donnie was two months premature, and the doctor told Lester's parents he wouldn't make it, but he did. Their father died the following year; grief made their mother an invalid, and it fell to Lester to run the farm and raise his brothers and sisters. He was big-hearted, smart enough to realize how intelligent Donnie was, and made sure that his brother took his studies seriously and that there was money to buy his books and school supplies.

Their sisters married and moved away; two of their brothers joined the Marine Corps and died at Belleau Wood, and finally, it was only Lester and Donnie and their mother. Lester sold half their acreage after Donnie graduated high school so he could go to college, and Donnie made him proud, graduated, got a job in the city, and wore a suit and tie to work. Donnie met Claire in the steno pool and fell in love, and Lester was the best man in their wedding, and two years later, Lester met Alice, and Donnie was able to reciprocate.

They became fathers within a month of each other, Donnie to a son, and Lester to a daughter, and Donnie bought a house just down the street from his brother so their children could play together.

Lester wanted a son, so his wife tracked her ovulation and took cough syrup before sex and ate blessed thistle and potato skins. Bo was born nine months later, one month before scarlet fever took Donnie's son. The brothers buried him together, and their wives wept and comforted each other, and after time had blunted their pain, Donnie and his wife began trying for another child. Seven barren years passed before they could announce they were pregnant, and on that night the brothers beamed and their wives' eyes were wet with joy, and there was brandy and a bottle of champagne, laughter, and more brandy. Lester let Ruby try both even though she was only fourteen, but he said ten was too young, and wouldn't give any to Bo, though he turned a blind eye when Ruby let her sister take a sip of hers.

Alice started knitting baby clothes the next day, and Donnie and Claire converted their guest room into a nursery, and the families attended the same church and sat in the same pew and shared their excitement with the congregation, and asked them to pray blessings upon the pregnancy.

Claire's appendix ruptured at twenty-two weeks.

CHAPTER FOUR

Bo wished it hadn't been open-casket: the thing lying in the coffin wasn't her aunt—didn't even look like her. It looked like it was made of wax.

Now they were in church again, at Mass.

"Saints of God, come to her aid!"

Bo had heard the prayer before, when other people in the church were sick.

"Remember, Lord, that we are dust: like grass, like a flower of the field."

Not grass, Bo thought, maybe a flower—a small smile—her aunt had loved dandelions. Bo used to go out in the yard and pick them for her, careful to grab as close to the grass as possible so that there would be lots of stem. She'd give them to her aunt, and her aunt would get the special vase from the highest cabinet and fill it with water and put the flowers in it and set it on the kitchen counter where everyone could see them.

"Merciful Lord, I tremble before you, ashamed of the things I have done."

Who was he talking about now? Bo thought hard, but couldn't think of anything she'd done that she was ashamed of—maybe one thing: she'd taken one of her mother's necklaces once, but just because she liked to hold it by one end and watch the diamond swing back and forth and the light leaping off of it. That was bad, but she'd told on herself and given it back, and her mother had thanked her and said that next time she should just ask, and that if she promised to be careful and only do it on Mother's bed, then she could play with it. So, no, Bo couldn't think of anything she was ashamed of, and her aunt certainly hadn't ever done anything she was ashamed of. Bo caught a glimpse of her uncle out of the corner of her eye; he was slumped forward in the pew, face empty, his hands limp in his lap. It was so unfair. He didn't have anything to be ashamed of either.

The priest must be talking to the other people.

"I know that my Redeemer lives: on the last day I shall rise again."

Bo wasn't sure about rising, and the last day seemed a long way off. She knew Jesus had rose, or risen—Fr. Hopkins and Fr. Quinn disagreed about that— but she couldn't think of anyone else who'd done it.

She liked Fr. Hopkins. He was tall and had a low, soft voice and big hands, and was very nice. Fr. Quinn was nice, too, but sad."I know that my Redeemer lives," Fr. Hopkins said. "And on that final day of days, His voice shall bid me rise again…"

So Fr. Hopkins would rise, too. "Rise," she said to herself.

"Lazarus you raised, O Lord, from the decay of the tomb."

Jesus, Fr. Hopkins, Fr. Quinn, and Lazarus. She'd forgotten about Lazarus. Suddenly, she was crying; she didn't want to forget her aunt.

"Into your hands, Father of mercies, we commend our sister Claire, in the sure and certain hope that, together with all who have died in Christ, she will rise with him on the last day."

She knew she was supposed to pay attention—it was church, and you were supposed to pay attention at church, but she couldn't.

"Merciful Lord," Fr. Hopkins prayed, "turn toward us and listen to our prayers."

Prayers, Bo thought. She had prayed for other people in church that were sick, but God hadn't listened or hadn't heard, or—a long ago Sunday School lesson popped into her head—God had decided not to answer them. God knows best, she remembered. God has a plan. Maybe that's why Fr. Quinn looks so sad, she thought, maybe Fr. Quinn wants God to answer more prayers.

"…We ask this through Christ our Lord."

People stirred, not her uncle. It was almost over; Bo felt sick. The last goodbye.

"Amen."

CHAPTER FIVE

Lester buried his brother's wife and child. Donnie stopped talking, started drinking. Their mother passed eight months later, and Lester buried her, too.

Lester had Alice cook for Donnie, and sent Ruby and Bo to clean his house.

CHAPTER SIX

"Ruby, Uncle Donnie needs you."

Ruby froze, feather duster quivering in her hand. She'd been humming to herself. She turned to Bo. "You should head on home and get ready for your camping trip."

"But I haven't done the kitchen or bathroom yet."

"I'll take care of it."

"Why?" Bo's eyes narrowed.

"Ruby…"

"Coming, Uncle Donnie." She turned back to Bo. "No particular reason."

"Nothing doing." Bo crossed her arms. "I'm staying."

"Bo…" Ruby glanced at the door to her uncle's bedroom, straightened one of the pillows on the couch.

"No."

"Fine."

It was only thirty feet from the couch to Uncle Donnie's bedroom— why was it taking Ruby so long? She seemed to be staring at the sliver of black between the door and the doorjamb, but Bo couldn't see anything. She pretended to be dusting so Ruby wouldn't catch her watching. Bo would know when Ruby had gone in anyway because Ruby would have to push the door open, and the hinge would bay something awful and Ruby would flinch as she always did when she walked into their uncle's room and the door made that sound.

If Ruby closed the door behind her, then Bo wouldn't be able to see anything, and would count to thirty before creeping up to the door to try to listen, but that never kept her attention for more than a minute or two, because whatever it was Ruby and their uncle did in there, it didn't involve much talking.

The bedroom door didn't always latch, though, and sometimes it even worked itself open enough that she could see in.

Once, Bo saw their uncle pinching the bridge of his nose as Ruby entered, wincing. "Uncle Donnie really needs you today," he said.

A couple times the door didn't latch, and Bo saw their uncle pull Ruby against his body before one of them pushed the door shut. Bo hated being the youngest, hated that Ruby got to go in and do something that she didn't get to.

And Ruby wouldn't even tell her what it was that she was getting to do, and the one time Bo had asked her straight out, Ruby had screamed at her and called her stupid and told her to shut up.

That was when Bo thought to climb the tree to get onto the barn roof. Bo bet she'd be able to see down into her uncle's bedroom if she crept around the side and kind of half hung off it.

So one day she worked extra fast to get everything clean, and she waited a couple minutes after Uncle Donnie called Ruby in, then slipped out a back window, climbed the tree, and shimmied across the roof on her belly until Ruby and their uncle came into view through the bedroom window.

Bo watched him beckon Ruby, pat the bed, the empty half where their aunt had slept, where Bo thought that maybe her aunt had once given him what he needed. Ruby sat, let her uncle bring her down to him.

She closed her eyes.

Bo watched them several times over the next two weeks, unsure what she was seeing, knowing only that it made her feel sick to her stomach to watch, and that Ruby didn't seem to like doing it.

Uncle Donnie always held her afterwards, fell asleep clutching her to his chest. That was when Bo left her perch to avoid being caught spying.

One day Bo heard Ruby shriek in pain.

Their uncle had her naked on all fours, was standing behind her.

Ruby shrieked and he stopped, and Bo thought maybe they were talking, but couldn't see their faces or hear anything. Then all of a sudden Uncle Donnie threw himself backward and crumpled to the ground, but Ruby just stayed as she was, motionless, and Bo could see all of her, even the parts she shouldn't, the parts no one should, and suddenly there were tears in Bo's eyes and she was angry and scared and sick and worried over Ruby all at once, and had to force herself to take twenty deep breaths in and out before she trusted herself to climb down from the roof without falling.

Then she ran to Ruby as fast as she could, calling Ruby's name, burst through the door into their Uncle's room, and found her sister dressed and sitting on the bed. "What's wrong," she panted, "I heard…"—she saw their uncle curled fetal on the floor—"I'll get Father!"

"No." Ruby's voice froze Bo in place. "No." Ruby swept the tears from her face with a hand. "We don't need to get Father. Uncle Donnie's heart is broken; he's crying because Aunt Claire's gone."

"But—"

"Get your coat. We're going."

CHAPTER SEVEN

"Something's not right with her."

"Ruby?"

They were sitting on the porch.

"She's completely withdrawn..."

"What're you talking about?"

"Look at her, Les—she hasn't turned a page in over an hour."

"Maybe she's thinking."

"She cries at night."

"She's always been like that. She gets in moods, gets herself all worked up."

"This is different."

Lester laid his paper on the table.

"How?"

"I don't know."

He stared at his wife until she turned away, then picked up his paper and resumed reading.

Alice kept on watching her daughter.

"Rose?"

"Yes?"

Bo was pulling her boots; she'd finished her chores and homework, and was eager to get outside and into the woods before it got too dark.

"Come here, please."

"I already did my—" Bo stopped short.

"Sit down."

She sat. It was her mother's serious face, the one that meant she was in trouble. Her mind raced, trying to think what she'd done: she'd read her sister's diary—but that was weeks ago—and she'd been good since, except for kicking Bobby Michaels in the shin, but he'd been smart with her and deserved it.

"I want to talk about your sister."

"Ruby?"

Her mother shot her an impatient look.

"Is she in trouble?"

"That's what I wanted to ask you."

"I saw," Bo had told her sister. They'd been folding laundry.

"Saw what?" Ruby asked.

"What you and Uncle Donnie did."

Ruby froze.

"I finished my chores," Bo told her, "so I was coming to ask if I could walk home, and then I heard something, and I saw you."

Bo hadn't been able to make herself look at her sister, so she didn't see her hand, only heard the abrupt snap of skin striking skin and felt her head blasted sideways, pain radiating through her nose and eyes.

"Don't you ever say that again."

Bo hadn't backed down from Bobby Michaels or George Wilson, and she'd been ready to fight Arthur Platz, but she shrunk from Ruby, stunned.

"Did something happen?"Bo's eyes fell to the kitchen table. "What do you mean?"

"I mean, did something happen to Ruby? Did she do something?"

Bo didn't want to lie, knew she shouldn't because it was bad and she was terrible at it, but Ruby had made it clear that—maybe it didn't count as a lie if she didn't say anything. She shook her head.

"Beatrix Rose."

Bo started to perspire—how did her mother always know? Her ears were burning like they always did when she'd done something bad—but she hadn't even said anything!

"Rose."

Bo jerked her head upward at the change in her mother's tone, soft now, worried—not angry.

"You can tell me. No one's going to get in trouble."

She looked into her mother's eyes and felt tears swelling up. Her mother was worried, and she and Ruby didn't talk anymore, not at night as they fell asleep, or at any other time. Bo used to watch the light shimmer in Ruby's hair while she brushed it out, Ruby smiling while Bo went on about her day and the things she'd seen and the fish she'd caught and the deer she was going to get one of these days. Ruby would weave her chestnut mane into one big braid that fell between her shoulder blades, and then one of them would choose a book, and Ruby would read it aloud.

"I know something happened," her mom said. "I'm not mad; I just want you to tell me what it was."

They'd been in the middle of *Look Homeward, Angel*, but it'd been so long since Ruby read to her that Bo couldn't remember whether Eliza was the wife, and Helen the daughter, or if it was the other way around.

"Rose, please."

Bo was afraid Ruby would never talk to her again if she told their mother what she'd seen, but Ruby never said more than two or three words now, anyway, to anyone, and she went to bed early every night. Ruby was kind to her, and dutiful to her mother, and helpful around the house, but she wasn't Ruby. Ruby wouldn't have slapped her—Ruby had once been grounded for three weeks because she'd refused to drown their barn-cat's litter in the river like their father said.

Ruby said please and thank you and smiled at everyone and laughed at every joke.

"Ruby and Uncle Donnie…"

CHAPTER EIGHT

"Lester?"

"Hmm?"

They were in bed. He was reading a catalogue, mulling over which seed to buy for the coming fall.

"Can I talk to you a moment?"

"Sure."

He kept reading.

"It's about Ruby."

"She's just going through one of her spells."

"No."

He dropped his catalogue and peered at her over his glasses, hackles rising.

"It's your brother."

"I thought it was Ruby."

"It's both of them." Alice felt tears rising in her eyes.

"You're getting yourself all worked up over nothing."

"No." She shook her head. "He did things to her, Les. Donnie—he made her do things."

"What the hell are you talking about?"

"Rose told me."

"No."

"She said—"

"She's wrong."

"Les—"

"God dammit, Alice! I said she's wrong."

"Les—"

"Not another word!" He raised his hand across his body.

She wouldn't let herself flinch, waited for the blow. It never came; he returned to his catalogue, chest rising and falling in heavy, ragged turns until she turned away.

"Goddamn rot," he muttered.

She cut the light on her bedside table and rolled onto her side.

He stood in the hallway watching her, light off but unnecessary because the sun had yet to set. Ruby was curled fetal beneath her blanket, facing the wall.He almost called out to her. *Ruby,* he would have said, wanted to say. *Yes, father,* she'd have answered; he would have gone and sat on the edge of her bed. But he couldn't think what he might say or do after that, so he stayed where he was.

"Where are you going?"Alice was putting a fresh loaf into the breadbox as he yanked his coat from its hook.

"Out."

"Out where?"

"Leave it."

He returned an hour later with one of Mr. Hanley's glass jugs. She knew better than to ask where he'd been.

They were in the last days of an Indian summer, the breeze passing through the window screen, thick with apples and sweet corn and winter wheat.

The light was on in his office; his silhouette tipped the jug over a tumbler, set it aside. The door was cracked, and she moved toward it, walking loudly, slowly, giving him a chance to speak; he didn't, and she turned to go.

"I don't suppose there's anything to be done?" he said to her back.

She was silent.

"No," he said after a moment, "I'd guessed not."

CHAPTER NINE

September 1929 brought the warmest September Maine had seen in eight years. It was Bo's job to bring the food her mother cooked to Uncle Donnie's and leave it on the doorstep, and they were two weeks into the month and she still didn't need a jacket. Two days of food went uncollected, and Bo told her father, who went to investigate and found his brother hanging from a rafter.

October arrived and the temperature plummeted; Bo started wearing a jacket. The Stock Market crashed, and suddenly half the days of the week were black, and Bo didn't understand why.

There was no funeral for Uncle Donnie; her father had him cremated on a colorless Wednesday, brought him home in an urn, and put him on a shelf in the back of the barn.

The radio was full of words she'd never heard, 'shanty-town,' and 'Hoovervilles,' and 'unemployment.' Newsmen called what was happening 'The Great Depression,' but people didn't seem to think it was so great. Everyone seemed sad and scared.

Her mother got sick in March, and a few days later President Hoover got on the radio and said the worst was over, and her father called him a damn liar. One newsman claimed people were starving all over the country, and another said that over 3 million men had lost their jobs.

December came, and Bo's father told them he was going to be gone for a while, though he didn't say why. Her mother told her everything was going to be okay, but Bo wasn't sure she believed her, and when Christmas came and went and her father still hadn't come back, she knew she didn't. She felt better when her sister explained about the Depression, and how everyone was poor now, and that their father had gone looking for a way to provide for them so they wouldn't have to eat such small meals, and could buy new clothes once in a while.

Their mother's illness lingered, but then it was February, and their father came back, and their mother got better, and things did seem like they were going to be okay, even if Ruby was still mostly silent and her parents were up late every night, whispering. Her father had come back with a trailer and farm equipment, livestock, and more seed than they'd ever had for things they'd never grown before, which confused her because everyone was supposed to be poor now.

She knew something was happening, but not what, only that she probably wasn't supposed to know, and that the things she wasn't allowed to know kept piling up. She and Ruby weren't allowed to listen to the radio anymore—and it was starting to feel like there were more things she didn't know than things she did, and she hated it. It wasn't fair. Her parents listened to the radio every night, and Bo's bedroom was directly above, and she would lie on the floor and press her ear to the vent, and try to catch what she could. In the past, Ruby would have scolded her and made her get up, but she was silent, now. Bo heard the man on the radio say 'food riots' and something about apple sellers and something else about deportations, but she hadn't been able to make out much else from the broadcast, so even after she looked up the word 'deported' in the family dictionary, she didn't know who or what was being deported, or to where, or why.

And so it went.

Suddenly nothing was right, and no one would tell her why, or if and when things might get back to good. And even though it felt like it had all started with their aunt, and spread to their uncle and Ruby, Bo sensed that it was bigger than all that now, bigger than them, and it seemed unfair and even cruel that her parents and sister wouldn't talk to her or explain anything.

It seemed unfair to leave her on her own.

CHAPTER TEN

"Bo."

"Yes, Father?"

They were patching up the wire around the rabbit hutch.

"You won't be getting a rifle this year."

Bo didn't respond. She already knew.

Ruby had taken her aside. "I need you to listen," she had said. "I know Father promised you a rifle this year, but it's not coming, and you have to promise me you won't make a fuss."

" But," Bo had started.

"No buts, Bo. I don't want to scare you, but we're in trouble, might be in trouble."

"It's not fair! He promised!"

"I know it's not, Bo, and I know he did, but he can't afford it. We can't afford it. The crops haven't come in yet, and no one's buying our rabbit or our goat's milk. People aren't even buying many of our eggs."

"But—"

"No, Bo. No but's. Remember how Uncle Donnie—" Ruby crashed to a halt, pallid.

Bo held her breath.

"Remember how he left everything to Father, how Father said he wouldn't accept a single penny? Well, he accepted everything, the house, the car, and the money. He had to."

"Goddamnit, girl!" her father yelled. "You damn well better answer when I'm talking to you!"

Girl. The word struck Bo like a switch.

"Yes, Father."

She felt sick, tears stinging the backs of her eyes, but she forced herself to look at him. Ruby would've known not to, would've left him a way to save face, but Bo didn't know better and kept looking at him until he fled her gaze, rage dried to dust and something in its place that she'd never seen before, something broken.

"I'm…" his voice trailed off. "You're too young, you're not ready."

"Yes, Father."

"Go inside and see if your mother needs help."

"Yes, Father."

Bo did, and her mother didn't, and eventually she wandered upstairs to her room.

"You okay?" Ruby asked. "You've been standing there for a while now."

"Oh."

Bo's eyes fell to her feet. She didn't know what she was feeling or how to say it, so she stayed silent, and her sister didn't press her.

"Sit with me?" Ruby asked after a while.

Bo didn't mean to crawl into her sister's lap, but she did, surprising them both, and they watched the moment carve itself out in space and time, silent, both of them aware of its fragility. Bo sat between Ruby's outstretched legs and mashed herself back against her sister, and Ruby encircled her with her arms, and laid her face against the crown of Bo's head. Bo felt the warmth of her sister's breath run across her cheek, inhaled notes of late blackberries and second-season raspberries and goat's milk.

"Are you okay?"

Bo's question.

"I will be."

It wasn't the answer Bo wanted, but she allowed herself to breathe again, allowed Ruby to continue holding her.

"What's Black Thursday?"

"The day the stock market crashed."

"Is that why everything's different?"

"Maybe."

"Is it why father can't buy me a rifle like he said?"

"Yes."

Bo thought a minute. "What's the stock market?"

"I'm not really sure, exactly. Something to do with banks and business."

"It's why we don't get the paper anymore, too, isn't it."

"We don't?"

"Father stopped it last week."

"I didn't realize."

They fell to silence.

"Are you going to be okay?"

"Yes."

"You'll tell me when you are?"

Ruby nodded.

"You'll tell me?"

"I'll tell you."

"Will it be soon?"

"I think so."

"You think so?"

Ruby nodded.

"Good."

CHAPTER ELEVEN

It was almost dusk. Bats charged from the shadows to wing and swoop as Bo walked through the field, bow in her right hand, two arrows in her left. They were farmers now, real farmers, not just rabbit farmers. Brussels sprouts and kale and asparagus and corn and carrots and potatoes—green everywhere. Green that required planting and hoeing and weeding and watering. She liked the tomatoes, which were huge and red and sweet, and the sugar snap peas because they looked like Christmas lights and were easily pilfered and stashed in her pocket, but the biggest reason they were her favorites was that they were both Ruby's responsibility. Bo could have done without it all; her father went camping less now, hunted less, which meant that Bo didn't get to go camping or hunting much anymore. She liked the plough horse he'd bought, but not enough to make up for all that she'd lost, the days and nights by the river and in the woods. And they had a milk cow now, an ornery old Holstein that kicked at her and tried to step on her foot every time she milked it.

Bo quickened her pace to clear the last rows of corn and put all of it behind her.

Sundays were the only good days to be a farmer. She'd run home from church, ditch her dress for overalls, and she and her father would load all the milk, butter, eggs, vegetables, and rabbit meat they could spare into the back of his truck and make their rounds. People paid if they could, bartered with goods Bo couldn't understand her father wanting, things he made her carry up into the barn loft, and which they'd never use. The widow Martinsson had four children under the age of five and cried every time she and her father came by, carrying crates overflowing with food into her kitchen, and refused her money. Bo didn't understand why her father wouldn't accept the praise people tried to give him, or the gifts, especially if times were as hard as everyone said. Mr. Spencer would slip her sweets when her father wasn't looking, and Nea Alen would give her satin ribbons and old kickshaw she could take to Ruby. Bo felt like a heroine riding next to her father, lugging crates with him, or at least the daughter of a hero.

Her father always gave her a penny when they got to Mr. Docherty's, and sent her to the store across the street. She wasn't exactly sure why, but suspected it had something to do with the bottles he hid behind the empty crates in the truck bed. Bo could get three pieces of candy for a penny; she gave one to Ruby, kept one for herself, and alternated the odd piece between them from week to week.

There was a sycamore just inside the northern tree line, thirty yards from a plat of clover-flecked grass hedged by wood, south and west. She crouched low beside the tree, shielded by sweet grass and cottonsedge, lay her arrows at the ready, adjusted the guard on her right arm.

Mr. Renaud had offered her the bow on one of their delivery runs, but her father wouldn't let her accept it. She'd begged, and he'd cuffed her so hard her ears rang and Mr. Renaud flinched.

She'd walked all the way across town to Mr. Renaud's the next time her father was away, told him that her father had changed his mind and could she still have the bow, and he'd said of course, and that it had belonged to an Algonquin Indian once, a Penobscot, and that his great-grandfather had won it gambling. Mr. Renaud had wrapped it in a blanket and handed it to her with care.

It was a man's bow, nearly as long as she was tall, and it was weeks before she was able to draw it to the wall. Day after day, she'd come home from school, finish her chores, then retrieve the bow from its hiding place in the loft, and pull and pull until her arms burned and her fingers were raw and bleeding.

A pair of owls played call and answer. Bo waited, stilling herself. A she-fox appeared between cornstalks, nostrils flaring as she scented the air. She glanced back over her shoulder before trotting off through the grass and into the woods, her kits stumbling after her.

Bo and Ruby went to the library every other Monday. You were allowed three books at a time, and on the Monday after Bo tricked Mr. Renaud into giving her the bow, she chose *Modern Archery* by a man named Lambert, *A Study of Bows and Arrows* by Saxton Pope, and *The Last of the Mohicans* in case someone asked her why she was getting books on archery. She'd been Catholic her whole life, and no one had ever told her the Pope was an archer. It made her think that maybe God would understand why she did what she did, and that maybe he wouldn't be too mad.

White flickered between the pine branches at the tree line, and a doe stepped tentatively into the clearing; Bo's breath caught in her chest. Not what she wanted, but where there's one… She thought of shadow and water as she reached for an arrow, her heart thumping so hard she was sure the deer could hear it.

Flow, don't move.

She nocked the arrow.

Two more deer stepped out, does.

Her chest was tight.

Breathe.

A buck.

She willed her heart to quiet, willed herself to stone—it was looking right at her—to vapor, anything a deer couldn't see. It took a step past the break line, toward her, another, turned south, away from her, stepped again, bent to the clover.

Bo'd only ever shot at one other deer, and she'd missed. Badly. She'd heard the arrow ripping through the leaves as the buck bolted. She'd lost over half her arrows before that, lost them before she even managed to hit the target she'd set up behind a cluster of trees at the boundary of their property, the top to a barrel that had long since disappeared and which her father wouldn't miss. Her arrows were old, maybe even as old as the bow itself, dogwood with stone tips and fletch that were brittle and pocked. A couple of the shafts were warped.

She realized she'd have to torque the bow as she sighted her shot, torque it or move and risk spooking the buck.

She wasn't good enough to torque it.

Flow, don't move.

She knew he'd beat her if she made the shot. Her father had barely spoken to her since she challenged him in front of Mr. Renaud, hadn't taken her with him on his deliveries in over a month, and when he saw the carcass and realized she'd lied and gone behind his back... The callouses on the thumb and forefingers of her left hand, and on the palm of her right would only make it worse; he'd see them and know she'd been deceiving him for weeks, and his eyes would narrow and his jaw would clench, and every word he said would have to cut its way past gritted teeth.

Bo took the bowstring to the wall as she rose. It wasn't right,—Mr. Lambert said you had to get in the proper stance, and then raise the bow, but she didn't figure she had the time for proper, and tried to flow and draw and rise all at once, and the buck saw her as she was one-one-thousanding the interval between wall and release, and sprang.

The arrow caught it mid-leap.

Bo ran to the deer, too close. She knew better—it might have lashed out in a final spasm of life and split her open with its hoof. But she was lucky; her shot had been true or the deer had leapt into it, and now she was looking down at her first deer. She watched as its eyes went dark, and the triumph and pride swelling in her chest were joined by remorse as she thought of all the fish she'd caught, and the deer her father had shot, and how the light must have faded from their eyes, too, and she wondered why it hadn't occurred to her before.

She'd get the belt. She'd get the belt, and her mother would cry and beg her father to stop, but he wouldn't until finally her mother threw herself between them like she'd had to do when her father had caught Ruby letting a guy put his hand up her dress behind the barn. The belt had hit her mother's cheek and mouth and split her lip and left a welt that had taken more than a week to fade away.

She knelt beside the deer, took the knife from the sheath on her belt and drove it into the deer's sternum, listening for the pop, pop of the knife puncturing hide and membrane, and working the blade towards the anus, taking care not to pierce the guts and foul the meat. Vapors of blood and death and offal rose in fingers as she scraped the cavity hollow, cutting out organs and yards of gut, the fingers tightening around her head as if to pull her in. She cut the diaphragm and felt a wash of blood on her hands. Anus and lungs and heart and liver, one by one into the woods, the heart last. She paused, cupping it in her hands; she'd read that Indians believed eating hearts made you more powerful. She lifted it to her face and inhaled, blood dripping between her fingers and down her arms as the organ piped vascular steam into the eventide. And she had no idea why she crushed it in her fists when she did, only that her mouth and lungs were thick with the metallic reek of blood. She clenched it so tightly her fists trembled, and when it was empty, she let it fall.

Her father's friends had talked about blooding. Should she blood herself? She made a move to, then thought maybe her father might want to be the one to do it, and stopped.

It was time to get him; she wouldn't be able to drag the deer to the house on her own.

Bo shook as she walked.

She'd been hiding on the stairs the time that Ruby got whipped. She'd heard the yelling and the doors slam, and crept as close as she dared, and though she couldn't see the belt hitting Ruby from where she was, she'd heard it—could still hear it. *Goddamned slut*, and the strap tearing air. *My own daughter*, and the sharp, wet crack of leather against flesh. *Filthy whore*, and Ruby sobbing and their mother begging. He'd been savage, demeaning, cruel, his voice rising with the lash and Ruby's frantic howls as blow followed blow, and it was only their mother's intervention that saved Ruby, that threw herself between her husband and her daughter. Bo couldn't see what happened, only heard her mother cry out, and then her father, *Alice!* he'd said. *Alice! Oh god! Oh god!*

Would he do that to her?

Would her mother save her if he did?

Bo had seen her mother holding her father later that night. The door to their bedroom was three inches open, and her mother's right eye was swollen shut. There was an icepack lying on the bed beside her, but she was cradling her father's head in her lap and stroking his hair as he sobbed.

I'm sorry, he said, over and over, *I'm sorry. I'm sorry. I'm sorry.*

Bo thought about leaving the carcass in the woods and was ashamed of herself. She took hold of two legs and dragged it as far as she could, hid her bow and arrow, and went to get her father.

Bo'd had to put salve on Ruby's back and buttocks and legs for over a week, after her morning shower and come nightfall. They'd go up to their room and Bo would clean her wounds and apply the ointment and rebandage her, and then she'd sit on her bed and Ruby would turn out the light, and Bo would stay with her until she fell sleep.

Her father had given Ruby twenty-one lashes.

Bo stepped out of the cornfield onto their driveway wondering how many awaited her.

CHAPTER TWELVE

"Pour me another."

They were in the living room, the girls in the kitchen, finishing their homework.

"Are you sure, Les? I'm worried you'll have an awful headache—"

"What did you say?"

She froze. She'd been standing behind him, kneading the knots in his shoulders and neck; her thumbs were red with exertion.

"I was just—"

"Goddamnit, woman."

"Upstairs, Bo," Ruby said. "Quickly."

"Les—"

"Shut your goddamn mouth before I shut it for you."

"I wasn't—"

The girls couldn't hear everything that was said, but they didn't need to hear the words to know how it would go, it'd be *goddamn*, and their father stomping into the kitchen and the hard, blunt sound of his tumbler slammed on the counter and the rattling of the pans hanging on the wall and the door slamming and the truck starting and their father driving off.

They'd wait a few minutes, then Ruby would go to her.

"What's a quim?"

"Something you don't ever say, Bo, not ever."

"But what—"

"A vagina."

"Why would Father—" Bo stopped herself; Ruby was shaking.

"You stay here."

She didn't. Their mother had gone up to her bedroom, and Ruby had gone after her, and so Bo counted to sixty very slowly and followed, walking as silently as she could.

The door was open; she'd heard Ruby knock.

Her mother was sitting on the bed staring into nowhere, hands folded in her lap. Ruby stood in front of her, unsmiling.

"He can't treat you like that," Ruby said.

"Like what, Darling? It was just a little misunderstanding."

"No." A sharp shake of her head, arms tight against her chest.

"Ruby, honey, you're trembling. Come sit with me." Her mother patted the bed next to her. "You know the stress your father's under, how I forget myself sometimes."

"I heard what he said."

"Honey, I haven't the fog—"

She stopped—her daughter's face—tried again, changing tact, but the words were stillborn on her lips. She forced a smile, begging her daughter for the same, but Ruby only glared.

"He has no right to treat you like that."

Her mother didn't respond, sat blinking on the edge of the bed.

"He's got no call to be like that—no decent person... he's a nasty, malicious—"

"He's your father!"

"He's vile!"

"Ruby!"

"A quim!"

The color drained from her mother's face.

"You let him talk to you like you're a whor—"

Her mother struck her.

Ruby closed her eyes as the pain expanded; her eyes watered and her nose ran.

"He hates us. I have scars from what he's done to me—he's split your lip and marked your face—"

"That was an accident!"

"He hates us. He only loves Bo because you let him treat her like a boy."

"He loves you, too! And me. He loves all of us."

"I don't believe you."

Ruby started to quake, her tears no longer autonomic, and let her mother guide her to the bed.

"You know your father's scar, the one that runs down his back?"

Ruby was silent.

"You were four years old; Uncle Donnie and Aunt Claire were here, and Mr. Harper and his wife from church, and another man I can't remember. I was cooking Easter dinner, and there was a pot boiling on the stove, and you got hold of the handle before we could do anything, and pulled it down on yourself. Everyone froze but your father. He was halfway to the dining room, but he ran faster than I've ever seen a person run, and threw himself between you and the water. I can still see the look on your face: you were so small, and you'd never heard your father raise his voice, and there he was, running at you, yelling. Your eyes were so big. He shoved you out of the way, and you hit your head against the kitchen cabinet and were crying. Your father was face down on the floor, scalded down to the bone, but he tried to comfort you."

"That doesn—"

"No, it doesn't. It doesn't make up for the things he says, and nothing can make up for what he did to you. Your father knows I will never, never forgive him for what he did, and I know it doesn't make it any better for you, but your father will never forgive himself, either. He doesn't forgive himself for the things he's done to me either. He punishes himself worse than you or I or any power in the world ever could."

"And keeps on doing it."

"Has he raised a hand to you since that day? Have you seen him raise a hand to me? To Bo?"

Ruby shook her head. "He doesn't need to. He has us all so afraid. He makes us feel stupid and cheap and dirty…"

"Do you remember how he used to carry you around on his shoulders? He'd pick you up and toss you in the air, and you'd laugh and laugh. He was the one that put a daisy in your lunch box every day. He used to take us for picnics on Saturdays—for ice cream and sodas after church."

"And then he just stopped! Why did he stop? What did I do? It wasn't my fault what Uncle Donnie…" Ruby's face fell into her hands. She fell to her knees, "It wasn't my fault! It wasn't my fault! I'm sorry! I'm so sorry!"

Her mother knelt beside her, pulled her to her chest, and held her there. Bo was crying too, hiding behind the door, and she kept crying even after her sister and mother stopped. Her mother called, and she came.

"How long have you been listening?"

Bo's face fell.

"You're not going to get in trouble."

"A while."

"And you heard what your sister and I were talking about?"

She nodded.

"What did you hear?"

"Ruby said Father hates us, and you said he didn't, and Ruby asked how he can be so mean if he loves us, and you told stories, and Ruby said it wasn't her fault, and started crying."

"Your father does love us."

"I know."

"And Ruby knows too, right, Ruby?"

Ruby turned away. A slight nod.

"And she knows he doesn't mean the things he says when he gets angry, that—"

Bo interrupted. "What does he mean?"

Their mother paused.

"He means things men aren't allowed to say, that he's worried for his family, and scared that he won't be able to provide for us, and he blames himself for not being strong enough."

Bo looked to Ruby for confirmation, but Ruby and her mother had locked eyes.

"There are things men can't say to women, because they think they're supposed to be strong. But they're never as strong as they think they should be, and they know that they need help, but they don't know how to ask for it, so they keep on floundering and hating themselves for being weak."

"And that's the part of Father that makes him get mean?"

"Yes."

Bo looked from her mother to Ruby; her sister was somewhere else, looking at the wall or the clock or a knot in the wood. "Why doesn't he just ask?"

"Because he can't."

"Why not?"

"It doesn't matter, Bo, he just can't. And it's our job to know that, and to understand that he doesn't always mean the things he says, and to remember that when he hurts you, no matter what."

"No matter what?"

"No matter what."

"Why?"

"It's our lot, Bo, what we're meant to do, what we're given."

"We?"

"Women. You, and I, and Ruby."

"What are we given?"

"A lifetime of men," Ruby said.

She spoke without looking at them. Bo didn't understand, and looked to her mother for an explanation, but she was staring at Ruby again.

"A lifetime of men?"

Her mother bowed and closed her eyes, and it felt an eternity before she opened them.

"Yes, Bo. A lifetime of men."

CHAPTER THIRTEEN

Bo woke up alone, her sister already downstairs or outside working at her chores. She pushed the covers away and was dragging her legs over the edge of the bed when she saw it, a smear on the inside of her pajama pants. Her hands flew to cover the stain, but they weren't big enough. She couldn't let her father find out—he already suspected that she was becoming a woman. Bo had heard him say so to her mother when he thought she was out of earshot; the look on his face made her ashamed of herself. She'd tried to stop it from happening, slept on her chest so her breasts wouldn't grow, hunted and fished and hiked through the woods, and played hard at hotbox and dodgeball and smear the queer and whatever else the boys did. She'd bound her breasts with fabric from the first day they appeared, two weeks before she turned eleven. She knew it'd only get worse. She'd watched it happen to her sister, watched her chest grow and grow and push her sweaters and the tops of her dresses up and out until she looked silly. Ruby's were bigger than their mother's now, and men looked at Ruby with glances that reminded Bo of the way she felt when she smelled her mother's roast chicken cooking.

This was worse than growing bubs. Much worse. Her mother did the wash, hung it out to dry on the clothesline or in an upstairs room, so her father and anyone who saw their wash would have proof that she was a woman, now, and she wouldn't get to go hunting or camping anymore.

Bo stared at the stains on her pant-leg and bed-sheet, felt the crust of blood and tissue that had dried into her pajamas and thigh; it itched and she wanted to scratch it, but she couldn't do that without touching it. The stains seemed to grow as she stared, to whip and reel with the room as her head spun. There was no way to hide it—she only owned one set of sheets and two pairs of pajamas, so she couldn't throw them away, and she didn't have any money, so she couldn't switch them out for new ones.

Ruby found her curled into a ball next to her bed, crying, shut the bedroom door, and sat beside her, waiting for her to speak.

"It's over, isn't it?"

"What is?"

"Father won't take me camping anymore."

"Day trips, maybe."

Bo shook her head, tried to staunch the tears massing in her eyes.

"I don't want day trips."

"I know."

"And I don't want dresses or ribbons or makeup—or to have to stay inside all day, or to bake or clean or sew. I don't even know how to sew, and I don't want to learn!"

"I know. Hush now, you're getting yourself all worked up."

"It's not fair!" The tears were streaming now.

"Bo—"

"No! He taught me to hunt and fish and make a fire without matches, and he said I was good at it, and bragged about me to his friends, and now he's going to throw me back in the kitchen and tell me I'm no better than y —"

Ruby clenched before Bo could swallow the word, face twisting.

Neither of them spoke for a long time.

Bo tried, "I—"

"It's okay."

"I'm sorr—"

"I know."

"I didn't mean—"

"I get it, Bo."

They were silent again, and Bo's shame doubled and tripled and wound itself into her flesh and cinched her gut in knots.

"It's okay." Ruby wiped at her eye with the back of her hand. "It's not your fault. How could you think any different?"

"What?"

Ruby's voice was vapor; Bo wasn't sure she'd heard her right.

Ruby shook her head. "Nothing, never mind." She forced a smile. "You've always been special to Father, and you always will be. Things may look a little different, but that doesn't mean they've changed. You'll still be you, and you'll hunt and fish and tromp through the woods, and Father will be proud when you come home with your haul."

"Promise?"

"Promise."

Bo nodded, bowed her head. "Ruby…" Her eyes stuck to the floor.

"What?"

"I really am sorry. About what I said."

"I know you are."

Bo looked up at her.

"And you're not mad?"

"No."

"Really?"

"Really."

"And you're not hurt?"

Ruby shook her head.

"Not even a little?"

Ruby smiled. "Maybe a little."

Bo nodded. "I really am sorry."

"I know."

They held each other's eyes uneasily until Ruby stuck her tongue out and made a face, and Bo smiled, and then Ruby smiled too, and Bo believed that things really were okay.

"I'm going to need one of those awful spider-belt things now, aren't I?"

"What?"

"A Modess thing" —Bo pantomimed a belt with straps and a pad— "like mother wears."

"Oh, lord." Ruby covered her mouth, snickering. "Goodness, no—they're for old ladies. They make internal ones, now. I'll give you one of mine."

"Internal means inside, right?" Bo looked ill.

"Trust me." Ruby led her toward the bathroom, opened the hall closet, removed a tampon, and held it out to Bo.

"Do you need me to show you how?"

Bo shook her head.

"Okay."

Bo stepped into the bathroom and closed the door behind her.

CHAPTER FOURTEEN

Bo sat on her bed, waiting. The sun wouldn't be up for another couple of hours, but she was already dressed. Her father had started moving around three-thirty, made coffee, eggs and bacon. The smells made her mouth water, but she didn't go down. He hadn't said she couldn't go, just didn't invite her, acted as if she hadn't been going with him since she was five years old.

She hoped he'd change his mind; her gear was all packed, stacked against the barn wall near her father's truck, visible, but out of the way.

Ruby turned over in her sleep.

The clock in the living room struck four.

Bo listened, heard the barn door open and the truck start, her father pull out of the bay. Each sound struck her like a blow.

Then it was quiet.

He'd really left her.

She lay back atop her covers, turned toward Ruby; the room was devoid of light so she couldn't make out even the lines of her bed. She listened: Ruby's breath was like rainfall on grass, oats shifting in a feed-sack, barely there, inaudible beneath the sporadic groans of the house.

Was this how Ruby had felt all those weekends she'd been left behind?

Bo sat up, pushed herself over the edge of the bed, and went down to the kitchen, found half a cup of coffee leftover, not quite cold, drank it down, and set the pot in the sink. She took her jacket from a hook in the hallway, pulled her boots on. She'd set up a blind at the west end of their property a year ago, in a small clearing that opened up near the river. She wouldn't make it before the deer started moving, but at least she'd be in the woods when the sun came up.

Ruby would cover chores for her.

Her things were in the barn where she'd left them, just beyond the reach of the light falling from the single bulb above the door. She couldn't really see; details trickled from the dark like drops of blood: the frayed rim of her sleeping bag, the length of her bow, the copper buckle on her canteen. There was something unfamiliar on top of her pack; she bent to pick it up, knew what it was the moment it touched her skin, a George Wostenholm IXL hunting knife that had belonged to her father's grandfather. She drew it from its sheath, held it out, testing its weight and balance, letting the dim light catch on its blade.

A bribe. Blood money.

An attempt to quell his conscience.

She sheathed it, reached to undo her belt, stopped.

Did he think this made up for what he was doing to her?

There's no way he could think that.

She left the knife exactly as she had found it, hurried out the barn door and into the woods.

He'd see it there when he got home.

She hoped it would hurt.

CHAPTER FIFTEEN

Tolan sets her e-reader down and rubs at her eyes. She's considering setting her mother's story aside. She's read a few pages each day ever since she found it on their computer, but she's dyslexic so the words swim and invert when she reads, and standing the letters up so they're in the right order and facing the right way so she can understand them is a brawl. She's a high school senior, now, and time's an issue: she's running cross-country in the fall, and track in the spring, competing in the 400-meter hurdles and the 10,000-meter.

It'd be easier if Sarah were around. She likes Bo, but it was Sarah that sucked her in, Sarah that she thinks might be her mother, and she has no idea how Bo connects to Sarah.

Maybe she'll skip ahead?

No, she's too compulsive for that.

Skim some?

That's doable. She'll get the gist of what's going on.

But things keep changing, little details, a character's name, the position Ruby and Uncle Donnie were in when Bo first saw them, whether Donnie was naked or just had his fly unbuttoned.

And why hadn't her mother mentioned she was writing a book? Tolan didn't even know she wrote, let alone that she was working on a novel.

She wonders where the details come from: Donnie, Lester, Ruby, the things that happen to them. Did her mother make them up, or were they borrowed from the lives of people she'd known? Cribbed from stories she'd heard?

Tolan knows she'll keep on reading, despite her struggles, and not just in the hopes of discovering things her mother has hidden from her, but because she cares about the characters, cares for these non-existent people.

Ruby turned nineteen and married the son of a shipping magnate against his family's wishes.

Alice got sick again.

Lester broke off his affair with the Martinsson widow.

Bo was on the verge of adulthood, and even though she had capitulated to her mother's entreaty to grow her hair out, she remained quietly indomitable, and Tolan wants to see what happens to her.

CHAPTER SIXTEEN

"Les." Alice was standing at the kitchen sink. "Someone's in the driveway."

He moved behind her. "Must be Bo's people. They're not from around here, at any rate. That's a Humber Pullman. Brand new, from the looks of it."

"A Humber what?"

"An expensive car. Where's Bo?"

"Getting ready."

"Guess I'd better go out there."

Lester met the man just as he and three other men were getting out of the car.

"How can I help you gentlemen?"

"Is this 208 Bayview Street?"

"It is."

"You must be Bo White. I'm Lowell, Charles Lowell. I've hired you out for the weekend."

"You've got the right place, but the wrong person. I'll get Bo."

"Thank you."

Lester nodded and left, found Bo in the barn gathering the last of the equipment.

"They're here. You have everything?"

"How'd they seem?"

He shrugged. "Big city royalty."

"They say where they were from?"

"Plates say Massachusetts."

Bo rolled her eyes. "Lucky me."

"You'd better get on out there; I'll help you with the gear. You'll need to borrow the truck again."

"Fancy car?"

"A real Jim Dandy."

It made Bo mad when she thought about it, so she tried not to, the know-nothings driving up from Massachusetts or New York or Connecticut to trip through her woods and play at hunting and fishing. They came in brand new clothes so stiff and loud they were audible from a quarter-mile, carrying rifles with polished-steel barrels that shone like beacons and that reeked of gun oil, and refused to rub pine or deer urine into their clothes to mask their scent and scuff up their rifles, and forced her to explain to them that the only deer they had hope of taking in their present state was a blind, deaf geriatric with a crippling head-cold.

All four men were standing beside the car when they came out. Lowell glanced at his watch. "I thought we agreed to meet at nine. Am I mistaken?"

"No." Lester smiled. "You're right on time."

Lowell looked from Lester to his friends and back. "I'm afraid I don't understand. Has Mr. White gone missing?"

"Not at all. Mr. Lowell, meet my daughter, Bo."

Bo extended her hand.

"There—" Lowell sputtered, "There must be some mistake."

"There's no mistake, Mr. Lowell. My daughter—"

"A girl?"

"Most daughters are."

Lowell stared.

"But a woman?"

"The first guide Maine ever registered was a woman."

"Well, it isn't proper—"

"You're under no obligation, Mr. Lowell. If you're uncomfortable, Bo will give you your deposit back, and you can be on your way."

Silence.

All eyes were on Lowell, waiting, Bo and her father squinting into the morning sun while the men opposite them felt its heat on their necks and the backs of their ears, and beads of perspiration rising beneath their leisure suits.

One of the men started chuckling. "This must be what William meant when he recommended we retain Bo's services. He said we'd be surprised."

"But—"

"Come now, Charles," the third man said. "Will spoke highly of her, and we've come all this way…"

"Well…" Lowell blinked. "Right. Yes, yes, of course." He turned to Bo. "Forgive me, Miss White, I meant no disrespect. We'd be grateful for your services."

"Good." Lester nodded. "Now let's get your gear into the truck."

"Truck?"

"We'd planned to take our car," one of the men interjected. "There's plenty of space for the equipment in the trunk, and room enough for your daughter in the backseat."

"And the deer you take, you're planning to strap them to the hood?"

The men stared at their feet.

Lester chuckled. "Don't worry, gentlemen, it happens all the time. We'll just get everything moved over to the truck, and you can leave your car here. I'll make sure nothing happens to it."

Lowell nodded. "We'd be grateful."

"Not at all."

Bo loaded her gear first, then helped the men with theirs.

Lester stood beside Lowell, watching. "They say the Landaulette can do upwards of seventy."

Lowell nodded. "They do."

"Any truth to it?"

"I'm afraid I can't say, speed limits being what they are."

"Of course, the law is the law."

Lowell smiled, minutely, reached into his pocket. "It occurs to me that I should leave the keys in case the need to move the car arises."

Lester stifled a grin. "I'll take good care of it, Mr. Lowell."

"Please do."

Bo turned out of the driveway and accelerated, her father shrinking in the rearview. Lowell sat beside her, the other men in the back seat, arms linked like lattice, thighs pressed together. Each bump in the road jostled them with violence proportionate to their velocity, but Bo pushed the speed limit anyway; they'd left an hour later than planned, which meant she'd have to set up camp in the dark. She didn't expect the men would be of much help. "Forgive our poor manners, Miss White," one of the men behind her said. "We've neglected to introduce ourselves. I'm Martin Jordan."

"Pleasure to meet you, Mr. Jordan. Call me Bo."

"Martin, then."

Bo caught his smile in the rear view mirror and nodded.

"You've already met Mr. Lowell—"

"Charles," Lowell corrected.

"Charles. The man next to me is Eduard Saltonstall, and tucked in next to him is my son, Parker."

"It's a pleasure to meet you all."

Silence followed, giving way to idle talk and restrained laughter as the men settled into the trip. Bo wanted her clients to feel they'd gotten their money's worth, so she'd point out prominent landmarks and places of interest, but otherwise she left it to them to dictate her involvement in the conversation. They had hours to drive: she had stories to tell if they wanted Maine color, the knowledge to answer any questions they might have about flora or fauna or Maine history, and the wherewithal to occupy herself if they chose to ignore her.

She'd had a letter from Ruby on Monday: Oliver was nearly a year old, now, and Ive's career was on the up and up. They were doing well in Tangier, but hoped to be in Paris soon.

Bo knew it broke her parents' hearts that they'd not met their grandson —they hadn't even met Ruby's husband. Ruby told them it hadn't been intentional, that she and Ive had fallen in love overnight, that he'd had to get to Tangier right away, and it just hadn't worked out for her to get home. She'd told Bo the same thing, and Bo had chosen to believe her, though she knew their parents didn't, and that her father blamed himself, and that their mother probably agreed. Bo missed Ruby, but knew that she was happier for having left Maine and the farm and her parents behind.

Sometimes she wondered if her sister might miss her a little.

Bo blinked twice, shook her head, focused her eyes on the road, and her ears on the men behind her. She'd had some characters in her truck: a big-talking Texas oilman whose fly was tangled in a tree as often as it was in the water, a man from New Orleans who'd fished and tracked and shot so well she couldn't figure why he'd hired her. One man had shown up with a case of moonshine—no fly rod or rifle—handed her a five dollar bill, and told her to go catch something for him to bring home to his wife and leave him be.

The worst had been the Pentecostal couple. Their first question had been was she saved, and after she hadn't known how to answer, the fact that she'd spent her life in church hadn't mattered. It was Jesus this, and the Holy Spirit that, and cleansed by the blood of the lamb; she'd been ready to convert just to stop them talking.

She'd had clients suggest using headlights or laying bait for the deer, and one hopeless fly fisherman had wanted to dynamite the fish he couldn't catch, but she didn't have many problems. She simply refused such requests, and if the clients persisted, left them where they stood, whether or not they had a car to carry them back to civilization.

"How do you like our chances, Bo?" Martin asked.

"Good, so long as it doesn't get too hot. It's great country, plenty of fowl as well as deer and fish."

"Martin's a little walleyed, though," Eduard said. "That has to hurt his odds."

Everyone laughed.

"How familiar are you with hunting?"

"Mostly fox," Martin said, "some falconry."

Bo didn't know how to respond.

"You're wicked," Eduard chided. "We know our way around a rifle, Bo. Especially Parker."

Parker smiled. "I was a boy scout."

"Pshaw," Eduard said. "Parker has been winning shooting competitions since he was twelve."

She saw Parker's smile widen in the rearview mirror, kept her eyes on the road. "I look forward to hunting with such distinguished company."

Parker blushed; the men laughed.

"What's that?"Bo turned; it was Parker.

"My bow."

"Bo's bow."

She ignored him.

"What's it for?"

"Brushing my teeth."

It was going on ten o'clock. She'd managed to get the camp set up, cooked dinner, and done the dishes afterward. Now the men were drinking brandy around a dwindling fire. Everyone except Parker.

"May I see it?"

She handed it to him; he took it, drew the string—"Don't!" She lunged, punching the bow from his hands, startling him and the men and the night to silence. "Sorry," she said, burning beneath the heat of their eyes. "I didn't mean to startle you."

The men turned away graciously.

"You were worried I'd snap my wrist?"

She nodded. "That bow tends to bite people."

"But not you."

He was a head and a half taller than her, his face a swath of black beneath the starless night.

"No."

"Here," he said.

The fire had burned down to embers. The bow was invisible until it pressed her palm.

"Thank you."

"I wouldn't have," he said, as they moved toward the others, "just so you know."

"You might have."

"What's this, now?" Martin asked.

"I offered Bo a bet, but she wasn't up to it."

"What?" Bo startled. "You did no—"

Martin smiled. "What were the terms?"

"He didn—"

"I told her I'd wager double her fee she couldn't take any game with that ancient contraption of hers, but she wouldn't take the bet. She doesn't think I'm good for it." Parker frowned. "She said I'd welch."

"That's an awful thing to say about a man," Martin scolded.

"I didn't—"

"Only one thing to be done, we have to protect young Mr. Jordan's honor. Will you guarantee his wager, Charles?"

Charles waved him away, "Leave me out of your nonsense."

"I'll guarantee it," Eduard said, grinning. "You can go out first thing tomorrow; it'll give us old folk the chance to sleep in."

"I'm tagging along," Parker interjected.

"Oh, are you now?"

"Someone's got to make sure she doesn't buy something off another hunter and present it as her own."

He broke out laughing, the men, too. Bo looked from one to the next, nonplussed.

"You'll have to forgive them, Bo," Lowell said frowning. "They're fools, all of them."

She knocked on his tent shortly before four, meaning to wake him, but he'd been ready, "I figured you might have it in for me."Bo handed him a vial of yellow liquid. "You'll want to rub this into your clothing and shoes."

"What is it?" He pulled the stopper and recoiled at the smell.

"It masks your scent so you don't scare off the deer."

She said no more, watched as he poured it onto his palms, worked the liquid into his boots, pants, and shirt.

"Don't you want any?"

"I did my clothes earlier—put a little on your neck and chin, too, you don't want your aftershave scaring off the animals."

He nodded, used the last of the liquid, wincing inwardly as it stung where he'd nicked himself shaving. He finished his chin, rubbed a few drops into his cheeks for good measure, and handed her the empty vial.

"Ready?"

She nodded. "Do you eat fowl?"

"Duck?"

Bo shook her head. "More likely pheasant or woodcock, turkey if we're lucky."

"No deer?"

"I'll leave them for you and your friends."

"Ah. Good business."

She nodded.

"Nothing to do with showing off, birds being smaller targets, and all."

"We'd better get going."

They set off, shivering and tired, and stubborn to conceal it, grateful for the cover of night. Bo's pace was malicious, but the length of Parker's legs allowed him to match it; soon they were sweating.

They'd put three miles behind them by the time she stopped.

"We'll head into the woods here." She gestured toward the tree line.

He nodded.

They were both short of breath.

He followed her off the road to the tree line, watched her lean her bow against a tree, shed her backpack and quiver.

"Coffee?" she asked.

"Coffee?"

"We made good time getting here."

She took a thermos and two tin cups from the bag, poured, held one out to him. He took it and yelped, wincing. "Christ, that's hot!"

"Hence the handle."

"You could have warned me."

"That coffee's hot?"

His lips parted, froze.

"Are you okay?"

"When'd you make coffee? I didn't see a fire this morning."

"Paraffin stove in my tent."

They finished a cup, poured another.

"So what's it like being a guide?"

"How do you mean?"

"Do you enjoy it? Is it much work?"

"Most of the work's up front, scouting and tracking and setting up blinds so you know where to take people once you get them here."

"Don't the animals move around?"

"Some."

"So how do you know they'll still be there when you come back?"

She brought the mug to her lips, swallowed. "You read the terrain."

"How's that?"

She took another sip of her coffee. "Animals aren't that different from us, really; they need food, water, shelter—somewhere to hide. Find a place that has those things, or where they're all nearby, and you're likely to find the animals."

They finished their coffee and stood, shook the cups out, and returned them to the backpack.

"Ready?"

"Waiting."

She rolled her eyes. "We'll leave the bag here, get it on the way back. Do you know how to walk without scaring off the animals?"

"Quietly."

She shook her head, stifling a smile. "Well, aren't you smart."

They were back in camp before nine, Parker grumbling cheerfully, a tom dangling from his shoulder, and Bo grinning, despite herself. The men were sitting around a fire drinking the coffee she'd left behind. Martin saw them first. "It appears young Mr. Jordan lost his wager."

Parker shook his head slowly, putting on a frown. "We hadn't been in place ten minutes when a turkey comes plodding out within spitting distance of our blind. The damn thing's looking right at us. Bo drops her arrow twice before she manages to nock it, trips standing up, sneezes as she's trying to draw the string, and when she finally gets off a shot it's three feet right, and four feet high, and I swear to god, the bird looks right at me, winks, and throws himself in front of the arrow."

Bo shrugged. "Better to be lucky than good."

The men laughed.

"Hold it out for us," Eduard said. "Go on."

Bo listened to the men razzing Parker, smiling as she took a griddle from the truck, eggs, bread, and bacon. They insisted that Parker do the cooking as a further penalty for his defeat, and his father promised to have the tom stuffed so Parker could admire it for perpetuity.

She moved to start another pot of coffee, but the men insisted Parker handle things, so she sat, leaning against one of the stumps surrounding the fire pit. It was cool and overcast, and the susurrus of the fire and its heat wove a womb around her as the morning's adrenaline seeped into the ground. A bead of sweat fell down her neck and back, and she shivered and moved closer to the fire. Parker greased a cast-iron griddle and set it in place, and soon the air was thick and rich, butter sizzling as fat strips of bacon spat and eggs fried, the whites curling brown at the rim. Bacon and eggs came off, passed out on tin plates as Parker dropped finger-thick slices of bread onto the griddle to toast. He handed Bo a mug of coffee, which she drank quickly to stave off sleep before pouring herself another to have with breakfast.

She ate quickly, finished ahead of the others. Watching Charles, it surprised her that he had been so thrown when they first met. He ate in the continental style Bo's mother had forced her to learn, knife in his right hand, fork in the left, tines downward: cut, spear, convey to mouth, repeat. Even his bacon. If he wanted a sip of coffee, fork was placed over knife in the center of the plate before he lifted his cup. Etiquette, even in the woods, countenance and comportment fit for the Ritz-Carlton. He would be methodical and precise with a rifle, and competent with a fly-rod, his casting too mechanical to be beautiful, but exact and efficient.

The other men were like horses freed from their plows, spirit flinging control aside as they ate, food falling off their forks, crumbs clinging to their moustaches and the corners of their mouths. They were likely to rush their shots, Bo thought, to try to put too much into their casts and end up with a tangled mass of line. Parker was harder to figure.

"I believe young Mr. Jordan should do the dishes, now, don't you think, Martin?" Eduard said.

"He'll be doing them for a month, given what he's cost me today."

There was laughter, mock protest, and further jeering as Parker gathered their plates and utensils.

"Why don't you change before we head out again, Parker," Charles suggested. "No need to mask your scent from the fish."

"Will do, Mr. Lowell."

They watched Parker disappear, turned back to the fire.

"Bo," Charles said, "might you have neglected to inform Parker that one need use only a few drops of deer urine to conceal his scent?"

Bo felt the men's eyes. "I might have," she said, face hot.

"Do you think you could rectify that before our next hunt?"

Another nod. "Yes, Sir—Charles." She paused to collect herself, willing the heat from her face. "I'll do that."

"We'd all be very grateful."

"Yes, Sir." Bo turned to go.

"One more thing, Bo."

She stopped.

"Well played."

She fought a grin. "Thank you."

"Bo."

"Parker." She turned to face him, squinting in the sun.

"May I speak to you a moment?"

"Sure."

They were standing in the parking lot of a penny-diner they'd stopped at on their way back to Port Haven. Parker was missing his usual grin, but she couldn't think why. Everything had gone well, everyone had seemed to enjoy themselves. Their fishing had been moderately successful: Charles had taken a deer; Eduard had missed a chance at one. Parker had shot a tom of his own, held it up for her to see with a Cheshire smile and a cheeky wink. She'd stuck her tongue out by way of reply, regretted it immediately, but he'd laughed and no one else had seen her do it, so she'd been able to play it off.

Bo followed him toward the corner of the parking lot, walking into the sun, head down for the glare; he stopped abruptly, turned, and she would have run into him if he hadn't caught her by her shoulders.

He laughed awkwardly, moved backward, tripped, regained his balance.

"Sorry." She blinked, sun-blind. "I didn't see you."

"It's awfully bright."

He moved toward her so she'd fall within his shadow, balked at the proximity and took a step back, raised his hand to shield her face.

"Thanks."

"There's something I'd like to ask you."

She waited.

"I was wondering if it would be okay, that is, if you would give me your permission to write you?"

"Write me?"

"To write to you."

"Letters?"

"I'd restrict myself to postcards if you'd prefer, or sonnets if your objection is a matter of form rather than length."

A sly smile, just enough vulnerability to prevent her from smacking him.

"Why?"

He shrugged. "Why not?"

She crossed her arms. "Why?"

His grin faded into seriousness. "I'd like to keep in touch."

"In case you want to go hunting again?"

He stared at her for a moment, eyes narrowing, mouth forming a question that would die unasked.

"Or in case you ever make it to New York."

"New York?"

"I'll be moving there in the spring, after I finish up in Boston."

"What would I do in New York?"

"The Empire State Building, the Statue of Liberty, Madison Square Garden, the Met… you could study at Barnard."

"I'm not much of a writer."

"I have very low standards."

"I'm shocked."

"I'm also very forgiving."

"How magnanimous of you."

"Magnanimity is one of my specialties."

"There you are," came Martin's voice. "We're ready to go when you are."

"Be right there."

She started toward the car, but Parker grabbed her arm.

"You didn't answer my question."

"We'll see how you do on the ride home."

"I'll be on my best behavior."

"See that you are."

CHAPTER SEVENTEEN

Tori knows something's wrong, has known all day, but Tolan just shakes her head when she asks. *Not now.* Not now before first bell, and at lunch, and in the locker room after school when they are changing for the meet.

Now they're almost to the race site, and Tolan should be focusing. Tori teases her about it, about how obsessive she is about her pre-race routine, how surly she gets; Tolan visualizes every step, every movement she'll make from the time she steps off the bus until she finishes the race so that when it comes time, everything that happens is an echo of something that's already taken place. She says she feels better that way, feels less pressure.

But Tolan isn't visualizing, today, only staring at the back of the seat in front of her.

Tori's not worried about the meet; she's being recruited by the best cross-country and track programs in the country, and she's already qualified for states. It doesn't really matter, though; her parents are going to make her turn them down. She's going to be a surgeon like they are, and they don't want anything distracting her. It'll be Harvard for undergrad, Hopkins for medical school, and Duke for residency, but for now they let her run, so long as she maintains her 4.0 and extra-curriculars. Tori knows how her life will go, and that Tolan doesn't, that she has no idea where she'll be in a year, and Tori figures that's why she's in a frenzy, because she can't afford to go to college without a scholarship, and having lost most of the season to mono, this is her last chance to catch someone's eye.

The bus leaves them in a car park behind the high school. The yellow lines demarcating parking space from parking space have bled out into the ether and left the asphalt to be battered by time and weather, to molder and pit. The girls dodge pock and rut as they make their way to the staging area, some silent, others babbling, either self-contained or lashing out at the sloe tailings strewn across the lot and sending them hiss and tumble into the grass.

Tolan and Tori pick a spot on the blacktop near the edge of the grass, apart from most of the team, but close enough that their coach won't object.

It's turned cold, but the blacktop's still warm with daylight, and the heat will help them get loose. They start with the major muscles, quads and hamstrings, stand, move on to their hip flexors and calves. Tolan pays attention; she started stretching near Tori even before they were friends, aping her movements, because she knew Tori had had a running coach since she was five. Tolan's wearing spandex and long sleeves as opposed to the shorts and tank tops that most of the other girls are wearing, because she likes to run hot. She learned that from Tori, too: Stay hot, stay loose. Tension kills.

Tolan's trying to keep herself calm. It's just a test, there's nothing to worry about.

It's just a test.

Her mother hasn't said anything because there's nothing to say, and she doesn't want her to worry.

It's just a test.

If it is breast cancer and they caught it early, it's highly treatable— she'd looked it up as soon as she heard the doctor's voice on their answering machine.

Her mother isn't dying.

She's not.

Bo's mother died without warning.

Aneurysm.

Dead.

One month before Bo started at Barnard.

Tolan shakes her head. She and Tori double back, now, hamstrings again, legs out straight, pulling themselves forward so that their foreheads rest on the tips of their shoes. Tolan counts silently: one, one-thousand, two, one-thousand, all the way to sixty, switches legs.

She and her mother and Bo are all intertwined somehow, now.

Tolan feels tears welling in her eyes thinking about Bo's father forcing her to go away to college only a month after her mother's death. Bo came home for Christmas and begged him not to make her go back.

Tolan stabs at her eyes with the blades of her fists.

Ruby had been in Lebanon when their mother died, and her father had been too upset to attend the funeral. Bo had had to bury her alone.

If her mother dies, Tolan will have to bury her alone, too.

But she's not going to die.

One last time, then put it away: She's not going to die.

It's just a test.

She and Tori finish their stretching and move on to their ABC drills, to butt kicks and skips and ankling, and finishing those, it's time for accelerations, starting with a slow jog and gradually increasing their speed until they hit a sixty meter sprint at about 90% of their maximal sprint. And now their bodies are a sheen of sweat, and the start of the race is only minutes away, and they're ready.

Tori takes Tolan's hand and bulls her way to the front, pulling Tolan behind her.

Tolan grits her teeth and tries to force them from her mind—all of them, Bo, and Bo's parents, and her mother.

Focus.

Race.

Calm.

Qualify.

States.

Scholarship.

"On your mark," says the official.

This is one of the longer courses they'll run this season, a 5k—essentially a three-mile anaerobic sprint.

"Get set."

The course is triangular, equilateral. Tori will finish near sixteen minutes; Tolan should lose sight of her for a maximum of seventy seconds at the first turn, and for approximately one hundred and thirty-five seconds at the second.

Their muscles quiver with tension.

Gun.

They don't hear it, only sense time's hesitation as the pins synch along a shear line. Tori's first steps are explosive, blasting her clear of the pack, her movements lithe and smooth and powerful. Tolan's are brutal, ugly, barely functional, seventy-two inches of legs fighting inertia and each other. She labors, fights for momentum. Fights herself.

Finish.

Get to the finish line.

But today isn't about finishing, she isn't running to anything, not trying to finish or to qualify for states or to land a scholarship. She's running from —from her mother, from Bo and her dead parents, from cancer—she passes the first mile marker, terror dissolving each into each so that Tolan is Bo and about to lose her mother, and her mother is Bo's mother and about to be torn from life—but she's not, because she might not even have cancer, and even if she does, the doctors will treat it and she won't die. Tolan is all of it and none of it—and she's wrong. She's blown it. They've run a mile and a half and she's only steps behind Tori. Her lungs are cinders, her throat char. She can't maintain—she's going to collapse. She runs harder. Tori is pulling away, hits the final turn, Tolan lashing after her. Bo doesn't exist. Her parents don't exist. They don't, they're not real—only her mother is real. And she's real, the pain, chest, head pulsing fire, the world now flicker and flex. Her mother's cancer. Might be real. But they'll kill it if it is, the doctors will, burn it to death; Tolan will never be Bo, never weep alone at her mother's graveside. Tolan's tears are scalding her eyes. Tori finishes, 16.10, another girl, 16.17. Tori's watching her. Three hundred meters. Two: kick, thrash, kick—throw the elbows. Her mother's walking toward her, but Tolan's blind, punches through the line at 16.59, shattering her personal best, breaking down as she decelerates. Tori catches her ten meters behind the finish line, keeps her from going to the ground face first, but Tolan shoves her aside, keeps walking, staggering, makes the tree-line before falling to her knees and burying her face in her hands. Tori kneels beside her without speaking, pulls her sideways into her chest, Tolan's head against her clavicle. Tori's rocking her gently, whispering in her ear when Tolan's mother spots them. Their coach is walking towards them, too, but Tori shakes her head; he looks from them to Tolan's mother, stops.

"Tolan?"

She freezes at her mother's voice, choking a sob mid-throat. "What are you doing here?"

"I wanted to see you r—"

"The shop?"

"Mrs. Chandler's there—what's wrong?"

"Mom?"

"What?"

"Mom..." Tolan is trembling, voice broken and breathy and shrill. "Mom..."

"What?"

"Mom!" Tears are falling hard.

"What! I don't know what you want, Tolan—what do you want?"

"What did he say?"

"Who?"

"MOM!"

"Who! What did who say?"

"The oncologist!"

Tolan's mother knits her brow. "Dr. Williams?"

"YES!"

"He said he'd be happy to sponsor this year's Race for the Cure."

"What?"

"The fundraiser for breast cancer research."

"What? You had a mammogram a week ago."

Her mother flushes.

"The doctor's office called. I saw your planner, and you had an appointment with an oncologist..."

"You thought I—"

Tolan nods, covering her mouth with both hands, unable to stop the tears.

"Tolan..." Her mother is shaking her head, slowly, back and forth. "I'm sorry. I'm so, so sorry."

Her mother's been standing, and now she's sinking beside her daughter, and there are tears in her eyes, and Tori's crying too, and the other girls' parents are leaving and trying not to stare, and the coach doesn't know what to do because the rest of the team is already on the bus. Tolan's mother sees him; *I'll take them home,* she mouths. He hesitates. He's not supposed to let anyone go for insurance reasons, and he starts to say so, but he's just out of school and unmarried and terrified of crying women, so he only nods, and hurries to the bus.

"Why didn't you tell me you were having a mammogram?"

"I didn't want you to worry. It was just a routine checkup; I have one every year."

"Mom!"

"I know. I'm sorry, I'm really sorry. I'll tell you next time."

"I'll worry about you all the time if I think you're hiding things."

"I'm not—I won't. I'd tell you—I will tell you from now on."

"Promise?"

"Promise."

Mother and daughter looking in each other's eyes, tacit agreement, silence, each retreating, collecting herself, wiping tears from her eyes, sniffling to stop a runny nose, standing and brushing grass from her knees.

Everyone else has gone. The sun is set.

They stop at Tolan's favorite sushi place for takeout on the way home, and Tolan knows that her mother is feeling guilty because it's been a rough year at the shop and she can't really afford it, so she orders the cheapest thing on the menu, as does Tori, and they drive home, and Tori calls her parents on the way and tells them that she'll be spending the night at Tolan's. The girls shower, Tori, then Tolan, dry off, put on pajamas, choose a movie.

They're on Tolan's bed when her mother comes to say goodnight. Tori's sitting with her back against the headboard, and Tolan is curled fetal beside her, her head resting on Tori's lap as Tori strokes her hair.

"She's asleep," Tori whispers.

Tolan's mother nods and smiles. "Are you doing okay?"

Tori smiles. "Always."

"Can I get you anything?"

She shakes her head, still smiling, holds up her water bottle. "I'm good."

"Okay." She starts to go, stops. "Thank you."

CHAPTER EIGHTEEN

Bo tried not to gawk.

Traffic was thick, motion difficult to come by, and even harder to sustain. The evening was a wash of horn blasts and brake dust and a thousand unintelligible voices. There were more people in the streets and on the sidewalks than she'd met in the whole of her life, and the buildings were bigger and rose higher than any she'd seen. The sun was setting, but the world around them grew brighter, gaslights firing and sweating vapor, and thirty-foot signs burning Planters Peanuts and Sunkist Oranges and Coca-Cola into the night in neon. Shopkeepers closed their stores and locked the doors behind them, and friends called back and forth across the street while young men whistled at the women walking by and newsies hawked the evening papers as traffic cops blew their whistles.

"What do you think?" Parker asked.

"It's... there's a lot to see."

Parker smiled.

"What hurrying human tides, or day or night!
What passions, winnings, losses, ardors, swim thy waters!
What whirls of evil, bliss and sorrow, stem thee!
What curious questioning glances--glints of love!
Leer, envy, scorn, contempt, hope, aspiration!
Thou portal--thou arena--thou of the myriad long-drawn lines and groups!
(Could but thy flagstones, curbs, facades, tell their inimitable tales;
Thy windows rich, and huge hotels--thy side-walks wide;)
Thou of the endless sliding, mincing, shuffling feet!
Thou, like the parti-colored world itself--like infinite, teeming,
mocking life!"

"You're quite pleased with yourself, aren't you?"

Parker paused as if to consider the question. She rolled her eyes, smiling.

"I am, come to think of it. Not often that one has the occasion to quote Whitman."

"I'd imagine one finds many such occasions when he's willing to contrive to create them."

"You wound me."

"I'm sure."

"You might try being nice to the man that drove all the way from—"

"I didn't ask you to," she said sharply.

"I was only teasing."

They made the end of the block in silence, then three more, and turned off Broadway. Parker drove aimlessly, unsure what to do next. She was to start at Barnard in two days; her father couldn't leave the farm, so he'd volunteered to drive her down. He'd intended to take her out for dinner, surprise her with a show afterward, take her around the city.

He drove into the dark along the river, let the throngs of commerce and neon fade behind them.

"I'm sorry," she said. "You were just trying to be fun and do something nice."

"It's okay. You're just tired. We've been driving all day, and it's hot, and the city can be overwhelming."

She shook her head. "I'm not tired. I've enjoyed the drive and the city... I just... I don't want to owe anyone."

Parker nodded. "I know what you mean. That's why I'm in New York instead of working at my father's paper in Boston." He glanced at Bo, back to the road. "Can I ask you something?"

"Okay."

"Why did you agree to come down with me?"

"I guess..." she started, fidgeting with the hem of her blouse. "I... I don't know."

"Play pretend with me for a second?"

"What?"

"Pretend with me. Just for a second."

Her face tightened in a question.

"Please?"

She nodded, finally.

"Lets pretend you're a nice pers—" She punched him in the arm. "Ow! See what I mean?"

She hit him again.

"You're not pretending!"

"You're cruising, buddy..."

"Pretend—don't hit me—you're a nice person. And the reason you agreed to let me take you down to school was that you knew I enjoy spending time with you, and as a nice person, you wanted me to enjoy myself."

She was doing her best not to laugh. "You've got about three seconds to turn this around."

"All I'm asking is that you keep on pretending for the next forty-eight hours." He paused, laying a hand on top of hers. "Forget about owing anyone, or charity; let me show you around the city, take you to my favorite restaurants, to a show, maybe even two."

She struggled, feeling the heat of his hand atop hers, the emotion in his voice—feeling a visceral, soundless shriek rip through her, demanding she refuse him.

"You'd be doing it for me."

Nothing.

"Remember, in this scenario, you're a nice person."

"Forty-eight hours." Bo made her voice grave. "That's it."

"Then you're back to being an ogre?"

"Jerk!"

They were both smiling, he unabashedly, she turning away in order to hide it.

"I'd better get us turned around and headed in the right direction now that I'm on the clock; Battery Park is the other way."

Parker slowed, made the turn. Looking at him, Bo felt a cut of surprise: he inhaled deeply, eyes closing, and opening again, brighter than before, his body transforming as tension fell away like beads of water on a window pane, the color rushing back to his knuckles as his grip on the steering wheel loosened.

She realized she liked looking at him.

She was as far from the woods and her bow as she'd ever been and she'd just seen more people and more colors and taller buildings than she'd seen in her life and she was sitting beside a handsome, smart, rich, and sophisticated man who talked about places she'd never even heard of, let alone been to, and ideas she didn't always quite understand.

But the way he was smiling now, breathing easy, resting his arm on the window so that his hand lolled about in the onrushing air, talking and teasing and telling her about all the places they could go—

"Hey," he chided, snapping his fingers, "you!" He jostled her leg, gently. "Nice girls listen to a guy when he's trying to talk to them."

"Even when they're jabbering on like a squirrel?"

"I can see we're going to have to work on 'nice.'"

"You first," she said, removing his hand from her knee.

He looked stricken, stared assiduously at the road ahead. "Would you believe it was an accident?" He gave her a furtive, sidelong glance.

"I believe I'm going to let you tell me about the place you're taking me to for dinner."

He didn't answer.

"Don't tell me you've forgotten already."

"Um," he stuttered, "no. I... er, I—"

"It's okay."

"I didn't mean to. I was jostling you, then—I left it there by accident."

Bo couldn't keep herself from laughing.

"It's true!"

"I know." She touched his arm. "I wouldn't have come if I didn't already know you were a gentleman."

Relief.

A small smile.

Her hand on his forearm.

"Thank you."

"You were telling me about the restaurant..."

"I was. Yes, I was. Well, the poet Christopher Morley..."

"Another poet?"

"Yes. He once wrote—"

"Seriously?"

"Seriously. He—"

"Does whatever you're about to recite to me have anything to do with where you're taking me?"

"Indirectly."

"How indirectly?"

"It's à propos."

"À propos?"

"Relevant."

"I know what the word means."

"Well, I—"

"If I let you tell me what Christopher Whirley—"

"Morley."

"If I let you tell me what Christopher Morley said—"

"Wrote." Parker fought the smile plucking at the corner of his mouth.

"What?"

"Wrote."

"Now you're baiting me."

"I'm not. He's a poet, so technically, he wrote it—"

"He might have said it."

"What?"

"Sometimes poets perform their work."

"True, but—"

"He might have composed it out loud."

"You're baiting me."

"I'm not if you're not."

They stopped to let a gaggle of people cross in front of them, eyeing each other dramatically, neither willing to be the first one to break.

"If you concede that it was written, I'll tell you what he wrote."

"If you concede that it might have been said as well, I'll listen."

The last of the people made it across; Parker broke off eye contact and accelerated, chuckling. "This is absurd."

"Almost as absurd as a man who subjects a woman to a rendition of something a poet once said before—"

"Wrote."

She threw up her hands.

Parker pulled alongside the curb, cut the engine, and got out. "Just a minute," he said, and he was around the car and opening Bo's door, offering his arm.

Bo shot him a look. "Can I help you?"

"Take my arm; it's how men and women walk together in New York."

"I'm sure it is."

"It's a very gallant city."

"I'll bet." She took his arm. "Happy?"

He smiled. "Quite."

It was late August. Wind ran in sporadic gusts, sweeping down high-rises and over the streets. Bo was wearing a long skirt and a thin blouse, and gooseflesh rose on her arms as she began to shiver. Parker pulled her against him.

"I'm beginning to think you planned this."

"I've no idea what you're talking about."

"How much farther?"

"We're almost there."

"I don't believe you."

"See that sign?"

"Delmonico's?"

"That's the one. It's fairly well known—they claim to have invented eggs Benedict and baked Alaska."

"I've never had either."

"You will."

"What was it you were going to share with me, again? Something Christopher Morley once said?"

"Yes. '*Remember, when you're writing about New York, faces are as important as buildings.*'" They walked up three steps, between two columns, through a door held open by a porter, and into the restaurant.

"I like that," Bo said. "It seems like good advice in general."

"Indeed."

CHAPTER NINETEEN

"Parker?"

He half raised a hand.

"What are you doing here?"

They were standing in the church vestibule in her hometown. The last of the mourners had left, as had the priest. A layman was cleaning the sanctuary. Her mother had died eight months ago, her father last week, while she was away at school. Heart attack.

Bo's last memory of him was of him sending her away, telling her she had to go back to school despite the fact that her mother had just died.

"I came as soon as I heard."

Parker was wearing his trench coat, holding a fedora in his hand. Water ran from his shoulders in drops.

"You didn't have to—"

"Can I give you a ride home?"

She nodded.

He found her coat on a rack in the corner and helped her into it.

Outside, the winter rain had stopped and an aperture of sky had begun to poke through the clouds. A father walked past the church, his child struggling to keep up. Across the street, a gnarled old man with a cane raised his face to the sun.

Parker's car was parked on the street. He opened the door for her, didn't say anything or try to take her hand or engage her in any way, only drove, remaining still and silent even after they'd arrived at her parents' house.

They sat in the driveway for a long time.

Bo wasn't crying, just silent, seatbelt wrinkling her blouse, hair coming loose atop her head, eyes unfocused. He watched her nostrils flare and relax, her throat muscles constrict when she swallowed. She had a hat in her lap. He had questions he wasn't going to ask: why didn't you tell me when your mother died, when your father died? Do you like getting my letters? Why are yours so short? Did you enjoy learning to drive with me, stalling and starting and lurching through Quogue, driving through Riverside and Flanders and Wainscott?

"Walk?"

He nodded.

"I should change first," she said.

They went into the house through the barn; he'd never been inside, and he wanted to look around, or at least to walk more slowly so he could soak up the details of the place in which she grew up, but he followed, matching her pace.

She left him in the kitchen. "I'll be right down," she said, returning in a jacket and slacks a few minutes later, her hair loose.

They went out.

"I took my first deer here." She pointed to the woods. "I'd gone behind my father's back to get the bow, and I knew that if I got the deer he'd find out, and I'd catch a beating."

"But you took it anyway?"

She nodded; he forced a smile from his face.

"That's my Bo."

He regretted the remark immediately, knew she'd find it patronizing.

"He didn't, though."

"Didn't what?"

"Whip me. He didn't even yell. He helped me skin it and tan the hide, showed me how to butcher it."

"It sounds like he was a good man."

Bo squinted up at Parker, realizing that she'd never asked that question, never asked herself who or what her father was, or tried to weigh the cruelty and violence and infidelity against the hunting and fishing and generosity.

"He did his best."

They wandered a short way into the woods, came back out, lingering in the field. A small shadow passed over them and they looked up to see an eagle riding a thermal.

"He clasps the crag with crooked hands;
Close to the sun in lonely lands,
Ring'd with the azure world, he stands."

"You and your poets."

"What? It's an eagle. They're majestic creat—"

A cut of bird shit burst on his hand, splattered onto his cuff, ran down his wrist.

"You were saying?"

"Never mind."

He was dabbing at his sleeve with a handkerchief when the sky went dark. The wind kicked hard, and the sun was swallowed by a surge of cloud; the air was instantly heavy with charge.

"We should…"

"Yes."

They were midway through the hay field when the first bolt of lightning struck, they ran along a seam in the crops and made it to the barn just as the heavens opened.

"By the skin of our teeth."

She nodded.

The wind roared. Rain pounded the street, hissing as it struck, and the storm bellowed, blotting out the earth beneath alternating smears of pitch and white.

It was gone as soon as it came.

"Incredible," Parker breathed.

"Welcome to Maine."

Chickadees and nuthatches appeared, a barn swallow; a pair of robins set upon the neighbor's yard and pecked at the worms raised by the storm. A blue jay shrieked, squirrels chattered, and family of chipmunks raided the birdfeeder.

"How long does it take to get here from Manhattan?"

"About twelve hours."

Bo counted backward in her head. "You drove through the night."

He nodded, tried to read her eyes.

"Why?"

"Your father died."

"So did my mother."

"I didn't—"

She shook her head, held out a hand.

"I only just found out. I came straightaway."

Her face fell. "That wasn't fair of me."

He shook his head. "All you've been through… why didn't you tell me?"

She looked up. "Why'd you drive through the night?"

"Why didn't you tell me?"

"Why would I?"

He had to close his eyes before he could answer, swallow, count to three.

"I know your sister lives overseas, and you've never mentioned any other family. I didn't want you to have to be alone."

"I was, now I'm not." She shrugged. "Doesn't really change anything, does it?"

He looked away. "I can go if you want."

She watched, expecting him to say something more, or to turn back to her, but he didn't. She might have said something if he had; part of her wanted to, but she didn't understand what she was seeing or feeling or where it came from, so she didn't know which words to use, or even what she might have said, and finally, she gave up trying to think it out, and in giving up, was seized by the fact that her father had died.

She felt more depleted than bereaved.

"Do you want something to eat before you go?"

A knife, stab and twist. He made himself gracious, "I could eat, but I don't need to."

"I could make you a sandwich?"

"You don't need to be in a kitchen right now. Let me take you out."

"To a restaurant?"

"Well, a pool hall wouldn't do, and they don't serve food at the library. You've just come from church, and a bar is no place for a lady."

"You really do think you're clever."

"To a restaurant. One of the nice ones in Portland."

"I'm not putting on another dress."

"One of the dodgy ones, then."

She rolled her eyes. "Mr. Crust has joined Mr. Clever."

Parker found a tavern in Freeport: hot roast beef sandwiches and steak fries, extra horseradish for him, and a beer. She tried both at his offering, and to her displeasure, discovered she liked them. He passed her the jar and ordered another beer, grinning.

"Quiet," she said. "It isn't that good."

The check came, and he settled it without a word.

"I'll pay you back as soon as I can," she said in the car.

It was nearly eight o'clock. He was very tired.

"Pardon?"

"I'll pay you back."

"I didn't realize I'd made a loan."

"I don't need your charity."

"What?"

It was the first time he'd taken a tone with her; she froze.

He sucked at his teeth.

"I only meant—"

"Stop it."

Silence. She stared out at the road ahead. He sighed.

"You mistake volition for charity, Bo, and in doing so you come off as ungrateful and arrogant."

"I didn't ask you—"

"Precisely!"

He pulled off the road and cut the engine, turned to her; she thrust her chin out to meet his gaze even as her breath caught in her chest.

"Why do you think I write you every week?"

She only stared.

"Please, Bo."

Silence.

"Please."

She shook her head.

"Because I want to. Because I've wanted to spend time with you from the moment I first saw you."

She could feel herself softening. Parker's eyes were rimmed sleepless-black, and he was reaching out to her, pleading with her, but she couldn't allow herself to hear him, wouldn't.

"You're fearless, Bo, smart and funny and strong, and independent in every way. You don't need someone to tell you what to think, or how to act. You know what you want, and you go after it, and you don't ask for anyone's permission."

She was losing: her jaw no longer thrust so hard or far, and her hands weren't clenched in fists anymore—she wasn't even angry, now, just alone in the world, and exhausted, and hollow.

"I took you to dinner because I enjoy being with you." Parker gestured to himself with both hands. "I *wanted* to."

She felt the beginnings of tears prick her eyes, hot and insistent.

"I wanted to take you out to eat for the same reason I drove up here, because it hurts to think of you being alone at your parents' funerals, and I thought that maybe if I could be here, share a meal with you, that it might help. I thought—hoped—I might even be able to make you smile, and that afterward, you might hurt a little less."

She had to turn away.

He waited for a response, and when none came, he turned the key in the ignition and pulled back onto the road.

"I'm sorry," he said when they reached her driveway. "You're dealing with so much, it wasn't fair of me to—"

His hand was between them, resting atop the stick shift, and she set her own over it, letting her fingers sink into the gaps between his and curl down until they pressed his palm; he stared as if he didn't understand what he was seeing, followed the line from her wrist up her arm to her shoulder and higher. She'd turned away from him again, trembling—crying, he thought, but he wasn't sure. They pulled into her driveway, and he brought the car beside the barn and cut the engine. He wanted to pull her to him, to hold her and feel her head pressing his chin, to inhale the scent of her hair, but he didn't move. He would do right by her, be a gentleman, a friend, a comfort. He allowed himself to look at her out of the corner of his eye, willing himself to capture every detail: eyes so brown as to be black, coffee with only a whisper of cream, her skin dark as a walnut, her pants khaki, belt brown, socks an olive green, a blouse she'd inherited or borrowed for the funeral and would never wear again, a dusting of freckles that swept across her collarbone to ascend the tender flesh of her throat. Her hair flew here and there at the nape of her neck and temples, fugitive wisps spun free of the pins and clips meant to bring them to heal, but too coarse to call beautiful, too rough-hewn and overlarge like her jaw and ears and hands, yet the desire of his heart, now and always. The only one.

"How long will you be in town?"

"I'll drive back tomorrow evening."

"Where are you staying?"

"I'm going to find a hotel."

"Stay here."

She said it quickly.

He wanted to.

"Bo... People..."

"Will talk."

"Yes."

Breaths passed in silence. Heartbeats. Chests rising and falling.

He watched her until she turned to him. Eyes hooded, and the round tip of her nose flared slightly beneath a flat bridge.

"Stay."

"Okay."

He got out of the car, went round to open her door, retrieved his suitcase from the trunk, and followed her into the house. She made up the guest bedroom, offered coffee, put the kettle on. They brought it out to the living room when it was ready, turned the radio on, sat down on the couch.

"Do you like jazz?" he asked.

"I like this."

"Billie Holiday."

"She has a beautiful voice."

"She does. I saw her and Ella Fitzgerald at the Savoy in January."

"What was it like?"

"Amazing."

"I think I'm falling asleep," he said, after a time.

"Let's just finish the program."

"Okay."

She took his hand.

They were asleep within minutes. He awoke shortly after midnight, holding her. Her head was beneath his chin, her arms tight against her chest. He'd been sleeping upright, holding her, head lolled back. His neck hurt and his arm was numb, and he was certain he should wake her and take her to her room, but he didn't. He let her sleep, watching her breathe until he drifted off again.

CHAPTER TWENTY

Bo awoke disoriented. Rods of moonlight cut through the window, bent across the end of the couch. Recognition came in pieces: she was at home; in the living room; the body beneath her was Parker; the thing pushing into her forehead was his shirt button; if she moved, his head would drop and he'd be startled awake.

"Parker."

Nothing.

A little louder.

"Parker."

He stirred; she reached up and touched his cheek, felt the heat of his skin and the coarseness of his stubble. He lifted his head, and she sat upright, letting her hand fall along his jawline down to his neck.

"We fell asleep," she said awkwardly.

She could only just see him, the line of his jaw, the shadow of his brow. No details. No color.

"I..." He paused, slid his hips back against the couch, leveraged himself upright. "I'm sorry."

"It's okay."

"I should, I'm sorry—I didn't mean—"

"It's okay."

"I should..."

Bo shook her head. "I'll take you to your room."

She took his hand, lead him toward the stairs.

"Careful of—"

There was a loud crack; he pitched forward, stumbling. She tried to catch him, but couldn't stop his momentum and was driven backward against the balusters just as he managed to get his hands outright and catch the banister to keep himself from crushing her. His clavicle pressed the bridge of her nose.

"The ottoman." The words came through grit teeth.

"The ottoman."

He pushed himself away, took a step back; the cold surprised her.

"Are there any other ottomans between here and the bedroom?"

She shook her head.

They ascended the stairs, and then they were standing beside the door to the guest bedroom.

He covered her hand with his own. "Bo…"

"I know."

"If there's anything I can—"

"I know."

Tears were stinging her eyes again.

"I mean that."

"I know."

She withdrew her hand.

"We should sleep."

He nodded.

"Goodnight, Parker."

They separated, changed into their pajamas. Hers had belonged to Ruby, once; his were near-new, brushed cotton, and monogrammed.

He'd been in bed for twenty minutes when she knocked.

"Yes?"

"Can I come in?"

"Of course."

He fumbled for the lamp on the bedside table as she opened the door.

"Move over." She slid into bed, turned the light out.

"Bo…"

"What?"

"Are you—your father just…"

"I know."

She worked her way beneath the covers, rolled onto her side, facing away from him. He waited, but she was silent. Heat emanated from the small of her back, expanded in the space between them until he could feel its gentle pressure against his thigh. He stared, blind, willing her to speak, trying to pull her from the dark of the room.

"Bo…"

"Lie down."

He did, slowly. She pushed herself backward until he felt her vertebrae against his ribs.

"Are you sure—"

"Yes."

He turned on his side, slid an arm beneath her neck, let his other arm fall over her body. For a moment, he thought she might weep, but she didn't, and he knew he'd been crazy to think that she would. She pulled his arms around her and gathered them under her chin like a blanket, one finger curling into his sleeve, brushing the underside of his wrist.

One kiss.
He could allow himself one kiss. A chaste kiss.
On the top of her head.
One kiss.
No more.

CHAPTER TWENTY-ONE

"You're reading a lot these days."

Tolan looks up from her tablet: it's nine-thirty on a Saturday morning; she's wearing sweats and a hoodie, folded up atop the window-seat in her room, reading her mother's book. She has been reading a lot of late, more than ever, and her mother's commented on the fact more than once. Tolan usually uses 'I hadn't noticed, hmm...' or 'I guess,' but once, without thinking, she'd said 'good book,' and her mother had asked her what she was reading. She'd only just extricated herself from that situation, gave a title she'd heard people at school mention, and made a note to ask Tori what it was about.

Today, her mother persists. "What are you reading?"

It's been long enough since the last time her mother asked that she should come up with a new title to give her, but her mind stalls.

"Sex," she says.

"What?"

"Sex."

Her mother blushes. "That doesn't even make sense."

She shrugs. Her mother gives her the squinty look that means *you're up to something, don't think I don't know it*; Tolan apes it back. They laugh.

"Well, I'm on my way to the shop," her mother says without moving.

Tolan sets her tablet aside, crosses the room, and wraps her mother in a hug. "Love you, Mom."

Her mother smiles. "Love you, too, Honey. Have fun with Tori."

"Always."

Tolan watches from the door as her mother walks down the hallway and disappears, then returns to her window seat. She hears the garage door open, an engine fire and catch, and if she looked out the window, she'd see her mother driving away, but her tablet's already in her lap.

She'd like it if she could spend less time reading, because reading is exhausting and makes her head and eyes hurt, but her mother is still writing, adding to the number of pages she hasn't read, and editing, changing details for reasons that aren't entirely clear to her, alluding to things then rescinding the allusions: did Bo and Parker... no, I guess not—an entire scene gone from the manuscript.

It's not all bad. She loves Bo's pluck, and Parker because he's gallant and funny. And she loves how they are with each other, their banter. She hopes they'll get together, though Bo doesn't seem interested.

Tolan finishes the chapter and sets the reader on her dresser. She should shower; she and Tori are going Christmas shopping at eleven.

It's early December, and their house is eighty years old and hemorrhages heat, so she walks to the bathroom and cuts the space heater on before returning to her room to change into her bathrobe and slippers. She folds her sweatpants and puts them back in her dresser, opens the closet to put her sweatshirt on a hanger—

There's a pair of khakis hanging between two of her shirts.

She's told her mother a thousand times not to try to put her clothes away. Tolan has a system: jackets, sweaters, shirts, pants, dresses, left to right. She doesn't own more than two or three of each, but each item hangs in the appropriate group, the hangers are equidistant apart, and the colors within the groups go from dark to light as they move right.

Her mother not only hung a pair of pants between two shirts, but she put the pants on a shirt hanger, and hung them so that one side dropped down further than the other.

And she bunched up the spacing.

Tolan would be mad if she didn't know how ridiculous she is.

Tolan's shivering by the time she fixes everything and makes it down the hall, but the heater has made the bathroom warm, and the trembling and gooseflesh dissolve into the arrhythmic start, stop, and spit of flossing, the whir of her electric tooth brush.

Finished, she takes a deep breath, steeling herself. It's not that she doesn't like what she sees—she's okay with her face, thinks she has nice eyes, and that the constellation of freckles on her nose and cheeks is cute—it's just that this is the part of her routine she dreads:

Their shower is directly behind the vanity, and the insert reaches from floor to ceiling; its sliding doors are full-length mirrors. The overhead light is bright and ceaseless and reflects off the mirrors and tile floor, and the hooks for her robe and towel are to the left of the vanity, which means that she has to pass naked through the glass gauntlet at least twice every time she takes a shower, to see herself with excruciating clarity, every blemish, defect, and inadequacy, and having seen them, she can't just continue on, can't just get in the shower, but has to inspect them and appraise the severity of their offense, and determine if the sum of her justifies the toleration of her flaws. Her toes are too long, but she has nice ankles—nice legs, really, from all her running, and she can't find the slightest bit of fat on her body, which is good, but also why she looks like a boy, why she has no breasts or butt.

Her arms are too skinny—she's too bony everywhere, really, but she does have nice shoulders, and a long delicate neck. Her face is her face, not exactly pretty, but not ugly. And then there's her hair: flame-orange as opposed to her mother's Irish setter red, thick and lush and coiling in large, playful spirals that remind her of the person she wishes she were, outgoing and fearless—wild, even—the person she thinks and hopes might exist beneath the shy, self-conscious girl she is. She loves and hates her hair, loves and hates that people are drawn to it, that they stare—hates that it isn't only on her head. Once, in middle school, before Tori explained about shaving down there and Brazilians, Tolan had been wearing a bathing suit, not even a sexy one, a one-piece, and a hair had poked out from underneath, and Sidney Cox had seen it and started pointing and yelling, 'The carpet matches the drapes, the carpet matches the drapes,' and she had been mortified and wanted to die, and he'd kept on yelling until she ran away in tears.

Tolan shakes the memory away, looks at the clock on the wall: Tori's picking her up in less than an hour. She gets in the shower.

She and Tori have done this three years in a row, always on the Saturday before Christmas break starts. At first they called it "The Yuletide Blitzkrieg" because Tori's last name is Quevedo-König, and Yuletide is fun to say, and then it became "The Christmas Campaign," or just "The Campaign." Tolan won't buy much, because she doesn't have much to spend, but even if she did, she only has her mother and Tori to buy for. Tori has a credit card that her parents pay off and is her family's designated gift buyer for more than a dozen cousins, six aunts, and seven uncles, so they'll be at the mall for seven or eight hours, staggering under the progressively increasing weight of the bags they acquire. Just before they leave, Tori will buy Tolan some embarrassingly expensive and amazing gift—always last, so she can make Tolan wait in the arcade while she buys it.

Specifically the arcade.

The arcade, because one time in their freshman year, Tolan's mother had dropped them off at the mall, and they had agreed to meet her outside Macy's at six, but something had happened and they still weren't where they were supposed to be at six-fifteen, so they had cut through the arcade to save time, and their hygienically-challenged, turbo-dork classmate Walter saw them. And because Tolan was near the "Wizard the Vampire Slayer" game when he saw her, he thought she was into Wizard and decided he loved her, and made her a Wizard-ess costume and asked her on a date to the Wildcat Comic Con in Williamsport, costume to be worn. She'd gone despite the fact that he was a freak with stringy hair and bad b.o., because she'd noticed that he only ever wore one of two shirts, a long-sleeved Oxford button-down in the winter and fall, and an off-brand polo shirt in spring and summer, and she felt bad for him, and realized that if her mother didn't buy her clothes and pay the water and the electric, she'd be grodie too. And if she hadn't met Tori and been admitted to the fringes of the in-club, people would call her a freak, too, because she's freakishly tall and freakishly pale, and shy.

And she'd never been asked out before.

Tolan rinses the shampoo from her hair and gets out, checking the clock as she towels dry. It won't take her long to get dressed; she hates the way makeup feels on her skin, so she never wears any, and because Tori's beautiful, and doesn't wear any either, and Tolan's her best friend, and they spend all their time together, no one says anything.

She's thinking about Bo as she puts on her robe, about how she dropped out of college after a year and a half. Parker had given her her first camera shortly after she arrived in New York. She'd hated college, missed Maine, and missed her time in the woods, and he'd said that photojournalism was like hunting, getting not just good pictures, but the right pictures, the ones that cut to the heart of things and revealed truths that people didn't or didn't want to see. He'd started a magazine a year before she left college, and after she dropped out, he'd convinced her that the magazine needed a photographer, and she should be it.

Tolan's not sure college is right for her, either, but she assumes she'll go, because it's what you do after high school. She tries to imagine herself as a photographer, tromping around the world taking pictures, and frowns.

She doesn't even own a camera.

Back in her room, she turns some music on, and by the time she's dressed she's smiling a little, excited for the day. She looks at the clock. She's got twenty minutes until Tori picks her up; her tablet's lying on her bedside table—It's 1939, and Bo's headed to Cuba.

Bo can wait.

Tolan lifts her guitar off its stand and sits down to play.

CHAPTER TWENTY-TWO

"Well, if it isn't Bo White!" Turner shouted across the bar into the lobby, waving her over. "Have a drink—Cuba libre!"

It was ten-thirty. She'd landed in Miami at eight, boarded a two-seater, and made it to Havana by mid morning.

"Ready to go?" she asked.

"Hello to you too, Bo."

"Shouldn't we be headed to the harbor?"

He gave a dismissive wave. "There's nothing to see, just a bunch of unlucky Jews."

"What?"

"Simmer down, little lady, I'm just being flip. The police aren't letting reporters near the *St. Louis*, so, seeing as we're without a story, Frank and I," —Turner gestured at the man on the barstool beside him, grinning— "decided to get a head start. Care to join us? The magazine's paying."

"I think I'll go up to my room and get settled."

"Suit yourself. Bartender," —he waved his index finger in a circle— "¡Más cubanos libres!"

Bo had been furious when she found out she'd been assigned to Turner, barged into Parker's office all sparks and rage. Parker had waited for her to finish, handed her a plane ticket, and told her that Turner would be waiting at the hotel.

Parker hadn't tried to defend himself; the magazine was just getting started, and Turner was the son-in-law of one of the magazine's principle investors and a friend of their editor in chief. Parker knew Bo was well aware of all of it, just as he'd known Bo would fight him anyway.

Turner was gone when she returned. Twenty minutes later she'd slipped the port authority's blockade.

———

Bo crept close to the wall, inching forward until she could see out the alley across the street. Motorcycles, pedestrians, a rickshaw, two policemen

—she caught sight of a cab and ran, crouching low and lunging for the door as the police began to turn in her direction. The cabbie stared, startled, as Bo lay low against the seat, breathing heavily, camera around her neck. Her hair was matted against her forehead, her blouse transparent from sweat.

"Hotel Nacional de Cuba."

The man didn't move.

Bo waited.

He looked from her to the policemen and back.

"Por favor."

The man smiled.

"Claro, Señorita. A mí tampoco me gusta la policía."

"Gracias."

Back at the hotel, she went looking for Turner, found Frank in the bar.

"Where's Turner?"

He took a sip of his drink before answering, eyes crawling over her.

"Gone to the bureau to cable his story to New York."

"Thanks."

Bo signaled the bartender over. "Can I borrow a pen?"

"Certainly."

She wrote on a cocktail napkin, folded it, and left the pen on the bar.

"Nice to see you too," Frank called after her, but she was already talking to the concierge.   "¿Puedes…?" Frustration, embarrassment. "I'm sorry, I don't speak Spanish."

"It's quite alright, Miss White. How can I help you?"

"Can you cable this to New York, please, the magazine, care of Parker Jordan. It's urgent."

"Right away, Señorita."

"And I'll need a cab."

"I'll have the bell hop call one for you."

"Thank you."

An hour and a half later she was in a café trying to communicate with a sailor in broken German and English. The man rubbed his thumb and forefinger together, and she slid two folded bills across the table, added three more when he made no move to take them. He put them in his pocket.

"Warten Sie hier," he said, and walked away.

An hour passed.

She ordered another drink.

Another hour.

The place was filling up, the waiter glaring at her, so she ordered dinner and a third drink, ate slowly, finished. The waiter brought her bill as soon as she'd swallowed her last mouthful of food.

No one was coming.

She left twice what her meal cost on the table and stood to go. It was hot outside, despite the late hour, the air thick and wet.

"Entschuldigen Sie," a voice called. "Fraulein."

She felt a hand close on her arm, jerked away, fists raised.

It was the sailor.

He stepped back, hands in the air, "Verzeihen Sie bitte! You are ready?"

She nodded, dropping her hands.

"I am Wilhelm. Please come. We go quickly."

They walked away from the cafe toward the docks, ducking into an alley. He produced a jacket and slacks from beneath his shirt. "You wear."

She stared.

"Quickly, Fraulein."

She undid the first button while he grinned, stopped, glared at him.

"Yes, yes," he said, turning away reluctantly. "Fine."

He waited.

"You have camera?"

"Yes."

"Gut."

They walked to the edge of the alley, looked left and right, hurried toward the docks, he in the lead, she close behind.

"Slow," he said suddenly, putting his arm out behind him. Sixty meters ahead a Cuban official sat in a small hut, smoking a cigarette.

Bo flicked his ear as hard as she dared.

"Warum zum Teuf—" He whipped his head around, saw his hand cupping her breast. "Zapp," he grinned.

She hissed.

"Okay, okay. You are mean. Nicht schön. Your arm on me."

"What?"

"Your arm." He gestured, pointing to his neck.

"Listen…"

"Betrunken… Drunk." He put his hat on her head, pulled it low over her eyes. "Arm." He looped it around his neck. "Slowly."

She understood. The guard saw them from ten meters; she leaned low and into Wilhelm, concealing her chest against him.

"Documentos."

"¡Por supuesto!" Wilhelm slurred, handing his over boisterously.

The guard handed them back without looking at them, bored.

"Y los suyos?"

Wilhelm squinted at the guard, acting confused. "Sie sind eine dumme und hässliche Person."

He held out his papers again.

The guard shoved them away.

"Su amigo."

Wilhelm stared blankly. "Und Sie sind faul, und Ihre Reißverschluss muss zugeknöpft sein."

"¡Documentos!"

"¡Ah! ¡Sí! Un momento, Señor. Por favor." Wilhelm shook Bo, "Fritz!" He poked her, slapped her cheek. "Fritz! Aufwachen! Dieser Idiot lässt uns nicht durch."

"¡Documentos!"

Wilhelm held up a finger. "Un momento, Señor." He undid the button on her breast pocket, reached in and fumbled around. "Fritz!"

Bo moaned, made herself gag and started to wretch; the guard leapt away—"¡Váyanse! ¡Váyanse! ¡Ahorita!"

Wilhelm smiled drunkenly. "¡Gracias, Señor!"

The guard watched them stumble past him, shaking his head.

"Pendejos borrachos."

They shuffled on, stumbling periodically until they were out of sight, then moving soundlessly onto the shore boat and pushing off from the dock. Bo's camera hung from her neck in a waterproof bag beneath her shirt. The boat shot forward when Wilhelm pulled, slowed in the lull between strokes. Looking down, she frowned, began re-buttoning the breast pocket he'd reached into.

"I ought to hit you."

He shook his head. "Bad to hit man in boat. Pech."

"I'm sure."

"You are safe on boat. If anyone sees, say you are for the Captain."

"For the captain?"

Wilhelm grinned.

"I'll say no such thing," she spat.

Wilhelm looked confused.

"He want help. He likes," Wilhelm paused, muttering. "Was sind die Wörter? Die Passagiere, die Juden."

"The passengers?"

"Yes. Passengers. He wants help them."

"Oh."

"Take pictures inside—not on the deck. Don't let the Kubaner see. I try take you back after... nachdem alle eingeschlafen sind..." He frowned, gestured to his watch. "After."

She nodded.

They were nearly to the ship.

"Das Geld war nicht für mich."

She shook her head.

"The money."

"I gave you all the money—"

"No!" He sulked. "Ich wollte es nicht behalten. Ich gab es den Beamten, den kubanischen Beamten. I give it for the Cubano."

"A bribe."

He nodded.

"I didn't… I'm sorry."

They rode the rest of the way in silence, passing a Cuban patrol boat before reaching the ship, hurrying to the captain's quarters once aboard.

"Vater."

"Wilhelm." The captain nodded abruptly before turning to Bo. "You must be Miss White." He extended his hand. "It's a pleasure to meet you, though I regret the circumstances."

"You speak English?"

"You sound surprised."

"My apologies, Captain, it's just that—"

The Captain followed her eyes to Wilhelm, who coughed once, and stared at the floor. The Captain sighed. "I think my son has been playing games with you. Isn't that so, Wilhelm?"

"I'm not sure what you mean, Sir."

Bo glared.

The Captain shook his head. "I'm going to be frank, Miss White," the Captain said. "The situation is dire."

"May I quote you?"

He nodded. "We set sail with 937 passengers, most of them Jews. When we docked here, we were told that the immigration laws had changed, and each passenger would have to pay an additional five hundred dollars if they wanted the Cuban government to stamp their visa. Those that were able, did, but most couldn't."

"Now what?"

"That is the question of the hour, or should I say of the last forty-eight hours."

"Will you return to Germany?"

His eyes creased in irritation, fatigue burning in his eyes.

"If we return to Germany, my passengers will most likely be arrested at the docks and sent to Dachau."

"Dachau?"

"A concentration camp."

She shook her head.

"Surely your intelligence agencies…"

She shook her head.

"They're like prisons, only worse. The Nazis round up people in cattle cars and ship them to the camps. Many are killed outright, gassed, or put into ovens, others are subjected to medical experimentation. Most are worked to death."

Bo was speechless.

"The Cuban government has given us twenty-four hours to disembark, after which time, if we are still in port, they will open fire."

"And our government?"

"You mean the American government?"

"Yes. The American government. Sorry."

"We're departing for Florida tomorrow, but they've yet to grant us permission to land, or promised my passengers asylum."

He turned away from her, ran a hand over his beard, took a breath. "I'm told Secretaries Hull and Morgenthau are advocating on their behalf, but we haven't heard anything definitive. Canada has already refused."

"Why?"

"We have been in port for a week now, Miss White. Eleven passengers were able to pay the fee, and five more escaped during the night. Two men slit their wrists and threw themselves overboard only to be fished out of the water by the Cubans, given the medical care demanded by their injuries, and returned to the ship. I've held negotiations with three countries to no avail, which leaves me with 231 crewmen growing more mutinous everyday, an indefinite number of SS and Gestapo spies, and a ship full of passengers that no longer trust me."

He turned back to Bo.

"What I'm going to ask you to do is illegal and dangerous, but I find myself without alternative. I have two small boats, each of which can take an oarsman and five passengers. I cannot go myself, and I cannot trust any of my other men for what I think are obvious reasons, but I'm sending Wilhelm in one—"

"And you want me to take the other."

"I do."

Their eyes locked.

"Okay."

He nodded.

"You'll be taking Mrs. Ulmann and her daughters."

"What about Mr. Ulmann?" Bo asked.

"There isn't room—"

"But just one more—"

"Enough!"

He stopped, closed his eyes, took a breath, opened them.

"The boat will be overfull as it is, which means it will already be riding low in the water, and correct me if I'm wrong, but I'm guessing you're not an experienced rower."

She shook her head.

"First watch ends at midnight; the watchmen usually leave early, and their replacements are always a few minutes late. You'll go north; Wilhelm will travel south. Row for an hour, then make land. It will give your passengers more time to run if you can get back to the ship before the lifeboats are missed, but don't take any chances. If you're not going to make it before first light, go ashore and lose the boat. Wilhelm, Mrs. Ulmann and her daughters don't speak English, so you'll have to brief them."

"Should we bring a weapon, Sir?"

The captain shook his head.

"If you're caught, you're to give yourselves up immediately."

They nodded. The captain started to go, hesitated.

"Miss White… You'll see to it that your magazine runs the story?"

"I'll do my best."

"Thank you."

The sea turned rough beyond the harbor, curbing their progress and forcing Bo to throw herself against the weight of the oars in order to drive the boat through the water. Never having rowed, her hands erupted in blisters, which tore against the rough-hewn scull and wept pus and blood. She was grateful, though, for her hands and the searing paroxysms tormenting her back and arms. The pain drowned out her fear and forestalled paralysis, reach by pull, until their destination appeared, and she ran the boat aground."Danke," the mother whispered, tears in her eyes. "Danke sehr!"

"Hurry."

"Ich kann nicht…"

"Go!"

Bo pushed the wife out, began handing her children to her as rapidly as possible.

Her daughter began to cry. "Weiß ich nicht—"

They were all out.

Bo shoved the boat back into the sea, jumped in.

"Danke!" the woman called after her.

"Ruhe!"

Bo was already rowing.

A cold wind had blown the clouds from the sky and the moon seemed to touch the water, turning the waves a luminescent silver. She could see for miles, but she didn't think to wonder if she were still in danger now that her passengers had disembarked, because she couldn't think.

Only row.

Row.

Dive beneath the pain.

Row.

Four hours had seemed ample time to make the trip, but her progress had become so incremental that she wasn't sure she would make it.

She rounded into the harbor and the *St. Louis* came into view, tranquil and safely at moor.

Only a hundred meters to go.

She felt crazy and exhausted and started giggling.

She'd made it.

Then a searchlight hit her.

Bo came to, head roaring. She tried to sit up, was jerked backward by the arm. She followed metal from her wrist to a pipe protruding from the wall.

She was handcuffed.

There was something on her head, a guard at the door.

The guard looked up from his book, met her eye, stood without a word, and left the room. He returned minutes later, resumed his position.

She awoke to the rattle of a key twisting in an iron lock, though she couldn't remember falling asleep. The man with keys wore a military uniform with a star on each epaulet, had a chair and a clipboard, and a white pencil-thin moustache.

"What are you doing in Cuba?"

"I'm a photographer. I work for—"

"We know who you work for, Miss White."

How did he know her name?

"I'm staying—"

"We know where you were staying."

"I don't under—"

"What were you doing in that boat?"

"I was trying to get on board the *St. Louis*."

"And how did you come by the boat?"

"I stole it. From the docks."

"So you're a thief?"

He wrote on his clipboard.

"I was going to give it back."

"And your hands?"

She looked down at them. They were wrapped in gauze.

"I hurt them rowing out."

"All that came from ten, at the most, fifteen, minutes of rowing?"

"I'd never done it before."

He set his pen down.

"I don't like being lied to, Miss White."

"I'm not lying."

"As you wish."

He capped his pen, stood.

"What happened to my head?"

He smiled wanly. "You resisted arrest."

They moved her from the infirmary to a jail cell later that night, shortly before she started vomiting. Twenty-four hours passed, forty-eight, more; she was in and out of consciousness. A tin plate with cold beans and rice appeared in her cell once a day, a canteen cup of water. There was a bucket in the corner she'd managed to use a couple times, excrement crusting on the cement from the times she'd missed. Fever radiated off her in waves.

She hallucinated, heard voices and footsteps, sounds. Her family appeared, speaking gibberish, receded into the ethers. Parker too. She told them she couldn't understand them, but they never responded.

And then Parker was there, pulling her out of bed, putting her arm around his neck, and lifting her off the ground.

"Thank you," she said.

Bo awoke at the Hotel Nacional. Parker was asleep in a chair at her bedside. Night shone through the window. She slid out of bed, crept to the bathroom, shut the door behind her, and felt for the light. She was startled by her face in the mirror: her lip split, closed up with stiches, her left eye swollen shut, her hair matted in snarls. The bandages on her hands and head were fresh. She raised the gauze up and saw a line of stitches running from eyebrow to temple.

She came out and found the lamp on her bedside table switched on, Parker looking up at her.

"How do you feel?"

"I'll be okay."

"The doctor says so."

"Good."

"Bo…"

She sat on the edge of her bed, turning away from his gaze.

"You were worried."

He didn't answer.

"There wasn't time to call."

Silence.

"You would have—" she stopped. "I had to do it."

"I know."

She turned. "You know?"

"Captain Schroeder called the offices."

"So you…"

Parker nodded. "You were brave and heroic." A tear welled up over his eyelid; he wiped it away before it reached his cheek.

"You don't have to worry about me."

"It was your camera that saved you."

"What?"

"Your camera. If you hadn't had it they would have executed you as a rebel."

"Oh."

"If you hadn't had it…" He turned away, pretending to look out the window.

"But I did."

"If you hadn't."

"But I did. I'll have the story to you by tomorrow afternoon."

"What?" He turned on her. "I don't give a—"

"It's a good story."

His shoulders fell forward.

"I'm sure it is."

"Thank you for coming for me."

He started to speak, stopped.

"I'm just glad to have you back."

"I'm glad to be back." She hesitated. "I missed you."

CHAPTER TWENTY-THREE

Mother and daughter sit together in a bookstore in the mall, reading, around them the sipping of coffee and tea, shoppers' smiles and grimaces, the intermittent conversation of disembodied voices, bells and bulbs and poinsettias gleaming on plate glass, Dean Martin singing *It's Beginning To Look A Lot Like Christmas*, parents wrangling children for pictures with Santa, and last minute shoppers weaving in and out of stores. Pan is clutching a mug, cozy beside a faux wood-stove. She's wearing jeans and a white sweater, and her hair is tied in a single braid; Tolan thinks she looks cute, and is about to say so when she remembers she's mad at her mother. She can't let her mother know she's mad because it's absurd that she is, and because her mother doesn't know Tolan's reading her book. Tolan's takes the elastic from her hair and lets it fall in secret rebellion, shaking her head so it's loose and wild.

"What?"

Tolan squints at her mother. "What do you mean, 'what'?"

"You're looking at me funny."

"Am not."

"Are, too, evil child. Quit making that face—people are watching. Why do you enjoy torturing your mother?"

Tolan laughs. "Because it's so easy!"

"You're an evil child."

"So you say."

They're both laughing.

"I really didn't mean to look at you funny. I was just thinking it's nice to be out with you."

Her mother smiles.

"Well, maybe not nice so much as not totally awful, kinda fun. Well maybe not fun, per se…"

"Evil child."

Tolan grins. "I prefer nefarious."

They finish their tea. Tolan collects their cups and takes them to the trash.

"Now I know you're up to something."

"What?"

"You're being helpful—you must be after something."

Tolan makes a face. "You just don't want to admit that you have the nicest, coolest daughter on the face of the planet, who's not at all evil, or…"

"Nefarious?"

"Right. That. Not even a little."

Her mother rolls her eyes.

They walk arm in arm toward the exit, holding one bag each. They'd separated so they could shop for each other, met back up at the bookstore. It's a big thing the two of them do, trying to sleuth out the gift the other got for them, and everything short of going through each other's stuff is fair game. Tolan's bag is dangling from her wrist, the store logo clearly visible. She went to a novelty store—the kind that sells itching-powder and penis-shaped toothpicks, and bought the cheapest thing she could find just so she'd have a bag. Her mother's real gift is a pair of Mikimoto earrings she'd saved for more than a year to buy. She's had them hidden in her closet for weeks. Tolan suspects her mother's bag is a ruse, too.

"Do you remember where we parked?"

"H-17," Tolan says, looking around. "Over there."

They walk in the direction of their truck. "It's snowing," her mother says happily.

"You're astute, you are. Blazingly observant."

"Oh, hush. You know what I meant, creepy kid."

"Want me to drive?"

Her mother's searching her purse for the keys. "Crash Aimes? Um… no. I have enough white in my hair already, thank you."

"When have I ever—"

"Once into the side of our garage—"

"I misjudged—"

"Once into the car behind us at the drive-in—"

"The front of his car was in our—"

"You ran over Tori's father's foot—"

"That was his fault! He admitted it!"

She found the keys. "I think we'll be safer if I drive, honey."

"I think we'll be safer if you get rid of this eight-hundred-year-old piece of junk truck."

"Don't be mean to Sham—he's been good to us."

"Harumph."

"You can drive another time; I just don't want to die before the holidays."

"Double harumph."

They got in the car.

92

"Want to make eggnog and sugar cookies tonight?"

"You're in trouble."

"Trouble?"

"Big trouble. I'm a good driver."

"You're a great driver, honey."

"Condescension. Now you're in bigger trouble."

"But if I weren't?"

"It might be fun. I like sugar cookies."

"And eggnog."

"Eggnog is overrated."

"You love eggnog."

"Harumph."

"You can invite Tori over."

"You're still in trouble."

Her mother laughs.

"We'll stop by the store on the way home."

Tolan smiles despite herself.

"I saw that."

"You saw nothing."

"Oh. Okay."

She takes her daughter's hand and gives it a squeeze, and Tolan squeezes back, and the snow falls in big, fat flakes that loop and flit in the wind. Soon they're pulling into the parking lot at the grocery store.

"Stay or come with?" her mother asked.

"I'll stay and call Tori if it's alright."

"I'll leave the truck running, then."

Tolan nods. "Thanks—hey, Tori's parents are going to be away on Christmas again, do you mind if she comes over?"

"Of course not."

She watches her mother go, not at all mad. She doesn't really care about the driving, and as far as the book, it's just that she really likes Parker, and wishes Bo did too. It could have been so romantic: the U.S. Government was rounding up Japanese-Americans and putting them in labor camps, so Bo and Parker flew west, charging off to take the pictures and write the story that would reveal the great injustice. Parker had bought a ring and memorized a proposal, and they sat down for dinner in the hotel restaurant their first night out there, and he was nervous and sweating and had a frog in his throat, but he took her hand across the table anyway and got it all out.

Tolan is near tears now, remembering. Parker had been so nervous he hadn't seen the look on her face, the dawning horror, and he'd stood up and walked around the table and kneeled beside her, taken the ring from his pocket, and she'd burst from her chair and ran out of the room with a hand over her face. He'd been too stunned to react right away, tried to play it off with a joke when he recovered—"I knew I should have gone with white gold"—but no one laughed, and he'd had to stand up, and return to his chair, and wait for the waiter to bring the bill.

"Tolan? Honey, what's wrong?"

Tolan jumps, stabs at her eyes. "Nothing. Sorry. I was just thinking about Tori, and how much it must suck to be left alone on Christmas."

Her mother puts a hand on her arm, moves it up and down, soothing her. "You're such a good person, Tolan, such a good friend, and I'm so proud to have a daughter who cares so much."

She does care. Deeply. She wants to grab Tori's parents and shake them until their teeth rattle, to scream at them and tell them what crappy people they are for leaving their daughter alone on Christmas. But she feels guilty, now, because these tears aren't for Tori, and she doesn't deserve her mother's praise.

These tears are for Parker, non-existent Parker, who had his non-existent heart smashed to non-existent pieces by the non-existent woman he loved.

CHAPTER TWENTY-FOUR

"Bo."

She hurried by with a handful of negatives.

"Bo."

Parker followed her into the photo closet.

"How long are we going to do this?"

It had been a week since she turned him down. They'd been back in New York for four days.

"I can't talk now, I've got to go get some pictures for a story."

She pushed by him, grabbed her coat and hat from the rack in the corner, and was gone.

He didn't move right away, stared blankly at the space she'd vacated. A dozen eyes fled when he looked up, the steno pool and a few beat writers, but he ignored them and crossed the open room toward the editor's suite.

He knocked on the door. "May I come in?"

His partner hesitated, momentarily confused. "Of course."

Parker shut the door behind him.

"This is about the article?"

"It is."

"Parker."

"Hank."

They locked eyes, dug in.

"We can't run it."

"We can."

"Our investors wouldn't stand for it."

"It's the right thing to do, Hank."

Hank pushed himself away from his desk, stood, and walked to the window, thumbs jammed in his pants pocket.

"There's a war on, Parker, a war we could lose. The country is emerging from the worst decade in its history."

"I'm aware."

"Well, this magazine is not going to add to its problems."

"No, we're not; we're going to illuminate them, so they can be recognized as such and dealt with."

"How? By giving people who might be in collusion with the enemy the freedom to sabotage our country?"

"Listen to yourself, Hank! That's rubbish and you know it—you can't even look at me."

Hank spun, lip curling in a snarl. "Are you calling me a liar?"

"I'm saying that you know as well as I do that what's happening is wrong."

"Are you done?"

"I wish I were."

Hank's suit jacket hung on a hook beside his hat; his tie was loose, his shirt open at the throat, vest stretched tight over a broad back and barrel chest. His sleeves were rolled to the elbow. He had steel-blue eyes, a jutting jaw, a cleft chin, and a pocket watch on a large gold-linked chain. He owned the ground on which he stood, annexed the space around him with the width of his stance and the hook and thrust of hands punctuating his proclamations.

Parker was wearing his suit jacket, was taller and thinner with satin-brown eyes. He spoke moderately, feet even with his hips, hands in his pockets.

"Our purpose is to provide our readers with images of the events unfolding in this country, and to set those images beside the ideals on which our nation is founded so that we may celebrate what is just and recognize where we have erred."

"Do you have any idea how self-righteous you sound?"

"That's precisely what I'm trying not to be, Hank. I have my convictions, but I recognize that finally, it's not up to me. I don't get to give the final word."

"I don't follow."

"If we kill this story, we're making a decision on behalf of the American people, that the denial of the rights of American citizens on American soil by the American government is immaterial."

"I don't see it that way."

"What way is that?"

"I don't see it as our government taking rights away from its citizens, far from it. It's protecting them."

"Have you even looked at the pictures Bo took? Have you seen them?"

"Is that what this is really about?"

"What?"

"All this sanctimonious talk about rights and obligations, and what you're really on about is the fact that we didn't publish your girlfriend's pictures."

Parker clenched, eyes narrowing. "Pardon me?"

The transformation hit Hank like a blow; he flinched, froze for the duration of a heartbeat, thrust his jaw out.

"This isn't about morals; it's about your infatuation with Bo."

"You're out of line, Hank."

"No, Parker, you're out of line. You've got a crush on an employee, and you're trying to dictate company policy accordingly."

"You actually believe that?"

Parker's voice was tight.

"I do."

Hank's eyes blazed.

"And you're going to kill the story."

"I already did."

Parker looked away out the window, down onto the streets, at cars like toys and people like pushpins. His disbelief rose like water, out of the streets and the storm grates and the gaslights.

He exhaled a single staccato laugh. "I guess that's that, then."

"That's what?"

Parker looked up at Hank. "Well, I can't imagine you'd want to carry on with a partner of such low caliber."

"Parker…"

"Excelsior, then, Hank." Parker extended his hand. "I wish you the best of luck."

"You're really going to do this? One little tiff, and you're going to blow the whole thing up?"

"Let's pretend for a minute that you didn't just denigrate my integrity with accusations you know very well to be baseless. Even forgetting that, we are left with the fact that you and I have a fundamental and irreconcilable difference of opinion with regard to the nature of the magazine's purpose and its obligation to its readers."

Hank rolled his eyes and looked away. "For Christ sake, I'll run it. I'll print the damn story."

"I hope you do."

Parker turned to go.

"What the hell do you want me to do?"

Parker stopped, hand on the doorknob. "The magazine is making money, Hank. Carlin will step into my role, and you can buy out my stake, or I'll find someone else to sell to. Our lawyers will work out the details."

"So you and Bo are done?"

"I have no idea what Bo will do, Hank, that's part of the fun." He forced a smile. "Good luck."

CHAPTER TWENTY-FIVE

"Would you come into my office for a moment, Bo?"

She nodded. "Have you heard from Parker? It's nearly noon, and I haven't seen him."

"That's what I wanted to talk to you about. Please—" He pointed to the chair in front of his desk, closed the door.

"When was the last time you talked to him?"

"Friday afternoon, I think."

He nodded, leaned against the desk, and scanned the room.

"Something the matter?"

"Parker left the magazine."

Hank hazarded a glance at her, turned away before they could make eye contact.

"What? When?"

"Friday evening. He came into my office, we quarreled, and he resigned."

"He what—why?"

"It was about the Jap roundup story. He insisted it should go to press, and I was adamant that it not, and one thing led to another…"

He stopped, closed his eyes a moment, opened them, and looked her in the eye.

"I said some things I shouldn't have, things I knew weren't true, and I didn't back down when he pushed back."

Bo waited.

"I told him his feelings for you were clouding his judgment, that he was favoring you, and that the only reason he was insisting we run the Jap story was because it was your piece."

The blood drained from her face. "That's bullsh—he never—I never—"

"I know! For Christ sake, that's why I'm telling you, so that when you hear about it from him you'll know that I didn't mean it."

"I'm a damn good photographer!"

"You are. There's no question. I was way out of line, and I know that. I knew it then."

"Parker never gave me—"

"A damn thing. I know. I looked back through my files; every assignment you've been given came from me."

"And I'm paid—"

"The same as every other photographer with your level of experience."

"So why—"

"I got hot! Parker wouldn't back down, and—I'm sorry, Bo, for Christ sake, I'm saying I was being a fathead—I'm trying to apologize."

"Can't you just apologize to Parker? Say what you just said and he'll come back—"

"He won't."

"But—"

"It doesn't work like that, Bo, not with men, and especially not with Parker. I've known him going on seven years; he'll abide many things, but questioning his integrity…"

Hank's face and voice fell, and he shoved his hands in his pockets.

"I not only called him a liar, but I brought you into it."

She screwed up her face. "So what?"

"So what?"

He squinted as if he were trying to bring her into focus.

"I can fight my own battles."

"You don't think he knows that?"

"I don't think this business has anything to do with me beyond the fact that I'm a woman. It's just more macho crap, two roosters trying to outdo each other, and I got caught up in it."

"That's not tr—"

"Look me in the eye and tell me that you would have accused Parker if I were a man, or that he would he have quit over it?"

Bo glared. He was silent.

"That's what I thought."

"You've got it all—"

"I'm getting it, is more like it. I had a job I liked working with two people I enjoyed until you two got going."

He ground his jaw, fought the edge creeping into his voice.

"I asked you in here so I could apologize, and because I wanted you to hear me say that I knew what I said to Parker was out of line."

"I know it was! And you can stuff your apology! I don't need to wait for confirmation of my worth from you, or Parker, or anyone."

"I guess not."

Bo stood to leave.

"You know, you've got me pegged—what I said had nothing to do with you. But you're wrong about Parker."

"Boy's club rules, Hank: when one of your buddies is caught in the wrong, cover for him."

"In the three years we worked together, Parker only made one request related to you. One. You know what it was?"

"No, and I don't care, Hank."

"He asked that I not send you to Europe to cover the war."

"I've had about enough of—"

"He cares about you!"

"Goodbye, Hank." Bo left, leaving the door open behind her.

CHAPTER TWENTY-SIX

Bo waited for Parker to contact her, but he didn't. Three weeks went by.

He couldn't be mad at her — it'd be absurd for him to expect her to quit her job just because he did.

Did he want her condolences?

It was press day, so she'd know soon. The staff always got together at P.J. Clarke's afterward.

But Parker wasn't on the staff anymore.

She was furious with him for messing it all up, missed having lunch together, trading hunches and stories and sharing ideas. She missed how the staff meetings had grown increasingly raucous as Parker played the straight man to Hank's wildcard. She'd always known when they'd have lunch together at Harold's, and when Parker was going to steal away to read beneath a tree in Central Park; he wore a tweed suit on those days, more worn than his usual clothes, with patches on the elbows that were themselves wearing thin. In the rare instances when he brought his lunch rather than buying it from a vendor, it was always roast beef on weck with extra horseradish. He'd have a book tucked in his jacket pocket, find a place just out of the sun's reach, sit down, read, and forget to eat. The book would be something esoteric, poetry or philosophy, and she'd make fun of him.

Bo left Clarke's after three bottles of beer, unaffected. She'd been teaching herself to drink since Cuba, building her tolerance and winning bets, drinking her male colleagues under the table. Parker rarely drank himself, but he'd taught her how to drink, which brands to ask for, cardinal rules: liquor before beer, etc.

She was worried about him as much as angry. Parker's father had been furious when his son declined the offer of a senior editorial position at *The Globe* in order to start a magazine; leaving the magazine would only antagonize him further.

It was unseasonably cold, began to rain as she turned onto 99th Street, the rain landing like metal rods, punching skin and fabric, clattering on the pavement. She pulled her hat down, tightened her coat, and kept walking. The night was dark, the street lamps buzzing loudly. The wind threw old newspaper and scraps of detritus into the air, rattled the vapor lamps so that the light they cast flexed and leapt. A can rolled down the street. The wind howled, and the rain gathered intensity, driving Bo off the street and into the nearest bar, O'Hara's, which was unfamiliar, but dry.

"Can I get you anything, Miss?" the barman asked.

"A Manhattan," she answered. "Up."

"Right away. Do you want to open a tab?"

Bo shook her head, handing him a dollar bill. "I'll pay as I go."

"As you like."

Bo lay her coat over one of the stools as the barkeep made her cocktail, and sat, grateful to have lucked her way into a clean, well-lighted place with transom windows, satinwood floors, and coffered mahogany ceilings. She wanted a drink or two, now that she was here, and maybe something to eat, and she didn't figure digs this classy and staff that wore vests and ties and cufflinks would allow anyone to harass her.

"Here you go," the barman said, handing Bo her drink.

Turning to thank him, she saw Parker sitting at a table against the far wall.

"May I sit down?"

He looked up from his book as if waking from a dream. "Bo. Of course. Please."

The waitress came; Bo ordered a dry martini, turned back to him.

"Where have you been?"

"Job hunting."

"Apologize to Hank—or just show up, he'll take you back."

He frowned and looked away.

"What? It's childish, and you know it."

The waitress came. "Can I get you another drink, Sir?"

Parker nodded. "Tonic water with a lemon twist. Please."

"You won't go back."

Parker's drink came, he nodded his thanks, rolled the glass in a slow circle, the liquid kissing the rim of the tumbler, sliding back into the main.

"You're really going to toss it all away over a rhubarb? You're better than that."

He looked out through the plate glass at the front of the restaurant at an empty street, the wind blowing the rain sideways.

He coughed, swallowed. "Have you been here before?"

She frowned. "No."

"My father was in town on business a few months before you got here. He stopped by the office and said he heard about this restaurant, the Blue Budgie, which serves the best steak sandwich north of Philadelphia, and did I want to have dinner later."

"Parker, I want to talk—"

"He had a stock holders' meeting to attend, and I had an article to edit, so we parted ways and agreed to meet at seven-thirty. I finished with the article sooner than I expected to, so I headed over early, figuring I'd read until he arrived. I took a corner booth and ordered a drink, and after a few pages this guy came in—the book was excellent, and I wouldn't have noticed him if he hadn't been so sauced—have you read Steinbeck?"

"Damn it, Parker—"

"Anyway, he more or less falls on the bar trying to order a drink, so George asks him to leave, and the guy does, so I go back to my book. Twenty or thirty minutes pass, the door opens and closes a few times, then all of a sudden KA-BAM! A gun goes off, catches George between the eyes —finis!"

"For God sake, Parker! We were working together at a job we enjoyed, having a good time. Everything was—"

He put a finger up. "I'm getting to the good part."

Bo scowled.

"Everyone's screaming, and there's this bird that the owner keeps beside the bar, and he's screaming, too, and afterward, no one can remember what the gunman looked like, only that the budgie kept screaming 'robber' over and over. A few months go by, and the investigation runs cold."

"Dammit, Parker."

"Just listen, it's a good story."

She crossed her arms.

"Anyway, this one detective won't let go — George had been a good friend. He walks into the restaurant one day—new owner, same budgie, and the bird calls out his name, and suddenly, he realizes that George had taught the bird to greet the regulars by name and he thinks what if the bird wasn't saying 'Robber' after all. The detective looks into it, and it turns out there's a Robert with an unpaid tab, so he tracks him down. The man confesses, but he wants to know how they found him, so the detective tells him about the budgie, and the guy says—wait for it: 'I never did like that bird.'"

She didn't laugh.

"Come on, Bo, it's a good story."

The waitress brought her another drink.

"Come back to the magazine."

"Talk to me."

"About what?"

"Bo…"

"I'm trying to talk some sense into you—you don't want to leave anymore than I want you to."

"Marry me."

"Parker…"

He winced, closed his eyes and bowed his head slightly. "Sorry."

She was silent.

"At least tell me why."

"I…" she began.

He leaned in.

"I can't."

He closed his eyes, briefly, then sat up.

"Please come back."

"I can't."

He reached into his jacket pocket and took out his billfold. "I start my new job tomorrow morning."

"Where?"

"*The Times.*"

"Doing?" Her voice was flat.

"Managing editor of the features area."

"Oh."

"I couldn't find anything on my own, so I had to call my father. I told him I'd left the magazine, but was staying in New York, and would he make a call on my behalf. He would, he said, but it was *The Times* or nothing—god forbid his son work for *The Post*. I told him I just wanted to be a reporter, but he said that was out of the question, I'd be an editor or nothing, end of discussion."

"Are you doing this because I didn't quit when you did?"

He stared at her.

"Because I won't marry you?"

Anger flooded his eyes.

"You're going to chuck a job, a magazine we built together, and our friendship for spite?"

Confusion.

"Our friendship? Who said anything—"

"Ask me again."

"Ask you what?"

"To marry you—anything. Whatever you ask, I'll do."

"Bo…"

"One time offer, Parker."

"Anything?"

"Yes."

"You promise?"

"Yes."

"Promise me you won't go to Europe to cover the war."

"What? No! I—"

"You promised. One wish. Whatever I wanted."

"I thought—"

"What, Bo?" Parker snapped. "You thought what? That I'd like having my proposal thrown back in my face? That I have such little regard for myself—for you—that I'd want to marry you knowing it wasn't what you wanted?"

Parker was rigid; Bo felt herself slipping, her face burning, tears like needles against the backs of her eyes, her lips trembling. He started to speak, saw her face, stopped, and looked down at the table, giving her time to compose herself.

"Look, I know Hank told you that I asked him not to send you to cover the war, and I know you're angry, but I'd do it again. I'm sorry, but I would. I know you don't understand why I can't go back to the magazine, and I know you think I'm being petty. I don't see it that way. I wish I could make you understand."

He looked down, spoke to his lap. "I know you care about me, and I don't understand why you don't want to marry me, but I'm willing to accept that, because I'd rather have you as a friend than not at all. But for God sake —you won't even give me a reason."

He paused, hoping, but she only shook her head.

He bowed, struggling to reign in his emotions, forced himself to raise his eyes and look at her. "I love you, Bo. I want to be a part of your life, and nothing, not your turning me down, or my leaving the magazine, is going to change that."

They stared at each other in agonized silence.

"It's not you."

"No," he shook his head, "it has to be. It has to be me, because as long as it's me there's hope. I can change. Who knows," he shrugged, "one day I might wake up, and be what you want."

"Parker…"

He stood and took his coat from the hook on the side of the booth.

"I left because it became clear to me that as long as I was there, you were never going to get your due. Hank said what he said to get a rise out of me, but there're others who believe it, and you deserve better."

He forced a smile.

"Call me if you feel like getting lunch sometime."

She watched him leave, ordered another drink. A man she recognized came in and ordered a beer, a detective from one of the Harlem precincts. A second detective arrived shortly after.

"You're late," the first man said.

"What a goddamn week."

The tavern had emptied out, the dinner crowd gone. Bo sat in her booth, the detectives at a nearby table, and an old man shelled peanuts at the bar. The detectives' overcoats were folded over the backs of the chairs between them, their fedoras hanging on the finials.

"You too?"

They grimaced.

The waitress came. "The usual, gentlemen?"

The men nodded. "Thank you, Alma."

She smiled, brought their order to the bartender, poached a drag off his cigarette.

"You catch a case?"

"Nah, just cumulative."

The detective nodded.

"Here you go, gentlemen." The waitress set two boilermakers between them. "Sandwiches will be right up."

"Gentlemen? You're calling this cad a gentleman? I thought you had better judgment than that."

The waitress rolled her eyes theatrically. "That'll never get old for you, will it, Gene?"

"Never."

She sighed, giving her head a slow shake. "I'll be back."

"Thanks, Alma."

The detectives turned back to each other.

"You?"

"Yeah. Wife killed her husband."

Glass against glass as they dropped shots into their beer, touched rims.

"A beer and a bump."

"A beer and a bump."

"Anyone we know?"

"Not personally. Vic's a guy by the name of Lovelace, though you didn't hear it from me. Goes to my aunt's church."

"Motive?"

"She said it was self defense."

"Was it?"

"Maybe. She'd definitely been worked over, scars."

They spoke and drank in turns. Bo wasn't trying to eavesdrop, but their words reached her nonetheless.

"Corroboration of motive?"

"Does it matter?"

The man shrugged.

For a brief interval neither spoke or raised their glass.

The waitress came with their plates.

"Here you go, boys, two roast beef sandwiches, extra *au jus* on the side."

"Thanks, Alma."

They took large bites, chewed intently.

"The thing that gets me is that they were all between her collarbone and her navel."

"The scars?"

The detective nodded. "A guy gets drunk and beats his wife, he grabs an arm, a wrist, chokes her... he ends up leaving something for someone to see, a black eye, scrapes, bruises. This guy—"

"Didn't."

"No."

Bo grit her teeth, finished her martini.

Three men burst through the door dripping bourbon and rainwater, jocular and raucous, hats askew.

Gene shook his head, killed his beer, motioned for another round.

"Kids these days."

"They charging her?"

"I hope not. Maybe."

The second detective shook his head. "Damn."

"God damn."

"What a mess." He shook his head. "You know, sometimes I wonder if we're even worth saving, the world going to hell like it is."

"I'll say, men beating the hell out of their wives, Japs bombing us, Hitler carving up Europe, Stalin lurking—a boatload of scumbag perps walking the streets." He frowned into his beer.

"Only God can save us."

"Come again?"

"Only God can save us."

"God?"

One of the men at the bar grabbed at Alma's ass as she walked by. The detective scowled. "He'd better hurry."

Their next round came. Bo stood, added to the money Parker had left, and stepped out into the rain.

CHAPTER TWENTY-SEVEN

It's not the seeking that Tolan's most aware of, or being found. Not the night on her bare skin or the heat of pressing flesh. Not even the hunger in Tori's eyes and lips and hands.

It's the blade of moonlight cutting across the hollow beneath Tori's neck.

She parts her lips.

Tori tastes like spearmint.

Tori caresses her, bites, gently, pulls at her arm and leg, and Tolan is straddling her, folding forward as Tori draws her down, kisses the hollow at the base of her neck, the flesh of her throat, pauses, closing her eyes and letting her cheek be still against Tolan's skin.

"You're sure?"

Tolan nods; Tori's hands are hard against her back, pushing downward, gooseflesh rising in their wake. They meet the band of Tolan's underwear, slip beneath it to the small of her back, the tips of her fingers brushing the first swell of her buttocks, leaving reluctantly, slowly, fanning out away from her spine and riding up over her hips, catching the fabric of her t-shirt and lifting it, rib by rib, hesitating at the base of her breasts, then taking the shirt over her head.

There's a strangeness to it: only an hour ago Tolan's mother had given her permission to spend the night at Tori's and to drink the champagne Tori's parents had bought to celebrate her committing to Harvard. They'd brought the champagne to Tori's room, jumped when the cork popped, giggled as it overflowed the bottle. Tori had poured a glass for each of them, tasted it, disappeared, and come back with Chambord.

Can I ask you a question? Tori had said.

Sure.

And here they were.

At night, not every night, one in ten or twelve, Tolan slips a hand underneath her pajamas and lets go, surrenders to the images that come: Daniel Craig rising from the Mediterranean, water clinging to his chest; Polina Semionova ascending in a developpé, lyric and impossible; Jake

Gyllenhaal; Anne Hathaway gasping beneath him. A boy she'd seen at the beach, once; his girlfriend, olive skinned, barely covered beneath a camo-print two-piece.

Now she is letting Tori kiss her, opening her mouth to her. She tastes the sweetness of the liquor as the champagne bursts against her tongue. Tori's mouth is descending, her lips and tongue whispering down her neck, the lightest touch of lips to skin, soft heat and cool breath; teeth between her breasts, hard yet gentle, jaws slowly closing, texture, a new sensation, being consumed, her flesh pulled away from her body, released reluctantly as Tori's kisses turn delicate over her abdomen, pause at her navel. She bites the bottom rim. Tolan presses Tori's head against her with both hands; Tori hooks her thumbs in the waistline of Tolan's pajamas, pulls them down, off, touches her forehead to Tolan's abdomen. The silk whispers against her nose, her upper lip; she breathes deeply, exhales. Tolan quivers.

"Wait."

Tori rises, turns the movie off, the lights on. Tolan starts to protest, squinting against the light, covering herself.

Tori places a finger over Tolan's lips. "Hush."

She pushes Tolan against the bed, moving her hands down her body, palms cupped, fingers apart, fingernails moving over her flesh, gentle rakes riding the slight swell of her breasts, catching on her nipples. Tolan's underwear is pale yellow. A finger slides beneath the band at each hip; air slips in, mouth, more, gasps.

She's a drop of water falling down Daniel Craig's body, a bead of perspiration at the nape of Polina Semionova's neck; she's Jake and Anne, and the air that boy and the girl with olive skin suck desperately into their bodies as they make love. She arches her back against the mattress, bucks her hips.

She's come, whimpers intermittently, bites her lip. Tori's beside her, kissing her temple, drawing circles around her areola with her finger.

"You're beautiful, you know."

Tolan smiles. "Am not."

"You are." Tori kisses her. "Lie there; I want to look at you."

Tolan does, squirms.

"Do I get to see you?"

"Do you want to?"

Tolan nods.

"I'm right here."

Tori rolls onto her back and opens her legs, lifts her arms over her head. Tolan undresses her slowly, reverent, scared, holds her breath without meaning to.

Tori's darker than she is, coffee with cream, flawless.

"You like me, don't you?"

Tolan is kissing her between her breasts, trying to mimic what she did for her, stops, lifts her head.

"Of course."

Tori smiles.

"But not the way I like you?"

It's Tolan's turn to hush her friend; she lays a finger over her lips, resumes kissing her.

Down.

She whispers into Tori's inner thigh, listening for her breathing, for a moan or gasp, a compass. She runs a hand between her legs, opens her to the night air; Tori gasps; Tolan presses; Tori writhes, bursts, falls.

When her breathing returns to normal, she leans in and bites Tolan's neck.

Tolan giggles.

Tori rises and turns off the light.

The comforter is down, the sheets, flannel. Tori pulls Tolan against her, kisses her on the forehead.

Tolan is warm and content, her body still giddy. She loves the scent of Tori's shampoo, lilac and vanilla, the feel of her body pressing her, of Tori's arm across her breast.

But melancholy is creeping, fear.

Tori will want to make love in the morning, and they will, and afterwards they'll shower together because Tori's parents are still in New York, and Tori will hold her from behind and bite her neck, and they'll laugh and talk. But Tolan's afraid that she might not be able to be with Tori in the way Tori wants.

She's scared she might be Bo to Tori's Parker.

Tolan wishes she were more like Bo, generally, just not like Bo was to Parker. Bo was fearless. She started winning awards for her photography, and told Hank she'd leave unless he let her write articles as well. He agreed; she was competent, getting better. She quit the magazine after Hank deemed her article on domestic violence "too divisive to print," took a job working with Parker at *The Times*. He proposed a second and a third time; she refused. They worked and traveled and ate together, recreated; she celebrated Christmas and Easter with his family, Thanksgiving as well.

Five years passed. Fat Man and Little Boy eradicated Nagasaki and Hiroshima; the war ended. Europe was divided between superpowers.

Parker proposed a fourth time, and Bo told him not to ask again.

Would it be like that for her and Tori? Tori's chest rises and falls with the slow rush of her breath.

"It's you, or no one," Parker had said, and Bo told him that that was too bad, and that he would be very lonely.

Tolan could never say that to Tori. It scares her.

Parker turned forty; his family stopped asking him when he was going to settle down.

Sleep is overtaking her, the warmth emanating from Tori.

How could she not have realized? How could she never have had a clue as to how Tori felt?

Why did Tori wait until now?

Tolan doesn't want to be Bo.

She'd never thought of a woman as a long-term option before.

Her eyelids are crushingly heavy.

She loves Tori.

She'll do whatever it takes.

She won't be Bo.

CHAPTER TWENTY-EIGHT

"Parker…"

"No, then?"

"You know, no."

He turned away; the sun was setting unremarkably over the harbor, the color choked in fog. Past the dockhands, an egret descended upon the water.

"Oh, well. I gave it the old college try."

"Why do you keep doing this?"

"Hope springs eternal."

"Don't be droll."

He turned back, forced a smiled. "You're right. I'm sorry."

"No, you aren't."

"Believe me, I am."

"You think I like saying no?"

A laugh escaped his lips.

"I should think you'd be rather bored with it."

"Stop."

"Right."

He looked down.

"Am I really so terrible?"

"I'm going to leave."

"No, you're not."

She bristled, challenged, dropped her napkin on the table, made to stand.

"You'd never pass on oysters Rockefeller." He didn't even make eye contact.

Bo stayed.

"Why are you having dinner with me?"

"You're a friend, Parker."

"We spend a great deal of time together... Walks, movies, theater…"

"We're friends—it's what friends do."

He nodded. "We have fun."

"Parker…"

"We laugh."

"Can't we just have a nice dinner?"

"Yes. Of course." He reeled himself in, met her eye. "I'm sorry."

"Parker..."

"No, no." He shook his head, "I'm ruining things. We have a great view, fog notwithstanding. I have a Delmonico coming, you, your oysters. We're drinking a wonderful red. Let's just put this behind us."

"You know I care for you."

"To an extent."

"I think I should go."

"You baited me into that one."

She frowned.

"Anyway, here comes our food."

They ate without conversing, ordered cordials out of habit.

"Parker," she began, "there's a reason I asked you here."

"You're leaving the country." He stared into his coffee.

"How'd you know?"

"Jameson called me."

"Carver? Why?"

"To get my permission to offer you the job."

"Why the hell should he need—"

"Professional courtesy." Parker gestured to the waiter for the check. "Christ, Bo, get over yourself and get off your high horse. You know damn well you've never needed it with me."

"I'm sorry."

"Enough to let me pay."

She glared.

"Of course not. Another transgression. Mea culpa."

"You weren't honest with me, Parker, from the very beginning."

A bolt of anger. "I've never been dis—"

"When you brought me here. You said the magazine needed a photographer, that I'd be helping you out."

"It did."

"It didn't."

"Maggie can't do every—"

Her face broke him mid-word; his anger died.

"Okay. Fine. I lied."

"Why?"

"You know why."

"Why?"

"Because I wanted you near me! Is that really so bad?"

"I'm not your play thi—"

"Enough." He stood, collected his coat and scarf.

113

"I have never, ever…"

He stopped, met her glare, counted to ten.

"Go to hell, Bo."

"You know what the ladies in the steno pool said?"

"What does that have to—"

"They called me a share crop. They didn't know I was just around the corner, and they said I got my job on my back, with my legs wide."

Parker was silent.

"When they saw I'd overheard them—it was all I could do not to slap the smirks off their catty little faces."

He grit his teeth. "I hope you're able to recover."

"You selfish son of a—"

"Good night, Bo." He walked past her.

"On my back!" she shouted after him.

He stopped, turned.

"Do you know what day it is?"

"What?"

"It's February 14th."

"So?"

"It's Valentine's Day, Bo. Valentine's Day. When you invited me to dinner, after what happened New Year's—I came here thinking…"

Nothing.

He shook his head. "Never mind." He opened his wallet, dropped a few bills on the table.

"I've made it abundantly clear—"

"Every night but one."

"Which I—"

"You did. You're right. The fault is mine alone."

"Parker…"

"When do you leave?"

She didn't answer; his eyes fell away to the baseboard, followed it until it disappeared behind another table.

"Okay." He made to go, stopped again. "Call me if you ever need anything. Please."

"I'll have the article for the weekly to you end of the day Thursday."

His face flickered, snapped back.

"Sure."

He left.

It was better for them both.

A car would meet her outside her apartment in the morning; she'd be in Cuba this time tomorrow.

CHAPTER TWENTY-NINE

Bo arrived at the hotel shortly before dinner, was greeted in the lobby by an effete man in a white tuxedo.

"Miss White, welcome." Theatrical bow. "I'm told you'll be staying with us indefinitely?"

She nodded.

"I've arranged for you to have a room overlooking the ocean." One side of his mouth curled slightly. "I hope that suits you."

"It does."

Silence passed between them. The man bowed deeper, expectant.

"Good," he said finally. "You'll be in suite 223. I believe Gary Cooper enjoyed the pleasure of Miss Lupe Velez's company in that room."

"I hope you've changed the sheets, then."

He choked a laugh. "Your key, señorita."

"Thank you." She took the key and turned to leave.

"One more thing, Miss White; I have a letter for you."

"A letter?"

"It arrived this morning."

She took it, recognized the handwriting, frowned.

He snapped, and a porter appeared. "Ernesto will take you to your room."

"Thank you very much, Señor...?"

"Raphael," he said. "Raphael Castellanos Sotolongo."

Another bow.

"At your service."

She smiled. "Please call me Bo. Thank you for all your help."

"My pleasure."

Ernesto led her to the elevator and took her up to her room.

"Put them on the bed, please."

"Sí, señorita."

"Gracias." She handed him three dollar bills.

"Es demasiado, señorita, no puedo—."

"Tómelo. Please. Por favor."

"Muchas gracias."

"De nada."

The porter left. Bo unpacked her things before reading the letter. Parker had used his own stationary, the stock of the envelope like cloth. She opened it to find his familiar Spenserian script:

Bo,

There is much I want to say, but I know you don't want to hear it, so I'll get to the point: neither The Times, *nor anyone else are interested in reporting the truth about Batista's Cuba. Too many people make money. My contacts tell me Havana is a mirage, that Batista arrests people at a whim, imprisons and tortures them or worse. I didn't ask you not to go, because I knew it wasn't my right, and I didn't warn you before you left, because I knew how it would look. I won't ask you to be careful now, but know that you'll be in grave danger from the moment you look behind the curtain.*

I know you'll come to this realization on your own in short time, and that when you do you'll start asking questions, but believe me when I say that you'll be killed if the wrong people overhear you.

I've arranged for you to meet one of my contacts at Sloppy Joe's this Friday night (forgive me if this strikes you as presumptuous). Enter the club at exactly 10:40, and order a Sazerac at the back bar. Wear a red cocktail dress. (Manzana de Gómez is a good place to shop for one.)

One more thing: Wilhelm Schroeder is in Cuba. Don't get too close. Batista's men are watching him.

With (chaste) affection,

Parker

CHAPTER THIRTY

Tolan's been wondering how she should feel about the turn her friendship with Tori has taken, and immediately thereafter, why she's always wondering if how she's feeling is the right way to feel, and who could possibly decide that, other than herself.

She's dizzy as she descends the stairs, choking on 'what if's': what if people find out? What if Mom finds out? What if Tori and I break up? What if we don't break up?

She hits the kitchen. Her mother is folding cheese, thyme, and red pepper into dough. Violently.

"Can I help with anything?"

"No thanks, honey; I've got it. I kind of enjoy this part."

There's a reading at her mother's bookshop in a little over an hour. A big name writer is coming, one of her mother's favorites. Nick helped her book him, paid the appearance fee. Her mother had protested, said she couldn't accept it, but ultimately did, unable to pass up the chance.

She'd gone shopping and did what preparation she could the day before, but most of the cooking couldn't be done until today, and she's running out of time, moving rapidly, a little manic. She slides the cheese puffs into the oven. There's a bouquet of fruit tulips atop skewers next to the sink; Tolan flinches watching her make them: the deft movements of the knife, the metal plunging into the fruit's flesh. Andouille-stuffed peppers are cooling on the counter; her mother decapitated forty peppadew cherry peppers to make them, crammed sausage into the cavities. Now she's preparing the Carpaccio, the long, crescent blade dropping slices of meat so thin they're translucent.

She's thrown back to the book.

It isn't the words that stick with her; it's the images becoming experiences as they swell and grow in her mind: she can hear Agata Schroeder bleating as García's men rape her in an alley, hear the rush of urine falling down Bo's leg as she's forced to watch. She smells the sweat of the men grunting and finishing into Agata. She knows she's at home, standing in her mother's kitchen, but she can feel the gun muzzle the soldier is jamming into Agata's head pressing her own, just above the base of her neck, smell the gun oil, hear the metallic click of the trigger—she's living it, can't look away, can't stop the nightmare even afterward, when the soldiers have gone and Agata's corpse is lying in the alley and Bo is standing next to it, and bits of Agata's brain are steaming beneath the streetlight.

Her mother is making another bouquet now, skewering Syrah-poached dried figs and sausage. She moves with delicate deliberateness, her face blank and her jaw unclenched.

It has to have happened—the story has to be real. After all the kisses and hugs and the cold washcloths her mother has pressed to her head when she was sick, after all the notes she'd put in her lunch box, and the trips to Philadelphia and New York that she'd scrimped and saved to pay for, just so Tolan could see symphonies and plays and ballets—after all the times Tolan had broken the rules or been bad or mean and her mother had responded with temperance and love, Tolan knows there's no way she could make up something so vile.

The cheese puffs are done. The oven's been switched to broil, and the artichoke hearts gratin are going in.

"Damn it!" Her mother jerks away, shaking her hand, kicks the door shut. "Damn, damn, damn!"

A crimson boil rises on her hand.

"Are you—"

"I'm fine," she snaps.

Tolan can see the tears in her mother's eyes as she runs her hand under cold water. Her mother apologizes for snapping at her a few minutes later, as she rubs butter over the burn.

In her mother's book, Bo has a dream. It's right after the rape. Bo's walking through a building she's never seen before—Tolan's there too, now, sick and desperate to leave, but caught in the spell: the walls are fluoride-white, the floor too, and the lights overhead are viciously bright. Bo is wearing a white hazmat suit with a glass face, and there's a door and a man beside her wearing the same.

Both Bo and the man are smiling—not beaming—they have the slight pinch in each cheek that's worn by those in the midst of upholding deeply held convictions.

"Bo," he says.

"Wilhelm."

"Bereit?"

She nods.

Tolan follows them through polished-steel doors into a cavernous room with massive rectangular windows that admit no light.

She doesn't know how she knows some of the things she does, that Wilhelm wasn't allowed to see his wife's body before it was cremated, that one of the soldiers that raped her had vitiligo on his penis—that Bo's been having nightmares in which the penis grows and grows and blots out everything until all Bo can see is one of the spots. Her mother hadn't written any of that.

The men are already laid out on the surgical tables, five of them in a row, equidistant from each other, bound to the table with leather straps, wrists secured at the top, ankles raised and bound in stirrups at the bottom. Two IVs have been placed in each man's neck; four half-dollar-sized spots have been shaved from their head. There are eighty-inch screens above each bed. Three feet of metal tools gleam on a surgical tray beside the first table: clamps, blades, hooks, pins, pliers. Some of the blades have thick, serrated teeth; some are fine and delicate.

Most of the hooks are barbed.

"Señor García."

The man's head is immobilized, but his pupils jump at Bo's voice, bound frantically about the perimeter of his eyes.

Tolan feels faint, backs away, only to find herself standing at the head of the bed, close enough to see the sweat beading on his skin.

"You should all know why you're here, but we've connected you to neuro-projectors just in case. They'll project the memory of your crimes onto the screens above you. Thereafter, they'll broadcast real-time video so you can see what's being done. We'll work on you one at a time, and the screens above you will show the video of the procedure in progress."

Wilhelm's turn:

"Pause for a moment, gentlemen. Feel the air caressing your skin, the gooseflesh rising on your arms and neck. Focus, and you'll realize you can even feel the light falling from the ceiling, and the reverberations of my voice against your skin. The IV in your left arm is delivering a drug that heightens your sensation even as it paralyzes you; the line in your right arm will keep you alive for as long as is medically possible."

Bo runs her fingers over the array of instruments on the tray in front of her.

"We'll start with these."

Two metal screws appear on the overhead screens.

Bo pounds the first half-inch into the arches of Garcia's feet with a mallet, screws them in while his eyes shriek.

"I've only one more thing before Mr. Schroeder takes over, a question." She holds up a steel rod a foot and a half long, three inches in diameter, and a jar of Vaseline. "When you raped Agata, did any of you gentlemen make allowances for her comfort?"

She puts the jar back on the table.

Tolan's mother saves her. "Are you okay?"

Tolan nods. "Mostly. A little queasy."

"You're white as a sheet. Maybe you should stay home tonight."

She shakes her head. "This is a huge deal for you. I want to be there."

"I have such a wonderful daughter."

"You don't need to tell me."

"Rodent."

Her mother swats at her across the counter.

"Help me carry everything to the car."

In her mother's manuscript the torture scene ends before the man is sodomized, but it's still going in Tolan's head.

She's not sure she can take it, not sure what's real. She knows she has two pans of food in her arms, and that her mother has left the door open so she could walk through it.

She knows she needs to slide the trays into the back of the car without spilling.

But she's not certain she knows her mother.

CHAPTER THIRTY-ONE

Tolan pulls up outside Tori's house, honks once, and waits. Tori emerges in jeans and a red sweater, carrying a backpack, gym bag, and two travel mugs. She's petite, has the curves Tolan will never have.

At least she isn't as tall as her mother, Tolan thinks, though she can't imagine that being 6'4" is that much harder than being 6'2."

She leans across the seat and pushes the door open. It's 7:15, and neither girl wakes up well, so they ride several miles in silence.

"Want to ditch today?"

"What?"

"We could get a pint of Turkey Hill and go home and listen to music."

"Tolan Aimes is suggesting we cut class?" Tori's voice is a whisper, her eyes wide.

"Shut up."

Tori laughs. "You know I'm always game."

"I know." Tolan shakes her head. "I don't know how you do it—you cut as many classes as you show up for, you never study, you write your papers in a single sitting, and you're still honor society… you suck."

"What can I say?" Tori shrugs, grinning. "I'm gifted."

"You suck."

"So I've been told."

"Thanks for the latte."

"Mom's new espresso machine is amazing."

"Tastes like it."

"So, we skipping?"

Tolan nods. "Sure."

"Where do you want to go?"

"Your house? My house?"

"Let's do mine."

"Okay."

Tolan continues driving, passes two streets and a parking lot.

"Aren't we going to turn around?"

"I'm going to swing by the bookstore and let Mom know."

"Seriously?"

"Seriously. Why?"

"You're such a rebel."

"But as long as mom knows, I—"

"We are so Thelma & Louise."

"Bite me."

Tori's lying on the overstuffed couch beneath the far window; Tolan's stretched out on the carpet beside her. It's a spacious room with high ceilings and long windows that flood the room with light. Tori took it over when her parents started sleeping in different rooms. They have popcorn and crackers, and a plate of hummus between them.

"So what's up?"

Tolan lifts her head. "What do you mean?"

"I've suggested we cut classes a million times, and you've never been game."

"I—"

"Is it the rumor going around about you and Alasdair?"

"Huh?"

Tori dips a cracker in hummus, pops it in her mouth; Tolan waits.

"He's telling people you blew him at the theater."

"What?! I did not! I—"

Tori waves a hand dismissively. "I know. A, you would have told me, and B, he's said that about at least three other girls."

"Asshole! I'm going to—"

"Easy, killer. It's not like anyone actually believes him."

Tolan shakes her head, presses her face into the carpet and screams.

"Boys." Tori rolls her eyes. "So if it isn't that, what is it?"

"Do you remember reading *Henderson the Rain King* in class?"

"Not really."

"Well, the guy who wrote it said, 'Fiction is the higher autobiography,' and I…" She pushes herself up into a sitting position. "Never mind." Tolan shakes her head. "It doesn't matter. It's stupid."

"Are you okay? You're acting really weird."

"I'm fine."

"Come on, T, something's up."

"It's just… I was reading this book the other day, and it was…"

She's squinting, looking for words: she can see clumps of them at a distance, but can't bring them into focus.

"… there's all these awful things, rape, torture, incest… the author tells you everything, right down to the color of the shit that comes out of this guy as a woman rips his stomach open with a hook, the sound it makes as it hits the ground… I can't stop thinking—it had to have happened to the author or to someone she knew—I can't get the images out of my head!"

She's seesawing between hysterics and embarrassment, tears shoving at her eyelids.

"I… it's—someone saw these things—someone lives with these images!"

Tori's frozen atop the couch, mouth slightly open, stunned; she wasn't ready for this, doesn't understand, tries:

"They're just word—"

"No." Tolan cuts her off. "No one could imagine things that awful—no would want to!"

"T, it's just a book."

"It's not! This one woman, Lewella, runs a safe house for abused women. There's this guy that's been beating his girlfriend with a belt…"

Tears, running hot and hard.

"The author describes the sound of the belt smashing into her face—the buckle—and of the woman's begging and crying. She escapes and Lewella takes her in, but the guy comes after her, and Lewella shoots him. She could've saved him if she'd called 911; he's lying there on the ground, moaning, but Lewella just stands there and watches as he chokes on his own blood."

Tori's scared, but she forces herself off the couch, towards Tolan. "Shush," she coos. "Breathe; take a deep breath." Tori's behind Tolan, twines her arms around her, pulls her against her chest.

"Remember that thing on Oprah—A Million Somethings—the one with the drug addict, and his girlfriend commits suicide."

She's stroking Tolan's hair as she talks.

"A little. No."

"The book was full of terrible, horrible things, and the author said it was autobiographical, but it turned out he made the whole thing up."

"So?"

"None of it was true, see? None of it really happened—the guy made it up. People do that—writers—they make up stories. *Silence of the Lambs, Requiem for a Dream, American Psycho*, the movie about that French guy who wrote S & M… *Quills*…"

Tolan's rubbing at her eyes, pushing herself back against Tori, groping for control.

Tori kisses her neck, rocks her gently.

"Sorry."

"For what?"

"I'm having a bad day."

Tori kisses her again. "That's allowed."

"I just don't understand how—"

"Neither do I."

"And why!"

"Shush." Tori strokes her hair. "Try to think of something else."

"Why would someone want to put those horrible images in people's heads?"

"I don't know, T, maybe they're just sick."

Neither of them speak; the words settle into the carpet.

"It's my mom."

CHAPTER THIRTY-TWO

Tolan is sitting in her room reading. She deliberated before sending her mother's manuscript to Tori, decided to send it in increments so they'd be going through it together.

She's been skimming since the rape: Wilhelm joined the insurgency after his wife's murder. Bo followed him deep into the Sierra Maestra and the Segundo Frente Nacional del Escambray, photographed Castro and Guevara, Batista's victims, the revolutionaries in their camps, the dead.

So many dead, the violence metronomic, a waltz: a rebel bomb exploded outside a casino; the Mafioso used garden shears to rip a vertical gash in the necks of those they deemed responsible and in the necks of their wives and sons and daughters, pulled their tongues out through the gaping pulp, and watched them asphyxiate; Batista's police herded men and women into allies, choked their bodies with bullets, left their corpses. More bombings, more blood. Cuba saturated and reeking and death begetting death as men with bombs and guns and machetes slaughtered men and women and children, armed or otherwise, their blood dripping into the distended belly of the earth only to rise like bile and force its way through the pores in the soil and the seams in the asphalt streets in a steady, ferric flow as the dead baked beneath the sun, coagulating in viscous graves.

Wilhelm was caught, arrested and condemned a traitor. They hung him on a chain, slowly lowered him into a cauldron of boiling water. Her mother wrote the terror in his eyes as he dangled over the water, naked, bruised and mutilated from torture. She described his body evacuating, his skin erupting in blisters, hissing as it burned. It'd made Tolan vomit.

It was several days before Tolan could pick up the book again. She'd dipped into Cuba's history in the interim, found the contours of most of the events her mother depicted, broad, suggestive details, names and places, possible analogues. She'd made Wilhelm die the way Jesús Galindez Suárez had, attributed Trujillo's crimes to Castro—why? She'd thought it might help, knowing what was real and what was made up, thought it'd be easier to deal with the pornographic violence and hate and filth if they weren't the product of her mother's imagination, but it didn't. It only raised more questions.

And what about Bo, now fluent in Spanish and ducking from safehouse to rebel encampment, minutes ahead of Castro's men? She'd been years in Cuba, gone years without speaking more than a few words to Parker. Would they catch her? How long would she stay?

Tolan felt a twinge every time she thought of Parker, an ache that she couldn't quite place, like someone had reached into her and grabbed her heart in a fist and made it so that it hurt to feel it beat in her chest.

She wished Bo would come home, or that Parker would go get her, even as she knew he couldn't, that Bo would never allow it.

CHAPTER THIRTY-THREE

Bo's plane landed in New York the night before Thanksgiving. She'd told Parker she was coming back to the States, but not when. She arrived, hailed a cab, and had it drop her at a cheap hotel, where she slept for a day and a half.

She'd call Parker later.

It had become obvious she'd gotten the story wrong even before she left Cuba; things didn't get better after the rebels won. The violence didn't stop. Castro erected kangaroo courts and held trials in barrooms and public halls and baseball stadiums, condemned thousands to death. *The Times* had suspended Bo in May after Castro declared Cuba a socialist state, but she wasn't ready to leave Cuba, to give up on the movement she'd followed and photographed and believed in. She'd found what meager work she could, slept on couches, in tents, subsisted. Then Castro ran out of traitors and started executing counter-revolutionaries, and she was forced to flee the country.

New York was bitter cold. Ten years in Cuba had thinned her blood, so she went to Brooks Brothers and bought a winter wardrobe: sweaters and chamois shirts, corduroy pants, and a heavy jacket. A hat and gloves. Her bosses didn't fire her, only told her not to come into the office, keeping her in limbo. She took day-long walks, wandering from Broadway to the Hudson through what had been Manhattan's radio row, along Cortlandt and Dey Street.

She meandered, got lost, didn't notice or care, walked the block of East 100th Street between First and Second Avenues, raw sewage burning her nose as people were shaken down and beaten up, narcotics sold. The tenements decayed audibly. Fliers and old newspapers rolled like tumbleweed, advertisements touting Robert Moses' efforts at resurrecting the old LOMAX plans. Swaths of Lower Manhattan seemed to have been abandoned.

Castro declared himself a "Marxist-Leninist" on December 2, and Bo was fired. She called Parker the following day and arranged to meet at noon at Highbridge Park.

It was cold, again, the city shivering beneath a crust of stale snow. The wind rose sporadically, throwing granules of grit and powder into pedestrians and against buildings and cars and trees. Parker was there when Bo arrived, offered his arm; they walked out onto the bridge in silence, their footfall and the water below them loud for the absence of words.

"How are you?"

She didn't respond immediately, and he didn't press.

"Are you mad at me? Is that why you've stayed away?"

She shook her head.

"I gave them the photos."

"You kept back the stories."

"Only some of them."

"Parker…"

He inhaled deeply, exhaled. "I did. I kept them back."

"Why?"

"Bo…"

"Why?"

"You know why."

"I don't."

"Your articles made Castro out to be the second coming."

"That's how I saw it. I thought he was a hero."

He shook his head. "No. You let yourself get wrapped up in a dream, imagined a holy war, and made Fidel into an archangel."

"So that's what this is about."

"What?"

"You're jealous."

"What? Of whom?"

"Fidel."

"Don't be stupid."

She stopped, let go of his arm, and turned to look out over the Harlem.

"I'm sorry," she said.

"I never asked you to be."

"So now what?"

He took her arm again. "Now…"

"They fired me yesterday."

He nodded. "There was nothing I could do."

"Christ, Parker." She rolled her eyes. "You don't need to save me. You're my friend, not my guardian angel."

"It probably won't be as bad for you as it will for Matthews; he'll never work again."

"And me?"

"After a time, maybe."

"Your father won't hire me?"

Parker shook his head.

A chunk of ice bobbed lazily in the river, the current too anemic to suck it under.

"Don't you need to be getting back?" she asked.

"What if I'd come down?"

"What?"

"What if I'd come after you? Would you have listened?"

She turned back to him.

"Did you?"

He didn't answer.

"I guess it doesn't matter, then."

She started walking again. He didn't.

"Bo."

She kept going.

"Bo."

She didn't turn.

"I did it for me."

She stopped.

"I didn't do it because I thought you needed saving, and I didn't do it because I thought you were wrong. I did it because I could read the lay of the land, and I knew what people at the paper wanted to hear. I knew that if you condemned Castro and it turned out you were wrong, you'd be forgiven, but that if you said what you were saying and were wrong, you'd be crucified. I wanted—was hoping—you'd come back, and we could work together again. I wanted to be near you."

Tears glistened at the corners of his eyes, formed in her own; she knew it wasn't the wind. She expected him to come to her, wanted him to, but he didn't.

"I couldn't do anything once Matthews got involved."

"Why'd they send him? I had things under control."

"It's a big story. They wanted another perspective."

"They didn't like what I was saying."

"No."

"But he saw what I saw."

Parker nodded.

"So why… "

"I tried, Bo. I fought."

"I know."

"I couldn't—I'm sorry."

"I don't need you to be sorry, Parker. Goddamn it, I don't want you to be sorry."

"I know," he said, "but I am."

"You should be getting back."

He nodded.

They walked to the parking lot in silence.

"Can I give you a ride somewhere?" he asked as he opened his car door.

"I'll be fine."

"I know."

A gust of wind lifted pebbles of snow off the ground, threw them at her back and his face, and was gone. Parker brushed the granules from his eyes.

"Matthews wouldn't have come near Castro if it weren't for me."

"I believe you."

"Then why—"

"What do you want me to say, Bo? What can I do? Everything I try is wrong." He paused. "Never mind."

"What?"

He shook his head. "Let's just—"

"What!"

"Why'd you go to Cuba?"

"I wanted a change. I wanted…"

"What?"

"I don't know: adventure, freedom, independence—"

"From me?"

"No."

"From what, then?"

"From everything."

"Come away with me."

"What?"

"Come away with me."

"We've been over this. I'm not going to marry—"

"I'm not asking you to."

"Then what? What is it you want from me?"

"I want to offer you a job."

"What, and be my boss? That's not going to work."

"Why are you like this with me? I'm not trying to put anything on you or take anything from you."

"I—"

"You nothing. You need a job, but you're not going to be able to get one until time passes and this blows over, at least not as a journalist."

"I can do something else, go back to being a guide, or work as a secretary—"

"You'd be miserable. And for what? To spite me? To protect yourself from me? When have I ever—Jesus Christ, haven't I earned anything, after all these years? If not your trust, at least the benefit of the doubt?"

"I don't think I need to protect myself—"

"Then take the job. It wouldn't be me paying you; it'd be the United States government. I'm not asking you to be my employee, share a hotel room, or even to let me pay for your food. It's a federal grant, a commission to write a report on domestic abuse. You'll get a per diem and travel and lodging costs."

Silence.

"What? What have I done now, now? How have I offended you?"

"I—"

"It's everything you say you want: travel, adventure, freedom, independence..."

The wind was continuous now, rushing off the river and burning his face. The water had begun to churn.

He turned away, and Bo followed his gaze into the distance and found nothing that might have piqued his interest, and looking back at him, found a dead thing with eyes bereft of life.

She started to speek, but he interrupted her.

"It was good to see you," he said.

He waited, but she didn't reply.

She had tears in her eyes.

He closed the door and drove away.

She accepted the job a week later, without *explanation. They traveled together for a year, produced a book the government ultimately refused to publish, which worked out for Bo; her research brought her into contact with Betty Friedan, who introduced her to the Guggenheims, and eventually the photos from the project became the substance of the one-woman gallery show that launched her into the rest of her life, America's Uncivil War.*

Parker returned to New York to write, but then his father passed away, and having shirked every filial duty, he couldn't evade this one, nor did he wish to, and so he made his inevitable, if long avoided, return to Boston, and took over his father's paper. He made sure his paper covered Bo's exploits, whether it was a new show opening, a local sheriff arresting her for obscenity as she traveled with *America's Uncivil War*, or her later efforts on behalf of Title IX.

They saw each other every month or so, and on holidays, which they still took together. One summer, Bo returned to Port Haven so she could photograph some of the few remaining local farmers and lobstermen for an article entitled "The Vanishing America," and Parker, who had always loved the Maine coast, accompanied her. He fell in love with a cottage overlooking the town harbor, and asked Bo if he could buy it, to which Bo replied, *Why would I care what you did with your money*, so he did. And a few years later, after a bad fall on the job, Bo thought it would be a good idea to have a source of income that didn't require an able body, so when she heard about a diner on the market in Port Haven, she bought it. The previous owner had had a stroke and been unable to manage his affairs, so the property had sat unused for three years and was rank with cat urine and mouse egesta, but it had two attached apartments. She had no interest in running the place, just wanted a revenue stream that would give her the freedom to move around and protection in case of another accident, so she looked up one of the women she'd photographed for *America's Uncivil War*, Lewella, and asked her to manage the building in exchange for a portion of the profits, and together they decided to keep one of the apartments free for women who were in a bind.

And as soon as Bo could travel again, she did, taking boats and planes and trains to various locations on four continents, shooting photography for whichever publications met her rates, and for the causes that stirred her.

CHAPTER THIRTY-FOUR

1977. Urban blight. Another meatpacking plant gone under on the south side of Chicago, a cement building in Canaryville grown varicose at the seams, white paint faded and fading gray, cracked and peeling. It was a boxing gym now, but the side of the building still bore a bull in profile, red on white. The bull's tail was gone, and one of the horns, and the letters had bled into the firmament long ago. Inside, the building looked every bit what it was, an industrial carcass picked clean. Lou had a smaller place before, but then the Union Stockyards closed, and he approached Walt about going into business together, and now they had eight full-size rings, free weights, weight machines, all manner of bags, and a locker room with a sauna. Exposed I-beams, metal, pipes, and rivets looked down at a cement floor stained with the blood of a hundred thousand slit-necked animals. It was frigid in the winter, sweltering in the summer, and smelled of sweat and old cigarette smoke year-round.

The dozen people training, jumping rope, sparring, and hitting bags were young, and Walt and Lou were old. The older men in the neighborhood damned, and the younger men fucked. The senior men resented 'fuck;' they goddamned and shitted, but they never fucked.

One of the other fighters stopped to watch a boy hit a bag.

"That Michael?"

No one answered.

"How old is he?"

"Fifteen."

"And he doesn't take nothing?"

Walt and Lou shot each other a look.

"No."

"Fuck me."

Lou stopped chewing his gum, frowned. Karl was new to the gym, a palooka whose face had launched more than a few careers.

Lou's son was holding the bag—trying to hold the bag, struggling to maintain his ground as Michael's blows knocked him back by increments.

"He's only fifteen?" Karl asked.

Lou ignored him.

"Fuck me."

Walt glared. "Why don't you take that trash some place else."

Karl shrugged, moved on. Walt turned back to Michael, settled into the din, feet scuffing over canvas, ropes sizzling in the air, bells sounding, coaches barking. The sound of Michael striking the bag rose above it all.

CHAPTER THIRTY-FIVE

Tori went with her even though it was just a regular checkup. Are you sexually active? The doctors only asked in order to know if they had to worry about pregnancy or STDs, so Tori knew how Tolan would answer.

It bothered her, but she wasn't going to say anything, not now, after what Tolan had read.

Tolan didn't say much on the way over, hadn't said much all day, but Tori didn't push, just took her hand while they drove. They went back to Tolan's house afterwards, because that was where her room was, and her bed, and her stuffed animals, and Tori thought the familiarity would be comforting.

Now they're sitting on the floor beside the bed, books and notes laid out in front of them; they have to give a presentation tomorrow, but Tolan isn't moving, just sitting, blank-faced.

"Tol?"

Michael Tolan.

Tori hadn't been with Tolan when she first read it.

Michael. Tolan.

She could only imagine how it must have felt.

"T?"

Tolan looks up slowly, fighting her way back from somewhere else. "Huh?"

"How're you doing?"

Her eyes pass over the comforter on her bed, following the seam as if the answer is at the stitches' end. She's still half in her head, five years old and asking her mother why she doesn't have a dad, nine years old, asking again, twelve, thirteen, fifteen.

"I guess now we know why Mom doesn't like talking about him."

"We don't know for sure that—" Tori stops. "What's she told you in the past?"

"Not much."

Tolan picks at the carpet.

"She said my father's name was Michael Donovan, told me a couple stories." Tolan smiles weakly. "She said that one time she fell and hit her head, and Michael" —she stops suddenly— "my father had to take her to the emergency room. She said he brought her home afterward and stayed up all night watching to make sure she was okay."

Tori nods.

"Mom had a wine tasting at the store last summer. She hadn't eaten much that day, so she was drunk by the second glass, and I had to come get her. We got caught at a light on the way home—there was this runner on the sidewalk next to us. He wasn't wearing a shirt, and Mom was looking out the window, staring, and I started teasing her, said something about how hot his body was. She said Michael's was better, just blurted it out. She was so embarrassed, she looked like she wanted to die. I couldn't bring myself to keep teasing her.

"She came into my room later that night and thanked me for letting it go, and I didn't know what to say, so I just told her I loved her. She said she loved me too, and goodnight, but she didn't leave, just stood there for the longest time, hugging herself. When she finally spoke, she said my father had been a boxer before they met, and that he still worked out like one when she knew him. She had this smile on her face that I've only seen once or twice. She said she used to watch him workout, and that he was handsome, and that she liked looking at him."

Tolan smiles. "She was so red."

Tori listens. Tolan looks up from the bedspread, forces another smile, shrugs.

"Mom said she chose my name because it sounded strong."

"That might be true, right? Him being strong? I mean, considering all it says he went through."

Tolan nods. "Part of me wants it to be true—wants it to be his story. That's sick, right?"

"No."

"No? For Christ's sake, Tor', his first words were 'Stop hitting her!'"

Michael had been four years old, at the time. He bleated the words through a stream of tears as his father beat his mother bloody. His father's eyes had narrowed into malignant slits. 'So you can talk now, you little shit,' he'd said, taking two steps toward Michael and unleashing a backhand into his face that spun him round and sent two teeth leaping from his mouth.

"No. It means that you want to know your father. You want the things your mother wrote to be true, because if they are, reading them is a way of feeling closer to him."

Tolan looks away. She can't imagine her mother striking her.

And the drinking. Tolan wracks her mind trying to think if there'd ever been a time when her mother had kept more than a bottle of wine in the house.

It had to be true.

"Do you think it's right?"

"Do I think what's right?"

"Mom writing about all this stuff."

"Why wouldn't it be?"

"Because it's horrible."

Tori shrugs. "Terrible things happen all the time."

"But why focus on them?"

Michael's father drank even more after he lost his job at the plant, grew even more violent. Michael did his best to antagonize him in order to draw him away from his mother and sister. Tolan felt admiration, empathy, and revulsion all at once, forced herself to continue reading, to confront every detail about what his father did to him, because if she turned away, if she skipped even a single sentence, then she was no better than Michael, would be abandoning him just like he had abandoned her.

So she read every word as he tried to protect his mother, as his father punched and kicked and choked him, threw him against walls and appliances until he was unconscious or immobile and couldn't do anything but watch and bleed as his father beat her.

"I don't know, T, maybe your mother's trying to understand things, to make sense of everything that happened."

"Shouldn't she want to get as far from it as possible?"

"Ignoring something doesn't mean it doesn't exist."

"And trying to understand it does what?"

Tori shakes her head. "I don't know. But let's say Michael really is your father and not just a character your mom made up. Let's say this is all true, that Michael really did go through these things, and that your mom loved him."

"You're saying she's trying to understand him?"

Tori nods. "Maybe."

"Do you think it has something to do with why they aren't together, like she's trying to figure it out?"

"Maybe."

Tolan is silent, tries to imagine not just the events, but being in them, being Michael.

According to what her mother wrote, Michael rarely spoke. His father called him a moron, and his mother held him out of school an extra year, and his classmates all called him a retard when he did start.

Only his sister was nice to him, his twin sister, who knew he wasn't stupid, and didn't try to make him talk. But then they turned ten, and his mother sent her away. His aunt and uncle from Peoria came while his father was off drinking. No one said anything, his mother just handed her brother-in-law a suitcase and put her daughter in the car, and then she and Michael watched them drive away.

His father beat the hell out of him when he got home, beat him and his mother so badly they spent the evening in the emergency room.

Michael began training the next day, flipped his mattress vertical against the bedroom wall and started punching it with the arm his father hadn't broken. One hundred punches twice a day.

Bo and Ruby and Parker and Castro and Michael and her mother and rape and death and hate.

Tolan's trying to hold on, staring at Tori because Tori's solid. There are tears in her eyes, but they're made of more than sorrow, of anger and fear and frustration, too.

"What does Mom know about any of this? What gives her the right? It's not like she's been ra—"

For an instant, the world crackles like a fifty year-old television, snaps on, off, on, off. Everything cuts out, and all that remains is a roaring pain ripping through her.

She tries to push through the thought, will her mind blank.

Rewind.

Rewrite.

"What right does mom have to put the most horrible moments of people's lives on display? People will read the story and think they understand, only they won't, because they can't, and the people that suffered through it will be even more alone than before."

Tori is silent.

Michael's father left just after he turned eleven. His mother did her best, worked three jobs to keep him clothed and fed, started him at boxing lessons to keep him out of trouble. She made sure he did his homework, and that he was kind and respectful, and she died just before he turned fifteen.

"How am I supposed to know what's real? Who my father is? Hell, who my mother is?

Tolan's looking for answers again, in Tori's eyes and lips, in the slope of her cheekbones and the scoop of her nose; her mouth is open, formed around a word, but emitting no sound, caught between speech and silence.

Tori pulls her to her chest, strokes her hair, kisses her ear. "Maybe we should stop."

"Reading?"

"Maybe it's too much."

Tolan presses herself against Tori, twisting, craning her neck back to kiss her, laying her cheek against Tori's head.

Tori tightens her arms around her.

They hear the garage door opening.

"Do you want to go down?"

Tolan shakes her head. "Not yet."

The brakes on her mother's truck shriek in protest, and the engine knocks and dies. The garage door squeals open, the engine turns over, the brakes screech again.

"I don't think I can stop," Tolan says.

"Then we'll get through it."

Tolan nods.

"We should get back to work."

"We should say hello to your mother, first."

Neither of them moves.

CHAPTER THIRTY-SIX

The frogs had buried themselves in the ditches on either side of the road, and the grasshoppers were hiding in the shade of the tall grasses and cattails, but the tall girl walked on. It was eleven and three tenths miles each way. The sun beat down on her in a vertical line. There was no wind.

Seven and a half hours round trip.

Her dress was threadbare, a fourth generation hand-me-down that chafed as she walked. At 6'4" and one hundred and twenty-three pounds, she was more than a foot taller and eighty pounds lighter than the dress's previous owner, and the excess fabric chafed her raw, which didn't hurt nearly as much as the safety pins biting into her back and side. She needed them to keep the dress from falling off.

There was a bus that stopped less than a mile from her house that could have taken her through Rockland and let her out across the street from the prison, but she couldn't afford the fare. She'd tried to earn money, but none of the fishermen would hire her, and at thirteen, she couldn't even bus dishes at Dave's. She did chores for the woman she lived with, Linda—more than was expected, and without being asked—but the woman had seven children of her own and struggled to make the rent each month.

She lived with Linda because her mother was in prison, had been since the tall girl was an infant. Her father was a fisherman and drowned at sea, and her mother had been sent to an asylum soon thereafter, after the second time she tried to suffocate her daughter with a pillow. She was sent from the asylum to prison for stabbing an orderly.

Visiting hours at the prison were between twelve and two, but her mother didn't like to be disturbed during lunch, so the tall girl arrived at 1:15 in order to be through the checkpoint by 1:30, and at the visitation table by 1:35. Her mother never spoke, and often left abruptly, but the tall girl always stayed in her seat until the door back to lockdown closed behind her mother. The guards never spoke to the tall girl, but the woman with the short-cropped silver hair was her favorite, because she'd let her mother stay until 2:05, sometimes. She didn't get to eat on those days: Linda set dinner out at 5:15, and there were nine other people and not much food, and no one ever saved her anything. She always did the dishes anyway, and sometimes she could salvage a bite or two.

Linda tried to dissuade her from visiting her mother. Does she speak to you? she would ask. The tall girl would shake her head. What do you do together? I tell her about school, or about you and Brad and your kids. Sometimes I read to her. That's it? Linda would ask, and the tall girl would have to nod. That's not much, Linda would respond, and the tall girl would shrug.

She went every week.

CHAPTER THIRTY-SEVEN

"Time's up, Smith," the guard called from the door.

"Love you, Mom," the tall girl said, standing.

"Put your hands on the table, Smith."

Her mother was silent, her hands in her lap, eyes fixed on the tabletop. The tall girl hadn't expected her to answer, but she watched her anyway, hoping.

"I'll see you next week."

She stood; her mother didn't.

"Hands on the table now!" Fire rose in the guard's eyes, his lip curling in a snarl, baring his teeth. "Now, inmate!"

"Earlier," her mother rasped.

The tall girl's breath caught in her chest. "What?"

"Earlier."

"Now!" The guard ripped her mother to her feet, dragged her out of the room.

The next week, she arrived at 12:30. "What happened to you?" the guard demanded, recoiling.

The tall girl was bleeding, chest heaving, her hair matted to her forehead; sweat ran down her neck and back and dripped off the hem of her dress. There were spots of blood where the safety pins had bit into her side, and at the backs of her ankles.

"I... I ran here."

The guard unlocked the door to the visiting area and motioned for her to enter, pressing himself against the wall so they wouldn't touch as she passed. The girl stopped midway, confused. "You're not going to search—"

"Go!"

She hurried through the door.

"What's the matter?"

The tall girl startled. It was after ten o'clock. Everyone was supposed to be asleep. She was in the bathroom, sitting on the side of the tub and dabbing at the bottom of her foot with a wet cloth.

Linda was groggy. "Let me see that."

She swiped, caught the tall girl's wrist and yanked it away from her foot, dragging the rough cloth over the broken skin and making her yelp.

"Quiet."

Linda pulled the foot up to inspect it, tipping her backward.

"Hold still."

The tall girl's foot was wet with pus and blood, and water from the cloth.

"What happened?"

"I was running."

"To the prison?"

The tall girl nodded, eyes on the floor.

Linda frowned. "That's going to need to be debrided."

The tall girl nodded again.

Linda left the room and came back with a stool, cotton balls, and a bottle of rubbing alcohol.

"Give me your foot. The other one just as bad?"

"I think so."

"Christ almighty, girl."

Tears filled the tall girl's eyes as Linda worked, and she bit her lip to keep from crying out. Linda wasn't kind or mean or gentle or rough, just weary, cowed. She had limp, thinning hair, rosacea, and eyes that had begun to sink into her face. She would have been fat if she could spare the flesh, but she couldn't, so it was just skin that hung from her arms and throat, swaying like laundry on a rope as she moved.

Linda finished the first foot, wrapped it with gauze, started on the second.

"You got cuts on your sides, too?"

The girl nodded.

"How bad?"

"Not bad."

"Don't you lie to me, girl—pull your shirt up."

The tall girl lifted her shirt: her boxers were blue with black stripes and had belonged to Linda's third son, and the welts on her side were red and dark-red, and had been cut by the safety pins holding up the boxers.

"We don't have no other clothes to give you."

"I like my clothes."

Linda's eyes narrowed with irritation.

"You get those taken care of, then clean up this mess."

She gestured at the bloody cotton balls.

The tall girl nodded.

Linda rocked back on the stool, forward, grunting violently and heaving herself up.

"And take that stool back to the kitchen."

The tall girl ran to visit her mother later that week, reopening scabs and blisters and turning her socks red yet again. She'd just turned thirteen, was gangly and uncoordinated, and after a few minutes of running her lungs felt as if they were being crushed beneath stone, and she had to stop and walk. But she kept at it, got better slowly, was able to run incrementally futher, week by week. She saw an old pair of sneakers hanging from a power line and threw rocks at them until they fell, caught one of Linda's sons spying on her as she showered, and came into possession of a pair of mesh shorts and a basketball jersey. The clothes were so large she had to gather the fabric at the sides of her hips and small of her back and knot it up with rubber bands, to keep them from sliding off. The excess shirt bounced behind her like a tail when she ran, and the fabric at her hips flapped like a pair of neon wings, and she knew from people's reactions that she looked absurd, but it didn't matter, because she was getting faster. After a year, she was able to hold a seven-minute mile pace all the way to the prison, two full minutes faster than she needed to run to make it on time. Her mother didn't say much more than before, and wouldn't make eye contact or answer questions, but over time and trial they achieved an understanding. The tall girl would begin talking, and her mother would shake her head or grunt depending on whether or not she liked what she was hearing. For the most part she stayed for the entire visitation period. Frequently, the tall girl read to her mother from a book her mother brought from the prison library. It wasn't much, but it was more than what she'd had before.

CHAPTER THIRTY-EIGHT

"Sit here a moment, honey; someone will be right with you."

The tall girl nodded and lowered herself into a cheap plastic chair. It was worn slick as a waterslide and threw her forward so she nearly fell. She'd sat for hours, marinating in fear, stomach torquing itself in knots as a plastic clock marked time from the wall. She'd run to the prison like always, but had been taken out of line at the first checkpoint and led into a side room. She'd been alarmed, at first, rather than afraid, but then they shut her in a windowless room and no one spoke to her or explained anything, and an hour went by and then two and she began to worry. She'd kept sliding out of her chair. Then she heard three short knocks, and the door opened and two men she'd never seen before entered the room carrying clipboards. They confirmed her identity, and led her through a door at the back of the room, and down a corridor into another antechamber, and left without meeting her eye. Another hour passed, maybe two, and a priest appeared, and she knew that her mother had been killed.

The chaplain was sorry, and she should let him know if there was anything he could do, and did she have any questions.

She did, of course, but she couldn't do anything beyond stare at the man and blink, nod when he asked if her mother had been Catholic. One of the men who'd led her to the room reappeared, and she was oddly grateful, but he just handed her a clipboard with a pen and a stack of paperwork, and left. The priest helped her fill it out, pointed to the places she should initial and sign, and promised prayers on her mother's behalf. Someone handed her a small, plastic bag and a manila folder with a form letter offering the warden's condolences and her mother's death certificate, and another took the papers she'd signed, and the priest led her to yet another waiting room.

"TIME OF DEATH," the certificate read. "12:17 PM."

The tall girl had been lazy that morning, woken up feeling queasy, and taken longer than usual to do her chores, so she didn't make it to the prison until twelve-thirty. She could have made it by noon, as usual, even with her late start: a seven-thirty pace would have had her there by 11:57. A seven-thirty pace—even an eight-minute pace, and she would have been talking to her mother at 12:17. She'd had it until mile nine, had it with room until a fist of pain jammed itself between her ribs so hard she couldn't breathe, and she cramped and heaved and dropped to all fours.

She'd walked the last two miles.

The tall girl looked down at the form. "FULL NAME OF DECEASED: Katherine Jane Smith."

She read it again: "Katherine Jane Smith."

She hadn't known her mother went by her middle name.

The clock caught her eye: 7:23. Linda would be worrying.

"Barb."

The secretary looked up from her book.

"Larry. How're you this evening?"

"Another day, another dollar."

Barb buzzed him through the door.

"Who's the girl?"

"Girl?"

He jerked his thumb behind him.

"String bean sitting in the hall."

"She's still here?"

"Guess so."

"Poor thing, her mother was killed today. Stabbed to death."

The man winced, shook his head. "I'll be damned."

"She's been here going on six hours."

His shift didn't begin for another twelve minutes, so he shuffled to the coffee pot at the back of the room and dumped non-dairy creamer and a long pour of sugar into a Styrofoam cup, added coffee, and stirred.

"Excuse me, Ma'am?"

Barb jumped, covered her heart with her hand. "You scared me half to death!"

"Sorry. May I please use the phone?" Her voice was barely audible.

"You haven't called anyone?"

She shook her head.

"You've been here for hours—your father's probably worried sick."

The tall girl shifted her weight awkwardly, foot to foot, staring at the ground.

"My father died when I was a baby."

Barb fought back tears and offered to take her home after her shift.

CHAPTER THIRTY-NINE

Tori's asleep beside her. The top of Tolan's head is nestled between Tori's breasts, her cheekbone in the hollow where Tori's ribs meet, her head rising and falling with Tori's breaths. There are many reasons why she can't sleep; one of them is that Tori can—is—so easily. They both think her mother suspects something. Tolan's scared because Tori's not, because she'd been so cavalier when Tolan asked her what they'd do if her mom found out. She'd just shrugged—the same way she'd shrugged when Tolan asked what she'd do if she didn't get into Harvard, and what if her parents got a divorce, and what if there turned out to be a pop-quiz in pre-calc.

Tolan can't sleep because Tori leaves for Harvard in less than five months and wants to have *the talk*, and because Tolan wants to have *the talk* too, and is scared of what she might say.

She can't sleep because her arm is draped across Tori's body, over the silk pajama top, her right hand clasping the flesh of Tori's left arm, and she feels like they fit.

She can't sleep because she hasn't heard from the colleges she applied to yet, and because she doesn't really care, but feels like she should.

And then there's her mom and her mom's book, but not just that.

Memories, too. Conversations and stories.

All of it in doubt now.

"Where'd the name Pan come from?" she'd asked her mom.

"From Greek mythology. He was god of the wild, shepherds and flocks, and music."

"He?"

"He." She nodded. "I guess my mother just liked the name. I hated it for years, because I got made fun of so much, but eventually I decided I was just glad that she hadn't named me Nymph." Tolan's mother shrugged, gave a little smile.

"Nuk, nuk. Where'd you grow up, again?"

"Belfast. It's a small town on the coast, near Rockland. Why?"

"No reason. Do you remember much of your childhood?"

They were in for the night, a mother-daughter evening with a rented movie, takeout Thai, and tea, brewed properly in her mother's favorite teapot, the white one with a purple orchid.

"Not really."

"What was it like growing up in foster care?"

Her mother looked away as she chewed, remembering. "I got moved around some, stayed with relatives for a while, with one of my mother's friends for a few years before I was sent down the coast. It was colder up north, especially in the winter. The house was always damp, but we got used to it."

"Friends?"

She shook her head. "Not so much. I was shy; I read a lot. A neighbor would take me to the library in the next town once a week, and sometimes ladies from church would give me books."

"Were there many other children?"

"Not after I moved down the coast."

Tolan nodded, let the last sip of soda roll around her mouth, enjoying the bite and tickle of the carbonation.

Her mother set her chopsticks down, dabbed at her lips with a paper napkin, and slumped back in her chair.

"I think I'm going to explode."

"Me, too."

They collected the leftover food, carried it to the refrigerator.

"When did you start running?"

"Umm, I think I was thirteen or fourteen. Malted milk ball?"

Tolan nodded, took the carton.

"What made you start?"

"You're asking a lot of questions."

"Sorry." Tolan put the DVD they'd rented into the player.

"No need, I'm just wondering why the sudden interest?"

"No reason in particular. I guess I'm just curious."

Tori mumbles something unintelligible in her sleep, extricates herself from Tolan, and the memory ends.

Did it happen just like that? Tolan isn't sure.

She needs to sleep.

CHAPTER FORTY

Tolan is stretching in the driveway when her mother gets home from work, moves to the side so she can pull into the garage.

"Didn't you go out this morning?"

Tolan takes an earbud out. "What?"

"I thought you ran already."

"I did." She continues to stretch. "I'm just feeling restless."

"Everything alright?"

Tolan nods.

"I thought I'd make a Cobb salad for dinner."

"Sounds good."

Her mother smiles, and Tolan puts her earbud back in, finds the track she wants, and presses 'play.' She's got track practice tomorrow and she shouldn't run again, but she needs to clear her head.

Her ponytail throws droplets of sweat as she runs, dark specks on the pale road. Six miles hasn't quieted her mind, hasn't stopped the line from repeating itself over and over: "You can't stay here anymore."

Tolan pictures her mother standing in Linda's kitchen. Linda is wearing coveralls over a man's flannel shirt, sitting down, because she's winded after walking from the living room to the kitchen. There's a cigarette between her lips, an ashtray on the table.

"Food, clothes, school," Linda says, "Doctor's bills... I can't afford— I've got my own kids to think about."

Her mother is confused, because she doesn't eat very much, and the only new clothes Linda has ever bought her are underwear from the five and dime, and her school lunches are subsidized by the state, and she's never once been to the doctor's. She wants to say that she'll eat less if Linda lets her stay, and that she'll find a way to pay for her own underwear.

Tolan throws herself sideways even before she's aware there's a snarling dog flying at her with its fangs bared; it misses. Tolan doesn't look back, accelerates. There's a woman sprinting toward her with a broken leash in her hand, screaming.

Tolan's heart is hammering. The adrenaline kicks her forward for another mile, her mind beaten blank by the concussive pulse reverberating in her chest and head.

The tall girl returns as the hammering recedes. She doesn't say a word, doesn't plead or protest, only packs her things in a pillowcase, thanks Linda for everything she's done, and lets a stranger drive her away from the only place she's ever known.

Is that her mother's story?

Tolan turns onto Main Street just past a dogwood. She's pushing it: the pain is exquisite, stone hands crushing the air from her lungs, pitch burning in her throat.

Dusk comes early and falls hard; she's a mile and a half from home, and the horizon is swallowing the last of the light. A runner passes her going the opposite direction, and the streetlights snap on with a pop, blink to luminescence. College students are walking in and out of the stores and restaurants in arrhythmic waves, clustering on the sidewalk.

Tolan moves into the street.

Guilt.

It hurts almost as much as her body. She wants the story to be true, because reading it feels intimate, feels as if her mother is sharing everything she's held back.

But if it's true…

She's beyond the last shop now, accelerating, only a mile from home, sprinting into the agony, legs like pistons, feet like hammers.

She wishes she could forget the manuscript and everything she's read, could leave the discovery of her ignorance behind and get back the mother she'd known for eighteen years.

Her arms punch forward, yank back, ripping fistfuls of air from the night and throwing them behind her.

But ignorance can't be bliss anymore.

What she knew no longer exists.

She needs something new to know.

A half-mile left.

Faster.

Who is her mother?

She's anaerobic now, eating asphalt, her stomach rising in her throat.

One hundred meters: she's pushed herself too far.

Fifty meters: acid burns in her mouth.

Twenty-five: lactic acidosis.

Ten: Fuck.

She collapses in her front yard, retches, stays down, watching on all fours as steam rises from her vomit. When she can breathe again, she pushes herself to her feet, wipes a cord of bile from her face, and goes inside.

CHAPTER FORTY-ONE

The sun hung low as they crested the hill, blinding them. A pair of dogs bounded in the grass to their left, chasing each other in turns as their owners stood by. There was wood and water to their right, asphalt beneath their feet; the river sounded soft static behind and between the trees. Bo's footsteps hit: one, two, one two; Parker's: step, cane, scuff.

It was too cold for crickets.

"It's a good thing you're doing."

She didn't answer.

"What's her name again?"

A wind rose, fell.

"Sarah. Sarah Smith."

"What's her story?"

"Shall we head back?"

They turned without another word, retraced their steps, descending into the lowland between them and the diner.

"How long will you put her up?"

"As long as she needs."

"Orphan?"

Bo nodded. "Girl's parents died, so she was living up in Rockport with the granddaughter of the old Martinsson widow, but the woman had eight children of her own, and couldn't afford to keep her."

"I'd like to contribute, grocery money or something."

"The ladies at church already took up a collection."

"Well then, I'll add to it. A college fund, maybe."

Bo gave no indication she'd heard him. They reached the end of the path.

"Care to stop at the bookshop for a coffee?"

"I've got coffee at the diner."

"But not lattes," he said, "or biscotti."

"I'll skip the biscotti."

"Okay," he said, dipping his head in a single nod.

"Parker…"

"You don't have to say it again." He forced a smile. "I know."

Neither spoke. They resumed walking.

"How about dinner," she said finally.

"Dinner at the diner, nothing could be finer…"

She ignored him.

"I'd have a slice of pie and scoop of ice cream."

"Nice try."

"Dr. Hariri told on me, didn't he? Damn Benedict Arnold."

"Did you remember to take your medication?"

"In my pocket." He patted his jacket.

"Doing you a whole lot of good."

"I'll take them with dinner," he said. "The biggest steak you've got, and fries with extra gravy."

"Why do I even bother?"

"Why do you?"

They continued walking, Parker leaning harder and harder into his cane as they climbed the hill, breath ragged for the pain, his limp growing progressively more pronounced.

Bo slowed, hooked her arm around his. The hill let out into a plane five hundred feet from the diner, but she didn't let go until they reached the door. Parker held it open for her, smiling as she went through.

Outside, the streetlights came on, and moths were born of the shadows.

CHAPTER FORTY-TWO

Sarah burst from sleep panicked, flailing for the lamp on her bedside table, found the knob, twisted: nothing; pushed it: no effect; pressed it: heard a click, and was driven into her mattress by a fist of light. There was something in the room. She searched for it, blinking madly behind the hand shielding her eyes. She couldn't see it, but it was there, watching her. She trembled, holding the covers beneath her chin in tight fists until her temples stopped pulsing, and the sound of her breath faded.

It was silence, she realized. She couldn't remember ever hearing it before. There hadn't been room with ten people living in a three-bedroom house.

Now she had a small apartment, a studio above a storefront. Lewella had outlined the rules of her occupancy—no men, no alcohol, no loud music, eleven o'clock curfew—and told her that she could pick up her allowance in the diner on the first of every month.

She caught sight of the clock: six fifteen. A bolt of panic ran through her: she had to enroll in school today, and she wasn't going to be able to shower. Then she remembered that she wasn't sharing a bathroom with nine people anymore, that she wasn't sharing one with anybody.

She rolled her legs over the side of the bed and stood up. The blood rushed from her head, and she fell into the wall, only just getting her arms up in time to keep from hitting it face first. She laid her cheek against the wall and closed her eyes: the plaster was cool on her skin, made her shiver.

She counted to ten, opened her eyes, and made the bed.

It was her first day.

She didn't mind being alone. It was different, full of unfamiliar sounds that leapt out at her without warning, but what really unnerved her was the plenitude. Everything she did felt somehow contrived because she could just as well have done a dozen other things. She couldn't decide whether to shower before or after boiling an egg because she'd had to be in the shower by five o'clock and out by five-o-five for as long as she could remember.

The linoleum of the kitchenette was cold beneath her sockless feet. Her pants were threadbare, sagged diagonally, dipping below her coxa, and the

154

legs were three inches too short. They'd belonged to Linda's oldest son, first, then to her fourth, and her sixth. She'd rigged a makeshift belt to keep them from falling down.

She decided to eat first, took a pot from an overhead cabinet, bent to take an egg from the refrigerator, and stood up, smashing her head into the still open cabinet door.

When she recovered, the egg was lying on the floor, shell fractured, yolk half out. She wiped it up, put the pot she'd intended to use back in the cabinet, and walked to the bathroom.

The bathroom light emitted a soothing hum, illuminating a porcelain tub, a vanity made of glass and metal, white tiling, and fresh grout. She stumbled again as she entered, caught herself on the sink basin. Looking in the mirror, she sighed, too tall, again, everything above her nose missing from the face looking back at her in the mirror.

Crouching, she saw a nasty welt rising on her forehead.

School started. People found out that she didn't have any parents, that she was not yet fifteen and living alone; they stopped what they were doing when she walked by, spoke in hushed voices. She'd known it would happen, if not with the first person she met, then with the second or third, and once them, everyone. Sometimes she let herself think that it was just the way she looked, that if her eyes weren't so green and her skin wasn't so pale, if she weren't quite so tall and thin, or her hair so red, that she might be able to blend in and go unnoticed. Sometimes she even let herself imagine that she was pretty.

She wasn't ugly, really, just too tall and too pale and too shy.

Too.

She made people uncomfortable.

She ran every day, morning and night, took long walks, got to know the town. She found places to read, to think, discovered a rope swing that, if she held her legs up as high as she could as she swung, would throw her into a languorous river.

And she found a bookstore.

CHAPTER FORTY-THREE

Hastings Bookshop had been a mill at the turn of the century, a brick and wood building laid out like a supine 'J', hanging over a lock at 1066 Hastings Street. Samuel's Great Dane, Bill, sniffed at a shrub as Samuel unlocked the door, then followed him in, tail wagging, along the short corridor winding toward the length of the 'J', inhaling the ghost-smells of lumber cut sixty years ago, and the sugar maple Samuel burned in the wood-stove. Ten feet along the scoop, then a corner, and the length of the spine that was the main of the shop; double-pane windows ran the width of the three main walls, beginning a yard off the ground and ending a foot from the ceiling.

The checkout counter faced east, and for a few minutes every morning the sunlight ran so hard through the windows and in such great abundance that it dissolved the lines of the books and the shape of his customers and the slivers of shadow differentiating one from the next so that they merged with each other in a world where all is light, and sorrow rises like vapors and is born unto nowhere.

It was Samuel's favorite time of day.

Bill found his dog bed, and Samuel went about preparing the shop for business, turning on lights, starting the coffee, re-shelving books. Ready, he poured himself the first mug, unlocked the door, and sat behind the register, a moderate smile fixed on his face, pen behind his ear, and an open book on the counter in front of him.

So his days began.

In the intervals between customers' questions and the shriek of the espresso machine and the clackity, clackity of laptop keys he could hear the rush and churn of the river beneath them. Part of Samuel resented the machine's noise, but he knew that it was the lattes and macchiatos and cappuccinos that kept him in business, and tried not to grumble. Such luxuries and the *New York Times* bestseller lists and Oprah's Book Club kept his bookshop in the black, and helped subsidize the poetry he loved. Hastings had the largest collection of poetry books in New England, and he invited poets from around the country to come and give readings, started a poetry workshop that met every other Thursday, and held an open-mic once a month for local artists to perform their work. He had a hard time keeping Eliot and Auden in stock, and occasionally someone came looking for Emily Dickinson or Sylvia Plath, William Carlos Williams or Allen Ginsberg or Charles Bukowski, but for the most part, the volumes he stocked remained ensconced on Hastings' shelves like Excalibur in its rock.

The bell rang, and Samuel looked up from his book. The girl who'd come through the door was tall and very thin; she turned red and buried her nose in her chest when he smiled at her in greeting. Bill raised his head and followed her progress across the store, then lay back down.

It was Tuesday, mid-morning. A half-dozen customers browsed, two men played chess. Mr. Dodd had a stack of magazines he wouldn't buy in the chair next to him. The line for coffee was three deep.

The girl caught his eye, occasionally, her hair flashing in his peripheral vision as she wandered amongst the bookshelves.

"Samuel!"

"Angela!" Samuel mimicked the woman's verve, laughed.

"How's my favorite entrepreneur?"

"Well. You? How're the girls?"

"We've just come from the groomers. They're in the car, looking like a million bucks."

"The book you ordered should be here by Thursday."

"Marvelous! Well—" She thrust her chin upward, magenta hoop earrings swaying with the movement. "—I'm off! People to see, and kingdoms to conquer."

"The world is your oyster!"

"Don't I know it!"

A flurry of movement, the door thrown open, the soft ringing of the bell as it closed behind her, silence.

The tall girl was frozen, staring at the space the woman had abandoned. Samuel caught her eye, laughed. "She's a force of nature."

The girl nodded.

It was five to seven when Samuel noticed her in front of him at the register. "How long have you been standing there?"

"A few minutes."

He knew it was longer: she'd been at the shop every day after school for almost two weeks, and the alarm on her watch went off at a quarter to seven.

"I'm sorry." He rubbed his eyes. "I must have dozed off. How embarrassing."

She handed him her dollar bill and fled, gone before he closed the register drawer.

"I'll be closing in five minutes," he announced to the remaining customers.

The browsers hastened their efforts; the men playing chess looked at each other and shrugged, shook hands, and disassembled their board. Another man finished his coffee in a gulp, wincing and twisting sideways as it burned down his throat.

Samuel rang up the last customer and followed him to the door.

"Take care, Parker."

"And you as well."

He turned the lock, flipped the sign on the door, and headed toward his office.

CHAPTER FORTY-FOUR

Samuel pushed his eggs around his plate, set his fork down, and picked up his coffee, put it down without taking a sip. He was the last of the breakfast crowd.

"What's on your mind, Samuel?"

He looked down into his coffee cup and smiled uncomfortably.

"Stomach's giving me trouble."

"And?"

"That obvious?"

"Just about."

"I was wondering if you knew anything about the new girl in town, tall and pale, red hair."

"I know the one."

"She's staying with you, right?"

Lewella nodded. Samuel waited, took a sip of coffee. She didn't elaborate, just wiped at the counter, tossed the rag in the sink, and stood with her arms crossed.

"She's at the store just about every day. Comes in, reads all day, switches out the novel she's been reading for a dollar paperback just before close, buys it, and leaves."

"And the problem is?"

"There's no—"

"Christ sake, Samuel—at least she buys something. You start making an issue of every customer that doesn't buy what he reads, and you'll be out of customers."

"There's no problem."

He spoke deliberately, chiseling the edge from his words before releasing them as he stood.

"I've just never seen her with anyone, never seen her eat. She's usually wearing the same clothes. I just wanted to make sure she was okay and to see if I could help."

Their eyes locked, Lewella's three decades older and watery for the years.

"And that's it? Nothing else to it?"

They stared at each other.

Sarah walked into the diner.

Samuel shook his head. "Go to hell, Lew."

He dropped a ten into the yolk on his plate and left.

Lewella took Sarah's order and gave it to Jesús, got her coat, stepped outside, and lit a menthol.

Forty minutes to get things ready for lunch.

Samuel hadn't deserved that.

CHAPTER FORTY-FIVE

"And how are we today, Sir William?"

Chuck, the bartender, flipped a biscuit at the dog as Samuel sat down.

"You keep calling him that and it'll go straight to his head." He turned to the dog. "Go lie down, Bill."

The dog loped over to the cushion set against the far wall and lay down.

"Guinness and Jameson?"

He was pouring before he asked; Samuel didn't bother to answer.

"How're things?"

Chuck snorted. "Same old shit. One son gets fired, one knocks his girl up. Daughter needs braces. Another kid wants piano lessons."

"Rough week."

"Week? Hell, that was this morning!"

Samuel winced.

Chuck rubbed at his temples. "Yeah."

"You eat breakfast at Lew's today?"

Chuck made a face. "Every day since I was sixteen, why?"

"She seem off to you?"

"When isn't she?"

A townsman hung his coat on a peg and sat at the far end of the bar. Chuck drew a beer and slid it in his direction.

"Two fries and a fish," he yelled at the kitchen. "Wings, Sammy?"

Samuel nodded.

"And a wing."

A half-dozen townies came in; Chuck drew their beer one by one: Coors, Bud, a pitcher of Yuengling. Samuel's wings came along with another wave of regulars.

"Don't worry about Lew," Chuck said when he'd worked his way back over. "The day she dies, they're going to cut her open and find nothing but piss and sawdust."

Samuel laughed.

"Another?"

"One more."

"That's what they all say."

Samuel opened his mouth, but nothing came out. "Shit," he said finally.

Chuck laughed.

"Well, at least we got a curse word out of you. We'll break you in yet, Sammy."

Chuck went on down the bar, working the patrons; Samuel finished. "Come on, Bill."

Bill stood, startling the man near him who jumped with a bleat and took off running, spilling beer all over himself.

The townies howled.

Chuck handed the guy a towel, wiped the bar, and poured him a new beer. "That would be Bill, Sammy's dog."

"Dog? That's a fucking bear!"

"Sorry about that," Samuel said, extending his hand.

The man took it. "No worries, bro. I just never seen a pet bear in a bar before."

"First time for everything."

"Night, Chuck." Samuel raised a hand. "See you soon."

"You should be so lucky."

Samuel gave a dismissive wave and left, Bill following behind.

CHAPTER FORTY-SIX

Samuel grit his teeth, sighed and set the book on the table beside his chair. He was three hundred and sixty pages in, and despising every word, but he would press on. It was a massive book, more than a thousand pages, each wet with uncut fat, loose words, and stilted prose, but the dust jacket bespoke genius, so he slogged on, feeling the dunce.

He lifted his tumbler, took a sip, wincing appreciatively as it bit.

The scotch helped.

Beyond the window a car made its way down the street. Samuel's eyes lingered on the phone sitting atop his desk.

He and his wife talked every other day, precisely at nine thirty when he knew she took her evening break. She was tenured at Harvard, spent the semesters in Cambridge, visited on the occasional weekend. She hadn't said he shouldn't call more frequently or at a different time, but neither had she invited him to do so. So he read, invented errands, and stopped by Chuck's or loitered at Hastings, anything to avoid staring at the clock.

He shut the light off, walked through the house and up the stairs to his bedroom. There were four paperbacks between the lamp and the alarm clock on his bedside table; he'd been rereading John Irving in the hours before he fell asleep, laughing at THE VOICE, Giants fans threatening to gangbang a transsexual ex-Raider, and surgeons slinging petrified dog shit at people rowing crew.

It was ten to eight. Neither bed, nor Irving appealed as yet.

Bill nudged his side, whimpering. Samuel looked down. "Outside?" Bill barked.

Samuel followed him downstairs and let him out, mixed wet food with kibble and a sprinkle of parmesan, set it by his water dish, let Bill back in.

Eight-thirty.

"What do you say, Bill, one more?"

Turning, he saw the dog had eaten and gone, so he cut off the kitchen light. Bill was on his dog bed, snoring.

I should offer her a job.

The idea came unbeckoned, but made more sense the more he thought about it. The tall girl—he didn't know her name—was always at the store anyway, and this way she'd make some money. He, in turn, wouldn't be so tied to the bookstore, and would be able to indulge in such perigrinations as he saw fit.

And it would piss off Lewella.

CHAPTER FORTY-SEVEN

"You know, you've never played for me." Tori pokes her. "We've been making love for three months, now, and…"

Tolan blossoms in scarlet.

"Awww," Tori teases, "you're so cute! Blushing because I've seen you n'ked."

Tolan yelps, writhes, dives beneath the comforter; Tori throws it off in hot pursuit and catches her, pins her arms above her head, bends to kiss her. Tolan allows her lips to part, knows Tori's will tease her at first, that their tongues will brush against each other, and that Tori will pull away, grin, before leaning in and taking one of Tolan's lips between her teeth, gentle and rough all at once.

Tolan likes knowing, likes the way they fit together.

"Why won't you play for me?"

Tori releases her arms, sits back, still on top of her as the morning light reaches into the room through a gap between the blinds. They're having a warm spring.

"I've never played for anyone."

"Not even your mom?"

Tolan shakes her head.

"How come?"

She shrugs.

"Play for me."

She shakes her head again.

"Alright then." Tori pounces, resumes tickling her.

"EEK!"

Tori pauses. "Feeling more compliant now?"

Tolan bucks and twists. "Hel—"

But Tori's pinned her again, is kissing her, harder and deeper and longer than either of them imagined possible, and Tolan's with her, answering kiss with kiss and crush with crush so that their bodies pulse with heat as they taste the salt in each other's sweat and drink the tang of their commingling arousal, refusing to break even as the giddy, flickering reel of unconsciousness closes upon their heads.

They break with a gasp.

"Sorry."

"Are not."

Tori manages a grin, her chest still heaving, still catching her breath. "Okay, maybe not that sorry."

Tolan laughs.

"Play for me?"

Tolan looks away. "I—"

"Play for me or we're going to have 'the talk.'"

"Getting my guitar."

Both girls force a laugh, turning silent as a butterfly of sadness flits through the room. They still have a few months before August.

Tolan's arms are shaking as she tunes the guitar.

"T?"

She looks up.

"Jesus—you're trembling. You don't have—"

Tolan shakes her head. "I want to. I'm just nervous." She strums a chord, twists a peg. "I've been working on learning a couple songs for you."

She swallows, forces a smile.

"For me?" Tori holds her hands over her heart.

Tolan nods.

The talk, looming.

She wants to play for Tori—she's been practicing the songs for weeks, but now she's scared, scared she picked the wrong ones—scared of the talk, because it hasn't happened, and because it will. The longer they go without having it, the more is said, the more is heard—in an act, a posture, a word or a silence. In a song. Saying and hearing, and saying and hearing, and no one certain—no way to be certain.

What does she want to say?

What does Tori want to hear?

Tolan feels as though she's standing back from herself, disembodied, watching words become things, visible, solid things with weight and heft.

Is she a lesbian?

Is she a lesbian because and only if she's sleeping with Tori?

She loves Tori—does loving Tori make her a lesbian?

Ani, Joni, Anne Heche: do people move in and out of it, or is it something they are?

Does it matter?

It matters.

Why does it matter so much?

What is she ready to say, what will she say, what can she say—what does she actually know?

Which song should she play first?

Joyful Girl.

She does, and well, but the song ends.

What's next?

She needs another song.

She still doesn't know.

One last needless twist of a peg, she risks a look at Tori, drops her head before their eyes can meet. "This is by God-Des and She," she says softly. "I played with it some so I could do it on guitar."

Tolan starts tapping her foot on the floor, marking time:

String: pluck, pluck, pluck—stop. Pluck, pluck, pluck—stop.

Body: hit, hit, hit—stop.

Fret: slap, slap—

Stop.

Fret, fret

Body, body

String, string…

The song's got Tolan, Tori too, her head's bobbing to the music, her eyes closed.

Tell Me…

Tolan never thought… she finishes the song, doesn't really stop, doesn't open her eyes, launches into the next—*Kiss That Counted*—voice no longer apologetic, raw and rich as she strums the harmony. Her voice dives where Catie's soars.

Tolan hits the final chord, kills the sound with a hand.

Tori claps. "Encore, encore!"

Tolan hesitates.

"Just one more. Please."

Tolan lets the sound bleed out this time, the strings vibrating to stillness. There's no clapping.

"I had no idea…" Tori starts. "You play… beautifully."

Tolan smiles, her hair wet at the temples and the base of her neck.

"I have an amazing instrument."

Tori's sitting on the edge of the bed; Tolan goes to her, lets Tori pull her into her lap.

"You're really tall," she says.

"You're really short."

They laugh.

Tolan closes her eyes, steeling herself. "I think we should probably have that talk."

"Shush."

"But…"
"Not now. Just let me hold you."
She does.
They can talk another time.

CHAPTER FORTY-EIGHT

It was a slow Saturday. Samuel was between books and uncertain what he wanted to read next. He read as much as ever, with Cate in Boston, read, and had the sense of being a conveyor belt of sorts, of moving along words and pages with something just shy of indifference.

He decided to close the shop early, cut the lights off, flipped the sign over, and called to Bill. He gave his truck too much gas coming out of the parking lot; his tires spun and spat gravel before catching and shooting him forward. He had to jam on his brakes to keep from running the stop sign. The girls' cross-country team ran by, the tall girl—Sarah, he'd learned— among them, her head and shoulders visible above the pack. He watched them run, the near-iridescent fabric of their spandex stretched against their bodies, neither concealing the parts men wanted to see, nor meant to. He waited until they passed, pulled onto Main Street.

It bothered him that the display stirred nothing. Ignoring the fact that the girls were about the same age as his daughter, he should feel something —if not desire, at least indignation.

Tomorrow, the whole of his truck would be loaded with the seven thousand volumes that had constituted the personal library of a wealthy New Hampshire eccentric. The lot had cost him fifty-two thousand dollars at the estate auction; fifty-seven hundred of the books had been inventoried, among them a first edition of *Catcher In the Rye*, a first edition, first printing copy of *The Cat In the Hat*, and a first edition of *The Hobbit*. All of the books, he was promised, were in good to excellent condition.

Samuel glanced at his watch: five-fifteen. The sun's white-yellow fingers were gone, the sky sucked translucent.

He'd never bought or sold rare books before.

Samuel took Route One to the gas station, filled his tank, and drove toward the water. He could remember telling his students: story requires conflict, conflict requires tension, and tension is created by the confluence of mutually exclusive intentions. That was what bothered him about his indifference to the girls. No desire, no intention; no intention, no tension; no tension, no conflict; no conflict, no story.

He was disappearing.

Samuel drove to the landing, loaded Bill into the kayak, and shoved off.

He'd wanted to write, had written, published. He'd wanted to continue writing, but stopped. He seemed to have let everything go but the wanting, a perverse desire divorced from the thought of action.

Cate was still in Boston.

He was not writing.

He laid his paddle across the mouth of his kayak, removed his glasses, rubbed his face with both hands.

"Damn."

Bill sat in the front seat of the double, caught a scent, lifted his nose to the wind. Samuel started paddling again: push right and pull left, push left and pull right. The spinning vortices his paddle threw faded into the sea.

The wine dark sea.

He laughed at himself, rounded a jut of land and slipped into the sound.

The wine dark sea.

The sound was empty, but not still, no gulls or people or boats, but the wind rough on the skin of the water and the particles of light enmeshed in it so that it seemed to run over and against itself.

Samuel pulled up his paddle, took a book from his pocket, and let the kayak drift slowly back out to sea.

"You going to stay today?" The store was closed. They'd cleaned up the coffee station. Sarah had set all the chairs on the tabletops and mopped the small tiled area, and Samuel had counted the register and prepared the evening deposit.

"Is that okay?"

"It's always okay."

"I like the books."

"I hadn't realized."

He smiled; she blushed.

"What are you reading today?"

"*Les Misérables.*"

"'Promise to give me a kiss on my brow when I am dead. I shall feel it.'"

"You know it?"

"It's a classic."

She nodded. "I've never read it before."

"Do you read poetry?"

"I haven't."

"If you like Hugo, you might try *La Légende des Siècles*, sometime, *The Legend of the Ages*. It's," he paused, eyes drifting away from her, "incomparable."

"Do we have a copy?"

"I'm sure. Let me check."

She watched him take the stairs, clutching her book in both hands.

"Paperback or hardcover?" he called down.

"Hardcover," she said reflexively, then winced. Hardcover would be more expensive.

"Here you are."

He tossed her the volume; she caught it, swayed with its heft.

"Could you take it out of my paycheck?"

He waived the question away. "Take it. It's been here since I opened the store."

"Are you— you don't have to…"

He frowned.

Her eyes fell to the floor. "Thank you."

"You're welcome." He smiled. "I have first editions of all three series at home: 1859, 1877, and 1883. Cate gave them to me on our first anniversary."

"In French?"

He nodded. "It's a beautiful language, and Hugo… Do you have any French?"

"A little. A bunch of the fishermen I grew up around spoke French, Québécois. I doubt I'd be able to read it."

"You could take classes."

She shook her head. "I can't afford to."

"Lewella told me Miss White wants to pay for any educational things you're interested in, books and classes and whatnot."

"The woman who's putting me up?"

He nodded.

"Do you know her?"

"Mostly by reputation. She comes by the shop every once in a while, when she's in town."

"What's she like?"

"Self-contained. You'd never know it, but she's been all over the world. She was the first foreign photographer allowed into the Soviet Union after the Iron Curtain fell over Europe, the first person to photograph Castro in Cuba."

"That's incredible."

Sarah put the Hugo into her bag, turned on a lamp. The sun hadn't risen that morning, wouldn't set.

Samuel was stepping into his coat.

"Lock up behind yourself."

Sarah nodded. "Will I get to meet her?"

"Miss White? I don't know."

"I'd like to thank her."

"You can always send her a note."

She nodded.

"You sure you don't want to get some dinner?"

"I have some snacks in my bag."

He left, and she read, falling into the rhythms of fin de siècle France until it was near ten o'clock, and without any real reason, she felt she should leave. She stayed late at the shop most nights after she worked. It was her favorite time, the hours spent alone with the books, first reading, and then, for the last twenty minutes or so before she left, walking amongst them, hands brushing the spines, occasionally rising up a cover, cresting its rim, and sliding down into it to finger the page-tops for the briefest of intervals. It made her feel warm and happy. She'd tried to tell Chelsea about it, her one friend, but the effort had gone awry almost immediately, so she'd stopped and let Chelsea change the subject.

Ten-fifteen. She'd walked the quarter-mile to her building, gone up the stairs into her apartment, and locked the door behind her. She made tea, took it and her book into the bathroom, and drew a bath. She had a piece of plywood, four feet long and two feet wide, that she lay across the top of the tub to act as a tray.

She lowered herself into the heat, her first bath, closed her eyes against the pain, made herself motionless as the water cooled and the pain passed into an excruciating luxury, opened her eyes when it no longer hurt, and began with Hugo: she decided to accept Miss White's offer to pay for her classes that night amidst the fever of heat and verse. It wasn't easy, and it wasn't hard, an indignity, but not a novel one; she'd been relying on others' charity her whole life. Still, she wondered what it was that made people feel sorry for her, whether it was her circumstances, or something deeper, some part of her that screamed *I need help!*

Her: quiet and shy, and unremarkable save for her height.

Her: someone who would be okay as long as she had books to read and a place to read them.

But maybe somewhere, in some other time, there was a version of her that didn't need help, that could do the things Miss White had.

CHAPTER FORTY-NINE

"Michael?"

Michael set his magazine on the tabletop and looked up.

Samuel.

They didn't really know each other. Michael bought two magazines at the bookshop every month: *Ring* on the first and *Boxing Monthly* on the fifteenth. He came in for an hour or two before or after work, bought a coffee, and sat at a table near the rear of the store. Samuel watched him read from the register, his brow always furrowed, face close to the magazine as he moved his finger slowly beneath the lines, forming each word in his mouth. They nodded their greetings each time they saw each other, but they'd never spoken.

"You work at the university, right?"

Michael nodded.

"I need to ask you for a favor: I usually take Sarah," —he nodded at her across the room— "down to campus for her classes, but I can't this evening. Any chance you could give her a ride?"

Michael looked at his watch. "I'll be leaving in thirty minutes."

"Thanks. I'll get her so I can introduce you."

Michael watched him cross the room and tap the girl on the shoulder, watched her startle, give an embarrassed smile. She'd been working for Samuel as long as Michael had been coming to the store, so he'd seen her around the shop, cleaning, shelving books, running the cash register. The color drained from her face as Samuel spoke to her, pointed to him.

Michael raised a hand.

"Thank you for driving me," she managed. They'd been driving for twenty minutes, and neither of them had spoken.

Michael shrugged. "I was headed there anyway."

"For work?"

He nodded.

"What do you do at the university?"

"I'm a janitor."

He knew he should say something more, put her at ease.

"Do you like it?"

"It's a job." He checked his mirror, changed lanes. "How about you?"

"Me?"

"What are you doing at the college?"

"I take a few classes."

"Which ones?"

"French and English."

"French?"

"I want to read *Les Misérables*."

He looked at her blankly.

"It's a book."

He nodded, knew it was his turn, didn't know what to say. They took the Forest Avenue exit, came to a light, stopped.

"You look young for college."

She nodded. "I'm not matriculated."

"Matriculated?"

"Enrolled."

He nodded, tried. "You must be smart, then."

She blushed, shook her head. "I just like to read."

The light changed; they resumed their progress. The campus emerged on the left, protruding from the fog.

"Where should I drop you?"

"I'll walk from wherever."

He didn't argue, turned into the staff lot and parked, pulled his thermos and brown paper lunch bag from the back seat.

"Where should I meet you?"

"Meet me?"

They stared at each other, confused by the other's confusion, beads of fog wet on their forehead and nose.

"So I can ride back with you."

"I don't get off work until midnight."

Her face fell; she hugged her books tight against her. "Oh…"

"There's no one you can call?"

She shook her head.

He squinted, wiped the water from his nose. "Come to the law school after your last class. I'll set you up in the break room."

※

It was raining when her last class ended. The classroom was on the opposite end of campus, and she didn't have an umbrella, was shivering by the time she made it to the law school, her hair wet and plastered against her skin, her clothes soaked through. Water dripped from her nose and the points of her elbows. "Hey," she said when she found him.

Michael set his mop in the water bucket and turned. "Hey."

"It's raining."

"Looks like it."

He led her down to the lounge, pointed to a plastic chair beside a particleboard table, and went to look for a blanket. He came back with coffee in a Styrofoam cup.

"I couldn't find anything for you to change into."

"That's okay."

He shook his head, unbuttoned his top button, second, third.

"You don't have to—"

"I've got a t-shirt on underneath." He took the work shirt off, held it out to her. It was navy blue, threadbare at the elbows, had his name stitched above the left breast in cursive gray letters. "Take it."

"But my name's not Michael."

"What?"

"Your shirt." She pointed, throat and face burning. "Your name..."

He followed her finger to his shirt, puzzled, saw the nametag and realized what she was getting at, laughed.

She looked relieved.

"Let me know if I can get you anything."

She nodded. "Thank you."

Her left her to her books, returned to his mopping. She finished her homework, kept going, working ahead, growing heavy-eyed as the hours passed.

He got her at ten to midnight.

"Ready?"

She nodded and collected her things.

Samuel had to be out of town the rest of the week, so Michael drove her to and from her classes. She brought him his shirt on Thursday, folded and fresh from the wash, got caught in the rain again, and had to re-borrow it. There was an oversized box in the passenger's seat of Michael's truck when he picked her up on Friday. She set it on her lap, had to tilt it at a diagonal to fit between her and the dash. "Open it."

"Open it?"

He nodded.

She did, tentatively, found a pink raincoat wrapped in tissue paper.
"Just in case."
She blushed. "It has my name on it."
"Now you'll be legal."

CHAPTER FIFTY

Samuel fed Bill, downed two fingers of scotch, poured himself another three, sat down. He'd wait for her to call this time. Nine fifteen came, nine thirty, nine forty-five; he finished the second drink and poured himself a third.

One chapbook of poetry: thirty-seven saddle-stitched pages with a robin's egg paperboard cover; one novella, forty-seven thousand three hundred sixty-one words published in four installments by a now defunct literary journal; one finished novel, published and largely ignored; one unfinished novel.

Scores of unfinished stories.

Artifacts.

He wished they'd rise like the vapor from his scotch and disappear.

The refuge of memory, of boyhood reconstructed, brakes grinding as his grandfather slowed to a stop, the window groaning against its rubber seals as he wound it down and the cab filled with the putrid-sweet sweat of rotting garbage.

Samuel remembered holding his breath as the gulls shrieked and fought over scraps of trash and the attendant pushed himself from his stool and began to move toward them, lame of leg and grinding grit and rock across the asphalt beneath a boot that never left the ground.

"Howdy, Howard."

The attendant gestured acknowledgment and pushed a button to lift the gate. They drove through, pulled up in front of the trash compactor, and cut the engine. Samuel watched his grandfather remove his seatbelt and open the door, did the same, holding onto the door handle with two hands, swinging his legs over the seat, and sliding down to the ground. The passenger door was bent and rusted, shut only after the boy threw himself against it. He was breathing hard when he met his grandfather at the tailgate, his shoulder throbbing.

"What took you so long? Take this."

His grandfather dropped a trash bag into his arms; Samuel staggered beneath its weight, wobbled forward.

"Damn thing's as big as he is, Roy."

"He'll be fine—Don't drag it, Samuel, pick it up."

He watched Samuel come back to the truck, climb up into the bed, push the remaining bins to the edge of the tailgate, jump down, and take each to the appropriate station.

"Shall we go to the library?" his grandfather asked when they were done.

Samuel nodded, looked at the resin on his hands, and contemplated wiping them on his jeans.

The library was a portable shed Howard had salvaged and whitewashed. Samuel's aunt had painted a sign to hang outside it. It was musty and damp, and the books inside weren't in any order, but Leonard straightened them once a week, half-organizing them by genre, mysteries on the left, romance on the middle shelf, business at the bottom left. The philosophy books sat on the floor along with other arcane subject matter, astrology and religion; whatever else they had went wherever there was space.

They entered the shed together, started at the extreme left and moved right, the boy following behind, mimicking his grandfather. His grandfather slowed at the poetry section as Samuel had known he would, moving his hand over the books, pulling the odd one halfway out to glance at its cover.

"Do you know this one, Samuel?"

The Poems of Browning.

Samuel nodded.

"*So glad it has its utmost will,*" his grandfather began. "*That all it scorned at once is fled, And I, its love, am gained instead!*"

"Porphyria's love," Samuel answered. He'd worked on saying that name over and over. "*...she guessed not how. Her darling one wish would be heard. And thus we sit together now...*"

"*And all night long we have not stirred,*" his grandfather said, "*And yet God has not said a word!*"

Samuel devoted hours to memorizing poetry as a boy. He didn't understand most of what he read, and he wasn't even sure he was saying it right, but his grandfather loved poetry, and loved when Samuel could recite poems to him.

They turned to go, his grandfather first through the door, Samuel making to follow, stopping to see if there were any books hidden behind the inward opening door, finding seventeen uniform, leather-bound volumes.

"What about these, Grandpa?"

His grandmother had been incensed when she'd come downstairs to find her floor strewn with milk crates and dust-covered books. "What's all this?" she'd demanded.

178

"A thousand years of language, Mary," his grandfather answered. "A thousand years of language."

Samuel let himself linger in the memory.

Samuel's publishings were stowed on the furthest end of the lowest shelf of a bookcase in his study. He would pull them from time to time, and thumb through their pages, knowing and not knowing why. There were notes in the margins, graphite slashes through words and phrases that had fallen out of favor, but the most recent of them was a decade old.

The chapbook contained a poem or two of modest worth. It was odd reading them, now, remembering what each stanza had cost in hours and anxiety, how they'd once moved him.

Bill sighed and rolled over.

Samuel frowned and turned from the window, pushed the door out of the way of the bookcase, and found his chapbook on the shelf. He took a hard swallow of scotch and opened the chapbook, read.

Nothing.

He felt nothing.

Once upon a time he'd been passionate, had written and made love and drank wine and argued about books and words like the fate of the world hung in the balance.

And then he was denied tenure—was that what did it?

He remembered the sterile days that followed, in which he wrote not a single word, and how they stretched into months, and then years.

But he couldn't remember when he stopped trying.

CHAPTER FIFTY-ONE

The door opened and the bell rang.

"No," Bo said without looking up from her crossword.

The old man laughed, ran a hand over his beard.

"You're sure?"

"As sure as I was the last thirty-one times."

"I'd take good care of you."

She ignored him.

Parker shuffled to the corner stool, leaned his cane against the wall, and unzipped his jacket and set it on the stool beside him, along with his hat and scarf.

"I'd hoped the thirty-second time would be the charm."

"Guess not."

Lewella watched Bo complete the puzzle, pushed herself up off the counter, and tucked the pen behind her ear. "The usual?"

"No egg—" Parker began.

"The usual," Bo interrupted.

Lewella brought him a mug, hot water, and a teabag. Jesús threw two pieces of rye on the griddle, dropped an egg in a pot of water.

"You're as bad as she is," Parker said, watching.

Lewella snorted.

Bo ignored him.

"You always have her bring me the egg—"

"You need the egg."

"I don't—"

"Hush."

Jesús pushed the egg and toast at him, grinning, "Cómelo ya, viejo."

Parker shook his head, cracked the egg, smiling as the yoke bled onto his plate. He picked up a piece of toast, tore it, and wiped it over the plate, pushing pieces of egg white up onto the bread with his spoon. He ate slowly, pausing to sip his tea as a couple at the opposite end of the diner finished up, pushing their empty plates and half-full coffee cups into the center of the table. Lewella rang them up and gave them their change, then bussed their dishes, and returned to the counter.

"No tienes corazón," Jesús scolded.

Bo ignored him.

"De edad, obstinada, y de mal humor."

Parker chuckled.

"You're fired, Jesús."

"¡Por fin, las vacaciones!"

Lewella laughed.

Lewella filled Parker's mug with hot water and brought him another teabag; he added milk, left the bag to steep as Jesús scraped the griddle. They worked and sat and thought in near silence, the only sounds those of the trade: coffee percolating, the motor of the pie display case, the whine of the lights overhead, the sporadic pop and sizzle of the griddle.

"Thank you very much," Parker said when he'd finished.

Bo waived the words away.

"Not you." He stood slowly, using both hands against the counter. "Jesús and Lewella."

He wound his scarf around his neck and put his coat on, set his hat on his head, took gloves from his pockets, and picked up his cane.

"Why on earth would I be thanking you?"

"Go home, you old bird."

Parker looked at Jesús and shrugged.

Jesús shook his head.

"Take care." Parker waved.

"Adiós, viejo."

They watched through the plate glass until he disappeared from sight. Bo turned to find Jesús watching her.

"What?"

He smiled. "Nada."

"What?"

"Nada."

"Shut up."

The door opened, and four people entered, stamping their feet and rubbing their hands together.

"Guess you'd better get to work."

"No quiero."

CHAPTER FIFTY-TWO

"How old is Michael?"

"I don't think it's said yet," Tori says, measuring out a cup of flour.

"Hmmm."

"Chocolate chip?"

"Toss it."

Tori sends it arching up in the air, and Tolan catches it in her mouth. "It's a little weird, though, isn't it?"

"What?"

"That he invited her to the movies. I mean, she can't be interested in him."

Tori shrugs.

"He's at least ten years older."

"You add the vanilla yet?"

Tolan nods. "He's interested in her, though, buying her things and talking to her, driving her all over. I mean, he can barely read, and he bought *Les Misérables*—it's like two thousand pages."

"It's definitely long."

Tori adds the last of the ingredients to the bowl and slides it across the counter toward Tolan. "You're going to have to stop waving that thing around if you want to mix the dough."

Tolan looks up at the electric mixer in her hand, points it at Tori like a gun. "I was making a point. It's weird."

She plunges the mixer into the dough.

"I don't know."

Tolan turns the mixer on, filling the kitchen with an electric scream and the harsh sound of metal crushing chocolate chips.

"So why'd she say yes? Think she's that lonely?"

"Maybe she thinks he's hot?"

"He's twice her age!"

"Maybe," —Tori grins— "Michael looks like Jake Gyllenhaal."

Tolan sputters—they haven't talked about boys since before they started—and Jake is—was—had been, her celebrity crush. "I," —she blinks dumbly— "Uh..."

Tori laughs, runs her finger along the rim of the mixing bowl. "Take it easy over there; you're allowed to have a celebrity boyfriend... just as long as you think I'm hotter." She brings her finger to her mouth, sucks the cookie dough off in mock-seduction.

Tolan sticks her tongue out.

They start spooning the dough onto a cookie sheet.

"You really don't think it's weird?"

Tori sighs. "I don't know."

"All done."

"Sweet!" Tori pushes the pan into the oven. "I can't wait—"

Tori gasps in surprise as flour bursts against her head, sneezes, coughs as the cloud dissipates, her hair and face and the side of her neck dusted white. There's an island between them, used measuring cups and the leftover ingredients. Tori takes an egg from the carton.

"You're in so much trouble."

They're squaring off on opposite sides of the counter when they hear the garage door.

"Mom! Help!"

Tori springs; Tolan runs. They're on the opposite sides of the counter again when her mother enters the kitchen.

"Girls? What's going on?"

"Your daughter's in trouble, Mrs. Aimes."

"Am not!"

Her mother looks from one to the other, from Tori's flour-stained hair and the egg in her hand, to Tolan's fear-stretched eyes.

"Just don't get any on the wall."

"Hey!"

"Don't worry, Mrs. A," Tori says, grinning at Tolan. "I'll be careful."

Tolan's nerves desert her and she bolts, shrieking. Tori is on her in half a dozen strides, tackles her a few feet from the stairs, sits on her as Tolan giggles and shrieks, pleading for help as her mother laughs.

"On her head or down her shirt, Mrs. A?"

"Neither! Eek! Mom! Help!"

"There's less chance of it getting on the carpet if you do it in her shirt."

"Mom!"

"But it might be funnier if you do it on her head."

"Mom!"

"I can't decide."

"Neither! Neither! I'll make it up to you! I'll make it up to you! Anything!"

"Anything?"

"Anything!"

"What do you think, Mrs. A?"

"Anything is a pretty good offer."

"Hmmm…" Tori looks down at Tolan, back to her mother, releases Tolan. "I'm feeling generous today, so we'll go with anything." She allows Tolan to push herself up off the floor, hands her the egg. "You can start by bringing this back to the kitchen."

Tolan, red-faced and teary from laughter, takes the egg, smashes it on Tori's head, and runs.

CHAPTER FIFTY-THREE

Sarah knew approximately where he lived, planned her runs accordingly. Michael had been driving her to campus for a few months; they'd been to a couple movies together, run into each other at the bookstore, and hung out a half-dozen times.

He worked out in his garage, kept the door open when the weather permitted; he was hitting a heavy bag as she passed, the metal chain grinding against screws and bolts. A few times he'd been using one that looked like an inverted balloon, black fists and black bag moving so fast they merged in an absence of line and color. Other times, he'd be jumping rope. Now, he was doing pull-ups, his back to the street, deep lines rising and falling, muscles quaking.

She'd never stopped before, didn't mean to now. His muscles gave out and he dropped, caught sight of her out of the corner of his eye and turned; her heart stopped, breath caught, chest, throat, and face flushed with fire.

"I—"

"Sarah," he said. "Hey."

Her eyes fell to the asphalt. "Hey."

She felt him watching her, felt the sweat running down her body.

"I've been meaning to talk to you."

She looked up, surprised.

"I thought we might catch another movie."

She smiled, couldn't meet his eye.

"I'd like that."

"*The Champ* or *Manhattan*?"

"Either."

She'd never seen a man's chest before except in a movie. It heaved, swollen and hard, sweat falling over his ribs, down the length of his abdomen, sliding diagonally down his hipbone into his shorts.

A breeze kicked up and goose bumps rose on her body.

"*The Champ*'s about a boxer."

"Let's do that one."

"You like boxing?"

Her eyes met his. A lawnmower started, children shrieked happily across the street, an ice cream truck rounded the corner.

She shook her head. "I don't know anything about it."

"But you want to see the movie?"

She nodded.

"Tomorrow?"

She nodded again.

"Earlier or later?"

"Later, probably. I work until seven-thirty."

"There's an eight-fifty."

"Okay."

"I'll see you then."

"Okay."

She tried not to run away too fast.

They sat in silence, alone in the theater. Sarah didn't want any popcorn or soda, and Michael wasn't hungry; he bent and folded his ticket stub and pumped his foot absently, tore his ticket into little pieces. The movie started off okay, was interesting enough to follow, had the boxing angle for Michael, and the actor playing T.J. reminded Sarah of one of Linda's kids, which made her smile.

There were a lot of tears, though, a lot of drama, and at times the score felt like an assault. Sarah found herself turning away, watching Michael instead. His expression didn't change much regardless of what was on screen, though he'd taken his jacket off and rolled his cuffs, and the muscles in his arms corded and twitched whenever a boxing scene came on.

He caught her watching him, once, or almost caught her, smiled at her. She smiled back.

"How you doing?" he asked.

"Good."

His smile brightened. "Good."

For a moment they forgot that they were in a theater and faced each other, but the suddenness of the eye contact startled them, and they fled back into the movie.

She was careful about watching him after that, lost his face in the flicker and shadow at the limit of her peripheral vision.

Nearly two hours in: the score swelled, trumpeting the arrival of the final fight, pimping the father's desperate gambit to redeem his past and ensure his son's future for all its worth. The emcee bellowed. The bell sounded. The fighters converged. Gloves tore the air, pummeled bodies, faces, lacerated flesh, loosed blood. The crowd roared: blows, breakage, blood, bell; blows, breakage, blood, bell; blows, breakage—

Suddenly she was blind. It took her a moment to realize what had happened, that Michael was blocking her vision with his left hand, that his right arm was wrapped around her shoulder, and his right hand entangled in her hair, that he was covering her ear and pulling her into him and pressing his forehead against her cheek.

She froze. His breath ran over her chin, the wash of his blood through his palm throbbed in her ear.

The fight ended; Michael let her go before she could decide how she felt.

The Champ was disfigured, lying on a locker room table. His son was exhorting him, "Wake up! Champ? Wake up!"

He didn't.

Sarah didn't cry. Neither did Michael.

"Sorry," he said finally. "I…"

His voice trailed off. The movie faded to black, and the credits appeared.

"I'm sorry," he said again.

They ran into each other at the bookshop the next day. "Hey," he said.

"Hey."

"How are you?"

"Good. You?"

"Fine. Good. Listen, are you working?"

She shook her head. "Not today."

"Any interest in driving out to Gray and going for a walk?"

Panic.

"Today?" she blurted.

His brow knit. "We don't have—I just wanted to apologize for—"

"I want to!"

She startled them both to silence, Sarah's face garnet, Michael's mouth open around a stillborn question.

"It's just,"—she shifted her weight, pushed a foot forward— "my ankle's a little sore from my last run."

His eyes fell to her foot, rose to her face. "Are you okay?"

She nodded, still flush.

"You're not mad about last night?"

She shook her head.

"I know it was weird, I—"

"It's okay."

He stared at her, unbelieving, but without any idea of what else to say. "Are you staying?" she asked.

"I can have a cup of coffee."

They chose a table. Michael pulled his magazine from his back pocket and unrolled it; Sarah took a book from her bag.

Twenty minutes passed. She felt his eyes moving over her and realized she hadn't once turned a page, did so, and fixed her gaze tight on the print, and even though she was screaming silent prayers to god that he wouldn't, she felt the air between them change, and knew he was going to ask if she was okay, and that she wouldn't be able to answer, even though she obviously wasn't. He would think that she was angry about what had happened at the theater, but she wasn't, wasn't worried about it at all, but she couldn't explain that, because then she'd have to tell him she was terrified of going for a walk with him, and he'd think she was crazy, because they'd walked together a dozen times, and it would only make it worse if she told him that there was a difference between walking *to*, and walking *for*, and that all their previous walking had been for the purpose of walking *to* somewhere, but now he was asking her to go walking for the sake of walking. For the sake of walking with him.

But Michael closed his mouth without speaking, and the air between them slid back into itself. Sarah exhaled the breath she'd been holding. She could see Michael reading out of the corner of her eye, mouthing the words.

She couldn't make herself read.

He spooked her, ten, twenty minutes later when he touched her, lightly, on the wrist.

"I have to go," he said.

"But, I thought we… Weren't we going to… It's Thursday, right? You don't work Thursdays."

"We are, if you still want to. I'll only be gone a few hours. I'm covering part of a co-worker's shift so he can see his kid's Little League game."

"Oh."

"Do you still want to go?"

She nodded.

"Pick you up after work?"

She nodded, smiled.

"Okay." He rolled up his magazine and stuck it in his back pocket. "See you then."

She watched as he walked away, counting his steps, gauging their length, until two children flew in front of him, forcing him to stagger and twist sideways in order to avoid a collision. Tears burned the backs of her eyes. How would she know how to walk with him, now? She threw her book in her backpack and hurried through the store, breaking into a run as she hit the open air.

Sarah slowed to a fast walk as she reached the town library, crossed the parking lot toward the entrance, took two steps into the foyer and caught her foot on the lip of the welcome mat, stumbling just as the door leading into the library opened. "Look out!" she yelled as she came through the doorway out of control, lurching sideways to avoid colliding with the woman leaving. Her legs tangled and she pitched forward into the circulation desk; three globules of sweat leapt in arcs from her forehead, landed on the librarian's lapel and keyboard. She stammered, tried to apologize, fled, clinging to the task at hand. She found the books she thought she'd need as quickly as she could, checked them out without looking at the librarian, and left.

Home, she took the books from her backpack and sat at her desk. Between *Galloway's Book on Running*, *Gray's Anatomy*, and the Army field manual on land navigation she learned that one could calculate the average person's stride by multiplying his height by .4.

Michael was sixty-nine inches tall.

She was seventy-six.

Seventy-six. Sarah hated the number; it spat at her: *Freak.*

She couldn't keep the tears at bay any longer, set her pen down, laid her head atop her arms, and cried into the table.

Afterward, she did the math.

Sixty-nine multiplied by .4 is 27.6; she marked out the intervals between Michael's steps on the kitchen floor. Seventy-six multiplied by .4 is 30.4.

She smiled.

She was only 2.8 inches from normal.

Sarah watched for him through the window; the sun sparked off the hood of his truck as he came over the hill, and she ran to the bathroom mirror one final time. She'd French-braided her hair into pigtails, because he'd said he liked them once. She was nervous, like she always was when they were together or about to be together, nervous and excited and afraid, but also happy. She knew that she'd be looking out the window of his truck, soon, trying to hide how worked up she was, staring through the window and feeling confused, watching the brick and wood and stone of the familiar world exist as they always had, but differently, too, now, gilt at the edges with some mysterious, not-quite-invisible quality. She and Michael would take roads they'd traveled countless times, pass the same people they knew from the bank and supermarket and gas station. They'd take 295 to Portland, get off at Franklin, and park near the movie theater. Or they'd head north to

Brunswick and the places they frequented there. Wherever they went, it would be familiar, but different, too: a wooden bench with a well-worn plaque overlooking the River, the Polish restaurant in the pale purple building that she'd walked past every day and never seen, the magazine rack tucked at the very back of the bookstore where Samuel had her put all the sports magazines, the dilapidated boxing gym on Forest Ave. New-old places and new-old things, things that she was just now noticing—like aftershave. It had been on the bathroom shelf with Brad's stuff, and in the grocery store next to the hairgel and fancy shampoo, and at the pharmacy beside the shaving cream. She'd fallen asleep during one of the movies she and Michael had gone to, woken up with her head on his shoulder, and there had been this scent that made her feel warm and safe, but also like her mind was carbonated. She asked Michael about it after the movie, said how good it smelled, and had he noticed it, and did he know what it was. He turned red, and Sarah was confused, and when he didn't answer, she assumed she'd done something very wrong, but then he smiled at her as they walked out of the theater a few minutes later, so that didn't make sense. It was near ten o'clock when they left the theater, and cold. Sarah was shivering, so Michael took off his coat and draped it over her shoulders.

And there it was.

Aftershave.

Michael wore it whenever they were together.

And now here he was.

"Hey," he said as she climbed into the truck.

"Hey."

He smiled at her, too much, looked away, embarrassed, put the truck in gear. They'd take route 115 out to Gray, pass a few farms, and wind through the pines until they got out near Libby Hill.

Her smile faded as she realized what he was wearing, a white sweatshirt beneath a brown canvas jacket, the hood pushed over the collar and falling down his back.

"You're going to need to change."

He laughed, put the truck in gear, and waited for a car to pass. "Not classy enough for you."

"Classy?" She squinted. "We should go back to your house so you can get something else."

"What if I like what I'm wearing?"

"You can't wear that."

"There's a dress code?"

"Sort of."

"You're messing with me."

"No," —she shook her head— "you can't wear that out in the woods right now. It's not safe."

His smile faded. "Not safe?"

"It's the wrong color."

"The wrong color?"

He turned left, headed toward Gray.

"Michael, please. You could get shot."

"Shot?"

"Yes." She nodded emphatically, made her hands into a gun.

His eyes narrowed. "For wearing the wrong colors?"

"Yes."

"By gangbangers?"

"What?"

"Gangsters."

"Who?"

"Viceroys, Black Disciples…"

She shook her head.

"Who's going to shoot me?"

"I don't know who."

"But you know I'd get shot for wearing brown and white?"

"It's November."

"Gang colors are seasonal here?"

"What?"

"What colors can I wear now?"

"Orange or yellow, like this." She pulled a neon orange stocking cap from her coat pocket and held it out to him. "Something bright."

"Or I'll get shot?"

"Possibly."

"Won't I be more visible if I wear orange?"

"Exactly."

"Won't that make me an easier target?"

She shook her head. "No one is going to shoot you if they can see you."

"You're telling me Maine gangsters only shoot what they can't see…"

"Not gangsters, hunt—"

"So I need to wear orange so that they don't not see me?"

She nodded.

He shook his head. "That doesn't make any sense."

"What?"

The lines around his eyes flexed. "How would they know where to aim?"

She was confused. "No one's aiming."

"But you said—" His voice disintegrated into laughter.

"What?"

He laughed harder.

"I don't understand…"

He tried to break it off, failed, covered his mouth with a fist.

"Michael? I..."

The tears welling in her eyes struck him stone sober; he pulled off the side of the road, turned around. They drove in silence until they reached his house.

"I was just playing."

She nodded, silent.

"I'm sorry."

She reined herself in as the moments passed; she wiped the tears from her eyes before they could fall.

"It's okay. I know you didn't mean anything."

"I didn't."

She gave a short, shy smile. "I know."

"Are you okay?"

She nodded. Another shy smile.

"Were you messing with me the whole time?"

"Not the whole time."

"When?"

His eyes fell to the floor. "Right after you said it wasn't safe. I remembered a story I heard on the radio last week."

She winced. "I can be very literal sometimes."

"What's that?"

"What?"

"Literal."

"It just means that I don't always get jokes."

"Then I won't tease you again."

"Yes, you will."

She spoke without inflection, face downcast, cut in a rueful mask.

A blade of pain cut through his chest, caught in his throat. "Sarah..."

She turned toward him, eyes large and wide, hesitant to been seen.

"I didn't mean—"

The corner of her mouth trembled. He waited for her to speak, but she wouldn't, covered her face with her hands.

"I would never hurt you..."

His voice trailed off. She was shaking. He didn't know what to do, lifted a hand to lay on her shoulder, dropped it, blanched. "Sarah, I— I'm sorry, I—"

She pulled her hands away from her face, grinning. "Gotcha."

He shook his head slowly, smiling despite himself.

She laughed.

"You're all kinds of trouble."

"I'm a quick study."

CHAPTER FIFTY-FOUR

"Tighter. Keep your hands up."

They'd been working out together for a while, three days a week. She was left-handed like he was, which made things easier. He circled slowly as she hit the bag: jab, jab, cross. Jab, jab, cross.

"Chin down, hands up. Protect your face."

He gave her his full attention, didn't train while he was training her. He took it slow, more slowly than she needed, but he wanted to be thorough. He showed her how to wrap her hands, how to stand, how to move, how to punch. He taught her to draw force up through her legs and into her core, and to exhale forcefully as she struck so that the energy charged up her arm and exploded into her target. He trained afterwards, while she watched.

"Time."

Sarah's hands dropped, her chest heaving. He helped her get her gloves off.

"Good job."

She nodded, sat on the weight bench, still panting.

"You get better every time."

She nodded, tried to smile through her fatigue.

"You still hit like a girl, but—"

She took a token swipe at him, arms leaden.

He smiled.

"Mean."

He laughed. "True."

She liked training; it made her body less of a prison, less like a cruel joke. She made it hurt, forced it through the pain, and it became hers, something she owned rather than something that owned her.

She'd wanted to run away the first time he'd taken her into the garage: the air was thick, smelled of him, of his deodorant and sweat, and of metal and leather. His gear was neatly set up and in its place, but everywhere, hanging from walls on metals hooks, and from the ceiling, sitting on stands in the corners, laying atop racks that ran the length of the wall: medicine balls, wrist wraps, leather jump ropes with wood and metal handles, a half-dozen pairs of boxing gloves. A heavy bag hung from the rafters on chains, and there was a speed bag bolted to two two-by-fours, dumbbells, a bench press, and weight plates. The gear was devoid of any flourish, all function. It all seemed hard and dark and menacing, and since she'd never seen most of the equipment before, she asked him to demonstrate how to use it. He forgot her presence even before he threw a punch, minutes into his rope routine, with sweat just beginning to lather on his skin. That might have been what had scared her the most, how totally he controlled his vision, how quickly he reduced his world. He rehung the rope, put on his wraps and gloves without acknowledging her, took up his stance, and erupted; the sound of his fists against the bag exploded against her.

His movements now were the same as then, the elements identical: sweat, power, and aggression, leather cracking beneath his fists, the chains going slack as his blows jacked the bag into the air, shrieking as the bag crashed back down, but familiar, now, even comforting.

"We should shower," she said when they finished.

He pinched his nose, stifled a laugh. "You should go first."

She was about to thank him, stopped short. "Did you just..."

He shook his head. "Never."

"Liar."

He waved away the air between them, wrinkled his nose.

"Mean," she said, smiling.

She stayed over for the first time that night. He washed his sheets and made up his bed for her, slept on the couch. They were both awake by five-thirty, Michael to workout in the garage, Sarah to go for her run. He was in the shower when she returned; she waited in the kitchen. "I put a towel and washcloth on top of the sink for you."

"Thank you."

His bathroom was meticulously kept, though the vanity didn't quite latch. She couldn't resist looking in: floss, a straight razor, shaving cream and a brush, aftershave, mouthwash, all equidistant from each other.

Light gleamed off the toilet and the sink basin.

She started to undress and stopped, looked around wildly; it felt suddenly as if the room had eyes. She turned on the water first, to build her resolve, waited for it to turn hot, peeled off her clothes.

The shower was pristine as well, grout and tub scrubbed white, a slight smell of bleach, washcloth and brush hanging from hooks. He had shampoo and conditioner on a shelf built into the corner. The fact that it was dandruff shampoo made her feel better somehow.

"Can I make you breakfast?" he asked when she was done and dressed.

"I could eat."

"Me too."

"Do you want help?"

"No need."

"What should I do?"

"Hang out."

"Okay."

She'd been over enough that she was comfortable, walked into the living room and stretched out on the couch with a book. Michael was almost always in motion, going through his checklist: doors and windows locked, blinds open if the sun was out, drawn if it was after dark, microwave and coffee maker and dish soap and the three pictures hanging on the walls all at right angles. He owned four coffee mugs he kept in the cabinet, evenly spaced, handles facing to the left, four plates, four bowls, four glasses, forks, knives, and spoons, and a dish drainer he never used because he washed and dried everything immediately upon use. She would read as he progressed through his list, often beginning again as soon as he completed it.

"Food's ready."

Her bookmark was one of the few artifacts of her mother's life that remained, a violet in ink and watercolor on stiff stock, two inches wide and six inches long. She placed it between the pages and set the book on the end table.

"Chocolate chip pancakes?"

He nodded. "The whipped cream's in the refrigerator."

"That's my favorite."

"I know."

"Thank you."

"Eat them before they get cold."

She put a dollop of whipped cream on each bite, held the pieces in her mouth until the chocolate and whipped cream melted, swallowed, and grinned.

"You look like you're having a good time over there."

She blushed, nodded.

"Good."

He wouldn't let her help him clean up afterwards.

"Do you have to work today?"

She shook her head. She knew he didn't have to either.

"Do you want to do something?"

She nodded.

"Anything in particular?"

She shook her head.

He finished the dishes, poured himself more coffee, joined her on the couch.

"Any ideas?"

She thought. "Bowling?"

"Bowling?" He frowned slightly. "Never been."

"Me either."

His eyes fell to the floor, came back to her. "Might be fun."

"I've always wanted to try it." She yawned.

"Sleepy?"

"A little."

"Want to take a nap first? I've got some stuff I can do in the garage."

She shook her head.

"No?"

She shook her head again, turned her body sideways, and laid her head on his thigh. Neither of them breathed.

He took the afghan off the couch and laid it over her, watched her tuck it under her chin, smile up at him, turn away and curl up. He set a hand on her thigh, removed it immediately, laid it on her arm, then on the couch back. He let his fingers touch her hair, brushed the backs of his fingers along her hairline.

She sighed and shivered, pressed her cheek into his jeans.

He touched her ear, ran his thumb and forefinger along the lobe, knowing he shouldn't.

Shouldn't.

Juan-Pablo Ortega: his first shouldn't, the first fighter to enter the ring with him, fall, and never get up.

Michael saw the blow that killed him, sometimes, when he closed his eyes. Ortega's eyes went dark just before the fist hit his temple; Michael heard bone shattering as Ortega's mouth guard shot sideways.

Ortega shouldn't have been in the ring with him. Michael knew it even before the fight. It was a career move—that was how it worked: sharks ate chum in order to get a shot at other sharks.

Ortega was the first, not the last.

Michael landed three punches before his opponents could throw one, all of them concussive, too hard, even. At twelve, he threw a punch with such force that it tore his biceps off the bone, costing him close to a year of training. Not all training, though: two weeks after surgery he was working on his footwork six days a week, grinding his teeth through the pain.

Ortega, Freeman, and Kowalski were the first three.

Up and comers, young, ambitious, hungry, just like he was.

Who knows what they would have become, given a little time.

He shouldn't have fought them.

Shouldn't.

CHAPTER FIFTY-FIVE

"You didn't come home last night," Lewella accused.

It was six o'clock in the morning. There were no preliminaries—Lewella didn't even wait for Sarah to sit down, just pounced as soon as she came through the diner door.

Sarah shook her head.

"Well?"

"I was at a friend's house."

"Curfew is eleven o'clock."

" I—I wasn't going to make it back in time, so I crashed at my friend's."

"Apparently you don't understand what the word curfew means."

"I—"

"It means your butt is in the apartment, in your pajamas, with the door locked."

"I'm sorry, I didn't—I thought it was so I didn't wake you up when I came in."

"No, young lady, it's to keep you from staying out all night and getting your pretty little butt in trouble."

"I... I really didn't know. I'm sorry—it won't happen again."

"You're damn right it won't, because if it does, I'm going to have to start docking your allowance."

"Docking it?"

"Fifty cents for every minute you're late."

Sarah stared.

"Am I being clear?"

Sarah nodded.

"I want to hear you say it."

"I understand, Lewella."

"Alright then. So who's this friend of yours?"

"Michael."

Lewella scowled. "Michael Tolan? As in, thirty something years old, lives alone, Michael Tolan?"

Sarah nodded.

"You spent the night with him?"

She nodded, saw Lewella seething, stopped. "No," she said quickly.

"Girl, you better start making sense or you'll be feeling the back of my hand right quick."

"No. I slept in his bed, and he slept on the couch."

"You slept on his bed?"

"He changed the sheets."

"I don't give a good god damn about the sheets!"

"He was on the couch!"

"Did he touch you?"

"No!"

The door opened and the bell rang, and two four-tops walked in, forcing Lewella to turn away from Sarah to tend to them, and since Sarah was a regular, and Jesús, the cook, had seen her come in, her order was up moments later.

She ate quickly.

"Ain't no running from me, girl," Lewella said, catching her in the act of inhaling her granola.

"I wasn't running."

"Right."

"It's just... I have a test today, and I want to get some studying in before school."

"What class?"

"Calculus."

Lewella frowned.

"I do. You can call the school."

"I just may."

Another group of customers entered, again drawing Lewella away. She returned in a more sanguine mood. "I'm sorry if I was a little gruff before," she said. "I forget how young you are, sometimes."

Sarah was silent.

"You haven't learned how things work yet, how men work."

"Michael's—"

"They do things, make you think that they're different than they really are."

"I don't understand."

"They don't tell you what they're really after up front, then they put pressure on you, make you feel like you owe them..."

Lewella's voice trailed off, but Sarah remained silent, uncertain whether she should speak and desperate to leave, but not sure she was allowed.

"I'm just trying to look out for you, is all," Lewella said.

"Thank you."

"Now go study, make those A's."

Sarah hurried away, out the door and into the dawning day.

"So when do I get to meet him?""Michael?"

Chelsea nodded. She was Sarah's only friend, an outcast, too, unlike her sister who was Miss Congeniality and the Homecoming Queen and everything else. Sarah was spending the night in order to avoid Lewella, but had made sure to leave a note at the diner telling her where she was, and giving her the number there.

Chelsea's mother had actually come into the room they were in to let her know Lewella had called. "She's a little intense," Mrs. Powers had said.

Sarah had only nodded.

"She wanted to know if there were going to be any boys visiting tonight, and I told her no. And then she asked specifically about a Michael Tolan. Do either of you girls know him? She says he's pretty bad news."

Sarah winced. "He's a friend of mine."

"Oh?" Miss Powers seemed interested. "A good friend?"

"We go to the movies every once in a while."

"Oh," Mrs. Powers said, taking a disappointed sip of the cocktail in her hand. "Well, that's no fun."

"Sorry about my mom," Chelsea said after her mother left.

"No problem." Sarah assured her.

Chelsea had gotten ahold of some vodka, mixed it with Kool-Aid, and after the first glass both girls' eyes were dancing, words falling clumsily from their lips.

"So," Chelsea said, "like I was asking earlier, when do I get to meet him?"

Sarah sat cross-legged across from her, holding her glass in her lap. "Um…"

"I can't wait to meet him—I hear he's hot."

Sarah laughed.

"What?"

"Nothing. I don't know—I don't think he'd be in a hurry to hang out with high school girls."

Chelsea screwed up her face. "Excuse me, all this time I thought you were a high school girl."

Sarah was staring down into her drink. "Exactly."

"You know what the best thing about you is?"It was Saturday, shortly before five o'clock; they'd fled Port Haven, driven an hour north along the coast.

Michael pointed at an apple dangling from a high branch. Sarah reached up and pulled it down, handed it to him. She waited for the answer, watching him as he scanned the tree.

"I don't need a ladder to get the good apples."

He might as well have hit her.

Michael finished inspecting the tree, oblivious, moved to the next.

Sarah made herself follow.

He shifted the bag from his right hand to his left and startled her by taking hers, by threading his fingers between hers, letting their hands dangle between them as her eyes combed his face.

"What?"

The sun was nearly gone. Fog ambled in off the sea, drops of water hanging in the air like Christmas bulbs, passing the hues of sunset from one globule to the next. They stopped walking, watched the fog envelop the apples and trees around them in quivering color.

"What?"

She shook her head, didn't answer. They watched the light bleed out of the sky, let the night swallow them. It was Sarah's dream realized in the conscious world: she was invisible. There was no world and no one else to see her; she wasn't too tall or too thin or too pale, only a hand Michael was holding.

"Am I your girlfriend?"

The words fell timidly despite the hours they'd spent together, the times she'd slipped out of her apartment late at night to spend the night with him. She'd stayed over enough over the past three weeks that he'd bought another bed and converted the office into a bedroom. They'd fallen asleep on the couch a couple times while a movie played, woken to find themselves intertwined. He always made them breakfast in the morning.

Sarah felt herself being pulled around at the waist, pressed into him, felt a hand slide up her back, between her shoulder blades, over her neck. She felt pressure, yielded, dizzy with their proximity and the scent of his aftershave, holding her breath as his mouth closed gently over her lip. His stubble scraped her chin. She kissed him until she wobbled.

"Am I?"

She let herself see movement in her mind's eye, feel the air flex.

Neither of them spoke.

Muted light hung in the distance.

—⚔—

Sarah tried not to be too obvious about her interest in Miss White. She'd asked both Lewella and Samuel about her, but neither of them had been willing or able to tell her much beyond a few cursory biographical facts, amazing though they were. Sarah had been by Miss White's old place on Bayview Street, but the property had been sold and subdivided into four plots, and nothing of the farm on which she'd grown up remained. Lewella said she traveled a lot, and that she mostly split her time between Florida and Boston when she wasn't. She appeared more frequently in Port Haven between June and September, but not usually more than one or two weekends a month.

She hadn't been explicitly told not to approach Miss White, though both Lewella and Samuel had described her as quiet, and very private. They'd said it would only embarrass her if Sarah thanked her for her generosity in person, and that even a thank you note was unnecessary, but Sarah had bought stationery and written her a detailed note thanking her benefactor for everything she'd done for her, and describing the classes she'd taken at the college on Miss White's dime.

She really wanted to approach Miss White now, but she had to leave for school soon, and she seemed locked in a rather intense conversation with the man she was with—Parker was the name Sarah thought she'd overheard—and Lewella seemed to be hovering nearby.

Finally, Sarah left, disappointed that she hadn't been able to speak to Miss White, but heartened, too, because from what she'd seen, she and Miss White weren't entirely dissimilar—yes, Sarah was freakishly tall, and Miss White was super short, and yes, Sarah had pale skin and red hair, and Miss White had dark skin and dark hair, but the point was that neither of them was what you might call beautiful, neither of them met any of the standards by which women might come to be considered ideal, and yet, Miss White had done all these amazing things, had built a life worthy of envy.

Miss White gave Sarah reason to hope.

She went to school, and from school to practice, and after showering, went directly to the diner for an early dinner. Lewella took her order as always and brought Sarah her food, and only after Sarah had eaten and her dishes had been cleared did Lewella tell her that Miss White had left something for her. Sarah had to wait until Lewella had a moment, which meant sitting on one of the counter stools for more than thirty minutes twiddling her thumbs, but then Lewella appeared with five large books: leather-bound copies of the photography collections Miss White had published, which Sarah hadn't known existed, but for which she would have been willing to wait for days.

CHAPTER FIFTY-SIX

Samuel rose and rose; Sarah trembled. "Please," she begged. "I need it... I need you. Take me—please."

He knew it was a dream. He was rising like a god, marble-hard, veined and throbbing.

"Please."

He touched her arm, her tiny shoulder, her belly. It was lightning and thunder; sparks leapt. She moaned, quaked.

He delved lower...

CHAPTER FIFTY-SEVEN

"Do you think he's above board?" Tori asks.

"Who?"

"Samuel."

Tolan lets the *Vogue* she's been reading fall to her lap. "Why?"

"I don't know, he's awfully nice to Sarah."

"He knows she's all alone; he's just being nice."

Tori's eyes fall away. "Maybe. But those fantasies—"

"Dreams," Tolan interrupts. "Fantasies are intentional. And he only had the one, and he was horrified."

"Yes, but…"

"But…?"

"Never mind."

"But…?" Tolan insists.

"Forget it."

"You think he does something, don't you? Something bad? What about Michael? He's the one trying to get in her pants."

Tori makes a face. "What do you mean, trying to get in her pants? He hasn't done anything except kiss her that one time."

Tolan's head falls with a hard sigh, breaking off eye contact; she stares, unseeing, at the magazine, lips pursed, head shaking minutely. She winces, looks up.

"This is really starting to fuck with me."

Tori nods. "How could it not? It's your mother."

CHAPTER FIFTY-EIGHT

January. They were in the garage, still gasping from their run, their breath freezing in the air.

"You're going to kill me."

She smiled, still shy despite months of movies and car rides, weeks of running and training together. He turned on the space heater and the overhead light, peeled off the polypropylene jacket she'd convinced him to buy. She removed her headband and unzipped her jacket, folded them, and set them in her gym bag.

"Have your wraps?"

She held them up, sat on the weight bench, and began to put them on as he watched.

"Tighter."

His eyes were serious, focused, his breath settled, chest rising and falling as normal, shirt clinging to his body.

"I know you don't like it," Michael said as he moved toward her, "but you're starting to hit harder now. You're going to get blisters if you don't do it right."

He took her hand, unwound what she had done.

"Stand up."

She stood.

"Like I showed you, loop over your thumb, wrap on the outside."

He motioned her to come around the bench, turned her so she was facing away from him. She felt heat before pressure; his hipbone pressed against the down-slope of her butt, his chest against her back.

"Sit back down, I can't see around you." She cringed. "Here," —he pointed— "on the bench."

She felt pressure on her shoulders and sat, felt his breath hot against her ear and cheek.

"Now carry it inside, up and over your wrist." He pushed closer to her; she felt the points of his nipples against her scapulae, his arms reaching under hers and pressing her ribcage. His stubble scratched her neck as he craned his head forward over her shoulder, holding her arm in his right hand, the wrap in his left. "Take it around your wrist again."

She felt his focus, the intensity of his concise, fluid movements. Sweat fell down her back, her ponytail damp against her neck; she imagined the droplets sliding from her back onto his chest, down his abdomen.

"Take it up along your hand and under your pinky finger." His movements layered fabric on her hand more quickly than she could follow. "Now bring it under your…"

Sarah looked at the heater, felt… dizzy, craned her head up, found his eyes full of… surprise? Fear? He fumbled the wrap and it hit the ground, rolled, unfurling across the cement floor. His arms collapsed around her, held her against him. Without losing his eyes, Sarah brought her free hand up and ran it down his cheek and along his jaw line; she pulled him to her until their faces touched and they could feel each other's heat and pulse.

Michael kissed her earlobe.

Sarah closed her eyes.

She was raising her head, feeling everything, the hum of the light bulb and the air running over her skin, his breath against her cheek, his stubble against her lips, the salt of his sweat on her lips, his arms and his chest pressing her.

He pulled her up off the bench; panic impaled her: she was too tall. She'd rise right past him.

It was over.

She was a freak.

But she wasn't a freak, at least not then. His hands were on her hips, and his fingers swept over the swell of her buttocks and down, cupped her, lifted. Her feet left the ground; her legs locked around his waist. There was a brace of frigid air as he opened the garage door, and the bite of the cold as he carried her toward the house. Inside, the sudden warmth made her dizzy. He laid her across his bed; they hesitated. She closed her eyes; he swallowed hard, leaned in.

She hadn't known you could taste heat.

She awoke disoriented, head rising and falling on his chest, the flesh of her cheek hot, sticking to his skin. Her senses asserted themselves piecemeal, in no particular order, yielded one detail at a time: there were curtains hiding in the shadows, a dresser; the pressure across her back was Michael's arm. His breath waxed and waned in a slow, hypnotic cycle; she followed a line from the darkness into a sliver of moonlight and found his right wrist, its fingers curling back over his palm. The air was thick with his scent, with hers—theirs—pungent and humiliating and exhilarating all at once. She lifted her head slightly, worried her movement would wake him, felt the morning air against her chest and realized she was naked, flattened herself against him. She was surprised at how neat everything was; in the movies the covers were always in knots, clothes strewn about the room, but everything was orderly, here, the sheets and comforter square on the bed, clothes in a neat pile on the floor beside them. She wondered how she might extricate herself and get to them.

"Time to run?"

She froze.

"Good morning." He spoke tentatively, asking.

She craned her neck upward slowly, not wanting to expose her breasts; he brought his hand to her face, traced its contours gently with the back of his fingertips. Her hair was loose, fell over her shoulder onto the bed.

"Good morning," she breathed.

They wanted to kiss. She would have to prop herself up on her elbow to do it properly, the way they'd kissed last night; she forced herself, focusing on his lips, their strength and warmth, trying to ignore the cold air and the fact that it was making her nipples rise.

"Going for a run?"

His voice was thick with the dregs of sleep, apprehensive, his eyes searching for her face beneath the shadows.

She nodded.

"Are you coming back?"

She nodded again, a short, subtle drop of her chin, smiled.

"Good."

She found him in the garage just over an hour and a half later, finishing his workout. She'd run thirteen miles; he'd lifted, jumped rope, and worked the bags. They were sweaty and shy and uncertain, shivering by the time they made it into the house because they'd stood so long in the cold trying to talk. He stripped off his shirt, meaning to switch it out for a dry t-shirt and make waffles and coffee, but he saw her watching him and stepped toward her instead, scooped her off the ground, and kissed her, leaned back, waiting, asking her something in a language she didn't know. She touched his face, and he smiled; she slid her hands around his head and into his hair, bent to kiss him. Then they were in the bathroom without knowing how they got there: he lifted her arms, pulled her shirt and bra over her head, stepped closer. She fumbled with the drawstring of his sweatpants, not looking down, untied it, and let them fall. Then they were kissing again, and he scooped her off the ground again, and she wrapped her legs around his waist again, neither of them thinking, only feeling him grow and press into her spandex. And then they were in the shower, naked, crushed against each other, the water pulsing, near scalding. And that was it.

No penetration, grind, or moan. No arched backs.

He kissed the top of her head, the hollow of her throat.

They held each other until the water ran cold.

CHAPTER FIFTY-NINE

Sarah locked the door behind her and turned to leave.

Lewella was at the base of the stairs. "Where are you going?"

"To a friend's house."

"At a quarter to ten? An hour before curfew."

Sarah nodded, gave a small smile, descended two steps.

"Which friend?" Lewella demanded.

"Michael," she said quietly.

"Michael Tolan?" Her eyes narrowed.

Sarah nodded.

"What's in the bag?"

Sarah looked at the strap of the backpack as if she were surprised to find herself carrying it.

"Clothes for tomorrow and my school books."

"You're staying the night?"

Sarah blushed, nodded, put her head down and attempted to walk past her. Lewella thrust her arm out.

"I'm not buying the separate bed bullshit, Sarah."

"Look, I'm just—"

"No! You look, girl. You have no idea what you're getting yourself into, what he's actually after."

"You have no idea what I know and don't know!"

"Okay, Sarah. Fine. Since you know so much, tell me why a man in his thirties wants to spend time with a sixteen year-old girl."

"He cares about me!"

"I'll bet he does."

"I don't know what you want me to say."

"He just wants to fuck you, you idiot! He wants to take you and use you and have his way, and when he's done, he'll toss you aside."

"That's not true."

"Don't you talk back to me, girl; I'm trying to help you."

"I don't need help."

"Yes, you do. You just don't know it yet."

"You're wrong! If he were like that, he'd be gone already!"

"What did you say?"

"I—"

"What has he done to you?"

Her voice was a rasp, anger rising through pinholed pupils over brown-black irises rimmed with copper.

"Nothing!"

Lewella stepped closer.

"Did he take advantage of you?"

She shook her head.

"Don't lie to me, girl."

Sarah tried to flee, ducked under her arm but Lewella caught her wrist.

"He did something to you."

She shook her head again.

"What did he make you do?"

Sarah flushed garnet.

"We'll put a stop to it—I'll call the police, I'll—he won't ever touch you again."

Sarah yanked her hand free and ran.

Michael picked up one of the books Sarah had left and looked at the clock. It'd been nearly an hour since she called to say she'd be right over. The doorbell rang; he set the book down and moved toward the door. It rang again."I'm coming." He hurried. "It's not that cold—" His smile vanished.

"Michael Tolan?"

The cops' uniforms were heavily starched, navy blue with yellow piping, badges shined and gleaming in the lamplight.

"Yes."

"You're under arrest for the assault and rape of Sarah Smith."

"What?"

There were two of them, a man and a woman. The he-cop twisted Michael's hands behind his back and cuffed him while the she-cop stood two yards behind with her hand on her gun. The metal bit into Michael's wrists.

"Who said that—did she say that?"

The cop-lights burned red and white as neighbors watched through their windows, eyes crawling over him until the officer shoved him into the backseat and slammed the door. A man came over.

"You know I can't tell you anything, Henry," the cop said, waving him away. "Go back inside."

The man shrugged and turned back, and the cop climbed into his cruiser, started the engine, and drove off. They turned left onto Main Street and disappeared from sight, and the neighbors closed their curtains.

CHAPTER SIXTY

She didn't know what else to do, who else she could go to—not Michael, not right now. She'd never been to Samuel's house, but it was a small town, and she knew he lived a mile or two beyond the shop, toward the sea. It was cold, but not bitterly.

"Sarah?"

She looked up sharply, startled; she hadn't noticed the headlights.

"Samuel?"

He motioned. "Get in, you must be freezing. In the back, Bill."

Samuel looked her over: her nose was running, she was pallid, her eyes and cheek were wet with tears.

"Are you okay?"

She tried to answer, couldn't speak, shook her head.

"What happened?"

She swallowed, rubbed the heels of her palms against her eyes, choked.

"I think Michael's in trouble."

"Michael?"

She nodded, eyes on the floorboards.

"Lewella thinks he did something to me."

"What? Why?"

Silence.

"Sarah?"

"I was going to his house. She saw me. I had a bag."

"When?"

"Tonight. An hour ago."

Color rushed to her cheeks as the heat revived her.

"She's going to call the police."

"I guess we'd better go down there."

Sarah nodded.

Samuel pulled into the next driveway and reversed course. Sarah watched absently as the street slid by. Ahead, the bank's digital clock read 12:4-, the last number obscured behind a maple. They turned off at the police station, parked, and walked through two sets of doors and into the harsh fluorescent light of the lobby.

"Karl?" Samuel said.

The night watchman looked up from his Sudoku and broke into a grin, set down the brownie he was eating.

"Samuel!"

The policeman brushed the crumbs from his desk into his hand and tossed them at the trashcan.

"Working hard, I see," Samuel teased.

The man laughed. "Someone's got to."

He looked from Samuel to Sarah and his face went grave.

"Miss Smith?"

Sarah nodded.

The clerk looked to Samuel. "Has she been to the hospital?"

"Is Michael here?" Sarah asked.

The policeman looked at her quizzically.

"Who?"

"Michael Tolan." Her voice quivered.

"We've got him locked up, Miss Smith. There's nothing to be afraid of. He can't hurt you."

"He didn't hurt me."

Her head dropped, her face burning scarlet.

"What?"

The clerk fumbled for a folder, opened it.

"It says here that he…" —the man looked at Samuel— "…that he… assaulted you."

"No," she said to the floor.

"But—"

"He didn't." She looked up, directly at him. "Can I see him?"

"But—there must have been an altercation…"

She shook her head.

"There's been a mistake, Karl, that's all."

"But—" He turned back to Sarah. "He didn't attack you?"

"No."

They held each other's eyes.

"But you said—" he looked at the report.

"I didn't say anything."

"Someone said—"

"Not me."

The man turned back to Samuel. "She'll have to make a statement."

Samuel nodded.

"Can I see him?" Sarah repeated.

The officer frowned, looked from her to Samuel, and nodded.

"One minute." He shuffled a few papers, disappeared into a closet, and came back with a ring of keys. "This way."

Sarah and Samuel followed him down a corridor to a staircase and into the basement, rounded a corner, and walked past a row of empty cells. Michael was at the far end, leaning against the wall.

"Michael?"

He turned.

"I'm so sorry."

She was crying as she walked, but he didn't respond, just looked at her, jaw set in a hard line.

"I didn't—"

Her voice choked, his silence violent as they stared at each other through the bars between them. Samuel stood at the periphery of the room, head down, shifting his weight.

"Are you okay?" Sarah's voice was thin, hoarse. "I—I'm so sorry this —"

The policeman entered the room frowning at a clipboard. "Everything alright here?"

Michael grit his teeth.

"Okay, then." The officer unlocked the cell door and handed a clipboard to Sarah. "Initial here, here, and sign here, and he's free to go."

She took the clipboard and pen.

Samuel stepped forward. "What happened, Karl?"

"We got a call reporting an assault and possible kidnapping."

Sarah's eyes darted from Michael to the policeman and back; she trembled, teetered; Samuel moved closer to her, just in case.

"Who?" Michael spoke without unclenching his jaw, tooth biting into tooth.

"I'm not at liberty to say."

"That's bullshit."

"Watch it, Mr. Tolan."

Michael set his jaw, silent. Sarah finished her paperwork and handed the clipboard to the policeman, who glanced it over and turned to unlock Michael's cell. "You'll need to come to the desk to sign for your things," the policeman said to Michael.

Afterward, the three of them walked wordlessly out of the police station into the cold and gathered by Samuel's truck. Michael moved unconsciously, stone-faced, and Sarah's eyes never left him. They stood in silence staring at the ground, the winter cold settling deep into their bones; Michael was absolutely still and blank, Sarah clutched herself, Samuel kicked at a piece of pavement into the grass.

"Can I give you a ride?" Samuel asked.

He spoke to the space between them.

Michael frowned, seeming to search for the origin of the voice, tracing it back to Samuel at great effort.

"I'll be alright."

Samuel nodded.

"Thank you."

"Sarah?"

"You should take her." Michael's voice was empty.

"I can walk," she said.

He shook his head. "It's cold."

"But…" she began.

Michael shook his head. "No. Not tonight."

Samuel's eyes moved from Michael to Sarah. "It might be better," Samuel said, "considering."

She nodded.

"Okay," Samuel said.

Michael was silent, stood motionless as Sarah and Samuel got into the truck and drove away.

CHAPTER SIXTY-ONE

"What the hell do you mean there's nothing you can do? For Christ sake, Mitchell, she's sixteen."

H. Mitchell Swenson's desk was mahogany, wrapped in burgundy leather, a gift upon his retirement from the Connecticut Supreme Court. A print of Doepler's *Forseti Seated in Judgment* hung on the far wall.

Swenson removed his glasses and pinched the bridge of his nose, pressed his fingers together, took a deep breath.

"He hasn't broken the law, Lewella."

She scowled. "The hell he hasn't."

The frames surrounding Swenson's diplomas were gilded, his pen set silver-plated, the pipes in his pipe-holder hand-carved. The room was paneled in walnut and teak. The blinds were drawn. He eyed Lewella from behind a migraine, accustomed to deference, resenting her presence.

"I don't like it anymore than you do, but from a legal standpoint there's nothing anyone can do; he's within his rights."

"His rights? The right to rape young girls."

"That's a big word, Lewella." The judge could barely see through the pain.

"So that's that, then. We're just going to stand by and do nothing?"

Her hands were balled in fists; she gnashed her teeth.

"There's nothing to be done."

"The hell there isn't."

"Come again?"

She shook her head and stood, shaking with anger. "I goddamn will do something."

"The man has the law on his side."

"Always."

She left in a rage.

The diner phone rang. It was only Lewella now, even Jesús had left for the night. She lifted the phone from its cradle. "Hello?""It's Bo. I'm at the airport, and my flight leaves in less than an hour, so I can't talk long, but I got your message."

"I'm so goddamned angry right now, Bo! It's bad enough they released Tolan within an hour, and that he managed to somehow coerce the girl into denying he'd assaulted her, but I went and saw Swenson, and he says the law can't touch Tolan because, technically, Sarah's of age.

"What's the girl say?"

"I told you, she denies he did anything."

"Maybe he didn't."

"Are you serious, Bo? He's twice her age! I thought you of all people…"

"There's always someone trying to put words in a woman's mouth, Lew—are you sure it's not you this time?"

Lewella shook her head, holding the phone against her ear. "Yes."

"What if this is what the girl wants?"

"She's sixteen! He's thirty!"

"She's seventeen, now."

"No," Lewella said, shaking her head again. "I've seen his type before, I'm sure of it. I've got his number—I've had so many women come through the shelter running from shitheads. I just wanted to let you know I'm going to give the girl an ultimatum."

"And if she won't leave him?"

Lewella started pacing. "I'm prepared to cut her off, to change the locks to the apartment."

"You're sure about Tolan? I could ask around, if you want."

"He's bad news."

"You know if you kick her out and cut her off, you're pushing her right into his arms, right? She'll have no choice but to move in with him."

"I figure he balks, most likely; he wants to take a child for a ride, not support one."

"And if he doesn't?"

"Things'll go to shit one way or another."

"I've got to go, Lewella. I know you want what's best for the girl, so do what you think is right."

"Will do."

"Just don't do anything extreme until you've made sure you're right."

"Have I ever?"

"Take care, Lewella. We'll talk soon."

CHAPTER SIXTY-TWO

"Never?" Chelsea asked.

Sarah shook her head.

"Not once?"

"No. Why? When did you start?"

"Just after I turned twelve."

"Oh."

"Do you want me to come in with you?"

Sarah hesitated, nodded, horrified and grateful.

"Dr. Pierce said it wouldn't take long."

"No worries," Chelsea waved the comment away. "I'm not in a hurry."

The doctor's office was on Main Street, just past the town hall. Sarah checked in with the receptionist and took a seat next to Chelsea to wait. She'd been bleeding for ten days before she got up the nerve to make the appointment. She hadn't told the doctor that it was the first time, her first period, or that it had started the day after she and Michael first had sex.

It'd happened in the shower. There'd been spots on her leg when she woke up, and on the sheets, and at first she'd thought it was just more of that, but then it didn't stop.

"Menorrhagia," the doctor said after Sarah had described the symptoms, "most likely due to an imbalance between your estrogen and progesterone levels. Basically, what happens is that the endometrium—the uterine wall—builds up unchecked, and when it comes time to shed it during menstruation, the bleeding is exceptionally heavy."

The doctor asked her how bad it had been, and Sarah had turned crimson and told her that she'd been going through almost a dozen tampons a day.

"Are you in pain?"

She shrugged. "It's uncomfortable."

The doctor consulted her clipboard. "Is your mother here? I'd like to talk to her about implanting an intrauterine device—"

"Implanting?"

"It's a very brief procedure, almost painless."

218

"Almost?"

"Some women experience mild to moderate cramping. Is your mother here?"

"My mother passed away last year."

"I'm sorry to hear that." She shoved a lock of hair behind her ear. "What about your father?"

"He died when I was a baby."

They looked at each other.

"Any family—"

"Just me."

"But—"

"I'm emancipated. Legally."

It took the doctor a moment to recover and begin explaining the procedure.

Sarah and Chelsea were back at the doctor's office, waiting. "Are you on anything?"

"Me?" Chelsea rolled her eyes. "No way, my mom would flip if I even mentioned birth control."

"Oh."

"Good thing I don't have a boyfriend." She made a face.

"Sarah Smith?" The girls looked up to see a woman in scrubs reading off a clipboard.

"Right here." Sarah raised her hand.

"Follow me."

The woman led them to an empty room, took Sarah's vitals, and left. It was cold and antiseptic, with bare walls somewhere between cream and gray. Dr. Pierce appeared shortly, face buried in her chart. "Sarah…"

"Hi."

"Your tests came back negative for any STI's, so we're good to go."

She nodded.

The doctor set the clipboard on the counter and began to wash her hands. "I'm going to do a pelvic exam first to determine the shape and position of your uterus."

"Okay."

The doctor took a pair of latex gloves from a box and pulled them on. "I'll be using a speculum to hold your vagina open, and a grasping instrument to steady your cervix while I take measurements. I'll place the IUD by inserting a narrow tube through the opening of the cervix into the uterus, and leave a short length of nylon string hanging from the cervix into the vagina, which will allow me to check that the IUD has remained in place in future visits, and enable easy removal when the time comes. Any questions?"

Sarah paled, shook her head.

"As I said before, some women experience mild to moderate cramping during the procedure, but the whole thing rarely lasts more than five minutes."

"Can Chelsea stay?"

"Of course."

Twenty minutes later, they were walking out the door.

"You okay?" Chelsea asked flexing her hand.

"Yeah. Sorry about that."

"About what?"

"Your hand."

"You were holding on pretty tight."

"Sorry."

"No problem, I'm sure I'll be able to feel it again someday. Hey, how come Michael didn't come?"

"Michael?"

"What? This was kind of a big deal, right?"

Sarah didn't answer, kept on walking.

"You didn't tell him, did you?"

Sarah couldn't look at her friend. "He had to work."

Michael stood blinking as the bookstore slowly took form behind particles of light, fragments of color and line congealing and becoming a cash register, books, a rack of postcards. Samuel. "Is Sarah working?"

Samuel looked at the clock, back to Michael.

"She starts in twenty minutes."

"Thanks."

Samuel nodded.

The men stood awkwardly; Michael shoved his hand in his jean pockets.

"How is she?"

"Worried."

Michael looked up.

"Worried about you, and that Lewella is going to kick her out."

"Is she?"

The bell on the door jingled, and both men turned. Sarah came around the corner, a hand shielding her eyes.

"Hi, Samuel." She blinked, saw Michael, froze.

"Would you mind getting me some pens from the office?"

"What?" She was confused momentarily, then understood, nodded, and headed to the office.

Michael followed.

"Hey," he said when the door had shut behind him.

She was silent.

"Are you okay?"

She nodded. "Are you?"

He nodded.

Their eyes met and darted away from each other. Sarah wore a heavy sweater over a turtleneck, had wrapped herself in her arms.

He kicked at an invisible speck on the carpet. "Haven't seen you for a minute."

"Three days."

She forced herself to look at him.

"I—"

"You needed time. You were mad."

"At you?"

She nodded. "For getting you in trouble."

He shook his head.

"You're not mad?"

"You didn't do anything."

She shook her head, sniffled, wiped at a tear with her sleeve.

"Then why—"

His eyes fell to the ground, returned to her. He shook his head.

"It's been three days!"

The force of her voice and the strength of knot gnarling in her gut startled her, threw her into retreat; she sat, buried her face in her arms.

And then he was holding her, pressing her against him, arms around her head, his canvas jacket rough against her cheek.

They held each other until they heard a soft knock at the door.

"Sarah?" Samuel said. "Can you watch the register? I have to pick Cate up at the airport."

"I'll be right there."

The door shut.

Michael took her hand. "I'll pick you up after work?"

"Okay." She rubbed at her eyes.

"Okay."

She opened the door and hurried to the front.

CHAPTER SIXTY-THREE

"There you are," Lewella said.

Sarah froze, Chelsea beside her.

"We need to talk."

Sarah looked to Samuel for help; he shrugged, busied himself with the register.

School had just let out. Her shift didn't start for a half-hour. She had nowhere to run. She led Lewella to a table at the back of the store.

Lewella leaned forward in her chair. "Talk to me."

Sarah watched her silently, clutching herself.

"Come on, Sarah, I can help you."

"I'm okay."

"No, you're not."

Lewella had already called Sarah's high school and child services, had had a social worker visit her. She asked the parish priest and the sheriff to check on her from time to time, and used her master key to let herself into the girl's apartment to check for drugs and alcohol. The school psychiatrist had called Sarah out of class to interview her, and then passed her off to the school nurse, who'd asked her about her eating habits and given her pamphlets about sexual abuse and eating disorders.

"What he's doing to you isn't right."

"He's not doing anything—"

"Yes, he is, and I'm worried about you."

"You don't need to be."

"The things he's asking you to do—he's twice your age!"

Sarah was silent.

"You need to stop seeing him."

Sarah's eyes were fixed on her lap.

"I'm not blaming you for what happened, Sarah, but you need to take ownership of your life and get yourself out."

Nothing.

"You're enabling him."

Sarah remained silent, flush with anger and embarrassment.

Chelsea approached at a distance, cleared her throat, "Sarah? Sorry to interrupt. Samuel needs your help for a minute."

Sarah hurried off.

"How is she really, Chelsea?"

"She's fine."

Lewella frowned. "You expect me to believe that?"

Chelsea shrugged. "It's the truth."

"Have you even met him?"

She shook her head.

"He's a grown man. Sarah's a child, and he's taking advantage of her!"

Chelsea bristled. "She's not a child, she's seventeen, and she's legally emancipated! It's her choice."

Lewella shook her head. "No."

Sarah returned. "I have to get to work."

"Me too," Chelsea said.

Lewella scowled, shook her head, stood up. "You're forcing my hand, Sarah."

"She's not forcing anything," Chelsea snapped. "You're butting in on something that's none of your business."

"I can't be a part of this." Lewella shook her head. "I'm not going to help you enable your abuser. I'm giving you until the end of the week…"

Sarah stared.

"…either it stops, or I stop. You quit seeing him, or you'll have to find a new place to live and a way to support yourself. I'll change the locks, and the checks will stop."

"I'm…" Sarah stammered, scared. "I thought the money came from Miss White?"

"It won't be coming from anywhere if you don't stop this nonsense."

"I… I…"

"I don't want to have to do this, Sarah."

"What are you going to do?" The girls had finished their shifts, were walking back to Sarah's.

"What can I do? I don't have anywhere else to go."

"You could stay with me. I'll ask my parents tonight."

"And the money?"

Chelsea was silent.

It was cold. They pulled their hats as low as they'd go, wrapped their scarves tighter, jammed their gloved hands deep into their pockets.

"You have to tell Michael."

Sarah nodded.

"How do you think he'll react?"

"I don't know."

CHAPTER SIXTY-FOUR

Michael stood in front of the coolers for a long time before choosing a dozen long-stem roses, grabbed a plush bear on impulse as he was carrying them to the counter.

"Would you like me to add some baby's breath?"

"W—what?" Michael stammered. "Babies?"

The woman laughed. "Breath. Baby's breath. Greenery and little white flowers."

"Oh." He stared. "Do I?"

She smiled. "I think it looks nice."

"Oh, okay. Please."

He paid and left, got into his truck, and set the flowers on the seat beside the bear, thought better of it, and stuck the bouquet between the seat and the center console so it wouldn't fall, wondered if he should have bought chocolate, too.

He looked at the clock; he'd left work early so he could stop at the florist's and surprise Sarah, take her to the park before her shift started, but traffic had been thick and slow for several miles, funneled into a single lane in the aftermath of an accident. It seemed to be picking up ahead of him, though, so he'd probably still make it.

Words shuffled through his head, thoughts vanishing before they'd formed. He didn't know what to do or what to say to her, only that he needed to say something, to do something, and that no matter what he said or did, it wouldn't be quite right.

Distracted, he took his exit late, veering laterally without warning and cutting off the car behind him. The driver lay on his horn, screaming and brandishing his middle finger.

Michael raised a hand in apology.

"Shit."

The house was empty when he got home. He stood in the kitchen, bear in one hand, bouquet in the other, eyes darting frantically about the room, searching for her, not wanting her to be elsewhere. He went out to the garage and found a vase among the things the previous owner had left behind. He sat the bear on the kitchen table, the flowers between its legs, and went upstairs to change. It was five-thirty—Sarah had work at seven. He wondered where she was, what she was doing, wished she were home. He came back down and stood motionless, rooted to the floor, staring at the flowers, feeling lost and stupid until, finally, he decided to go work out. The bags were different. He always knew what to do with the bags. He didn't have much time, but he knew how to adjust, warmed up with the rope, quickly, ten minutes, just enough to get hot, and switched to the speed bag. He was sweating in no time; it was falling in rivulets as he hit the speed bag, pouring off his body by the time he switched to the heavy bag. He stripped off his shirt, tossed it aside, and unleashed a flurry of punches: hook, hook, uppercut, the final blow jerking the bag upward, sending the chain slack, the links shrieking hard into each other as metal tore into metal.

"I don't see him in the house," Sarah said to Chelsea. "I'll check upstairs."

"I think there's someone in the garage."

Michael didn't hear them. His workout had built to its crescendo, the power shots long past, fatigue clenching his muscles as he forced himself through a series of combinations, twenty-second salvos, crucibles of will.

"He's in here."

Chelsea saw the last interval, shrank back. Sarah entered as his final punch bent the bag in half. Spent, he removed his gloves, turned, and saw her.

"Hey," he said softly.

Chelsea followed his smile to her friend's.

"Hey."

They looked at each other, cautious, hopeful, Michael's chest heaving as he tried to catch his breath.

"This is Chelsea."

He nodded. "Michael. Nice to meet you."

Chelsea forced a smile, hung back.

"Samuel just hired her."

"Nice."

He felt Chelsea's eyes moving over his body, ignored them, held Sarah's gaze, trying to make his eyes as soft as he could.

"Work at seven?"

"Seven-thirty."

"Can I drive you?"

"I need to talk to you about something."

"Okay."

"Now?"

"If you want."

"I think it might take longer than that."

"Is everything okay?"

She shook her head.

"Is it me?"

"Lewella."

Michael ground his teeth, instantly dark.

"She's kicking me out unless I stop seeing you."

He stared, waited.

"I don't want to."

Michael stifled a smile. "Then don't."

"Don't?"

"Stay here."

"Stay?"

He nodded.

"With you?"

"Yes."

"You're serious? But…" She was smiling, trying not to cry.

"No buts. We can talk more later."

"Okay."

"I should probably shower before I take you guys to work."

"Yeah—" Chelsea turned red. "I mean…"

Michael choked a laugh. "I'll be quick."

He brushed the back of Sarah's hand with a finger. She nodded, didn't pull away.

"Shall we?" He pointed to the door, followed the girls out of the garage.

"Whose truck is that?" Sarah asked.

"Mine."

"What happened to your old truck?"

"The engine blew."

"Blew? Wasn't it only a couple years old?"

He nodded. "Bad luck."

"I'm sorry."

"Me, too," Chelsea said.

"Thanks." Michael held the door as the girls entered the house. "You guys stay in the living room, okay?"

"What?" Chelsea looked at him oddly.

"Please."

Sarah nodded.

"Wow, he's hot," Chelsea said, then froze. "He's upstairs, right?"

Sarah smiled. "Yes."

Chelsea exhaled, relieved. "I didn't know real people looked like that."
Sarah made a face, cocked her head to the side. "Like what?"
"Seriously?"
Sarah shook her head.
"How many boys have you been with? Other than Michael?"
Sarah blushed, shook her head again.
Chelsea looked horrified.
"What?"
"Life's not fair."
"Why?"
"You aren't kidding, are you?"
Sarah just stared, waiting, embarrassed.
"They don't all look like that."
"Like what?"
"His body—all that muscle…"
"Oh."
She felt heat rise in her chest and neck, felt her ears start to burn.
"Look at you turn red," Chelsea laughed.
Sarah buried her face in her hands.
"Do you have anything to eat?"
"What do you want?"
"I don't know—can I forage?"
Sarah frowned. "Michael wanted us to stay in the living room."
"Yeah, that was a little weird—why?"
Sarah gestured at the window.
"The window?"
"Yeah."
"What about—oh!" Chelsea's eyes went wide. "Me?"
Sarah nodded.
"He thinks people would…"
"Yes."
"People really—"
"Everything."
"Since Lewella?"
"That didn't help."
Chelsea screwed up her face. "That's so weird."
Sarah shrugged. "Granola bar?"
"Sure."
"I'll be right back."
She returned with two bars, flipped one to her friend.
"There're flowers on the table," she said, unwrapping hers.
"Flowers?"
She nodded. "Roses," —she chewed— "and a bear."

Chelsea's voice rose an octave. "He got you flowers and a stuffed animal?"

Sarah shook her head.

"He didn't say anything."

"Who else would they be for?"

Sarah looked sad. "I don't know."

"They're for you, idiot."

"I don't know…" Her head dropped.

"He bought you flowers! And a bear!"

She wanted to believe it.

"He didn't say anything because I showed up—he hasn't had a chance."

"Maybe."

"Go ask him."

"Don't you think—"

"Ask him!"

Sarah smiled despite herself. "But—"

"Sarah Smith! If you don't, I will."

Alarm swept across her face. "I'll be right back."

She took the stairs two at a time, clinging to her resolve. The door to the bedroom was closed; she knocked, waited, heard nothing, forced herself to go in. She could hear the shower behind the bathroom door, started to knock, froze, heart pounding, knocked. The water cut off.

"One second… come in."

She pushed the door open. He was standing outside the shower looking at her, a towel wrapped around his waist. She blanked.

"Hey," he said.

"Hey," she managed.

Questions passed across the space between them. Her hair was down. His skin was flush from the hot water. Both of them held their breath.

"Are they for me?" she said to the floor, bashful, unable to meet his eyes.

"Who else?"

She looked up; his voice—the way he was looking at her. He hadn't been like that since his arrest, his eyes soft and warm, pulling her into him, making her nervous and giddy all at once.

"But, why—" Her voice faltered. "Why now?"

The question hung in the air; he wanted to answer, couldn't, felt frustrated and dumb. He went to her, reached out and swept the backs of his fingers over her temple and along her hairline, wove his hands into her hair, and pulled her down to him. He lifted her off the ground with his other hand, set her atop the sink and leaned into her. Their mouths met hard. She pulled herself against him, his hair thick in her hands, protruding between her fingers. He was still wet, but she pressed herself against him, and when she couldn't kiss him any longer for want of breath, she clung still, safe and warm against his heat, dizzy beneath the kisses he let fall on her neck and ear and temple, inhaling him.

"We need to go," he said without loosening his grip.

"Yes."

He didn't let go; she didn't unwind her legs. Finally, he took one last kiss, long and hot and gentle, and pulled away, letting her climb down from the sink.

"Okay," she managed, smiling, breath uneven.

"Okay."

He took a step toward her.

"Michael, we—"

He lifted her off the ground again, pinning her against the wall, and she wrapped her arms and legs around him and leaned down and met his mouth.

"We have to—"

His kiss smothered her protests.

He pushed her away. "You're terrible! We need to go. You need to get to work!"

"What?"

"Here I am trying to be responsible, and then you—"

"Me?"

"You can't just blow off work, Sarah—"

"But—"

She realized he was teasing her, and smacked him, laughing.

They arrived five minutes late; Michael told Samuel it was his fault, and Samuel waved the apology away, said it wasn't a problem. "So," Chelsea said, "were they for you?"

Sarah couldn't keep from grinning, hung her head, embarrassed.

"You girls okay by yourselves?" Samuel asked.

"Yes," they said in unison.

"I'll be back in time to lock up."

The door swung shut behind him.

"You were gone a while," Chelsea said as they worked.

"Sorry," Sarah looked up briefly. "We were talking."

"No problem."

They finished the row, moved on to the next.

"You came down wearing a different shirt."

Sarah paused. "I wanted to wear something nicer for work."

"A flannel shirt?"

"Something warmer. I meant warmer."

"Oh."

They continued, shuffling books, turning them the right way up.

"Michael was taking a shower, right?"

"Yeah. Why?"

"No reason," Chelsea smiled sweetly. "It's just that your hair was wet."

"What?"

Chelsea saw the color rising in her friend's neck. "When you came down. Your hair was wet."

"Oh." Sarah stared intently at the books.

"Any idea how that happened?"

She shook her head.

Chelsea laughed.

"You look like a tomato."

"I think you should be nice to me."

Chelsea laughed again. "I think someone's been particularly nice to you."

"You're mean."

"Just jealous. I wish some hard-bodied stud would throw me down on top of a sink."

Sarah choked.

"You had an imprint of a cursive 'C' on your lower back." Chelsea's grin nearly split her face. "I saw it when you climbed into Michael's truck."

Sarah croaked.

Chelsea smiled.

They went back to shelving.

Sarah was sure she was about to burst into flame.

"How was work?"Michael held her hand as they drove, let it go only to shift, retook it at the first opportunity. He was nervous, knew he'd have to talk again, that he wouldn't know what to say.

"Good. Slow. It's nice having Chelsea there."

He nodded.

It was a starless night, the moon hidden. She watched him as he drove.

"Sarah, you're shaking." He reached for the heat.

"I'm a little nervous."

He looked at her, back to the road.

"Why?"

"I just am."

"We don't—I hadn't even—"

"I want to."

They were both surprised. He started to speak, stopped.

"Do you?"

He felt her eyes, pulled up at a stop sign, turned to face her. Her eyes shook him somehow, made him feel off-balance.

He nodded.

"Can you say it?" Her courage faltered, and she looked away. "You don't have to."

"Sarah..."

She turned back to him.

"I really want to."

"But..." she said.

He stared straight ahead, brow furrowed, struggling. Sarah followed his gaze.

Michael swallowed. "I love you."

Neither spoke. The words remained, their echo.

"Sarah?"

She was crying.

"What's wrong?"

"Are you sure?"

Her voice was timid, barely audible. They reached the house, and he pulled into the driveway, cut the engine, and took her hands. The garage lights came on, light sparkling in the tears she was trying to hide.

"Sarah."

She turned to face him.

"I'm sure."

"And you want to be with me?"

"Yes."

She broke, threw herself against him over the center console, weeping, and clung to him.

"I love you, too."

He hadn't meant to say the words, hadn't even thought them, but having said them, he knew they were true, and that true had no bearing on the ultimate issue, on right or wrong or whether it was within his rights to love her.

He closed the door behind them without letting go of her hand, pulling her against him so he could feel her breath on his skin and inhale the scent of her shampoo. They walked into the house hand in hand, up the stairs, and into the bedroom.

"On or off?"

She hesitated, wanting both to hide and to see, meek and nervous and curious.

"On."

He dropped his finger from the light-switch, wishing she'd said "off," doubting he was ready to see her again, the angles that in time would blossom into curves, but which now, by their absence, marked her as a child.

He felt the doubt slipping away as she kissed him, her fingers enmeshed in his hair, hands hard against his scalp. He kissed the nape of her neck, felt hands sliding over the swell of his shoulders, along the flare of his lats. Her thumbs hooked under his shirt and he lifted his arms so she could peel it off; she stopped halfway, surprising him, leaving his eyes covered, his arms bound above his head. He felt her lips press his chest, the tip of her tongue brush over his skin, her mouth working its way upward, slowly, until their lips locked. Still she refused to free his arms, to uncover his eyes, ran the blade of her free hand down his back, took his pants, his briefs; there were scars on his back and abdomen and arms, jagged cuts from broken bottles and cigarette burns like small, dark flowers, a thin, straight line cutting diagonally across his chest, a swath of road rash. She ran a finger over each scar, uncovered his eyes, freed his hands.

"Did they hurt?"

"Some of them."

"I'm sorry."

"You didn't do it."

He smiled at her; her eyes swept over him and she smiled back bashfully.

"What?"

"Chelsea says not everyone looks like you."

She kissed his solar plexus, his abdomen, the flesh beneath his navel.

"She says I'm lucky."

Bright.

Pure.

Young.

He winced.

"Did I hurt you?"

Her voice was brittle with nascent panic.

"No."

He lifted her off the ground for the third time that day, and for the third time she twined her legs around him, locking herself in place. He sat on the edge of the bed; she had to lean down to kiss him. She lifted her arms, felt cool air climb her skin as he peeled off her shirt in an achingly slow progression. The collar was just under her nose when he stopped.

"Hey!" she said.

"Payback's a bitch."

He bit her; she felt his breath on her chin, on her lips, strained, but couldn't reach him. He kissed her face, the valley beneath the swell of her lip, her nose through the fabric of her shirt. She struggled, pressing herself forward, mouth moving, lips reaching for him. She found him, her kisses hungry, more than a little violent.

He shucked her shirt and threw it to the floor.

She wasn't wearing a bra.

He tried to focus on her navel, her runner's body, the firmness of her abdomen, her heat, her scent; he lay her on her back, dropped soft kisses from her neck to the band of her underwear, down her sternum, down the center of her stomach, lower, slower, viciously slow, until she gasped, arching her back, her pants and underwear gone in a single, fluid sweep. He inhaled deeply, picked her up again, drunk on her presence, hungry. They rolled, clinging to each other, their flesh mashed together, searing into each other, their eyes locked, breathing ragged, she on top now, he sitting beneath her.

It isn't right.

The voice was unassailable, and for a moment her body disappeared, she disappeared, pleasure disappeared—even the air was gone, and there was only the malignance of his actions.

He shut his eyes so tight it hurt.

She wanted to be with him; he could feel it, smell it.

"I love you, Sarah."

He fell backward on to the bed, and she fell forward, hard, the air driven from her lungs in a sharp explosion of breath; they moved and mashed and meshed, and there was hot and wet and hard, and the wild pulse of their hearts.

CHAPTER SIXTY-FIVE

Sarah woke when the window shattered. She'd fallen asleep on the living room floor. The brick landed thunderously and cartwheeled, catching the meat of her cheek as it ripped over her brow, crashing to a halt against the couch behind her. The clock ticked, baseboards creaked. She heard a car, a dog, nothing, pushed herself off the ground; a shriek of pain ripped through her as a shard of glass bit deep into the flesh of her palm.

She went into the kitchen, turned on the light and called the police, a jagged blood stripe beginning a half-inch in front of her ear and running to the corner of her eye. Her hand bled freely; she held it in front of her face and watched the blood swallow her palm and wrist. She ran water into the wound, pulled the shard of glass from it, inhaling violently at the spike of pain, found peroxide, used it with grit teeth, wrapped the wound with paper towel.

She was eerily calm.

Two squad cars came, four policemen. She answered the door, took them to the living room, pointed to the window and then the brick.

"Are you okay, Miss?"

"Smith," she said absently. "Sarah Smith."

"Are you okay?"

The question surprised her. The policeman gestured toward her hand, her face; she looked down and saw that the bandage was half-saturated, looked up and caught her reflection in the glass covering the picture on the wall, a nautical scene she'd given Michael on his birthday, and saw the bruise expanding over her face and her eye swelling shut.

"I think so."

The policeman looked at his partner.

"Would you like to sit down?"

"Okay."

She lowered herself onto the couch, shivering. One of the policemen called for a blanket.

"Did you see who threw the brick, Miss Smith?"

"No." She shook her head, winced. "I was asleep."

"Alone?"

She nodded, staring through the shattered window into the night. No one could find a blanket, so one of the officers draped his jacket over her.

"Thank you." She drew it tightly around her.

"Any idea where Mr. Tolan is?"

"Michael? Probably on his way home from work."

The policeman scribbled.

More questions:

"Is there anyone you'd like to call?"

"No."

"Anyone we should—"

"No."

"Can we take you to the—"

She shook her head, nearly passed out.

"Do you have anything to cover the window?"

She looked at them blankly.

"A trash bag, maybe?"

She found one, some duct tape, held them out to the policeman.

He frowned, looked at his partner. "Won't Mr. Tolan be able to fix it when he gets home?"

Sarah blanked, stared at the materials she was holding. "I thought— right. Sorry."

"Not at all, Miss Smith," the other officer said, taking the tape and bags. "We'd be glad to help." He shot his partner a sidelong glare. "Jesus, Frank."

"Thank you."

The policemen did what they could to tape up the window, shut the door behind them on their way out. She could hear them conversing as they walked to their cruiser.

She watched the men through the flashing light and felt a wave of panic, remembering the last time those lights had been here, and how Michael had been arrested, and that that too was her fault, like now, and that the policemen had written about her on their clipboards, and called about her over their radios just like they were doing now. She was terrified by the time Michael pulled up—he'd be mad at her, and they'd stop talking again, and he wouldn't even look at her.

But he wasn't mad. He saw the window and ran toward the house, calling after her. "Sarah?" he yelled, "Sarah!" He flew to her. "Are you okay?" He knelt at her side, a piece of glass cutting into his knee. "It's okay, I'm here. Everything's going to be okay."

"Someone threw a brick through the window."

He scooped her up, leaned back, wincing as the shard of glass drove deeper into his knee, stood.

"I've got to get you to the emergency room."

"I'm sorry."

"What?"

"That the police came. I didn't do anything… I was asleep."

"Shush. Let's get you into the truck."

"I'm sorry, Michael, I didn't mean to make trouble for—"

"You didn't. You don't have to worry—Christ, you're really bleeding."

"Mr. Tolan?"

"Yes, Ma'am." He stood. "How is she?"

"She's resting. We gave her some blood, stitched her up. You'll want to put an icepack on her when she gets home."

Michael nodded. "Yes, Ma'am."

"She's lucky the glass didn't sever the tendon."

Michael nodded.

"We'll bring her out shortly. Here's a scrip for antibiotics—make sure she finishes the whole course. These are instructions for changing her bandages." She paused, pointed. "You should have that looked at."

He looked down at his knee, the smear of blood that soaked through his pant-leg, scanned the waiting room.

"It'd be a while."

"Probably." The nurse shrugged. "Triage."

"I want to get her home."

"Suit yourself."

He took the papers. The nurse left. Twenty minutes later they wheeled Sarah out.

He drove her home, carried her into the house, to bed, found every blanket they owned, and covered her with them. She smiled, ate a cracker, fell asleep. He stayed up watching her, fear melting into relief. Hours passed. He began to shake, softly at first, then with increasing intensity, grinding his teeth, hands balled in fists.

CHAPTER SIXTY-SIX

How do you write the tide?

It began as an amusement, continued as a discipline, became habit. Cate did it too, in certain moods. Also: how do you write the fog, Christmas Eve, a father arriving home from work and seeing their infant child for the first time that day? How do you write any of the thousands of mundane and magical moments that comprise a human life? What detail makes this room this room as opposed to a hundred-thousand other such rooms in a hundred-thousand other such places? Where do anger and embarrassment and fear lie if not in balled-up fists or red cheeks or wide eyes?

Cate was good at it. Better than he was.

Samuel had had the nightmare again last night, was trying to beat it, to keep it from ruining the day. Bill ambled along behind him, nose to the ground, stopping and smelling and lifting his leg as Samuel walked.

How do you write the tide? Its motion is the most frequent invocation: the tide as mechanism, advance and withdrawal, as celestial dance, the press of the moon's palm against the naked back of the earth. Sea as blood, tide as pulse. Samuel steered to sound and smell, breath. The gentlest tide leaves a skin of ocean ashore, stranded, hissing in the sand. You can smell the rush and retreat of the brine, feel it in the flesh of your throat and on your tongue.

Cate would be eating lunch now.

He followed Bill's progress along the beach, left off, looked out to sea. The sun hadn't been out all day; it was gray and darkening and there was little to see. Behind him, his truck was fading into the gray. Sarah and Chelsea worked three nights a week now, ran the shop more smoothly and precisely than he did. Chelsea handled the coffee bar, Sarah the register; both girls left messages on sticky notes in looping script, telling him to order more napkins or coffee cups or paper rolls for the cash register.

Business was steady.

He remembered again how lucky he was, kicked at a loose rock and made himself do the rundown. He had money, good health, a successful business, a beautiful wife, and an exceptional child.

His eyes reached out across the bay as he came to the end of his thoughts, waited. A tern flew across his vision.

What was he waiting for?

Nothing.

"Bill!" he called.

The dog came bounding toward him, launched himself into the truck; Samuel shut the door behind him and headed toward Chuck's out of habit.

CHAPTER SIXTY-SEVEN

"Come to Boston with me."

Vaguely ethnic bombshell is running across the flat-screen in Tori's living room.

"What?"

The heel of her boot catches a villain's face, spins him sideways.

"Come to Boston with me."

Tall, blonde, and handsome crushes bad guy number one's larynx; tall, dark, and handsome uses a Glock to take out bad guys two-five.

Tolan tries to turn, but Tori holds her fast. Is she serious—she's never serious.

"I can't."

"Why?"

Tolan laughs. "What do you mean 'why'?"

Bang, bang, kick, kick, stab, punch; groans. The screen is littered with bodies, but there's no blood. The villains are cleanly fallen and the heroes triumphant, breathing evenly, hair in place. Leading man number one's makeup suggests a bullet or knife or fist grazed his face, but it could just be the lighting.

"Why?"

"Well, college, for one."

The heroes emerge from gun smoke and shadows, congregate.

"You don't even want to go to college."

"I—" Tolan stutters, shuts her mouth, tries to turn again. "I don't not want to go."

The good guys have won again.

"But you don't want to go, either."

"I—" She shakes her head. "Everyone goes to college."

"Come to Boston."

Suddenly, Tolan can't hear the smile. The television disappears behind the silence.

"And what?"

"We'll get a place in Back Bay."

"A place in Back Bay?"

"Yes."

"And then…"

"We'll be together."

"And then…"

Tolan's trying to keep it light.

"I'll go to school, you can… we'll figure things out."

Tolan squirms; Tori lets her go.

"And after Boston?"

"Med school, some place warm—maybe Duke or Stanford." Tori puts on a grin, plays the rake. "You'd look great in a little orange bikini."

Tolan lets herself smile briefly, winces as she feels the smile crushed.

"And then you'll be a doctor."

"Ana Victoria Quevedo-König, MD. No worries, though, you can still call me Tori."

"And I'll be…"

"With me."

"And when you meet someone?"

Tori's head tilts and drops, and her mouth opens, but she doesn't speak.

"Come on, Tor," Tolan closes her eyes, opens them, looks away, "We're going to—whatever we call what we're doing—forever?" She shakes her head. "You're going to go to med school and become a doctor like your parents want, and then you're going to work and get married because that's what people do. You'll make beautiful children who'll call me Auntie Tolan, and we'll see each other from time to time, and I'll dote on them. And maybe we'll be able to steal a long weekend once a year to reminisce about all the fun we had…" She lets her voice peter out.

"Fun?"

Tolan nods, stops, shakes her head.

There are tears forming in both their eyes.

"That's all this is?"

"No."

They sit in silence, blink back tears. Tori shuts the TV off.

"Your mother will want us back soon."

Tolan shakes her head.

"No?"

"No."

Pause.

"Hot tub?"

She nods. "I'll call mom and tell her we'll be over later than normal."

"I'll start the jets."

Tolan reaches for her phone as Tori walks away. Tori's parents are out of town again, so they have the place to themselves.

They soak, shower.

Tolan's mother is asleep by the time they get home. They're tired, get in bed and cut the lights, intertwine. Each of them knows the other is awake, but neither of them have found words for the things they want to say, so all they do is breathe, waiting for sleep, inhaling the lingering notes of the shampoo they'd used, the body wash.

Tori kisses her. "Sweet dreams."

Tolan can smell their scents, too, subtle beneath the vanilla and lavender; it draws August closer.

August. College. Boston.

"I love you, Tori."

"I love you, too, Tolan."

There it is.

And now what?

Tori is spooning her.

Tolan thinks she feels tears on her neck.

CHAPTER SIXTY-EIGHT

Michael spent the night staring at her, picked up the phone, realized he didn't have anyone to call, and no idea what he would say, and set the phone back in its cradle. He knew he had to wake her every three hours, but the care instructions didn't say anything about how much light there should be in the room, or what temperature the room should be. He turned off the lights, but left the curtains open, cracked the window, and put another blanket over her; the room was flooded with silver light, and he could see his breath, make out the rise and fall of her breathing beneath the covers.

She took up all and none of the bed, her feet hung off the end even as it swallowed her, as she lay almost apologetically atop it, occupying a fraction of its width. The moonlight shifted and shadows crawled across the wall as she slept.

He wanted to go to her, to touch her, to take up a position and defend her against all threats, real and imagined.

He wanted to kill.

For her.

Eventually the anger subsided, and he stopped wringing his hands.

He woke her every three hours, asked her what her name was, and what the date was, and who was president, and she answered, and sometimes she'd smile or take a sip of water before turning onto her side and curling fetal, falling asleep again. Once, on impulse, he lay his hand over her forehead, cupped her cheek; she reached up from the depths of sleep and pressed it against her, and he stayed there, bent over, perched on the edge of the bed, until she let go.

A clock he'd never noticed before ticked like drops from a broken faucet. He woke her at six; she answered, slept. Moonlight withdrew at dawn's approach, turning silver to white, and then morning came, and white was obliterated by gold.

He nodded off as the room filled with sun, woke at 9:03.

"You missed one," she said, smiling.

He startled awake, shook his head, and rubbed a hand down his face, eyes chapped raw, capillaries like lines on a map. "I'm sorry, I must have—I made it until six."

"How come you didn't come to bed?"

"Your head, and hand—I didn't…"

"Michael?"

"Things keep happening." He stared at his feet. "I keep getting you hurt. Maybe… you're seventeen, Sarah. Maybe they're right."

The clock ticked. Outside, chickadees chattered back and forth.

"I've been seventeen the whole time."

He raised his head, and she was looking at him, emerald eyes, irises minute.

"And things keep happening; you keep getting hurt. You've lost your apartment, your income, been to the hospital."

"So?"

"I'm twenty-eight."

"I know."

"People won't ever—"

Her eyes stopped him short. She'd pushed herself up against the headboard.

He wanted to speak, didn't know what to say or how he felt, hadn't had practice at any of it. He made himself get up and move toward her, stand beside her, taller for once, so that no matter how far back she craned her neck, she couldn't see all of him. She pressed her cheek against his chest.

"Wouldn't it be easier if…"

His voice trailed off, she didn't move, didn't speak, only pressed her face harder into him, clinging to the strength of his muscle, the softness of his shirt, the heat rising through it.

"It's only my age?"

Her voice: a petal about to fall.

"You've got to—I've got to let you…"

She felt his hand push up beneath her hair, felt the flesh of his thumb brush against her, felt his hand tighten around a fistful of curls and press her into him.

"I've got to let you grow up."

He was pressing her so hard it hurt, crushing her to him, smothering her, but she didn't say anything, didn't want him to let go.

"I will."

She felt the world slide and start to spin, faint from the strength of his grip, the pain. He let go; she gasped for air.

"I need to sleep," he said.

"You stayed up all night."

"Do you need any codeine?"

She nodded. He brought her water, two pills.

"Come to bed?"

He knew it was wrong to lay down next to her, but he didn't have the energy to fight it. Sarah took his hand, and soon, they were asleep.

CHAPTER SIXTY-NINE

"Thank you for your time."

The men stood, the banker's suit crisp, tailored, navy-blue with gray pinstripes, Michael in khakis and an Oxford button-down. Michael extended his hand.

"I'm sorry we couldn't help you."

Michael forced a smile. "Me, too."

Saturday, late-morning: he stepped over a patch of dirt-gray slush, took out his keys, and fit them into the truck door. The wind kicked up, making his eyes water. He slid into the seat and started the engine.

Sarah had spent the night at Chelsea's. Michael had woken at four-thirty and put in four hours at a temp job he'd found clearing debris on Orr's Island, then driven south to Freeport and started hitting banks when they opened at ten.

He pulled out of the parking lot onto Route One, and the stack of mail in the passenger's seat shifted: "Application for credit denied," two bills marked "FINAL NOTICE."

Sarah had told him her allowance would stop coming, had picked up as many hours at the bookstore as Samuel was legally allowed to give her. Michael hadn't been worried, but then he was fired, and the hospital bills hit.

He didn't have to pick her up until 1:30, so he had time to try a couple more banks.

Michael accelerated, five minutes away from where he was supposed to be, already ten minutes late, cursing himself. The girls would be freezing after their run, soaked with sweat. "Fuck."

He saw the cop too late, got pulled. The trooper took his time, told him he'd clocked him at eighteen over. "Yes, sir," Michael said, handing over license and registration.

"Those aren't good." Michael followed the man's gesture to the notices on the seat.

"No, sir."

"Slow down, okay?"

"Yes, sir."

Michael arrived twenty-five minutes late. It was gray, spitting, and the wind was hard, the ocean dotted with whitecaps. A seagull unleashed a long, shrill cry and began to beat the air with its wings.

Sarah was nowhere in sight.

She was standing at the sink when he pulled into the driveway. He hadn't been worried until he'd driven home the first time and found the house empty. He'd been searching for her for two hours, canvassing every route she might have run, a clot of terror lodged in his throat. But there she was. A bolt of rage ripped through him. "Where the fuck have you been?" The door hadn't even closed behind him. "I've been looking for you for hours."

She was sitting on the couch; he towered over her, apoplectic, jaw clenched, voice low and guttural.

"I… I got a ride with Chelsea's mom."

"You what?"

She flattened herself against the couch. "We finished early, and it started to rain. Chelsea's mother was there."

"You weren't here when I got back."

"Chelsea's mom took us to lunch."

"So fuck me? I drove an hour to get you, but fuck me."

"No! I—"

"You're a goddamn child."

She recoiled as if he'd hit her.

"You do whatever the fuck you want to do, and don't even think about how it affects me." Michael moved closer and closer, fists balled at his side; Sarah held her breath, tried to force herself through the back of the couch. "Fuck." He stepped backward, turned away, pressing his fingers into his temples. "This is insane."

"I'm sor—"

"I shouldn't even be upset. You're just a kid."

"I'm not a kid."

"I'm an idiot for expecting a child to act like an adult."

"I'm not a child!"

He turned back to her as if surprised to find her there.

"I'm not a child."

She pressed herself forward, away from the couch.

His voice dropped, got uglier. "You damn well act like one."

She stood up. "I'm not a child."

"You have no fucking idea—" He grabbed at his hair with his fists. "This is so fucking stupid. What the hell am I doing?"

He stormed out.

CHAPTER SEVENTY

Michael headed into Hastings. He'd thought of getting a six-pack for Samuel, but decided against it. It would have looked like an attempted bribe, pathetic.

Michael opened the door to the shop, and the bell jingled.

"Samuel." Michael nodded.

Samuel looked up from the cash register.

"Sarah doesn't start for another hour."

"I know."

"Oh." Samuel set his glasses on the counter. "What can I do for you?"

Michael shifted his weight. "I need to ask a favor."

A customer approached the register, and Michael stepped to the side. Samuel ran her credit card, smiled, and chatted idly with her while they waited for the charge to go through.

He turned back to Michael. "Did you want to talk in my office?"

Michael shook his head. "Here's fine. This won't take long."

Samuel nodded.

"I want—I was hoping—I need to ask you for a loan." Michael wore workpants and a thick shirt, a canvas jacket, looked tired. "I'll pay you back, sign something."

Samuel stared.

Michael sighed. "I know what I'm doing. We're not friends, and it's probably not exactly good for business for you to be seen with me." Michael paused, looked away. "I know you probably think I'm taking advantage of Sarah." He kicked at the ground, clenched his jaw. "I was fired the month before last, no explanation. I didn't tell Sarah because I knew she'd think it was her fault. Last week someone torched my truck. I told Sarah the engine went, borrowed money from a friend, and bought the cheapest clunker I could find. I'm a month in the hole, and I've been to every bank within thirty miles. The insurance company still hasn't cut me a check, so I haven't been able to pay my friend back. I won't be able to make the mortgage this month, and the gas and electric companies are threatening to shut off the heat."

Samuel was silent.

Michael forced a laugh, jammed his hands into his pocket.

"No hard feelings; I didn't expect you to say yes."

CHAPTER SEVENTY-ONE

The sign was coming up on his right: "Martin & Sons, L.L.C., building homes since 1930."

Samuel pulled into the lot and parked.

"Gene."

"Samuel."

"How's Marian?"

"Fine. Giving me hell like always. Cate?"

"She's well."

The conversation came to halt. A clock ticked on the wall; a bandsaw whirred in the shop behind them. The men stood looking at each other, Samuel uncomfortable, Gene waiting.

"I need to ask a favor."

"Uh-oh."

"You know Michael Tolan?"

"I've heard the name."

"I'd like you to consider hiring him."

Gene raised an eyebrow.

"As a favor."

"I haven't heard much good about him."

"Lewella?"

Gene said nothing.

Samuel shook his head. "I'm sure you haven't."

The man waited.

"He's a hard worker, Gene. As for the rest of it… I don't like it, but it isn't my business."

"The girl?"

"It's what she wants."

"She works for you, right?"

Samuel nodded.

"How well do you know him?"

Samuel exhaled, drawing it out, long and slow.

"Not all that well."

"But you're willing to vouch for him?"

Samuel frowned, "Someone shat in his truck two weeks ago, then last week, they set it on fire. He was fired from his job the month before last without explanation. He's been to every business within thirty miles looking for a job, and gone to every bank trying to get a loan. He even came to me, knowing how I felt. He's not going to make his mortgage this month, and the gas company's threatening to cut his heat, but he's still with her. That's quite a price to pay if you're only interested in taking someone for a ride."

Gene listened, impassive.

"Give him a chance, hire him to do whatever, and I'll pay his salary."

"And if my business suffers?"

Samuel winced. "Then let him go. You'll have done all you could."

The men stared at each other.

"I'll think about it."

"Thank you."

Gene nodded.

CHAPTER SEVENTY-TWO

Samuel watched him yelling at her through the window. Maybe not yelling. He couldn't hear anything, just see the contortions of his face. She was crying, would open her mouth to speak, get shouted down. She started dabbing at her eyes, got out of the truck, and started toward the shop. The bell jingled as the door opened; she came into view, eyes red. She went to the bathroom, came back, and took her place behind the register.

Samuel closed the door to his office and reached for the clipboard hanging on the wall. Michael was still sitting in his truck, the night closing in around him. Twenty minutes later, Samuel's order was finished, checks and bills sealed in stamped envelopes, ready for posting. Michael hadn't moved. It was too dark to make out anything but his outline. Samuel hung the clipboard back on the wall, grabbed the stack of envelopes, and turned out the office light.

"For Dale?" Sarah asked as he handed her the envelopes.

"All but this one. Give that to the delivery man when he comes tomorrow."

She nodded.

He thought about telling her that Michael was still out there, waiting for her to get off work, shivering in his truck.

"You okay?" he asked.

Her head dropped slightly.

"Just tired."

"Okay."

It was cold outside, still. Even the wind had frozen, fallen to the ground. Samuel raised his hand in Michael's direction and Michael gestured back, stepped out of his truck.

"I wanted to thank you," Michael said.

"Oh?"

"For vouching for me with Mr. Martin."

"How's that going?"

"He keeps letting me come back."

"Good."

The men stood awkwardly in the cold.

"Anyway, thank you. I owe you a couple beers."

"Glad to help." Samuel hesitated. "I'm headed that way now, if you want."

"Chuck's?"

Samuel nodded.

"Sure."

Samuel threw his truck into drive. It wasn't what he wanted, but he didn't have anything more pressing, didn't have anything, really. Chuck's and beer weren't hard to swallow, and Michael—he was ambivalent about Michael. The image of his face turned on Sarah, etched with anger, flashed through his mind; he hadn't liked seeing that, a man yelling at a girl.

But couples fought. It wasn't any of his business.

Couples.

The word made him uncomfortable: a seventeen-year-old girl and a twenty-eight-year-old man weren't a couple.

Something, but not a couple.

He and Michael drove their separate miles, parked, walked in together.

"What's your drink?"

"Anything. Guinness?"

"Sure. Shot?"

Samuel started to shake his head, reconsidered. "Jameson."

Michael came back with two glasses and a bottle, pushed the pint and tumbler toward him.

"Thanks for coming."

Samuel nodded.

Michael looked down into his beer, took a sip, set the bottle down, and began working at the label.

"Sarah tell you Lewella kicked her out and cut off her funds?"

Samuel's eyes rose. "No."

Michael nodded.

"She's living with you now?"

"Has been awhile."

Seven-thirty on a Thursday, the bar half full, twenty people getting a jump on the weekend. A group of lobstermen harassed the new bartender as Chuck laughed; they bought shots and pints with bills fresh from the ATM, knit hats pushed back on their heads. An old man sat in a corner booth by himself, drinking black coffee. A couple in their sixties ate Reubens at the bar, watched the Pick Six numbers appear on a small TV mounted on the wall.

A group of women came in, laughs and smiles, done up, big hair, big earrings, heavy makeup. The lobsterman followed their progress to the bar.

"I'm not sure what you want me to say," Samuel said.

"I don't want you to say anything."

The men's eyes locked.

"I can't give you permission."

"I don't need it."

No malice, just a statement. Samuel's eyes fell to his pint glass.

Across the bar, one of the lobstermen nodded to his friend and gestured at Michael.

Michael drained his beer, looked at Samuel's.

"Mind if I have one more?"

Samuel's was nearly full.

"Go ahead."

Samuel watched him walk up to the bar and wait for Chuck, realizing he knew nothing about Michael, only that he was an ex-janitor and involved with Sarah. Sarah, who would be sipping Perrier or a Shirley Temple if she were here.

He took a sip of his beer, warm now, pleasantly bitter. Michael was leaning on the bar, sleeves rolled up above his elbow, his forearms thick and corded, muscle and veins visible even in the lowlight. Samuel was struck by the width of his chest as he came back, the power in his arms and legs.

He frowned.

Too much. Too much power for a seventeen- year-old girl.

Michael took a long pull from his beer and set it down on the table.

"I don't mean to keep you here."

"You're not." Samuel indicated his beer. "I'm still working."

The men held their drinks, avoiding eye-contact.

"I just wanted you to know that I'm not just taking her for a spin."

Samuel looked at him quizzically.

"That I care about her."

Samuel nodded.

The lobstermen mustered their courage in turns, approaching women, buying drinks and flirting, but the night was stubborn, the bar wouldn't quite fill. Chuck would leave a poorer man than he could have been, and the lobstermen would go home alone. Samuel finished his beer, waited, and Michael, seeing his empty glass, took one final pull and stood up.

"I don't mind if you finish your beer."

Michael shook his head. "I'm good."

"Hey you!"

They turned. One of the lobsterman was pointing at them.

"That's him, Keeb, right? The one that's messing with the girl?"

Keeb stared dumbly.

"The kiddie-raper—you fucking disgust me, asshole."

"Let's go," Michael said.

Samuel stood frozen; Michael grabbed him by the arm and pushed him toward the door.

"Stop right there, chicken shit. Tuck, don't let him leave."

Tuck was 6'4," wore a thick beard, a denim vest over a flannel shirt, and outweighed Michael and Samuel together. He stood in front of the door, arms crossed.

The lobstermen advanced rapidly, gnashing their teeth.

"You like raping kids, asshole?"

The man shoved his hands into Michael's chest, spittle hitting Michael's face as he was driven backward. The rest of the lobstermen were standing now.

"What's going on, Kenny?" one of them called.

"This is the asshole Lew told us about."

"Who?"

"How about it, asshole: you a kid-raping piece of shit?"

"I didn't rape anyone."

The lobstermen continued to advance, forcing Michael backward.

"That's not the way we heard it."

The heel of Michael's back foot touched the wall. He pushed Samuel sideways toward the bar. The lobsterman ignored him, closing on Michael.

"I didn't rape anyone."

There was a lull, the jukebox between songs. The air crackled, coiling like a viper. Michael's voice was low and calm, his jaw unclenched, hands in front of his chest, palms out.

One of the women at the bar laughed loudly. Samuel motioned for Chuck.

"Like hell!"

The words were feral; the lobsterman pivoted, cocking his fist— Michael's jab snapped the man's head back before it could start forward, followed by an overhand left that dropped the man like a piece of meat.

Michael spoke to Keeb across the body, lowering his hands. "We don't need to do this—I've got no problem with you."

Three other lobstermen stood within a yard of Keeb. Tuck remained motionless in the doorway. Samuel spoke into Chuck's ear, then pointed, and Chuck's head jerked upward.

"Fuck you!"

Michael ducked the wild punch, broke two brutal hooks against Keeb's ribs, and shattered a third man's orbital bone before the remaining men tackled him, driving him into the wall, his head whipping viciously into the wood and sending him to the ground, semi-conscious, the men on him in an instant. His nose exploded in blood as the bone snapped sideways, a ring opened his brow. Chuck was yelling for them to stop, held back by the other lobstermen, Samuel at his side. A man was kneeling on Michael's chest, throwing punches; Michael dropped his chin so the man's fist hit the bone of his forehead, heard the fingers break, and felt the man recoil in pain, rolling off Michael's arm. Michael hit him twice, knocked him sideways against his friend, rolled hard left and spun to his feet; the remaining lobsterman charged head first, spit frothing over his lip, nostrils flaring. Michael smashed his fist into the man's temple, and it was over.

Most of the men had regained consciousness by the time the cops showed up. Michael sat on a barstool holding a bag of ice against his head while the police talked to Chuck, and then Samuel. They made Michael remove the icepack, took pictures of his face from different angles, took his statement.

"Did you want to press charges?" the policeman asked him.

"No."

The cop raised an eyebrow, made a note on his form.

"You should get that looked at," he said without looking up, his ballpoint pen scraping loudly across paper.

Michael gave no reaction.

"He will," Samuel said.

"He's going to need stitches."

Samuel nodded his agreement. Michael stared straight ahead, his face colored with bruises and blood in various stages of drying. The cop gave a snort and shook his head, returned to his clipboard.

"And someone's going to have to set his nose."

Samuel and the policeman looked at each other.

"Thank you, Glenn."

Samuel watched the policeman leave, turned to Michael. "You shouldn't drive."

Michael dropped the icepack in the garbage can. "Yeah."

"Can I take you to the hospital?"

Michael nodded.

"Sarah should be closing up the shop about now."

"Yeah."

"Did you want to pick her up before we go?"

Michael steadied himself against Samuel's truck, his vision fading in and out, stomach hollow.

"We can just call the shop and let her know. She can walk home."

"You don't think she'll worry?" Samuel said.

Michael looked at him, lips pursed, lines creasing his forehead. "I don't want her to see me like this."

Samuel grimaced. "Okay."

CHAPTER SEVENTY-THREE

"Do you think I'm a child?"

Samuel paused mid-motion, set the book in his hand back on the cart, and turned to look at her.

"How do you mean?"

Sarah looked up briefly, back to the shelf.

"Is this about Michael?"

He watched her, but she gave no reaction.

"Sarah, you and Michael ... that's beyond me."

She kept shelving.

"It just seems hard," Samuel said. "For both of you. I don't know how you guys do it."

"It's not that hard," she said softly, "not always. People look at us funny, but they've always looked at me that way."

"And Michael?"

"What about him?"

"With everything that's been going on... the pressure has to be getting to him."

"Yeah, the truck was bad luck. You don't expect the engine on a three year-old truck to blow out of nowhere like that. It had been having some problems, though. And as far as quitting his job, he'd been talking about wanting to do something different for a while. He's a lot happier with what he's doing now."

Samuel stopped what he was doing.

"What?"

"They burned his truck, Sarah," he said gently.

She stared at him blankly.

"The reason it'd been having problems was that people were putting sugar and ball-bearings in the gas tank."

"He said..." Her voice trailed off. "Because of me?"

"No," Samuel said quickly.

"Why, then?"

Samuel shook his head. They continued shelving in silence.

"Do you think Michael thinks I'm a child?"

"Does he say he does?"

"Only when he's mad."

Samuel frowned, started to speak, and stopped.

"I'm not a child."

"Chuck.""Professor."

"How're you?"

"Too early to call."

Samuel looked at his watch. "It's ten-thirty."

"I run a bar."

Samuel scanned the room: a half-dozen regulars were shooting darts, a trucker was mopping up the last of the vinegar from his fish and chips with the last of his french-fries.

"In Port Haven, ME."

"The night is young."

"You close in an hour and a half."

The door opened, and two young girls appeared in heels, shivering, thin jackets wrapped tightly around their bodies. Chuck grinned.

Samuel shook his head.

"I'll have the usual."

"Double prune juice coming right up."

Samuel watched the women take the corner booth and order drinks.

"One brew, one shot," Chuck slid the drinks across the bar in Samuel's direction.

"*Gracias.*"

"You're welcome-o."

Samuel shook his head.

"Snob."

The men laughed.

"Tolan's a friend of yours, right?"

Samuel threw his shot back. "Not really. An acquaintance."

"But you knew what last night was about?"

Samuel nodded.

"People aren't too happy about the fact that he's living with that girl."

"No."

"Did you hear someone torched his truck a while back?"

"Yup."

Chuck took a few swipes at the bar with a rag and tossed it in the sink. "Pissed and shit all over it, first."

Samuel remained impassive, stared down into his beer, emptied the stein. Chuck pushed him another.

"Was it the same guys that attacked him?"

Chuck made a face.

"Sorry," Samuel said. "Question withdrawn."

Chuck waved away the apology.

"You know them both, right?"

"Sarah and Michael?"

Chuck nodded.

"Sarah works for me at the bookshop."

"You think it's okay what he's doing?"

Samuel grimaced. "Hell, Chuck…" His eyes fell to the bar top. "I don't know—it's legal."

"Right and legal ain't always the same thing." Chuck leaned back. "If it was your daughter, would you—"

"No, I wouldn't. But so what?"

"So what?"

"She's not my daughter."

Chuck's eyes narrowed. He picked the rag out of the sink and began rubbing hard at the bar.

"What am I supposed to do?"

Samuel's voice stopped him short; he dropped the rag.

"It's what she wants."

"She's seventeen, Sammy."

"I know."

A group of fishermen came in, already drunk, amiably raucous, beards thick, sleeves rolled.

"Shitty situation," Chuck said.

Samuel nodded. "For everyone."

CHAPTER SEVENTY-FOUR

"Did you know they beat him up?"

"That's not what I heard."

Sarah nodded. "They broke his nose and everything."

"Yeah, after he kicked six of their asses."

"What?"

"Obie's brother was one of the guys that rushed him. Michael put three of the guys in the hospital. He didn't say anything?"

"He didn't tell me."

Chelsea shook her head. "The cops came and everything."

The girls took a sip of their tea.

"How come he didn't get in trouble?"

"The other guys started it."

"Why?"

"They said he was a rapist."

Sarah cringed.

"Sorry," Chelsea said. "I'm an idiot."

"It's okay." She made herself smile. "How do you know all this stuff?"

"Everyone knows."

Sarah cringed. "He's not, you know," she said, eyes on the floor.

"Not what? Who?"

"Michael. He's not a rapist."

"I know."

Sarah's eyes filled with tears, but she blinked them back. "And I'm not a child."

"I know—"

"I love him," Sarah said, tears falling despite her efforts.

"And he loves you."

CHAPTER SEVENTY-FIVE

"Do you think you could do it?"

Tolan and Tori are watching the sunset, curled up beneath a blanket with mugs of hot chocolate.

"Of course we could do it," Tori chirped.

"It'd be tough, though. Everywhere they go, everyone's against them."

"Chelsea's not. Samuel's not."

"He's not really for them, though, either."

"They've made it a year."

"Yeah." Tolan swallows the last of her cocoa, tips her mug all the way up and hits the bottom several times trying to jar the marshmallows loose.

"Sometimes all you can do is try."

They girls look at each other.

"Yeah," Tolan says softly, looking away.

"It doesn't have to be like that for us, T." Tori takes her hand, gives it a squeeze.

"I know."

CHAPTER SEVENTY-SIX

Michael stood at a distance, watched the bus pull up and disgorge Sarah's cross-country team with a hydraulic belch. She was the last one off the bus, paused at the top of the stairs to consider the best means of making her escape: duck forward and go down the steps head first, or lean back and limbo her way to the asphalt. Michael bit on his back molars; it was hard to watch her sometimes, all timid, angles and length, limbs at cross-purposes. It wasn't so much that she was clumsy as that there was never enough room for her in the spaces she tried to disappear into. He'd come home to find her crying more than once: she'd tripped on the edge of a carpet, on her own feet, ducked going through doorways to avoid hitting her head and banged her elbow on the doorjamb, ran into a filing cabinet. Once, she fell in the cafeteria in the middle of lunch, in front of everyone, and her tomato soup splattered all over the cash register.

It had rained earlier, a cold pre-summer rainfall. Michael hung back from the crowd of spectators; Bangor was far enough from Port Haven that he was less concerned about encountering hostile parents, but he remained on edge, uncertain as to where to stand, whether or not to wave. He hadn't been to a race in nearly a year.

It had been warm the last time he'd gone, perfect, the sun full and bright, a gentle brace of salt air sweeping in off the harbor. Michael had stood along the course next to everyone else, kept to himself, but it hadn't mattered. A woman two people to the left had nudged her friend, and the man next to her had leaned in close to them. Michael hadn't been able to hear what was said, but they both looked over at him afterward. Within ten minutes the people on either side of him had moved, so that Michael stood in the middle of a thirty-foot gap in the wall of spectators lining the course. He hadn't seen the group of parents approach the town policeman, hadn't see them point to him, or the parents' outrage when the policeman frowned and said there was nothing he could do. Sarah had waved as she approached the starting line, smiled. He'd smiled back. The race had started and ended. Sarah had come in third. Michael was waiting for her by his truck when the men approached, introduced themselves brusquely, an attorney in Eddie

Bauer and a BMW hat, a man in a suit, and a third man, short and powerful with a weather-beaten canvas jacket and calloused hands.

"We'd appreciate it if we didn't see you here again," the attorney said. "It'd be better for everyone."

Michael didn't respond.

"You're not welcome," the attorney said. "If you persist…"

The men looked at each other as the sentence trailed off into its implications.

"I'm just here to watch her run."

"You won't be here again. If you are, we'll take legal action. Furthermore, if you continue to endanger our daughters with your presence," —the attorney paused, looked to the other men— "we'll be forced to take steps to remove your motivation for coming."

Michael's eyes narrowed.

"We've already talked to the athletic director and the principal."

Michael frowned at the memory, kicked at a rock. He hadn't told Sarah; she'd been hurt when he stopped coming. He frowned again, looked for another rock to kick. He'd blamed work, and she had said she understood, and hadn't complained. A month went by, and she started asking him to come again, then another month went by, and she stopped asking. The season had ended.

Now it was her senior year, states again; he'd asked his boss if he could take the afternoon so long as he went back to work afterwards, and stayed as late as he had to in order to finish.

Michael looked around the parking lot, followed the trickle of parents and friends toward the race course.

"You look lost," a man laughed.

"What?"

"Best place to watch is over there." He pointed. "It's a two lap course, so you'll see them start and finish, and once in between."

Michael nodded. "Thank you."

They walked toward the course and took up their spots. The girls were stretching or running in place, still in their warm-up gear. Sarah was bent forward, arm out, standing on one leg, the other leg pulled backwards up over her head.

"Looks painful," the man said, frowning, running a hand down his beard.

"Yes."

"That one's mine." The man pointed at one of the girls, waved.

The girl gave him a curt nod.

"She's a senior, wants to run in college."

"I hope it works out."

"Thanks."

The girls were on the move now, taking their places at the line in a slow scrum. Despite her coach's prodding, Sarah still let herself be pushed to the back of the group, would have to begin amidst a tangle of limbs.

He felt a crush of anger, forced it down, felt his gut turn to acid.

Assholes.

The assholes that kept him from watching her run, the asshole family and foster family that abandoned her, the assholes that bullied her at school, the assholes she was convinced were so far above her, the assholes that pushed her off the starting line—himself, an asshole who couldn't or wouldn't say and do the things he should for her. He wanted to pummel them and himself, to obliterate every last asshole and obstacle in her way, and finally give her something she needed.

"Sarah!"

He hadn't meant to do it, but it was too late; her head lifted, already a foot above the others, searching for his voice, pushing herself forward towards him. He held his hand up, a still wave; she hesitated in disbelief, lit up the space between them with her smile.

"Hey," he mouthed.

"Hey," she mouthed back.

"Good luck."

Warning was given, stances assumed, the gun fired. Michael saw her break from the pack, three strides, her long, spindly legs eggshell-white; he watched her chase the horizon and the distance between them grow until she was no more than a smear of color bleeding into shadow and sky.

"Your sister can run."

Michael's eyes remained fixed at the point where he'd seen her last.

"She made nationals last year," Michael said softly.

She'd come in fifth and never said anything. He only knew she'd been at all because Samuel told him.

"What's her name?"

"Sarah Smith."

"Speak of the devil."

She appeared alone, twenty seconds ahead of the next runner. If she saw him, she gave no indication; her face was expressionless, flush with blood, the myriad of blunderous angles gone, the graceless length and gawkish limbs that rendered her a clownish, encumbered mess. It was what she was always trying to do, to cease being the tall girl, the shy girl, to ceasing being awkward, and become pure motion.

"Sarah Smith?" the man asked.

Michael nodded.

He loved watching her run, the change. It surprised him every time: suddenly she wasn't afraid of anything, didn't need anything.

"Does she want to run in college?"

"Yes."

A cluster of runners rounded into view, the man's daughter amongst them. The man clapped and cheered, watched until she was out of sight.

"Which schools is she looking at?"

"She hasn't really talked about it."

"Here she comes."

The men turned as Sarah hit the last straightaway, watched her accelerate, burst across the line into the embrace of her coach.

"I'm going to go say hello." Michael pointed. "It was good to meet you —"

"Bob," the man said, extending his hand. "Bob St. Pierre."

"Michael Tolan."

They shook hands.

"Take care, Bob."

Michael made it a few yards before the man called him back. "Wait—I thought you said your sister's name was Smith?"

"Different fathers," he said over his shoulder.

Sarah was looking for him.

He felt a grin spreading across his face, lifted her off the ground and spun her around as she squealed. He slowed, steadying them, letting her slide down him until her feet were on the ground again.

"Hey," she said.

"You were amazing."

CHAPTER SEVENTY-SEVEN

"*Sixteen Candles*?"

Sarah smiled. "I've never seen it."

"Never?"

She shook her head.

"Oh, Sarah… what am I going to do with you?"

She shrugged. "More vodka and Kool-Aid?"

"Of course!" Chelsea smiled wickedly, cradling her fingers and tapping them against each other. "Another innocent corrupted."

They talked, drank, laughed.

"Michael's out of town?"

Sarah nodded.

"Working a job in Vermont."

"Oh."

"They send him to the jobs farthest from Port Haven so no one recognizes him and gets upset."

Chelsea winced. Sarah looked at the ground. The alcohol was thick in their heads; the light danced and the room rocked slightly.

Chelsea started to giggle.

"What?"

"Michael."

"What about him?"

"What's it like?"

"What's what like?"

"Michael."

"What about him?"

"Sarah!"

"What? OH!" She turned scarlet.

"Sarah Smith…"

She curled into a ball on the floor, covered her ears. "I can't hear you!"

"Oh yes you can!" Chelsea pinched her lightly. "What's it like? Give it up! I want details."

Sarah looked at her friend, saw her staring back intently, eager.

"Have you ever?"

Chelsea shook her head.

"Oh."

"What's it like?"

Sarah's head swam with vodka. She pushed a lock of hair from her eyes, lay back on the carpet. "Big," she said to the ceiling. "Scary at first."

"Scary?"

"The first time hurts."

"Hurts?"

Sarah nodded, "At first, then it feels… full, and you aren't sure you can take it, but then he… withdraws, and you can't take that either. You're breathing him the whole time, but you can't really breathe, and his arms are around you, and you're sweating and a little dizzy from the heat, so you can't really think, and… he's inside you, and it's impossible and unbearable, and he keeps moving, and—"

"Easy girl."

Sarah blushed.

"But it's good?"

Sarah nodded, lambent amidst a vodka haze, eyes dancing and wearing a smile so broad and bright it hurt her face, and realizing only belatedly how she must look and sound, turning red again, and burying her face in her hands.

Chelsea giggled.

"I'm jealous."

"Don't be." Sarah hadn't meant to say it. "I'm not sure that he really wants to be with me."

CHAPTER SEVENTY-EIGHT

It's springtime, just before seven. Tori's the stronger runner, so Tolan's setting the pace, but she's pushing hard, harder than she should. They'll run just under forty miles over the next three days. Tori's parents are taking her to Paris for two weeks after they get back. Tolan could have gone, but declined, said her mother needed her help in the shop, which wasn't entirely true, but true enough that Tori couldn't be mad at her.

Tori's hair is twisted in a French braid, and Tolan's wearing pigtails because she knows they're Tori's favorite: a gesture; she hasn't given her an answer about Boston.

Their bodies are slick with sweat, but the trail they're running is cool and dark beneath a thick canopy of leaves, and the hair on their arms is standing on end. Bars of sunlight penetrate the cover sporadically, churning with dust and pollen and throwing evanescent specks.

Neither girl is wearing headphones.

They emerge from the wood onto a ribbon of asphalt hedged by cut grass and loud insects. The path widens, winds eastward into the sun, and their gooseflesh melts and the hair on their arms reclines. Belmar bridge: Tori and Tolan slow, stop at the midpoint, walk to the rail.

"How long are we going to ignore this?"

Tolan doesn't answer right away, continues to watch the river. She's been accepted to a college in Maine, and one in New Hampshire, was rejected by Boston College and Boston University. She told Tori, but she's not sure any of that really matters.

"I still don't know about Boston, Tor, I'm sorry."

"It isn't about Boston anymore."

Tolan turns, surprised.

Now it's Tori who won't make eye contact, whose eyes latch onto the river.

"It was wrong of me to ask you to give up college, and I'm sorry."

Tolan waits.

Tori swallows. "This is harder."

"What?"

Tori looks up, locks eyes with Tolan.

"I want to come out."

A dragonfly bombs between them, scything the air with its wings, tearing a corner hard left. There's a half-dozen ducks in the water, an otter floating on its back, and a snapping turtle sunning itself on the riverbank; a trout ruptures the skin of the water, falls back with a mayfly in its mouth. They don't turn.

"To who?"

"Whom."

Tolan ignores her, waits.

"My parents. The track team. The people we spend time with." She pauses. "Your mom."

Tolan's gut clenches and twists. "You'll tell them..."

"That I like girls, that I'm a lesbian."

"A lesbian?"

Tori nods.

"And what? That we're together?"

"I'd like to."

A bicycle whips by behind them, vibrating over the slats.

"I don't know if I'm a lesbian."

"You're with me."

Tolan nods.

"But that's not the same thing?"

"I don't know."

"I'm going to tell people the last week of school."

Tori's voice is gentle, hits Tolan like a fist to the throat.

"You're not asking."

Tori's eyes fall to the ground. She shakes her head.

"Then why..."

"So you know it's coming. So that you have time to distance yourself if you want to."

"Like that would help? People would assume—"

"They already do, T."

She hadn't considered that.

"My mom..."

"Don't you think she already knows?"

"She doesn't think like that."

Tori raises an eyebrow.

"What? She's almost asexual—she doesn't even date."

Tori frowns. "Don't you think it's time we rethink her a little?"

"What'd you mean?"

"Seriously, T? Your mother is a 6'4" orphan who wrote a book about an orphan called 'The Tall Girl' who grew up in a town in coastal Maine just like she did, and worked at a bookstore in high school, just like she did. And in her book, the tall girl has an affair with a man twelve years older than she is, gets pregnant her first year of college, and leaves him—maybe you don't know her as well as you think."

Tolan recoils as Tori talks, biting her lip, tears falling down her face.

Tori looks away, takes a deep breath and lets it out slowly, turns back. "My point is that she probably knows more than you think, and that she'll understand, because she's been there."

"We don't know this is a true story."

Tori stares at her, clenches her jaw. "I know this is hard for you, but…" Her voice trails off. "We should start again. I'm getting chilled."

Tori takes the lead, picking up the pace; Tolan trails behind, certain she's being punished. She doesn't want it to be a true story anymore, not even a little. She wants her father to be dead and her mother to be the person she's believed she is for eighteen years. She wants the ugliness arising between Michael and Sarah to be a product of her mother's imagination.

Selfish bitch, Michael called her.

He punished himself later, punched his heavy bag without gloves or wraps until the bag was wet with blood and some of the bones in his hand had cracked, but what did it really matter?

Another time: childish bitch.

He hurt himself for that, too, apologized profusely, but it didn't erase the words.

Her mother had hurt him, yes, but Tolan doesn't think she meant to, knows he did.

Once, the worst: *Dumb, fucking whore.*

Punishment for one night, something that may or may not have happened.

Her body brings her back, the strain and throb, the pain. She doesn't know what she'll do, or what she wants to do, and soon the run is over and they're back at the campsite, showered and changed and cooking veggie dogs over an open fire as the sun sets. There's so much between them, so much unresolved that the air is charged with an electric current, yet they're sitting next to each other in silence.

The present is undoing the past, conversations and reasons and memories crumble to silt.

"Hey Tor? How come you hooked up with Pádraig?"

"The accent."

"Shut up."

The fire is throwing shadows, the firewood hisses and spits.

"I didn't really."

Tolan makes a face.

"We only went to third-and-a-half base."

"I wasn't aware there was a third-and-a-half base."

"It's after third base, but before home plate."

"Thanks for that."

"Thanks for reminding me."

"About Pádraig?"

Tori doesn't answer right away, stares out over the fire. They're wearing sweats and hoodies, siting on damp logs, a cooler between them, graham crackers and Hershey bars atop the lid, freezer packs and ice cubes halfway to melt and a dozen 802's beneath it. An open bag of marshmallows leans against one of the sides.

"Was it that bad?"

"Damn it." Tori's stick is on fire; she tries to shake it out, pitches a parabola of fire into the night.

"Nicely done."

"Don't be a bitch."

It's more than Tolan deserves, but she doesn't apologize or speak or turn. She fixes her eyes on the flames as the night swells with cricket-song and the wing and swoop of bats, while a pair of owls play at call and response, and the murmuring of the adjacent campsite falls upon them in unintelligible whispers.

Tolan stands, reaches for their empties, one each, dumps what's left of the bottle in her hand, pauses a moment.

Nothing.

"You'll get the fire?" Tolan asks.

A dog barks in the distance. One of their neighbors calls out his beer order to a departing friend.

Tori is silent. Tolan turns for the tent.

"Run wear you out?" Tori asks.

Tolan ignores the question, unzips their tent, and takes a toothbrush and toothpaste from her backpack, floss. Done, the items go back into a Ziploc bag. She curses herself for leaving the tent flap open while she brushed, enters the tent, closes it behind her, and crawls into her sleeping bag, lies there listening for the mosquitos she's let in. She's tired, but she won't sleep; her mind is racing and the ground beneath the tent is hard and uneven.

And Tori will be two feet away, not speaking to her.

Tolan's bag is rated for sub-zero temperatures, and soon she's wet with perspiration, peeling off her sweats and hoodie, her t-shirt a few minutes later, folding them neatly.

Tori is as quiet as one can be when she enters, but the zipper is loud. Tolan's lying on her side, her back to the entrance, isn't sure whether she wants to feign sleep or talk.

"It was bad because it wasn't what I wanted."

Tolan doesn't move.

"I was ashamed afterwards—I still don't know why I did it. It's the one thing in my life I can say that about."

Tolan rolls onto her back now. Little light penetrates the tent; Tori is line and shadow and circumspection, no substance.

"How long have you known?"

"That I like girls?"

Tolan is silent.

"Always, I think."

"Always?"

"In a way."

"Did getting with Pádraig help you figure it out?"

"No."

"No?"

"I knew."

"Then why..."

"I don't know, I really don't. It felt... wrong. Not bad, but wrong."

The elusive obvious, descending like a war hammer.

"It's not college, is it?"

Tolan shakes her head, wonders if Tori can see.

"You don't know..."

Tolan's made of shame: blood and bone and sinew are shame.

"So what we've been doing is..."

She doesn't know.

"An experiment?"

"No."

"Sport fucking?"

"No!"

"Then what?"

"I don't know."

"What are we doing?"

"I don't know!"

"You don't know." Tori sucks her teeth, starts to speak, reins herself in. "How do you expect me to feel, T?"

"Badly."

"Badly."

"I wish it were different."

"Me too."

Tori peels her sweatshirt off, crawls into her bag without another word. Tolan tries. "You know I love—"

"Don't!"

It's a bleat, a short sharp exhalation of pain; Tori takes a deep breath.

"Just don't."

CHAPTER SEVENTY-NINE

"How's Brian?"

"Well, he's no Michael," Chelsea teased, "but…"

"Hush." Sarah swatted at her; Chelsea laughed.

"Four months now."

"Nice."

"Cotton swab?"

"I think I got it all."

Chelsea scrubbed at her toenails.

"We've been getting naughtier and naughtier…"

Sarah was focused on her toes, trying to get the base coat all the way to the edge of her nail without smearing it on her skin. "We have?"

Chelsea gave her a look.

"What?"

She rolled her eyes.

"Which color?"

Sarah surveyed the choices. "Green."

"Green?" Chelsea put on her most indignant look. "Please! It's 'Mystical Sea Mist.'" She laughed, took the polish. "Brian and I."

Little lines appeared on Sarah's face as she painted.

"What?"

"We've been getting naughtier and naughtier."

"Oh."

Sarah dipped the brush back in the bottle, pulled it out.

"You have no idea what I'm talking about do you?"

She looked up at her friend, startled, searched her face for an answer, shook her head.

"Sorry."

"Sex, Sarah, I'm talking about sex."

Sarah stared, opened her mouth, shut it.

"You know, for someone who's been getting it longer and more regularly than anyone I know—"

"Stop!" She buried her face in her hands, looked up. "I was distracted."

Chelsea was laughing.

"I'm going to die if you don't stop."

Chelsea tried, dissolved in a fit of giggling, tried again. "I can't," she said, fanning herself with both hands. "My face hurts."

"I..." Sarah began.

"I can't breathe," Chelsea gasped, tears rolling from her eyes. "I'm laughing too hard."

She gave up, resumed painting her nails.

"I'm sorry," Chelsea said when the laughter subsided.

"Harumph."

"Who am I supposed to talk to about these things if I can't tell my best friend?"

"You can," she said quickly. "Er, so, you and Brian... did it?"

"It?" Chelsea choked off another fit. "No, not yet. I let him go down on me, though."

"Oh," Sarah stammered. "I mean... good, er... how was it?"

Chelsea fell apart, couldn't help herself, rolled on to her side doubled over in laughter.

"I'm trying," Sarah said meekly.

"I know. I'm sorry."

"You look like a tomato," Sarah said.

"It was amazing."

"Good," she smiled. "I like it, too."

"Now you look like a tomato."

They finished their nails, picked out a movie, *An Affair To Remember*.

"Can I do your hair while we watch?" Chelsea asked.

"Sure."

Chelsea collected her combs, a brush, a mirror and a few elastics, and sat behind her friend.

"You've got beautiful hair."

Sarah smiled.

Both girls loved Cary Grant; they'd seen the movie a dozen times, kept the volume low so they could talk. Chelsea's mother came up to check on them.

"You girls need anything? Your father and I are going out."

Chelsea shook her head.

"There's some champagne in the refrigerator if you girls want to make mimosas. Don't tell your father."

"Thanks, Mom."

"Thanks, Mrs. Eliot."

She left, and the girls returned to the movie.

"Is Michael going to Virginia with you?"

Sarah shook her head.

"Hold still."

"I haven't asked him yet."

"Things still aren't going well?"

She shrugs.

"I'll bet he does—I can't believe he's selling his house for you! That's so romantic—things can't be that bad between you."

Sarah frowned. "His truck has been acting up. The new one. Well, new to him."

"Whatever. You don't sell your house to buy a car."

"I think he's still trying to catch up from before."

Chelsea wove the final lock into the braid and cinched it with a hair tie. "What do you think?"

She held a hand mirror up for her.

"I love it."

"It's a French braid. Mom used to wear them."

"Michael will love it."

"Love taking it out."

Sarah flushed, forced a smile. "That too."

"Would you go without him?"

Sarah stiffened.

"Sorry. I shouldn't have—"

She shook her head. "It's okay."

The girls' eyes met in the mirror.

"I..." Sarah's voice trailed off, and she looked away, out into the room or into herself. "No."

Chelsea watched her in the mirror.

"I don't know."

"Things really are bad, aren't they?"

"I haven't told him I got into UVA. He doesn't even know I applied."

"Why?"

Tears welled up in Sarah's eyes. "I don't think he loves me."

"What? Why would you even say that?"

Sarah shook her head and began to sob.

CHAPTER EIGHTY

She was cross-legged on the couch when he got home, clutching a mug of tea in both hands, a book spread over her lap.

"Hey."

She looked up, surprised. "Hey. You got up early for a Saturday."

"Had to get a few things. Worked out and showered, too."

"When?"

"While you were on your run."

"Oh."

He leaned against the doorjamb. A cut of sunlight crossed the room, parting the morning shadow and falling diagonally across her face so she had to close one eye to look at him.

"Are you doing anything today?"

She shook her head, squinting, pushed a lock of hair out of her face; she'd left it down to dry, waves of orange and red, strawberry blonde highlights Michael had never noticed before falling over her shoulders and down her back.

"I was hoping to kidnap you."

A cloud interrupted the sunbeam as he spoke, and she was able to open both eyes, to see him looking at her, the gentleness of his posture. She dropped her eyes, head tilting, hair falling over her face as her dimples rose and teeth emerged, a smile pulling at her mouth.

"What?" he asked.

She shook her head, smile flowing into a soft laugh.

"What?"

"You're not very good at kidnapping."

"Really?" Michael raised an eyebrow.

"Nope."

She shook her head again, curls swinging, pushed her hair back over head, met his gaze, the sun still behind a cloud, her eyes live, color and light swirling around the iris.

"I'm pretty sure kidnappers can't have permission."

"Is that so?"

She giggled.

"I'm pretty sure that, by definition, you can't kidnap with permission."

He'd swept her off the couch before she could blink, tossed her over his shoulder, and carried her toward the stairs as she laughed, protesting playfully, kicking her feet and slapping his back.

"Put me down, you big bully!"

"How about now? Am I kidnapping you now?"

"Nope!" She stopped struggling instantly. "You have my permission."

Michael held her there, slung over his shoulder. "You think you're pretty smart, don't you?"

"If the shoe fits…"

"I think you may be in trouble."

"Nope," she giggled. "Definitely not, no trouble happening here."

"Big trouble."

He started carrying her up the stairs.

"Put me down, you big creep!"

"Now you're definitely in trouble."

"Help!"

He had her pack a few things, and ten minutes later, they were in the car.

Brunswick ended, became Bath, became Wiscasset. They drove through Damariscotta, Nobleboro, Waldoboro, the intervals between buildings growing, signs less and less corporate, increasingly handmade, from Jo-Ann Fabrics to Andy's Gas, Grocery, and Bait. Michael was quiet, but smiling, took her hand for miles at a time, window rolled down, her hair kicking in the wind. Her smile died when they hit Thomaston. "I was thinking about the other day, the goofy grin you got talking about that hot dog you won on a bet with that fisherman."

"Goofy?"

"Very goofy."

She smacked him, feigning gaiety.

"Ow," he laughed.

"Teach you to be mean." She made a face. "You'd better watch it, mister. I'm fierce."

He put his hands up in mock surrender.

Thomaston slid by at twenty-five miles per hour, rows of white colonials with black shutters, a prison, a city block's worth of businesses, two church steeples, and a bank. She grew paler and more tense with every foot.

Michael noticed. He cringed, remembering her mother. "Shit."

She turned, puzzled, waited, watching him intently.

"I'm sorry."

"For what?"

"I should have asked you first."

"Asked me what?"

"If you wanted to come here. If it was okay to bring you."

The softness of his voice, the concern that clung to each word only made it harder; she turned away from his gaze, blinking back tears, looking out the window as they drove, Thomaston disappearing behind them as they headed toward the sea, the streets and businesses painfully familiar.

She recognized Mr. Aaltonen outside the bank. He'd worked at the supply store Brad bought from. Old man Ray was shuffling toward the hardware store.

She was grateful they hadn't seen her.

Michael tried again. "Are you okay?"

She nodded, sniffed, rubbed at her eyes.

He continued driving, watching her out of the corner of his eye, trying to be unobtrusive and failing.

"We could skip the hot dog?"

She shook her head. "Take a left."

Main Street pulsed with movement, bumper to bumper traffic, and throngs of shoppers carrying bags that shimmered in the light and reflected off the glass storefronts on either side of the street. All of it disappeared within a mile, replaced by dirt-streaked siding and peeling paint on their left, the docks and the ocean on their right.

"Go left at the fork." She pointed. "See it?"

The smell of onions and hot dogs and peanut oil hit him half a block from the stand, made his mouth water.

"You sure you want to—"

"Try and stop me."

"Good," he said. "I'm starving."

She was trying to smile. They parked, got out, and stood in line. A child tugged at the hem of his mother's skirt and pointed. *I bet she's on a basketball team*, Sarah heard a woman say to her husband. *Must be awful to be that tall*, said another woman. *She's six inches taller than the man she's with. I'd hate that.*

Michael frowned, put an arm around her waist, surprising her.

"Want to eat down by the water?"

She nodded, tentatively covering his hand with her own. They waited, ordered, walked down to the water with their hot dogs and root beer, and sat.

She paused as she brought the hotdog to her mouth, inhaled deeply, eyes closing, an involuntary smile spreading across her face. Michael stifled a laugh. She took a small bite, chewed at length, holding the hotdog in her lap, swallowed, opened her eyes.

"Laugh all you want."

"I don't think I've ever seen you this happy."

She made a face.

"It's almost…"

She readied the hot dog for another bite.

"Orgasmic."

She stopped mid-bite, saw herself through his eyes, turned red, face, neck, and chest burning, eyes tearing up.

Michael bit his tongue until he tasted blood.

"I'm not talking to you."

"Sorry."

"You should be."

He finished quickly, pulled her to him so that her back was against his chest, wrapping his arms around her as he ate.

"I'm still not talking to you," she said when she finished, leaning against him and craning her neck.

"Okay."

They watched the water shimmer in the sunlight, listening to the gulls. The tide was out. A cool wind ran inland.

"Why does it bother you so much?"

"Being tall?"

It was easier, facing out to sea, away from everyone and everything. There was nothing to stop the words once they'd been spoken, so if they were the wrong words, neither of them had to see the hurt in the other's face, and if they waited long enough, the words would go so far out to sea that they'd be out of sight and out of mind, and they could try new ones.

"I stick out. Everyone stares. All I want is to be like everyone else, invisible, but I can't be; people see me, and they talk…"

Her voice trailed off.

To their right the harbor was dotted with boats, kayaks and yachts and sailboats riding the wind, lobstermen humming along in their diesels. A barge was making its way toward the docks, two schooners heading out to sea.

"Maybe if I weren't so tall… people would leave us alone."

He pulled her tightly to him, said nothing, looked out to where the dark blue sea met the translucent blue sky.

"I—" Michael began, stopped. He'd never seen an ocean, never even been out of Chicago, until an aunt he'd never met died and left him the place in Port Haven. He'd crossed Lake Shore Drive several times, sat on the concrete, staring out across Lake Michigan, but this was different.

"You're not a freak."

Her word.

She didn't respond.

He held her, suddenly nervous, trying to put things together, thoughts and words, failing somehow, again. It was always like this with her: what was right was also wrong, and up was also down, and left, and right. He wanted her, needed her, and needed to get as far from her as he could—for her sake. It was never just right, could never be right no matter how right it felt, the points of her vertebrae pressing his chest, his arms around her, the heat of her body, her hair tickling him as she lay her head in the crook of his neck.

Elements of love intermingled with base desire, and no matter which predominated, he knew it would still and always be wrong.

But the day was brilliant and bright, and the sun-baked granite beneath them and the breeze lolling in off the ocean freed them from their struggles and filled them with an inarticulate and ineffable hope. The excitement with which he began the day colored everything, past and present, turned buying supplies and packing and driving her to get the hot dogs she'd always wanted, but only once been able to have, into reasons to believe they could have a future together.

"You're beautiful," he said.

The words came without forethought. He felt her twisting, turning toward him, saw her eyes, large and wide, looking at him. Her breath touched his neck. A smile stalled on her face, hit a question. She had freckles on her cheeks, her nose. He brushed a finger lightly over her lips.

"I like looking at you," he said, feeling foolish.

"Really?"

He nodded, looking away as she watched him.

"I've never seen anything… so light. I think—"

"Sarah Smith?"

They turned, startled, disentangled quickly, and stood, following the voice back to a bearded man in his sixties.

"Well, I'll be, it is Sarah Smith. What're you doing up here—I thought I heard you moved south."

Sarah nodded. "Port Haven."

He turned to Michael. "Chet. Chet Alfven."

"Michael Tolan."

They stood in awkward silence, squinting into the sun, Chet looking at them.

"I've known Sarah since before she could walk. I used to pay her to fix some of my traps for me."

"Really?" Michael turned to Sarah. "She never offered to help me with mine."

"I—" she stuttered.

"Woah… Didn't mean to start anything," Chet said, taking a step back, both hands raised in, palms out.

Sarah held her breath, both men laughed, and she exhaled.

"So how do you guys know each other?"

Sarah's eyes ran from the man to Michael and back. "He doesn't even own a boat."

Michael laughed, Chet's face flexed minutely, eyes narrowing, brows knit for half a moment, then normal again. She watched the men take measure of each other on either side of polite smiles.

"Well, I best be getting back," Chet said.

Michael extended his hand.

"It was good to meet you, Chet."

"Take good care of her."

Neither man let go immediately. Their eyes locked, the muscles in their forearms taut.

"I will."

Rockland, Rockport, Camden. They walked the galleries on the harbor, stopped for ice cream. He took her hand, surprising her again, and she led him toward the docks, taught him how to differentiate between yachts and schooners and catboats. She pointed to a clipper at moor, sails trim, three masts rising to the sun. "Isn't she beautiful?"

He followed the line of her arm.

"I used to dream about them," she said. "They're the fastest, sail the closest to the wind."

He looked down at their conjoined hands, the contrast in size, the roughness of his own, the delicacy of hers, the gentle sweep from her forearm to the blade of her wrist, the valleys between their interwoven fingers.

"I sailed into the horizon with a faceless crew."

She turned back to him when he didn't respond, his face fallen beneath the shadow of a passing cloud.

"Michael?"

He looked up, forced a smile, gave her hand a squeeze.

"You okay?"

"Better than."

She looked at him for a long time. He looked back at her.

"Ready to pick out our campsite?"

She frowned.

"I'm fine, Sarah, I promise."

She nodded, didn't speak. They started walking up the hill toward the truck.

"You should see yourself," he said, looking down at the asphalt. "By the water, talking about those boats. You looked like you were eating hot dogs the whole time."

He glanced at her, saw her looking down at him, head cocked to one side, face questioning.

"You were smiling," he said quickly, embarrassed.

"I like boats."

They walked on, hands swaying between them.

"I like you," he said finally, hesitant, afraid of the words.

They reached the truck, drove to the park in silence, hands still joined, secured a campsite. They climbed Mt. Battie, emerging from the shadow of a canopy of pine and spruce onto an expanse of grass and flower beneath a sky opalescent with cloud and sunlight, the Penobscot Bay shimmering below them.

"Michael?""Hmm?"

"Has something changed?"

The fire was dying, the night sky the color of tar. He'd surprised her again, lay with his head in her lap, eyes closed, let her stroke his hair.

"What do you mean?"

The warmth of the fire, fatigue, and her touch encased him; his voice was thickening with the onset of sleep.

"The hand holding. The kisses. This."

His eyes opened; the fire popped. Something near a smile played at her face, joy made piquant by sadness or uncertainty. Disbelief.

She looked away, stared out into the night, he, up at her.

"I think I know, sometimes," she said, "then days go by and you won't touch me, won't even look me in the eye. I tell myself, I need to let go. That you don't love me, and that I need to move in with Chelsea and let you find someone who doesn't make things so difficult.'"

"That's not—"

"Days like today are amazing. I feel… the way you look at me, the things you say—" She turns back, smiles down at him, sadly. "Days like today, I think it doesn't matter if it goes away, or what else happens, or if you won't hold me or tell me you love me most of the time. Days like today, it feels like these moments are enough, proof that you do love me, and that we'll be together."

She looked away again.

"But it isn't true. I know that even before the day is over, before you change back. I remember what it feels like, how lonely I am so much of the time, and how much it hurts." She stopped, closed her eyes, and swallowed, reopened them. "What it feels like to be disgusting to the person you love."

Silence fell, his turn to speak, but he didn't. Couldn't.

"Chelsea said I could move in with her."

"Is that what you want?" Michael's voice was barely a breath.

Her mouth dropped open, her eyes widening and filling with tears. "What?"

He didn't speak.

"I need to sleep," she said finally, standing.

He managed to nod.

"I love you, Michael," she said, and disappeared into the tent.

CHAPTER EIGHTY-ONE

She was reading when he came home.

"Hey," she said, cautious.

He forced a smile, eyes bleary, lips stretched thin; she relaxed: tired, not angry. He sat down on the far side of the couch.

"How was your day?" she asked.

She knew the look on his face. He didn't want her to be a child tonight.

She touched his face, expecting and hoping he would put his hand over hers, pull her to him, kiss her, go from there, but he didn't, didn't react at all, stared straight ahead with an unfamiliar expression on his face. She reached out to him, and he let himself be pulled sideways, his head laid in her lap. Looking down she saw the part in his hair, his cowlick, traced a finger along his hairline, took his ear between her thumb and forefinger, light pressure on either side, drew her fingers up and down its length, something she'd seen Linda do for her husband at the end of a hard day, to her children when they were sick. He gave a grunt, and then her left hand was massaging his scalp, his hair protruding through the space between her fingers, and she felt his breath, hot and damp against the flesh of her thigh, waited for his advance, stifling her anger—yesterday I'm a child, she thought, now you're horny, so I'm a woman—but the advance didn't come.

She wanted consistency, for Michael's actions to confirm her status rather than shunting her back and forth between child and woman.

She continued kneading him, damp went to wet, not just the condensation of breath, actual drops of something liquid falling down her inner thigh; she was thrown, her anger gone, fear and curiosity rising with the mystery of the event. He didn't move. She brought her hand flush against his cheek, cupping the contour of his jawline, his stubble rough beneath her palm.

He'd yelled at her two nights ago. She wasn't sure if she'd deserved it, was sure that he didn't have the right to call her a child again. She and Chelsea had been sunning themselves; Michael had come home to find them in the living room still in their bikinis, blinds up, visible to all.

Now he was crying.

She thought he was crying.

It scared her more and more as she thought about it: Michael had yelled at her a half dozen times, but she'd never seen him cry. He was neutral, for the most part, stolid and strong. He didn't touch, didn't hug or kiss until she did, and then he was awkward, tentative. He was good at sex, she thought, flushing, more confident, never embarrassed. But that was somehow different for him.

And now he was asleep.

She leaned forward, incrementally, so as not to wake him, peered over his head, down at her thigh, searching for the residue of his tears. She didn't find them, couldn't see underneath his head, lay backward as slowly as she'd come forward until she felt the back of the couch. She didn't know what to do. Her book was within reach. Should she read while he lay there? Watch him while he slept? Stroke his hair? She listened to his breathing.

Should she turn out the light?

Did he mean to sleep?

She wasn't tired.

His head felt heavy in her lap, warm; his hair brushed against her leg, tickling her. She tried not to squirm. They rarely did this, anymore, rarely cuddled except in a bed, before or after sex. Possible reasons ran through her mind like ticker tape.

Something must have happened: fear.

He came to me: surprise; hope.

They moved in concert in her head, she and Michael: mirrors, lovers, poles, equals, opposites; she blinked, shook her head, blinked again.

Had he really been crying?

"Hey.""He was awake.

"Hey," Sarah said. She was in bed, his bed, the bed he'd given up and come back to, and given up and come back to, again and again. She was on the left side of the bed; the right side was empty, but had been slept in. She was still wearing yesterday's clothes, her collar, loose and sagging, had dropped over one shoulder. She looked up at him, blinking sleep away. He was in jeans and a white t-shirt, his hair disheveled.

She propped herself up on her elbows.

"We fell asleep on the couch." He was smiling. "I carried you in."

"Oh." Her hair ran everywhere, wild with sleep.

"There's Dunkin Donuts in the kitchen." He looked away, down at his feet. "I got you a bear-claw."

She pushed her legs out from under the covers and over the side of the bed, followed him into the kitchen and sat at the table, smiling.

"There's hot chocolate, too."

He bent down to kiss her, lightly and quickly, but she caught him, her hand on the back of his head; he hesitated, kissed her, moved to pull away, but she stopped him. He kissed her again, waited for her to release him. She didn't. He kissed her again, waited, again, pressing his lips against hers, first slowly, then opening them and taking her lip between them; she kissed back.

CHAPTER EIGHTY-TWO

"Michael?"

He looked up from his book, smiled.

"Hey."

She was standing in the doorjamb, eyes downcast, half looking at him, half looking at the floor. She wore one of his old training hoodies and a pair of his sweat pants. He closed his book and set it beside him.

"I thought you'd gone to bed."

She shook her head. "I couldn't sleep."

"How's your headache?"

"Michael…" Her nose crinkled as she thought, tiny lines appearing on her forehead. He waited, watching her. "Do you want me here?"

Their eyes locked.

"Sarah—"

"Do you want to be with me?"

"I am, aren't I?"

"Are you?"

She looked him full in the face, eyes wide, green, flickering.

"Sarah…"

"I know it's been hard."

Michael stared; she looked away.

"You think I don't know, but I do. I didn't for a long time, but I do now."

"How?"

"Chelsea told me some, Samuel."

"How long?"

"A while."

"I didn't want to worry you."

She didn't look up. "I'm scared you don't want to be with me."

"But I'm here!"

"You don't touch me."

"Sarah…"

"You don't talk about the future."

Silence.

She turned on him, eyes welling over with tears. "Do you want to be with me or not?"

Nothing.

"I can't be a woman if you won't let me."

"Sarah... look, you're tired, you haven't been feeling well. You should sleep, we can talk about this later."

She looked at him for a long time, searching, tears swelling in her eyes.

"Okay," she said finally.

CHAPTER EIGHTY-THREE

"Are you sure?"

Tori had left for Paris on Thursday; Tolan called Walter on Saturday. They hadn't talked since freshman year.

"Yes. You're not going to tell anyone?"

"No."

"No?"

"I won't tell anyone."

"Did you bring a condom?"

"Yes."

Tolan holds out her hand.

He gives it to her.

"You're sure?"

"Yes."

"You're shaking."

"I'm nervous."

"Me too."

"I've never."

"Is that why you want to?"

She nods. "Is that okay?"

"I was hoping you were in love with me—a wizard spell or something." He tries a smile.

She shakes her head, wants to reciprocate, isn't sure it'd be right to. "Sorry."

"It's okay."

They've driven to the next county, parked in a field by the airport. They get out of the truck; she has a blanket, opens the tailgate and climbs in, shakes the blanket out, spreads it across the truck bed, waits for him.

"This isn't going to work with you out there." She forces a smile.

They're both looking around to see if anyone's coming; it's only dusk, so it's not quite safe, yet.

"Sorry." He gets in.

"Pants off."

"Right. Sorry." He unbuttons his fly, fingers his zipper. "Can I keep my shirt on?"

She nods. "Have you ever?"

He shakes his head.

They remove their pants without looking at each other, pause, gooseflesh rising, the hair on his legs, her arms.

"The moment of truth," he says weakly.

They're hunched, halfway between sitting up and lying down, trying to conceal themselves. It's a warm night, but the metal is cold, even through the blanket. They lie back, push their hips in the air, pull their underwear to their knees, sit up, push it the rest of the way off.

Her curiosity gets the best of her first; he covers himself.

She looks up at him. "I've never seen one before."

"Never?"

"No."

"Not even online?"

She shakes her head.

She realizes her legs are crossed, forces herself to open them. His eyes fall; she's surprised: being exposed is easier than eye contact.

"You don't have any hair."

"I shave."

"Oh."

She holds the condom up. "We should get this on you."

"Okay."

Foil crinkles. "How old is this?"

"Old."

The latex touches him, he jumps, laughs awkwardly, settles. Pressure.

"My cousin gave—"

"Dammit!"

"Broke?"

"Damn."

Silence. Stillness.

"Does this mean…"

She shakes her head.

"But—"

"You're a virgin, right?"

He averts his eyes, nods.

"I'll take the morning after."

"But…"

His voice peters out into the night. It's dark now. They sit in silence.

"Do you want me to be on top?"

He nods, ashamed, remembers the dark. "You probably should."

"Did you want to…"

"What?"

"Touch me, or something?"

He does.

She does.

They hear a car, flatten themselves against the bed. The sound passes, disappears. They wait. She peeks over the side.

"Okay?" he asks.

"Okay."

She pushes herself to her knees; he scoots forward, lays back.

"You're sure?" he asks.

She doesn't answer, lowers herself; he inhales audibly, holds his breath. She freezes, waits: no pain, yet, just discomfort, stinging.

"It's okay," he says. "I'm okay."

She holds a moment longer, starts to move. His hands rise to her breasts.

"Can I…"

She's not with him, feels bad.

"Yes."

He slips his hands beneath her shirt. She's waiting for the tearing she's heard about, the searing hot thrust, but it only stings. She stops, waits for it to pass; he doesn't seem to notice, kneads and pulls, squeezes.

Then, "I'm—do you want me to—"

She buries him as deeply as she can. His moment comes with a grunt, a burst of heat; she feels herself clench involuntarily.

She counts to thirty, pushes herself away from him.

"Was it…" he asks.

No pop, no tear, no sear.

She nods. "For you?"

"Amazing."

They dress, move out of the truck bed, into the cab.

"Did—would you like to get dinner before you drop me off?"

"Um… I—"

"Never mind."

"I—"

"Don't worry about it."

"Another time?"

"It's okay."

"I'm sorry."

"For what?"

She fires the engine, turns her headlights on, backs up, puts the vehicle in drive and pulls onto the road.

"You shouldn't feel bad."

She doesn't answer.

"This is a fantasy come true for me—I've had a crush on you since junior high."

She blushes. "We talked about this, Walter..."

"No, I know—just listen."

She does.

"I," he starts, "You..."

She waits.

"We all thought you were gay."

"What? Who thought?"

"Leo and Harvey and I—other people. It's..." —his eyes fall to the floor mat— "...kinda what everyone thinks. You and Tori Quevedo live together don't you?"

She wants to tell him he's an asshole, that he's just saying this because she isn't into him, because he couldn't rock her world, but his voice is too kind, and she knows it's not true.

"It's..."

"You don't have to say anything."

He's waiting, watching her; she looks back briefly, sets her eyes on the road.

They drive.

"You were honest with me," he says finally, "so even if I hoped for more..." His voice trails off.

She's silent, processing.

"Besides, whoever heard of a wizard-hat-wearing, comic-book-toting fanboy who wasn't carrying the torch for some out-of-reach beauty?"

He makes a face.

She laughs.

Twenty minutes later, they're stopped outside his house, engine idling.

"Maybe we could get together for coffee sometime?"

He gives her a half-smile, rolls his eyes. "I'll hold my breath."

"Seriously."

He opens his door and gets out. "You know where to find me."

"At comic-con," she tries.

"There's more to me than just comic books," he says tersely.

"I'm sorry—"

He's glowering at her.

"I didn't mean—"

"I'm also a level forty-four wizard."

"I... I don't know what that is."

His lips quiver, then his deadpan breaks, and he's laughing.

"We'll have coffee sometime soon."

"You really don't have to."

"I'd like to."

He smiles. "I won't hold you to it."

He starts to close the door behind him, stops. "I know this sounds weird given the circumstances, but thanks."

"Thank you."

"Okay, then."

"Walter?"

"Yeah?"

"I kept the costume you made me."

He smiles.

"Take care, Tolan."

CHAPTER EIGHTY-FOUR

Tori's in Paris for four more days. Tolan's an hour and a half from Nick's bookstore, feeling shy and more than a little embarrassed because she hasn't seen him since she was eleven, and because she knows how great a debt she and her mother already owe to him.

She drops a gear and accelerates around a Volkswagen bus, trying to distract herself from the impending confrontation, half-wondering if she'll be able to distinguish the books she'll sort and shelve and sell this summer from those she's helped her mother sort and shelve and sell for years, from those choking the shelves lining every wall of the house she's grown up in, piled on countertops and coffee tables and desktops.

She's tired, but she's only forty minutes out. She veers off at a rest stop, fills her tank, buys a Powerbar and a sugar-free energy drink, and pulls back onto the highway. She'll make it just before the shop closes.

This whole trip happened in a day. She was playing Tori's speech about her mother over in her head for the hundredth time, and decided she believed it. The book was true. She'd told her mother Thursday evening that she wanted to visit a college she'd heard about in Maine that had rolling admissions, and her mother had given her permission and lent her a hundred dollars, and she'd left after school on Friday. She didn't tell Nick she was coming, and she doesn't know if she'll confront him immediately or in the morning, or how she'll do it, only that Nick is Samuel, that her father's alive, and that Nick knows where he is.

She'll start talking straight from the door, enter just as he's closing the shop and start talking and throw him off guard.

He'll have to tell her after she's driven all this way.

And Tori—what about Tori?

Everything is accelerating.

She isn't sure if she's going to tell her about Walter. Tolan did what she did—it never had anything to do with Tori, and now it's over and past.

Why would she tell her?

Except that she feels she should, for some reason.

It makes Tolan feel better that she's thinking about Tori even though she's pretty sure she's about to meet her father, but worse, too. Better, because it means she loves her, worse because that love wasn't enough to keep her from cheating on her.

But did she cheat, really?

Maybe she'd done what needed to do, and whether or not she learned anything in doing it was irrelevant.

What she was doing now was the real betrayal, going in search of her father without her, without even telling her.

They hadn't talked much since the camping trip.

What would Nick do?

He'd have to tell her.

Would she go to her father's directly?

Maybe.

She feels lightheaded.

Does her father know she exists?

That's a new question, one she hadn't thought of until now.

What would he say if he knew she were a lesbian?

Has she decided she's a lesbian?

Too many questions.

Her exit is up ahead, her confrontation with Nick imminent.

Compartmentalize.

Tolan rolls the window down as soon as she's off the highway, turns right onto Route 1, stops at a traffic light. There's a filling station ahead, a small storefront across from it. Moths wing and wheel beneath the streetlamp beside her; she can hear them hitting the bulb. The night air is thick with clover and honeysuckle, a breath of gasoline. Tolan looks left and right, ahead: no one. She waits, but the light doesn't change, so she runs it, not wanting to lose her nerve before she gets to the bookstore.

Red and blue lights.

Her heart stops, her breath.

"License and registration."

"Yes, sir." She reaches for the glove box, takes out the quart-sized Ziploc bag with her registration and proof of insurance, pulls her ID out of her purse, and hands them over.

"Do you know why I pulled you over?"

"Yes, sir."

The policeman is silent; Tolan wonders if he's waiting for an explanation, "I—"

"I'll be back."

He walks to his cruiser, runs her plates, returns. "I'm giving you a warning for running the light and citing you for having a trailer hitch that obscures your license plate. It's a non-moving violation, so your insurance won't go up."

"Thank you, Sir."

"Don't run any more red lights."

"Yes, sir."

Tolan watches him walk back to his car, starts her engine, waits to see if he's going to drive away, checks her MapQuest printout, pulls back onto the road. He follows her until she turns off, corkscrewing down a ramp, taking a left onto Main Street, another onto Hastings, a right into the bookstore parking lot. She opens the door, steps out of the truck, checks her reflection in the window, smooths her shirt, rakes a hand through her hair.

She can see him through the shop window, takes a deep breath.

A bell sounds when she opens the door. Nick is writing out a receipt. "We close in five—" he says, raising his head. "Tolan?"

"Hi, Nick."

He manages to get a book and its receipt into a plastic bag, hands it to the customer. "Have a good night, Sally."

He waits until the customer is gone to turn back to Tolan, smiles. "What a surprise! For a moment, I thought you were your mother."

"I get that a lot."

"What brings you all this way?"

She starts to speak, but her voice catches in her throat and she squeaks, flushes with embarrassment, swallows hard, coughs.

"Glass of water?"

She shakes her head, hand over her mouth.

Nick waits.

"Is my father alive?"

He goes rigid, blinks. "Wh—does your mother…"

"I need you to tell me where he is."

He's still blinking, leaning over the checkout counter, holding himself up with his hands.

"Does your mother know?"

"Please, Nick."

"She doesn't, does she?"

Tolan holds her ground, eyes locked on his, arms tight against her body, hands gripping her elbows.

"How long will you…" His voice trails off.

"Please."

He turns away. "I'll get his number."

"His address. Please."

"You don't want to…"

She shakes her head.

"Watch the counter for a minute."

He returns with an index card. "Anyone give you any trouble?" he laughs weakly.

"Thank you."

"You must have questions."

She waits, staring at him, seeing something else, a tangle of deceit, a league of liars; she's clenching her teeth, her hands balled up in fists, eyes narrow.

"Why?"

"Why what?" Nick finds himself backing away.

"All of it."

"Tolan…"

"Why?"

"You should call your mother."

She catches herself, unclenches her jaw, un-balls her fists, takes a deep breath.

"Does he know about me?"

"Mich—your father?"

She nods.

"No."

"No?"

"Not unless she told him."

Tolan turns away. "I should get going."

"Where?"

Tolan holds up the notecard.

"That's at least five hours from here."

She looks at the card, brow furrowed. "Oh."

"Do you have a place to stay?"

She shakes her head. "I'll throw my sleeping bag in the bed of my truck."

"Why don't you stay at my place—or here if you prefer. There's a cot in the back."

She shakes her head. "I should be fine in—"

"It's no trouble."

"I'll be fine."

"What if I promised not to tell your mother you'd been here?"

"Why?" Tolan studies his face.

He doesn't answer right away, stares, considers. Finally: "I'd worry."

"I'd probably stay."

"Okay, then. Here or at the house?"

"Mom used to work here?"

"All through high school."

"Here."

He's relieved.

"Thank you."

She nods.

———✳———

Tolan can't sleep, doesn't sleep well without Tori, now. And this is where the scene took place, the one her mother had written and rewritten, and finally cut. It was there, then one day, she went to send herself the latest version, and it was gone.

Gone, but not erased.

She's wandering about the shop. She was never entirely sure what happened in the scene, if it was real or made up or a dream—and if it was a dream, whose dream it was. Or whose nightmare?

Tolan walks over to one of the over-stuffed couches, stands between it and the coffee table. The wine bottle—or bottles—one in one version, three in another: one empty, one two-thirds gone, and one untouched—had fallen from or been knocked off the coffee table, landed on the area rug, and rolled beneath or behind the adjacent chair. Her mother had pushed Nick—Tolan is pretty sure it was Nick—it definitely wasn't Michael—down onto the couch and straddled him, or Nick had sat down beside her and started stroking her hair.

Tolan sits on the couch, sinks into it, leans back. Her mother's bra ended up hanging off a bookshelf in one version, laying on the floor in another. Tolan pulls the t-shirt she's wearing over her head and throws it on the floor, retrieves it, hangs it up, returns to the couch, and pushes herself down into the position her mother had been in, looks around. She isn't sure what happened next, her mother wrote sensations, not acts. Tolan closes her eyes, pulls her pants down. There's a draft; it lands on her just below her navel, moves over her body like a spirit. She presses her shoulder blades down, coccyx rising off the couch, and the spirit becomes a serpent, slithering up over her underwear—her mother kept her underwear on in every version, over her mons, coiling around her thigh, then slithering up over her ribs, scapula, and clavicle, spreading out, swelling at the base of her throat.

Tolan remembers a Sunday afternoon: she was young, coloring in the living room while her mother read. She pressed too hard and snapped her crayon, gasped, tears welling in her eyes, and looked to her mother, but her mother had been reading, oblivious, reduced to eyes darting left and right over the page. Tolan feels the tears running down her face, only now they have nothing to do with a broken crayon or the hole it tore in her picture, and everything to do with how light the book is in her mother's hands, how content she is, and how gracefully she turns the pages, with the totality of her absorption, and the way that she grows translucent as she reads, fading into the air and escaping herself. Books can never do that for Tolan. She'll never experience what her mother does when she reads, never know what it feels like to be free like that.

Her mother's normal, neuro-typical, not dyslexic like her. She doesn't have trouble with letters or numbers or directionality, with linking letters to phonemes and diphthongs.

Her mother remembers every word she's ever read.

Tolan can't.

She starts to use her hands, her body a divining rod, searching for her mother, for the things and feelings she's written. Tolan should know the scene is fiction, a dream or a nightmare that her mother made up and wrote for god knows why, but she doesn't, not anymore. The closer she gets to her father, the further she gets from her mother, and she's terrified and hates him for that. But she can't stop, now.

She has to know.

Tolan remembers, wiping the tears from her face before her mother could see them, and turning to a new page in the coloring book, choosing a new crayon.

Maybe what her mother wrote had really happened, and the tall girl had woken early the next morning, collected her clothes, and slipped out before Samuel was awake, gone back to face Michael, or maybe they'd woken up together and talked about what happened, agreed it had been a mistake, and never to mention it.

Maybe Sarah told Michael, and maybe he forgave her, or maybe he didn't, and that's why they broke up.

Her mother never wrote those scenes, though.

But, maybe it was only a dream. Maybe that's why she'd erased it.

Tolan gathers her clothes and puts them back on, walks back to the office.

She'll be gone by five, a thank you note next to the register.

CHAPTER EIGHTY-FIVE

It's not yet ten-thirty, but he's more than five hours into his day, his mind blank, poured into his tools, his world reduced to chisel, planer, and sandpaper, to the wood taking them where they need to go. He works and works and works, but only on one project at a time. It's inefficient: he should do all the sawing at once, all the planing, all the sanding, but he can't. One project at a time. He cuts the power to the bandsaw and takes a pull at his coffee—it's black, instant, not particularly good. He won't spend money on it because all he needs it for is to scald himself awake as it falls the length of his gullet and dissipates through his stomach and chest.

He hears gravel crunching beneath tires and looks out through the door into the glare of sun reflecting off late-season snow. The dog by the woodstove lifts his head, cocks an ear, lays back down. He just showed up one day, no collar, emaciated, and followed him into the house.

Michael sees something out the barn door, red and white flickering between the trees, sets his coffee down, and moves toward the driveway. A truck comes into view, red with white panels, a driver, no passenger, disappears into the sun; he raises a hand to shield his eyes, but he still can't see. The truck slows, gravel crunching and the brakes shrieking. He can make out the shape of a head turning to look at the house, then back at the barn, at him. She—he sees long hair now, colorless in the sun—has to turn away, eyes singed by the light. She goes clockwise around the turnaround, stops. The truck looks like one he used to own. The driver pushes a pair of sunglasses atop her head, pulling red hair away from her face, opens the door, steps out, and walks toward him.

"Excuse me, are you Michael Tolan?"

He can't answer.

"Nick Wiley gave me your address."

He's trying but he can't, reaches behind him for the barn wall, flailing for something to steady himself against.

"I think you knew my mother, Pan Aimes."

He's barely able to nod.

"I'm her daughter, Tolan."

Michael falls backwards, hits the side of the barn, stays upright.

"Do you have time?" she begins. "Can we..."

"Tolan?"

She nods.

He'd only had his bell rung once in all the time he'd fought, but he'd been taught what to do, to focus, to focus on one thing and tie a rope to it. Pull yourself out.

The sunglasses: they're dark brown, flair at the sides, pinch in the middle. The arms disappear into her curls.

"You're... am I... I thought..."

"You thought?"

He shakes his head, grasping, fighting.

"I'm...You're my?"

"I think so."

CHAPTER EIGHTY-SIX

"Don't go."

He only looked up after he'd said it, voice wrecked, hands in his jacket pockets. He was failing again, wasn't supposed to say that.

"Why?"

Sarah was standing at the kitchen table, reaching for the cordless phone. She took it from its base, had it in her right hand. He was supposed to be letting her go. The priest he'd talked to, and Samuel, they'd told him he needed to, that it would be best for her.

He didn't answer; she started to dial.

"Please."

He was staring at her; she avoided his eyes.

"Why?"

"Because…"

His voice trailed off. He knew they were right. Let her go, let her be young, let her grow up at her own pace, meet someone in her own time, someone her age, fall in love.

"Right."

She forced a hard, abrupt exhalation, squeezed her eyes shut as hard as she could, shook her head.

"I'll still be seventeen," she said, dialing again. She was shaking, hit the wrong number, and had to start over.

"Sarah—"

"WHAT?"

He shrank back.

She paused, grit her teeth, closed her eyes, opened them again. "What?"

"Please don't go."

He was fucking it up, failing her like he'd failed her on so many days. Bile rose in his throat, his mouth running with saliva like he was about to vomit.

"Let me drive you down like we'd planned," he found himself saying. "Let me come get you for Thanksgiving. Let me take you back to school after, get you for winter break."

"Why?"

"Don't leave."

"Why, Michael? What's the point?"

He opened his mouth to answer, came up empty, shut it, opened it to try again.

It wasn't too late, he told himself. Let her make her call, let Samuel or Chelsea come get her, drive her down.

Let her leave.

She was shaking her head. "Nothing's going to change. I have to—" She started dialing.

"Is this what you want? Do you want to go?"

"What?" She froze, thumb hovering above the talk-button, voice like crystal.

"Do you want—"

"What?"

Tears.

"I—"

"What did you say?"

Anger.

"Please don't go."

Shame and shame and shame.

They stared at each other, stunned and heartbroken beholding terrified and ashamed.

"Why?" she asked.

Anger and pain.

And pain and pain and pain.

"Tell me why."

"I—"

"What?"

"Please..."

"Why?"

Don't you fucking do this, Michael.

"Please, Michael, please—tell me why."

He was silent, steeled himself. He wasn't going to do it. He'd do what was best for her, let her go.

"Because I want you to stay." The words leapt from his mouth. "Sarah, I want you to stay."

She wouldn't look at him, started shaking her head, side to side.

"No," she said. "No. No, no, no..."

He stepped toward her; she backed away.

"I want you to stay."

He took another step; she retreated further.

"No," she said. "No."

304

"Yes."

Her back hit the wall, and he took her hand.

"I want you to stay."

"I can't..."

Her head downcast, shaking. She wouldn't look at him.

"You can."

He put his hand over hers, over the one he already held.

"I'm only... still..." She was trembling.

"Sarah..."

"I can't..."

"Sarah."

"You don't... and I do... and I can't."

She was trembling, voice and body.

"Sarah."

He put a finger beneath her chin, lifted it, pointed her eyes at his.

"I can't let you go."

"Why?"

This was it. Not merely failure, betrayal.

"Because I love you."

Her eyes were wide and wet, her face ghostly; she dropped the phone.

"I love you, Sarah."

Betrayal.

She crushed herself against him, sobbing. "I love you so much."

"I love you."

He held her as tightly as he could.

"I love you."

CHAPTER EIGHTY-SEVEN

Michael pulled the dust cloth away, stood over the chair, his face a pool of shadow reflected back at him on the fore of its bowed arm. It was his first. His boss had lent him the know-how and the tools, let him use his workspace after hours, monitored his progress. Michael had put over a hundred and seventy hours into it: a bow-armed Morris chair, black walnut, a lustrous espresso streaked with accents of light. There were flaws; he saw them immediately after it was too late to fix them, the spindles not quite flush, one notch imperfectly sanded beneath the finish. Somehow it didn't bother him. He'd had a local artisan upholster it in oxblood leather, the seatback and the middle third of the arms done in nail-head trim.

"How long are you planning on leaving that here?"

"Taking it home today, Mr. Martin."

His boss nodded. "Good."

"We're going to start on the Behuniak place today."

"I'm good to go whenever you're ready, sir."

Mr. Martin brought a Styrofoam cup to his mouth, tipped it back and winced, frowned into the cup.

"Go ahead and get started without me; I've got a few calls to make."

Michael didn't move or speak, stared. His boss looked up from his coffee cup. "Any time now..."

"Yes, sir," Michael said, shaking his head. "Sorry."

Michael walked from the building to his truck, keys jingling in his hand, crushed stone crunching beneath his boots. The rain was frigid, driven sideways by the wind and biting into his face, but he didn't notice. The Behuniak account was a big one, old money looking to build a summer home: ten bedrooms, custom woodwork throughout.

It was his first unsupervised job.

He left sore. He'd opened his thumb with a chisel, had had to work later than he'd wanted to in order to make up the time he'd lost. The job-site was forty-five minutes from the office, and he still had to drive back and report to his boss and punch his timecard.

"You've got another think coming if you think I'm paying you overtime," his boss said as he walked through the door.

"Oh, hush." Mrs. Martin shuffled into the room on a crippled leg, wearing corduroys and a flannel shirt, her hair up in a bun, a pen stuck through it. She answered phones, kept the books, and handled payroll.

"Tight as a tick, that old codger," she smiled.

"Marian—"

"Don't you 'Marian' me!" She wagged a finger at her husband, turned to Michael. "You make sure he gives you everything you've earned, and if he gives you any trouble, I'll be in my office."

"Thank you, Mrs. Martin."

They watched her shuffle away, Mr. Martin shaking his head.

"What happened to your hand?"

Michael frowned. "Stupidity."

Mr. Martin nodded. "Been there. You need help getting that chair into the back of your truck?"

"I'd appreciate it."

Michael had made it for Sarah, started on it as soon as she'd left for college, designed it to be big enough for her without looking massive, given it sleek, graceful curves, a high, slender back, and a seat-cushion and arms that flared at the front so she could sit cross legged without her legs banging against wood.

It was late November, and though Sarah only had a few days for Thanksgiving break, it was after eight by the time Michael pulled into the driveway. He could see her through the front window, reading, so engrossed she hadn't heard him. She leaned forward over her book, a lock of hair swaying pendulously with the rhythm of her breath. He was smiling watching her, realized it, and smiled wider. He got out and moved toward the bed of the truck, undid the ties holding the chair in place and pulled the thick plastic sheeting off. The blankets came next, faux-velvet squares designed to protect the wood from scratching; he folded them and set them atop the sheeting, slid the chair along the remaining pad until it rested on the tailgate, cautiously lifted it out. It was heavy, solid in his hands, cool against his skin. He carried it over his head, letting its weight rest against his skull, came around the back of the truck toward the house. She was still there, still reading. Beautiful.

He smiled.

He would set the chair in the grass by the side door. The grass was wet, but he'd put three coats of sealer and five coats of poly-satin on the chair, and then waxed it, so the water wouldn't be an issue. He'd set it down, open the door, and call to her, tell her he had a surprise for her, and that she had to stay where she was, and she'd ask whether 'staying where she was' meant staying on the couch, or merely remaining in the living room, in which case she'd be within her rights to walk to the very edge of the room, hang onto the wall, and peer out into the kitchen where he'd be coming in, but he wouldn't answer because he'd be setting the stopper on the door so it wouldn't shut on him as he carried the chair into the kitchen. He'd tell her to close her eyes, and to keep them closed, and then he'd take a cloth and wipe the water from the grass off the chair, and carry it into the living room, set it down in front of her and tell her to open her eyes.

He smiled.

She'd blink once or twice as her eyes readjusted, squint, see the chair, get all wide-eyed. Look at the chair. Look at him.

He gave her one last gaze through the window, forced himself to walk past it.

She'd smile. She'd smile at him, and her eyes would be big and green and sparkling, and she'd see the chair and understand and start to cry, and he'd sit down beside her, and pull her into his arms, and she would crush herself against him, and he would kiss the top of her head.

CHAPTER EIGHTY-EIGHT

"Fancy a movie?"

"Do I ever?"

"Every so often."

"No."

"I know an old movie house that plays the classics: Buster Keaton, Garbo, Cary Grant…"

"No."

"Another time, then."

Bo shook her head. She was seventy-eight and he was eighty-five. They'd met for breakfast twice a week for over half a century. He'd stopped asking her to marry him years ago. Mostly stopped. She had to be gruff with him when he was in certain moods, or he'd ask again.

They always came towards the end of the breakfast rush, took their time. He would have taken them somewhere else, someplace where he could order duck confit Benedict, or florentine crepes and fresh-squeezed grapefruit juice, but she preferred the diner.

He could still get her laughing after all those years, and not just with his Harold Lloyd and Charley Chase impressions.

She'd never tell him to his face, but she thought his witticisms rivaled Twain's and Russell's.

"What about a walk this evening?"

"Maybe."

She always said maybe. He'd taken a nasty fall and broken his hip two years previous, and didn't walk very well. A half-mile took a quarter of an hour and left him grinding his molars in pain.

"Just down to the harbor, a kindness to an old man?"

"Tomorrow, maybe."

"What about to Gifford's?"

"I don't drink soda."

"You could have an ice cream."

"It's too cold for ice cream."

"The tavern? For a sherry?" One of a half-dozen conversations they had in cycles.

"I don't drink sherry."

"Gin and tonic, then."

"One."

"Wonderful. I'll have my driver pick you up at eight."

"I'll meet you there at eight-thirty."

"Eight-thirty it is."

"Did you remember to take your pills?"

"What pills?"

"Take your pills."

"They give me heartburn."

"Suit yourself."

"I'll take my pills."

"You always do."

"Only because you ask."

"I don't ask."

"You take good care of me."

"I don't take care of you."

"Of course not."

Lewella watched it all from a distance. She liked Parker. Bo hadn't come around much until she got older, and didn't say much, so Lewella didn't know many of the details of her life, only that she'd traveled the world, and had her pictures in magazines, and had been a champion for women. Lewella had had several of the women who came through the shelter Bo funded in Portland work in the diner.

"Ready?"

"My man won't be here until half-past."

"Of course he won't."

"He never is."

"You're shameless."

"May I have another cup of tea, please, Lewella?"

She brought him more tea, filled Bo's coffee cup.

"Reading anything these days?"

"*The Kingdom and the Power*."

"A bit of a knave, Talese."

Bo shrugged. "Good writer."

"True. Hey, you'll never guess who I ran into in Boston the other day."

"Probably not."

"Sarah."

"Sarah?"

"The girl you had in the apartment a few years back. Tall, red hair…"

"Smith, Sarah Smith."

310

"I ran into her at the Boston International Antiquarian Book Fair. She was with Samuel."

"Oh? What's she up to?"

"She told me, but I've lost the details. This old brain, you know. But you certainly made quite an impression on her—all she wanted to talk about was you."

"Really? I don't know that I ever even met her in person."

"Evidently you gave her some of your photography books at some point."

Bo nodded.

"She said they meant more to her than she knew how to convey."

"Well, that sounds a little dramatic."

"She didn't seem to think so."

Bo shrugged. "Well good, then. I'm glad she enjoyed them."

"She said that she learned from you that it was possible to live on your own terms, no matter how unlikely or untenable they might appear to others."

"I think that's enough of that."

"Oh wait, it's coming back to me now… yes, she has a little bookshop and is trying her hand at writing with an eye toward becoming a professional writer—says it was you that inspired her and gave her the courage to pursue her dream."

Bo rolled her eyes, "Oh look, your driver's here. What a shame. I really hoped you could stay and embarrass me a while longer."

Parker looked out through the plate-glass window. "So he is. I'll see you tonight then. Eight o'clock sharp."

"Eight-thirty."

"A quick question, Bo—"

"No."

He smiled, shrugged. "You can't blame a man for trying."

"Yes, I can."

He pushed himself upward, slowly, collected his coat and hat from the tabletop. "Thank you for breakfast, Lewella."

Lewella nodded, watched him turn and shuffle from the door to his car.

Bo stared down into her coffee.

CHAPTER EIGHTY-NINE

"So, umm, what do you do for fun?"

They're sitting in his living room, grasping for conversation as the logs hiss and the flames flicker in the hearth.

"How do you mean?"

"You don't have a TV."

"No."

His living room consists of a couch and a recliner, a coffee table, and a couple of lamps and end tables. The drapes had been white once, and the walls are white, bare.

"Do you hunt?"

"No."

"Do you read?"

She hadn't seen any bookshelves in the house, but she hadn't been in his bedroom.

"I have a few books."

"Don't enjoy reading?"

He shrugs.

"Are you dyslexic?"

"What's that?"

"Words run together or split up wrong, and sometimes letters transpose. It makes it hard to read."

A spider scurries up the wall as he considers the possibility.

"I always thought I was just dumb."

"We haven't ruled that out."

He starts to reply, sees the corners of her mouth quivering and laughs.

"You almost got me."

Her face gives way and she allows herself to laugh.

"You're better at that than your mother. She could never really pull it off."

"Still can't. She's easy to get, too, never realizes you're messing with her."

He remembers, starts to drift, catches himself.

"You're in college?"

"Almost. Maybe. I got in, but I'm not sure I want to go."

He nods.

"Did you go?"

"No."

"What'd you do instead?"

"I was a janitor."

"Oh."

"I started training as a carpenter after I met your mother."

They fall to silence.

A coyote howls, another answers. An old truck grinds its gears as it turns, spitting oil as it comes out of it, straining to accelerate. They sit, quiet in the warmth of the wood stove.

"I work, mostly, hit the bags and lift weights, run when it's not too cold. I split logs and take walks. Sometimes I'll go to a bar to watch a fight."

"Friends? Family?"

He shakes his head.

She stifles a yawn. "Sorry."

"Getting tired?"

She shakes her head. "It's the fire."

"Sometimes I'll sit down and watch it, and an hour or two will go by. I don't fall asleep, but I don't remember anything either. The cold snaps me out of it. I come to and the fire's turned to ash and a few coals."

"Sounds like how Mom describes running."

"I used to watch her when I could."

"Mom doesn't have any family either."

"She's got you."

"But no one else."

"She's not seeing anyone?"

"Not—"

He cuts her off. "It's none of my business."

"She keeps in touch with Nick. He helped her start her bookshop."

Michael nods, his face blank.

"Mom cares a lot about him," she tests.

"He's been good to her."

"He supported us for a long time, paid for me to go to private school, for my tutors."

Michael turns away, puts another log on the fire, stokes the flame.

"Why won't you tell me?" she demands.

"Tell you what?"

Their eyes hold each other; she has a birthmark near her ear, half hidden by her hair, eyes that land like haymakers.

He has scars on his chin and nose, one that runs from his crow's feet to where his jaw inserts into his orbital bone.

"That you've been sending Nick money to give to her for years."

He looks at her questioningly. "Nick told you that?"

She shakes her head. "I guessed. Why else would he have your address?"

He shrugs.

Her eyes catch every move, every blink, frown, and twitch.

"Did you know about me?"

"No."

"You didn't know about me?"

"No."

"You didn't have a hunch?"

"No."

"You didn't suspect anything?"

He hesitates, but she misses it. "No."

"Then why?"

"I—"

"Why send money to someone you broke up with?"

The timbre of her voice changed: the pitch rose, the breath carrying the words ran frail.

"It was the only way."

"The only way to what?"

He turns away, a pain he'd almost forgotten opening a gash from his throat to his chest.

"I was a rapist and she was the innocent school girl I was taking advantage of—everywhere we went. Even Nick didn't think we should be together."

"Were you a rapist?"

He jerks his head back to her. "No."

"Why the money?"

A dozen answers run across his face, but he can't see them, and Tolan can't read them, so he sits, mouth open to speak words he doesn't have.

"I knew it would help," he says finally, "that it'd be a good thing."

"But eighteen years…" She looks around at the bare walls and the cracks in the ceiling, the second and third hand furniture.

Tolan watches his face fall in on itself, his skin jaundiced in the lowlight. Minutes pass in silence, fifteen, twenty, and she excuses herself and goes to bed. She wakes around two o'clock, thirsty, and goes to the faucet, sees a sliver of his neck and head around the wall dividing the living room from the kitchen, but he doesn't react to the sound of the cupboard opening and closing, or to the pipes knocking as she fills her glass. She hopes he'll turn and see her, but he doesn't, and she refuses to announce her presence. She drinks half of the glass, refills it, takes it into her bedroom, and shuts the door behind her.

CHAPTER NINETY

Parker put on two adult diapers and dressed in his best suit, took a dog-eared book from his bedside table, the pocket-watch and cufflinks that had belonged to his great-great-grandfather from atop his bureau, and moved toward the kitchen. He had to stop in the bathroom on the way to vomit, couldn't bend down to lift the toilet seat, and disgorged into the sink, wiped the blood from his mouth, and turned the tap to clean his hand and the washbasin. He made it to the kitchen only to change his mind, shuffled through each room one last time, making certain that everything was in order. He'd set a letter for Bo and his last will and testament on the kitchen counter the night before.

He took a syringe from the drawer next to the stove, removed it from the plastic wrapper, took his insulin from the refrigerator, pierced the rubber top, and pulled the plunger until it was full, began to put it away, thought better of it, and filled another syringe. He put the discarded wrapping and syringe caps in his pocket, and went out through the sliding glass door.

It was too cold out to be on the deck, too damp, but he didn't mind. It was still beautiful. The quay was quiet, the boats idly at moor. A soft drizzle fell through the fog.

Let beauty redeem ugliness till kingdom come.

He could taste brine on his tongue, feel the sea and the fog in his nostrils. A tern dove for a fish, a seagull cried, another, birds screeching and leaping from their perch, flying out to sea.

There was only the one matter that kept everything from being as it should. Bo.

Tears came, and he let them, not weeping so much as shedding the last tears he had left.

He regretted the cancer, the years it would deprive him of, but nothing else. He'd been lucky in life, was lucky to die here.

Reaching into his jacket, he found the syringes, took them out.

He hadn't believed in God since he was a child, but as he injected himself, he let himself entertain the thought that God would allow him to come back as tern or a gull. Maybe He'd take care of Bo, too, Bo who had never allowed anyone to care for her, but who, with his death, would be alone in the world. He hoped that, even though Bo had never let him marry her, God would let his love for her have mattered in some small way.

The pain was unbearable, the constant vomiting, but he said nothing of such things, only thanked her for a life spent, if not together, at least in proximity. He told her that he loved her, and that he hoped that now that he was gone and there was nothing left to be gained by his profession, that she would know that he'd always meant that, and nothing more.

CHAPTER NINETY-ONE

Michael wakes before the sun as always, a bed set to finish, an armoire to start. The coffee maker switches on at 4:45, and is set to beep when it finishes brewing, but he cuts it off so it doesn't wake Tolan.

He fills his mug, pours the rest of the coffee in a thermos, and decides he'll start with the bed set, wincing as the first bolt of coffee sears his mouth.

He works from five until eight, then breaks off to check on her, but her truck is gone.

Gone.

He stumbles, walks back toward the barn. He can see patches of gravel where her tires had been, half of a boot-print in the mud beside them.

The barn is holding him, the only reason he's upright.

The clouds are motionless. A hawk soars; Michael follows it until it vanishes behind the pines, and his eyes fall to the crows pecking at the grass along the tree line.

He knows nothing, intends nothing, feels nothing and shattered all at once.

Time plods.

His breath freezes in the air and falls to the ground. Though there is no wind and no snow left on the ground, only a hard crust of snow come and gone. His eyes leak tears for the cold. Steam rises from his coffee cup, thinner than his breath.

A half-mile away Charlie's delivery truck brakes, shrieks metal on metal. Michael exhales, takes a final sip of coffee, dumps the rest, and heads back into the shop.

He breaks for lunch at eleven, and finds Tolan's truck back in the roundabout. She's sitting at the card table in the kitchen when he comes in, and he doesn't know if he's allowed to ask her where she's been. She smiles shyly, seeing him, and he realizes he's not smiling and grimaces, and she thinks he's grimacing at her and her face falls to the tabletop.

"I was thinking I should leave tomorrow. I've got—"

"Don't."

The word leaps from his mouth, startling her.

"I don't want to be in the way."

"You're not."

She stares at him, her eyes moving back and forth over his face.

"I want you to stay."

"Really?"

He nods, but she holds back, uncertain.

"Yes." It is nearly a plea—is a plea, he realizes. "Please stay."

She smiles. "Okay."

"You smile like your mother."

He hadn't meant to say it, but it gets him another shy smile. "People say that."

"How—" He cuts himself off.

"Is she?"

Michael nods, looks away.

"She's well." Tolan watches him as she speaks. "She owns a used bookshop, reads, and does her marathons. Sometimes we run together."

Michael nods.

"She did her first ultra this past fall."

"Ultra?"

Tolan nodded. "One hundred miles. The Pine Creek Challenge."

"Why?"

"Why?"

"Why'd she run a hundred miles?"

Tolan shakes her head, looks away.

"She's quiet," she says.

"She always was."

They fall silent, neither of them knowing what should come next, what they can say, and what they shouldn't.

"You two," she hesitates, "were together?"

"What has your mother said?"

"Nothing," Tolan says quickly. "Not much."

She looks down, tracing a finger over one of the knots in the faux-wood of the tabletop. She's wearing her hair in two low braids, and the contrast between her hair and the skin visible at her part strikes him like a blow. He forces himself to take a breath, turns, takes the coffee can from the cupboard.

"Do you drink coffee?"

"A little," she says, then shakes her head. "No, not really. Do you have any tea?"

He shakes his head, measures out three scoops and dumps them into the filter, pours water into the side of the machine.

"Your mom drank a lot of tea."

"She still does."

"Are you hungry?"

"A little."

He starts opening cupboards, looking for something to feed her, then the fridge, the freezer.

"You don't keep much in the house."

"No. A few steaks and some microwave dinners."

Tolan scans the room. "You don't have a microwave."

He looks around as if to confirm the fact, shakes his head. "I put them in the oven."

He finds a loaf of bread, some peanut butter and a banana. "There isn't much."

"Was that oatmeal in the cupboard?"

A blank look.

She points. "The one next to the sink."

It was; she eats oatmeal and a sliced banana while he drinks coffee.

"I got your mother some tea things for Christmas, once, a ball and a little pot and some loose-leaf tea." He looks down into his cup, frowning at the grounds floating in his coffee, looks up to see Tolan smiling. "What?"

"She still has them, I think."

"Really?"

"The pot's white with a single purple orchid?"

He lets himself smile, shyly. "The shop woman had to help me out; I thought all tea came in bags."

Michael finishes his coffee.

"I should get back to work. Will you be okay?"

She nods.

"I have to make some headway on an order, but I figure I can knock off early, and we can go into town for dinner, if you're interested."

"She said you died."

It wasn't surprising, but the words were unexpected. It took him a minute to answer.

"How?"

"A car accident."

Tolan is looking about. Michael keeps his house pristine, but it isn't much: the walls are cracking and the windows are small and don't stop the cold. There's no sunlight, and the overhead lights are dim.

Michael stands, collects his mug and her empty bowl, and carries them to the sink to wash.

"I need to get to work," he says, doing the dishes and setting them in the drying rack.

"I'll go for a run."

"We'll leave for dinner around five-thirty?"

320

"Okay."

Work is a relief. The band-saw demands total concentration, and the wood is solid and familiar and silent. But then it's ten after five; he closes the barn, locks the door, and heads for the house.

Tolan is at the table again, doesn't hear him come in. He stands in the doorjamb, watching her: she's leaning forward, chin resting on top of her hand like her mother used to do when she read, though her brow is more deeply furrowed, and her nose crinkles and smooths as her eyes move back and forth across her tablet. She looks up without warning and catches him staring; scarlet streaks from her sternal notch up her throat, and into her ears and cheeks. He turns away.

"I'm going to shower quickly, and then we'll go?"

She nods.

He walks down the hall to his room, sheds his clothes, covers himself with a towel, and heads into the bathroom. He cranks the knob, waits for the water to turn hot, listening to the pipes knocking in the wall, the reverberations making the water droplets on the shower door leap and quake. A minute passes, two, he tests the water again. It's so cold it burns. He realizes he'd forgotten to tell Tolan his water heater only holds ten gallons. He needs a shower, though, can smell himself through his deodorant, feel the salt on the back of his neck and the sweat in his hair. He grimaces and steps in, gasps as the frigid water hits, holds himself beneath it with grit teeth. He is numb and shaking by the time he towels dry.

"There's only one restaurant," he says after he's dressed. "It's not fancy."

"That's okay."

"Mom's writing a book," she says as they drive.

"A book?"

"A novel maybe, or an autobiography."

Michael's silent.

"I found it on her computer. I don't think she meant for anybody to see it. It's how I found you."

"I'm in the book?"

"You're one of the main characters."

Silence again.

A street lamp comes into view, disappears behind them.

"Hey, Michael, how are you?""Hey, Vickie."

He can see the questions forming in her face, the curiosity in the tilt of her head, the slight pause as she takes two menus from beside the cash register. He's never brought anyone to the restaurant before, and Tolan is a stranger, pretty, decades younger.

She sits them at a table in her sightline, smiles at Michael. "I'll bring you your coffee and a water."

She waits expectantly, but he only nods. "Thank you."

She turns to Tolan, appraising her. "What can I get you?"

"Just water, please."

"Okay."

She lingers a moment. Tolan forces a smile; Michael stares heavily at the tabletop. Finally, she leaves.

Tolan opens the menu. "What's good here?"

"I always get the hot roast beef sandwich."

She smiles. "I like roast beef."

"It comes with mashed potatoes and gravy."

"Even better."

"I usually order a side of steak fries, too."

"Meat and potatoes and potatoes?"

He laughs awkwardly. "I like to dip the fries in the potatoes."

Vickie brings their drinks, takes their orders, serves the food when it's ready, lingers.

"She keeps looking at us."

"We don't get many strangers up this way."

Vickie checks on them after they finish, brings their pie and a hot chocolate for Tolan, and tops off Michael's coffee.

"I think she likes you."

"Why are you here?" He made his voice as soft as he could.

Tolan jerks her head up, her fork freezing midway to her mouth. "What?"

Barely a breath, tears welling in her eyes; Michael cringes, forces himself to look at her, to see her tears and eyes and the light catching in the tears. "I didn't mean it like that, just that you came a long way."

Her eyes run over his face, but she doesn't speak.

"I'm glad you're here, I want you to stay... as long as you can, but I don't know... what I can do."

"I just wanted to see you, to meet..." —the tears spill over now, slowly — "my father."

Father. He manages a nod, hears the bell of the cash register as Vickie rings up a customer, her *thank you* as she accepts the money, her *here you go* as she gives the man his change, and *have a nice night* after the man has tucked the bills in his wallet.

The man helps his wife into her coat, guides her through the door, letting in a brace of cold air; Tolan shivers.

He drops his eyes to his coffee cup. "I'm bad at this."

322

She laughs, and he looks up; she's wiping at her eyes with her sleeve, smiling. "I can see that."

He snorts.

She scoops a bit of ice cream and a bite of apple pie onto her fork, lifts it to her mouth, doesn't chew, lets the flavors merge with sensation, sweet, cold, tart, hot, the flesh of the apples, the evanescent crust.

"Can I ask how old you are? You don't have to answer."

"I'm—"

"Older than mom."

He nods.

"Ten years?"

"Twelve."

He half expects her to slap him.

Vickie refills his coffee again. "How do you like the pie, honey?"

"It's really good."

"We bake it ourselves."

"It tastes like it."

Vickie leaves.

Neither Michael nor Tolan speak. The refrigerator hums, grease spits in the fryer, a customer clears his throat, hawks into a napkin.

"Your mother was sixteen when I met her. I was twenty-eight."

He watches for a reaction.

"Why'd you break up?"

"I—"

She waits.

"I'm not sure."

She nods, unsatisfied, doesn't pursue it, thinks of Tori and what she might say in thirty years if someone asks her why they aren't still together.

Michael drinks his coffee; she sips her hot chocolate, takes another bite of pie. They finish, Vickie collects their plates, leaves the bill. Michael takes it and stands.

It's cold as they cross the parking lot to his truck, unseasonably cold, the night black as pitch. What light there is falls like snow from three dim bulbs mounted on the side of the diner, tottering and twisting in the darkness. Tolan is shaking by the time they reach the truck.

Michael cranks the key in the ignition, turns the heat all the way up; her teeth chatter as they drive.

"Heat doesn't work very well."

"That's oka—"

"Shit!"

Michael rips the wheel to the right, slamming on the brakes. Only once they've stopped does she see the deer bounding away, their headlights catching on its tail.

"Are you okay?"

She nods.

"Christ."

He pulls back onto the road.

"Michael?"

"Yeah?"

"How come you didn't introduce me to the waitress?"

"I didn't know—I wasn't sure what to say, what to call you."

"Your daughter?"

"I didn't know if you'd want that."

"Do you?"

"Do I what?"

"Want to tell people I'm your daughter?"

He nods.

"I'd like that, too."

Conversation continues in disconnected bursts, both of them facing straight-ahead, eyes tight on the road.

"You're a cabinetmaker?"

They're nearly back to the house.

"More or less."

"Can I see your work?"

"Sure."

Five minutes later, they're rattling the length of the driveway, pulling up in front of the barn.

"Do you want to go inside and warm up before I show you the shop?"

"Please."

She's clutching herself.

"We can wait until tomorrow if you want."

She shakes her head.

They go inside. He's carrying a plastic bag with the teapot, tea, and honey they'd bought in town and sets it on the counter.

"I've got a few things to take care of in the shop so I'll head out. Come over when you're ready."

"Okay."

She appears a half-hour later, still shivering. He takes his coat off and drapes it over her shoulders.

"You don't have to—"

The coat is short and three times too wide. He smiles, "It was the same with your mother."

"Yeah."

He turns to survey the shop. "How much do you want to know?"

She shrugs. "What's that?" Her arms are wrapped beneath his coat so she gestures with her chin.

324

"An electric planer. It's for reducing the thickness of larger pieces of wood, shaping them and smoothing them out."

She stands next to the machine, following its lines and bevels as he looks on, following the ribbed hose running from its back, the wires, taking in the gleaming metal tray and the teeth of the blade. He'll show her the band saw and airdrop tomorrow, explain their uses if she's interested, but it's too cold now, and he doesn't want to bore her. He follows her sightline to the far wall where his tools are hanging, metal, lacquered wood, and rubber grips in various permutations. He keeps them spotless, and they're catching the light, throwing it from various angles.

Tolan stares at them for a long time.

"Do you use all those?"

"More or less."

"Meaning?"

"Different styles of carpentry use certain tools more than others. Most of what I make is Scandinavian or Early American Colonial, relatively simple styles, so I don't use the fancier tools all that much."

She turns back to the wall, swaying gently side-to-side so that the light and tools seem to undulate.

"Do you have anything finished?"

"A few pieces in back."

He can't tell if she's stopped shaking beneath his jacket.

"I can show you in the morning if you're cold."

"Are you?"

"No."

"I'd like to see them now, then, if it's okay."

A shy smile.

"Sure."

He leads her toward the back of the shop. "I do most of my sales online, but sometimes people want to see my work in person before they commission a piece, so I bring them in here."

He unlocks a door, flips a switch, and lights come on. It's the only finished room in the shop, twelve-by-twelve with taupe walls and burgundy trim, his work evenly spaced along the perimeter. He flinches as she steps into the room, and she sees him, freezes, retreats, takes her boots off, and sets them outside the doorjamb. Michael's face is hot with embarrassment, and he starts to apologize, but she's already in the room.

"What kind of wood is this?"

"Mahogany."

She looks around the room. "You like mahogany."

He nods. She moves from a chest of drawers to a table, reaches for it, stops.

"Can I touch it?"

He nods; he can polish it later.

She turns back to the furniture and he braces himself against the doorjamb: her eyes and the sway of her hair as she turns, and the way she moves, awkward and elegant all at once; emotion fills his lungs like water. His eyes widen as her fingertips move up the apron of the table, the arch of her arm extending and her fingers sweeping over the table's edge and running lightly along its length. She moves to the next piece.

"You made Mom a chair like this, didn't you?"

"Yes."

"She still has it. I used to get in trouble when I was little," she says, running her hand down its back and along an arm. "The chair was one of the only things she wouldn't let me touch. She kept it upstairs, and she'd be downstairs cleaning or doing the dishes and call for me thinking I was playing in the next room, and when I didn't answer, she'd go looking and find me in the library. I'd be playing in the chair, touching it or turning it on its side so I could look at it from different angles. I'd breathe on it and watch my breath condense, then fade away. She brought it to the bookstore after she found me sitting in it with a coloring book and a box of markers."

He nods.

"What's this one?"

She's standing at the far corner of the room in front of something covered with a heavy cloth.

"It's a Queen Anne desk and chair."

"Can I see it?"

"Sure."

He gathers the cloth at each corner, lifts it slowly.

An inaudible gasp, a slight parting of her lips. Tolan lowers herself to her knees, reaches out, touches it gingerly, traces the backs of two fingers along the belly of the cabriole.

"You made this?" she whispers.

"You sound surprised."

"A little." She looks up at him without breaking contact with the desk, her hand cupping the claw-and-ball.

"I finished it about seven years ago."

"I'm surprised no one's bought it."

"It's not for sale."

"Why?"

He shrugs.

Her eyes are her mother's, her complexion, her freckles.

"There's a scene in Mom's book where…"

Tolan's voice falters. She swallows, starts again.

"You're fighting someone, boxing. The guy gets lucky and knocks you down—doesn't really hurt you, just makes you angry."

She won't look at him.

"You beat the hell out of him after that. You could end the fight at any time, but you don't. Your manager is yelling at you to finish him, but you won't. You keep hitting him until he can barely stand, then backing off just before he falls. The guy's defenseless by the last round, and you…"

Her voice is breaking.

"You let him stumble after you for a while, and then,"—Tolan looks up suddenly—"you kill him. With one punch."

She wraps herself in her arms, trying to steady herself and hold his gaze, but tears are rolling down her face.

"That's why I was surprised, because this is beautiful, and that's horrible, and I don't understand how you could do both."

They stare at each other.

"It wasn't like that."

"Did you kill him?"

"It wasn't like that."

"Did you kill someone?"

"Yes."

He didn't blink.

"Did you mean to?"

"I hadn't even met your mother then. She couldn't have written what happened because I never told her about it—"

"Tell me."

"It's not that simple."

Eighteen years ago is now. Tolan is Pan. The pale skin and the wet eyes, the way he has to tilt his chin up to meet her gaze—the way they need words that he doesn't have.

"You won't understand—I was in prison. I've never told anyone!"

Michael pauses, trying to read her face, realizes his hands are throbbing, that he's been gripping the molding so tightly the blood's gone out of his fingers.

"I was sixteen when I got sent to Menard. I rode transport with a guy doing his fourth stretch. He said I was a fish, and that fish get tested, and that I couldn't back down, or they'd tear me apart. He said I should hit the guy testing me as hard as I could, and not to stop hitting him until the guards broke it up."

Michael's eyes fall away.

"It happened my second night, at dinner. A guy came up to me and told me to give him my tray and fuck off. I didn't. He swung at me, and I ducked the punch and started hitting him. Everyone was yelling and stomping their feet and pounding the tables, but the guards just stood there. I heard the guy's face break, and he fell. I paused, waiting for the guards, but they didn't come, and I didn't know what to do, only that the convict had said not to stop, so when the guards didn't come I got on top of the guy and started hitting him again, and then he wasn't moving, and my hands were covered in blood, and the guards still hadn't moved. They locked me in solitary for three weeks, and when I got out I found he'd died in the infirmary."

Michael meets her eye, looks away.

"Some of the guards were running fights out of the prison. Admission cost a grand, and there were no rules, and people drank and bet, and the guards took a cut. They told me they'd have me killed if I didn't fight."

His voice is distant, without affect. "Sometimes it was enough just to hurt the people I fought, sometimes the guards wanted more."

"How—"

"Five. I killed five people."

"That's not what I was going to ask."

Gut, heart, and strength go with her words; he realizes he's released his horror into her world.

Five.

He'd traded five lives for his own, and that was how he'd thought of himself, ever since, as "Five."

What would it do to her, the knowledge that men spat and cheered and made money at other men's deaths, that her own father had participated?

The air is heavy and his body weak; he feels his knees buckling and has to brace himself against the wall.

"I was going to ask how you survived, how long you were in jail."

"And why?"

Her eyes fall to the floor. She nods.

"My father left when I was a kid, and my mother died, so I went to live with my best friend, Gianni. His father used to hit his mother. He didn't usually hurt her, just slapped her around, but one day he started beating her with this belt that had a brass buckle on it. He tore her face to shreds and there was blood everywhere, but he wouldn't stop, so I hit him. He fell down the stairs and broke his neck, and Gianni and his mother testified in court that I was lying, that Mr. Rossi hadn't hit her. It was my word against theirs, so when the prosecution offered a deal, my lawyer said I should take it. I got two years."

He can see questions etched in the tension in her face, waits, forcing himself to slow his breathing.

"I need to know," she tries, falters, doesn't bother to wipe away her tears, "I read—Mom wrote that you... Did you ever... were you—is that why she left?"

"You're asking if I hit her."

She doesn't answer, won't look at him.

"What does the book say?"

"What?"

"What does the book say?"

"I'm asking you."

"Why?"

"What do you mean why?"

He's there and he's not there.

"The book says 'yes,' I say 'no'—then what?"

"I didn't say it said you did."

"You wouldn't have asked if it didn't."

A solid, simple statement, like getting a leg back, helping him stay upright.

"Can't you just answer—"

He shakes his head. "You need to tell her."

"What?"

"Tell your mother you found her book."

Tolan stares at him.

"Do you think she loves you?"

He doesn't know where the words came from.

"Of course."

"Do you trust her?"

"Yes!"

"Then let her tell you, let her answer your questions."

He can see the light bend over the tears in her eyes, flit in the gossamer-thin residue of those that fell, but her jaw is setting, thrust forward the way his used to get when he was angry; her eyes are her mother's, but the fury churning in the irises is his, curling and rising.

She folds her arms across her body. "All I want from you is the truth."

Michael turns away, walks toward the door.

"Did you hit her?"

He stops, head down, says nothing.

"Did you hit her?"

Each word undoes him further.

"Michael!"

"Once."

Silence. He forces himself to turn, look her in the eye, is sick at what he sees.

"Why?"

"It doesn't matter."

She stares at him.

"Did you hurt her?"

He shakes his head. "I pulled it."

His voice is a breath.

"Did she do something?"

He hesitates—half a breath. "No."

"What she'd do?"

He doesn't answer, stares at his boots.

"Is it why you broke up?"

Michael looks at her.

"What did she do?"

"I..."

He feels himself shaking, the familiar failure, panic. Her eyes look so much like her mother's.

"I... wasn't right for her."

Pan is there, flickers before his eyes, is gone—he always wanted to be what she needed, knows he never was, and now he's looking at Tolan, fighting, shaking his head, desperate to be what she needs.

"I wasn't right."

Tolan covers her mouth with a hand. The tears come sudden and hard and silent, and her whole body is shaking and Michael wants to go to her, to hold her, but he doesn't know if he is allowed to.

"I loved her," he wants to whisper.

"She ends the scene abruptly," Tolan says. "It doesn't say you did it."

His face falls.

She stands there.

"I apologized," he says after a long silence. "It doesn't make it any better, but I never did it again."

"Did you have the chance?"

"What do you mean?"

"Did she leave you right away?"

"No."

"When did she leave you?"

"After."

"Why?"

He looked at her.

"Because of me?"

"No."

"Why?"

"I don't know."

"What do you mean you don't know?"

"She never told me."

CHAPTER NINETY-TWO

He cranks his hips taut as his forearms rise, extending until they're nearly straight and the axe high above his head, then rips his hands and hips and axe downward. The log explodes; the axe-head is three inches deep in the stump. He leaves it there. He's split three cords of wood in two hours; there is a trickle of blood and pus sliding down his finger, and his chest is tight, his throat burning. He's sucking and sucking, but can't get any air. He knows Tolan is watching through the window, though, so he won't let himself clutch his chest or fall to his knees.

He didn't think she'd be here when he woke up, but his alarm had gone off, and he'd made his coffee and gone out to the barn, and there it was, her truck—his truck—still in the driveway.

CHAPTER NINETY-THREE

Michael opens the door to her truck and pushes her bags into the back seat.

"Are you mad at her?"

Tolan is sitting in her truck, but the door's still open. His eyes narrow and his lips purse; he shakes his head quizzically. "For what?"

"For not telling you about me."

He doesn't answer right away, looks past her, past the truck, at the woodpile.

"Yes," he says, finally. "No."

She blushes whenever he looks at her directly, just like her mother.

"I'd like... to have watched you grow up."

"But..."

"But I couldn't."

"Couldn't?" Her face is suddenly taut, ugly with anger.

He doesn't know what Pan had told her or what she'd written, only that he doesn't know what to say or how to say it, and that if he doesn't say something she'll be gone.

And he knows that even if it were his right to tell his side, he isn't sure anymore what happened or why.

He wants Tolan to have her mother.

"You always knew she loved you, right?"

"Always."

"And you grew up happy, and she was happy?"

"Yes."

He kicks lightly at her tire.

"But I'm your daughter! She kept me from you for eighteen years!"

"Tolan—"

"How can you not be angry?"

"Because you're here," he says, meeting her eye, feeling naked and stupid. "Because you were both happy."

Tears fall from her eyes. She isn't happy or sad, only standing before a man she doesn't know, listening to words she doesn't understand.

"I loved your mother."

Tolan gets out of the truck, throws herself against him.

"I have to get something," he says, fleeing, bewildering her. He's choking back tears, makes it through the barn door before losing it, collapsing against the wall. He'd wrapped the desk and chair in bubble wrap and cloth the night before, not quite daring to hope she'd be there in the morning.

Tolan's leaning against her truck when he comes back. "I'd like you to have these," he says, "if you want them."

Her eyes widen. "The Queen Anne?"

He's already turned back, reappears moments later with the chair.

"Are you sure?"

He nods.

She embraces him.

"Will I get to see you again?"

"What?" She pulls back, staring at him.

"I'd like to—if you want—you could visit again."

She doesn't answer immediately, and he waits, head down, unable to look at her, knowing without a doubt that he doesn't deserve the hope he's clinging to.

"I'd like that."

He opens her door, and she gets in, rolls down the window.

"I left my cell number on the kitchen counter."

He doesn't really understand, can't blink back his tears, has to turn away.

"I'll call you when I get home so you know I got in safely."

He nods.

She turns the key in the ignition and drives away.

CHAPTER NINETY-FOUR

"What are you doing today?" Lewella asked, warming Bo's coffee.

The diner was empty, still and calm in the lull between lunch and dinner.

"Isn't it Wednesday?"

"Yes."

"So Parker and I..."

Lewella caught Jesús out of the corner of her eye.

"I'm going into Portland after we close, if you'd like to come with me."

"No hay nadie que quiera ir a la ciudad contigo," Jesús smiled, "vieja cabra desagradable."

"Shut it."

Bo shook her head. "No. Thank you. I've got some... things I have to —errands."

"Ves? Solo digo la verdad."

"You remember it's Park—"

Bo shook her head.

"But it's..."

Bo frowned.

Jesús looked at Lewella and shrugged. "Puedes guiar a un caballo hasta el agua..."

"Are you sure you don't—" Lewella started, but Jesús touched her arm, shook his head minutely.

Bo was silent, staring off into nowhere, and Lewella couldn't say whether she was ignoring them, or lost in a world only she could see, only that she seemed very far away, more and more.

Bo had always kept her own counsel, and they were never surprised to learn that she'd been in Montreal when de Gaulle issued his defiant *Vive le Québec libre,* or in Morocco covering the Green March and Spain's surrender of the Spanish Sahara.

They knew she rented a small house in San Sebastian every April, and that she'd traveled extensively in Vietnam, but that was because Parker went with her.

334

He'd been gone for years now.

Almost seven.

Lewella worried Bo was slipping into the shadows.

The bell on the door rang, and a couple stepped into the diner. Lewella sat them and took their order, filled their coffee cups. Another couple arrived ten minutes later, and another shortly thereafter, followed by a well-dressed woman in her twenties. Her eyes touched every face and corner and surface, until they found Bo. The woman blossomed in a wide, electric smile, ran to embrace her, and was embraced in return.

"¿Quién es ella?" Jesús asked.

Lewella grit her teeth.

"This is Margeaux," Bo said. "Parker's granddaughter."

"¿Sabías que tenía un hijo?" Jesús asked Lewella.

Lewella folded her arms across her chest. "There's no way..." she muttered.

"Parker and I take her sailing," Bo said.

"Sailing?"

"On the Hudson, mostly. It'll be a shorter trip today."

"That sounds lovely!" Margeaux said, then turning to Lewella and Jesús, she added, "I'll be staying with Bo for a while. I want to help her get situated, now that she's moved into Papa's old place."

"We might go to the movies, this afternoon, if the weather's bad," Bo said. "There's a place in Portland that Parker loves where they play the classics: Buster Keaton, Greta Garbo, Cary Grant..."

Lewella arched an eyebrow.

"Shall we?" Margeaux asked.

"I'm ready."

"It was a pleasure to meet you both." Margeaux smiled.

"Who the hell was that?" Lewella asked Jesús after the women left.

"Margeaux, aparentemente."

"My ass..."

Jesús shrugged.

"Who?"

"No sé."

"I'm asking you to speculate."

"Speculate?"

"Especular."

"Todo es posible cuando se trata de la Sra. White."

"But this?"

"Todo."

"I'm worried."

"Tal vez hay un corazón enterrado en alguna parte de ese viejo cuerpo crujiente tuyo."

"How sick do you think she is?'

"No sé."

"I just can't—she always puts flowers by his grave on his birthday."

"Tal vez ella no necesita hacerlo nada más."

"What the hell does that mean?"

"Tal vez ya está con él."

"Parker's dead, Bo's alive, and you're too old to be this stupid."

"¿Te casarías conmigo?

"Casarías? Wait—what?"

Jesús laughed. "¿Ves? Nuestro amigo podría estar más cerca de lo que piensas."

"Casarías?"

"Es un tipo de animal. Muy fea y gruñón y rencoroso."

"Something's not right."

"¿Qué?"

"I mean, if is Bo sick—what if that woman's taking advantage of her?"

"¿Qué pasa si está tratando de facilitarle las cosas?"

"What things?"

"Ha vivido una buena vida, Lewella, ha dado tanto a tanta gente."

"So?"

"Tal vez ella se está preparando."

"For what?"

"Tú sabes."

She shook her head.

"Estar con él."

"Shut up."

"Nunca."

"I'm going to look into this Margeaux and find out what she's really up to."

Jesús shrugged. "Haz lo que quieras."

"Damn right. But first—" she reached into her apron "—I need a cigarette."

"Rasparé la plancha."

"And the dishes."

Jesús sighed. "Y los platos."

"What—is it a hardship for me to ask you to do your job?"

"Sabes que soy la única persona que te ha conocido por más de cinco minutos y no quiere estrangularte, ¿verdad?

"Go fuck yourself."

Lewella moved to go, but Jesús caught her hand and held firm so she couldn't yank it back, held it between both of his own.

"What the hell do you think you're doing?"

"Va a estar bien, Lewella. Bo va a estar bien."

"Because you say so?"

"Te lo prometo."

She pulled her hand free. "I'm going for a smoke."

"Ya lo dijiste."

"She's either sick, or that leech is trying to bleed her dry—either way, I'm going to get to the bottom of this."

"Ya dijiste eso, también."

She stormed out the door, and he retreated to his work, humming as he scraped and swiped and cleaned.

Bo had helped him escape Noriega, had introduced him to Parker and to Lewella. They were what they were, a family, sometimes close, and often not, but always a family. Then Parker died, and they all retreated into themselves to mourn in secret, to wither. And now it seemed they were about to lose Bo, and though it saddened him, Jesús hoped it would be better for her. He hoped that she would find Parker and they would be easy together, and that all that had stood between them would fall away.

Once upon a time, Jesús had been sixteen, and he had stood between a chicken and a burro and married his sweetheart, and they were with child that very season. She was six months pregnant when she died, and he was only seventeen, but he still thought of her from time to time, and hoped he'd see her again, in this life, or the next.

Now, he and Lewella were all that was left, and watching her light her second cigarette with her first, her third with her second, and her fourth with her third, he knew she was in pain. He was, too. And he hoped that Lewella would allow him to help, to be what Parker would have been for Bo, had Bo allowed it.

CHAPTER NINETY-FIVE

Tolan's sitting cross-legged on her bed with a photo of Michael on her lap. She wants to touch it, to trace her finger along Michael's jaw and upward over his cheekbone and temple and into his hair, but she doesn't dare, because the photo's already more than twenty years old and fading.

She wants its solidity, perhaps more than anything. She wants to hold the picture in her hand and know that this past weekend had happened and that she'd met her father and that her father and mother had loved each other once.

So she stares until she breaks, and then she pulls her sleeves up over her hands and scoops the photograph off the bed, and it sits so lightly atop her hand that it seems it might evaporate, yet is somehow thick, too, and sharp at the corners.

Tolan brings the picture nearer her face, willing every sweep and line and angle of Michael's face to inscribe itself in her mind's eye, then collects the photos he gave her and puts them in their shoebox and slides them under her bed.

Tori will be home tomorrow.

She wants to be ready.

There was a scene Tolan's mother had started a half dozen times without finishing. It doesn't appear, in part or in full, in the novel that now exists, and which seems—at least for now— to be complete and final. She'd prayed for a scene that would tell her what had happened between her parents, whether Michael left, or her mother, and if they would still be together if it wasn't for her.In one version, Sarah decided to leave Michael as she was looking at the pictures Bo took documenting the prevalence of domestic abuse in America; in another, it was as she leafed through a collection titled *The Fairer Sex*. Both scenes were aborted early on, before her mother had marked out the horizons of her story, when her characters were no more than a series of rough-hewn images. The most developed version of the scene was a letter Sarah wrote to Michael in which she said that she loved him, but that she wanted a life of her own, and that that couldn't happen if they were together.

In another take, her mother left Michael to become a writer and bought an old used bookstore so she could devote herself to reading and writing.

Tolan hated this version most of all, had cried for days after reading it, because if it was true, it meant she didn't really know her mother, and that her mother had lied to her for eighteen years, because how else could she not know that her mother wrote, that it was her lifelong dream.

She'd always thought of her mother was just a pathological reader, an English nerd that dedicated her life to books and tea and other flights of fancy.

But the scene is gone now, off to wherever it is that writers shunt the words they deem unworthy, and Tolan's of a different mind, curious, but peaceful, and lowkey proud of her mother for all she's accomplished.

Michael had found Tolan at the kitchen table on their last day together. He'd had a faded blue shoebox under his arm. "I thought you might like to have this," he said, handing it to her. "It's probably better if you wait to open it."

"Will I know what it is?"

"I figure so."

"Can I call if have any questions?"

"I'd like that."

Her favorite picture is a Polaroid Michael bought from a panhandler, a candid of himself and her mother.

The photographer doesn't try to conceal her mother's androgyny or the size of Michael's nose or his droopy eyelid, doesn't even allow them to settle into the world before he snaps his shot, or into each other, but photographs them trying to situate themselves against a tree leaning into Michael's back and pushing him forward so that her mother has to fight to fit herself into Michael's chest.

It's not a flattering picture. Her father's strength looks bullish and crude, and her mother appears anemic by comparison, and it would have been different had the photographer shown his subjects a modicum of kindness, had he taken a moment to notice her mother's eyes and Michael's smile.

But Tolan likes the photo as it is, likes that Michael's fingers are woven into her mother's, and that you can see the scars on his knuckles and a smudge of ink on her mother's thumb.

She likes that they're unaware of the camera, and that they're smiling, even though they're contorted and neither of them can see the other.

It means the smiles are real.

A smile of her own blossoms, for her mother and Michael, and Tolan feels a wash of quiet joy as Tori rises in her mind, as she pictures the swell of her nose and the vale between her shoulder blades which she'd dappled with so many kisses. She loves the way Tori laughs with all of herself, the way her eyes crackle with mischief and the way they are together. The Polaroid begins to grow in Tolan's mind, extending and expanding so that there's a before and an after and layers to the during: Michael's just kissed the flesh of her mother's neck, and her mother squeezes his hand and presses herself into him so that there's no longer any space between them.

They love each other, and in a moment, they're going to brush the grass from their pants and go home and make love, and they'll lie in each other's arms afterward and laugh and play.

She wants that for her mother and for her father, wants for them to have shared it.

And maybe they had. Maybe she and Michael had made love a thousand times and hatched twice as many plans, and it was only storm and circumstance and bad luck that came between them.

But there's no way to know, and no way to know if she and Tori will make it apart from trying, no telling whether or not they'll notch their thousandth tussle.

Tolan picks up her phone. She'd set the cutest picture she had of Tori and her as the wallpaper, and she looks from Tori to the Polaroid and back, as if to divine her now and then and future in the space between them, and she looks longer than she meant to, longer than she is aware, and then she comes to and finds that her phone has gone black and she is alone in her room with a picture of her parents and not a few fears and questions to last a lifetime.

Her parents were young once, and maybe that's all Tolan really knows, that a man happened upon them in an apple orchard, and that they were holding each other, and that they were happy.

About the Author

Ciahnan Quinn Darrell is an Instructor at Kings College, Wilkes-Barre, PA and a contributing editor at *Marginalia*. His short stories and essays have appeared in several journals, most recently in *The Columbia Review*, and his story, 'What Remains,' was nominated for a Pushcart Prize.

A Lifetime of Men is his first novel.

Girls, Inc.

Girls Inc. is a non-profit organization committed to training up women who will transform society through their accomplishments and through demanding that they be regarded in the fullness of their value as human beings. Operating in 350 cities across the US and Canada, Girls Inc. has served girls ages 6-18 for more than 150 years, providing research-based programming and professional mentorship to promote the intellectual and physical well-being integral to leading a rich and fulfilling life, while also engaging in advocacy work to fight for equal opportunities for women and girls. Girls Inc. encourages girls to dream without limit, while providing a support system and the technical training that enable them to bring those dreams to fruition.

I am proud to donate 10% of the author's proceeds from this book to Girls, Inc.

Ciahnan Darrell

Inspiring all girls
to be strong,
smart, and bold

For memorable fiction, non-fiction, poetry, and prose,
Please visit Propertius Press on the web
www.propertiuspress.com